W9-DEJ-409

WITHDRAWN

On Rotation

On Rotation

ON ROTATION

A Novel

SHIRLENE OBUOBI

THORNDIKE PRESS
A part of Gale, a Cengage Company

Copyright © 2022 by Shirlene Obuobi.
Thorndike Press, a part of Gale, a Cengage Company.

ALL RIGHTS RESERVED
This is a work of fiction. Names, characters, places, and incidents are products of the author's imagination or are used fictitiously and are not to be construed as real. Any resemblance to actual events, locales, organizations, or persons, living or dead, is entirely coincidental.
Thorndike Press® Large Print Black Voices.
The text of this Large Print edition is unabridged.
Other aspects of the book may vary from the original edition.
Set in 16 pt. Plantin.

**LIBRARY OF CONGRESS CIP DATA ON FILE.
CATALOGUING IN PUBLICATION FOR THIS BOOK
IS AVAILABLE FROM THE LIBRARY OF CONGRESS.**

ISBN-13: 979-8-8857-8113-8 (hardcover alk. paper)

Published in 2022 by arrangement with Avon, an imprint of HarperCollins Publishers.

Printed in Mexico
Print Number : 1   Print Year : 2022

For the Black nerdy girls who were led to believe that who they were was an anomaly. For the 4 percent of medical students in the United States who are Black women. For the dark-skinned girls for whom self-love is a continued, arduous process. For me, at age twelve, scouring the shelves for books about girls who looked like me, whose suffering wasn't supposed to be the subject of discussion in English class. For all my girls who spent their youth reading about other people falling in love and making no effort whatsoever to experience it themselves. This one is for y'all.

ONE

The worst thing I ever did was grow an ass. It announced its presence loud and clear before the rest of my body could figure out what was happening; one day, I was skinny thighs and gangly arms and protruding belly button, and the next, my thighs were bursting the seams off my jeans and my ass was projecting out so far from my back that you could fit a pencil bag down the gap, fit an orange, fit an asshole thirteen-year-old boy's hand. No belt could contain it, and spandex-polyester-blend "curvy"-fit Levi's didn't stand a chance. The Ass had taken over. It didn't care that it was 2002 and asses were out of style. It didn't care that it had robbed me of the chance to be that girl from the movies, the one scrutinizing her slim, toned body in her full-length mirror, peering over her shoulder and asking her bum of a boyfriend "Does this dress make my butt look big?" Because for me, the answer would always be yes, and it would be unjust to blame the dress.

(*No, sweetie,* movie boyfriends always say. *You look great.* Three minutes later, they'll complain to their boys about how annoying it is when she asks questions that have no right answer. They'll make fun of the fat chick, for no reason other than *fat girls are funny,* in the scene after that.)

Real men, the ones who existed off-screen, had no quarrel with the Ass. I knew what it meant to know that a guy was fucking you with his eyes before I knew what fucking was, knew enough to feel sticky-sick from their sleepy, half-lidded gazes and curled lips and *damn, mama*s. I learned to clutch my fists tightly over my barely budded chest and shuffle out of sight, legs clamped together to keep the Ass from jiggling too much, not that it helped. The Ass had tossed me into womanhood without my consent, thrown me out on a platter for consumption, and left me there to smile vapidly at the Uncle Who Was Just Visiting as his eyes went hooded and he said, "Ay! Angie! All grown up, I see."

For a while, no man who wasn't "hood" would ever fess up to being into ass, not until the time when ass came into style and every other Instagram post featured some skinny-waisted, big-bootied video vixen in a bodycon bandage dress. I would have given the Ass a pass for all the trouble it brought me if only it had remembered that I didn't have the right phenotype. Big asses were glamour if you were Kim K or a light bright Dominicana, but on a dark-skinned nappy-headed ho like me they were too jungle, too much Saartjie Baartman and not enough Marilyn Monroe.

Frederick, my (first ever!) boyfriend of six months, loved the Ass. He liked to rest his hand on the small of my back and stroke down the satin-smooth skin until the high, round cut of it was cupped in his palm. Momma had always said I was lucky — my ass came from my back on a steady slope, not jutting out assertively like so many of my aunties' did — and Frederick enjoyed that incline, resting his hand along it when we were watching Netflix or falling asleep on his double.

I think the Ass might have been the only thing he actually liked about me, in the end.

"I'm . . . not coming with you."

I hoisted my duffel bag higher onto my shoulder, giving my soon-to-be ex-boyfriend an appraising look. Frederick looked sheepish, leaning against his perfectly-parallel-parked Lexus with his hands shoved into his pockets and his gaze directed determinedly into the distance. He was the kind of guy whose fashion sense swung dramatically between runway sharp and basement-dweller sloppy, and today, in his sun-bleached high school debate tee and raggedy sweats, he was flagrantly going for the latter. It was an outfit barely acceptable for bed, let alone for meeting my judgmental Ghanaian parents. I still remembered what he'd worn on our first date: a blue blazer, starched white button-down, gray slacks. That outfit, paired with his sculpted frame, even brown skin, and thick-rimmed glasses? He'd looked good enough to eat. I'd taken one look at him, thought, *Oh, you'll do,* and praised the geniuses behind the Hinge app algorithm for bringing his existence to my attention. Everything about the way he presented himself in public was so deliberate, and once upon a time, that effort had been attractive to me.

But now? I knew, with certainty, that he had specifically chosen this monstrosity of an outfit to signal to me that I would be driving to Naperville alone. He'd probably spent thirty minutes hunting down the rattiest tee in his dresser just to get the point across. He would've done better to spit at my feet.

"Clearly," I said with a defeated sigh. "So. What are you doing here, then?"

We both knew the answer to that question. After all, Frederick had been playing the Nice Guy game for weeks now — the one little boys play when they want to break up with their perfectly fine girlfriends but don't want to bear the responsibility of hurting her feelings, and so drag things out and misbehave until the girl loses patience and breaks it off first. And he'd played it so well: responding to my complaints about my Step exam* with a halfhearted "that sucks," commenting at large on how hot he found women who looked nothing like me, finding reasons to be too busy to see me that somehow were not present for his boys. He'd been *mean,* when all he'd had to be was honest.

And my dumb ass had allowed it. I'd convinced myself that I was being oversensitive, that I needed to give him space, that

---

* Step 1 — aka every medical student's white whale. You get to take it one time, and if you pass, you're stuck with your score forever. (You can retake it if you fail, but that doesn't look great on your application.) Mess up, and you can kiss your dreams of being an orthopedic surgeon goodbye. No pressure, right?

he didn't owe me the commitment he'd promised me. And because of my own negligence, Frederick was going to end us in the cruelest way possible. Not that he thought he was being cruel. Knowing Frederick, he probably figured that dumping a girl an hour and a half before meeting her parents was being magnanimous. *I need to do it to her face,* he'd probably told himself, *that's what a good guy would do.* Even now, his expression was tortured, like someone was slowly driving a screw into his back. As if the burden of dumping me was one he was brave to bear.

"I'm sorry," he said. He looked me up and down like he couldn't help himself. "You look great."

In contrast to his shabby outfit, I had chosen a dress that I knew he would like: midi length and navy (classy, conservative) but form-fitting (so that everyone in the vicinity would know Frederick's girl had *body*). But physical attraction had never been our problem, had it?

"Thanks," I said. I crossed my arms, waiting for him to gather his nerve. Frederick mirrored my stance, avoiding my gaze as the silence thickened. Eventually, he cleared his throat.

"You know, I really was touched when you

asked me to come meet your parents," he started. "It was nice to know that you wanted me to see you with your tribe."

His delivery felt rehearsed, the heavy pause and pained swallow all part of a performance.

"But even then, I wasn't sure," he continued. "I said yes because I thought I should. It felt like the right thing to do. But —"

"Now it doesn't," I said, cutting his speech short. No need to hear his final arguments when I'd already accepted my verdict. "Okay, cool."

I pulled out my keys and took a sharp left, marching toward my car. Not a second later, I heard the heavy footfall of his steps behind me.

"Come on, Angie," Frederick tried. "Let's talk for a bit. I feel like I owe you that much."

I swung around to look at him one last time. Even in this getup, Frederick was handsome. Smart. So woke that he probably taped his eyelids open at night. He was everything I thought I wanted in a man, the perfect other half of the Black power couple I'd always dreamed of. *The Barack to my Michelle.*

But, yet again, I'd gotten ahead of myself. What about Frederick, aside from his nice car, his impressive CV, his *swag,* had convinced me that he could be the One? Sure, he checked off all the boxes, but every guy I'd fallen for checked the boxes too — except the one that required them to actually give a shit about me.

"You're breaking up with me, right?" I said. When he didn't answer, I nodded, understanding. I threw open my car door, tossed my bag in the back seat, and gave him my most beatific smile. "Don't worry; you don't owe me anything. We're good. Have a nice life, Freddy."

When I drove off, he was still standing where I'd left him, dumbstruck. I smirked. *Small victories, Angie,* I thought. *You dated a lawyer and still managed to get the last word.*

14

TWO

The drive up to my childhood home was mercifully smooth for a Thursday morning in Chicago. It was as if all the city's rowdiest drivers had decided to cut me a break and sleep in; I got cut off only once merging onto the expressway and swerved out of the way of only two souped-up Dodge Chargers going 90 down I-55. I turned on my favorite true crime podcast, careful to avoid any cases involving jilted lovers or angry exes, and when I tired of murder, switched to a playlist conveniently devoid of Girl Power songs and breakup anthems that could get me all up in my emotions. Today was about my baby sister. Whatever feelings I had about Frederick would have to be bottled up, boxed, and left in a cellar to ferment.

Too soon, I pulled into the driveway of my childhood home. With its brownish-red brick, charcoal roof, and well-manicured lawn, my parents' house looked like a clone of all the others on our cul-de-sac. Still, I could make out the small additions they had made in anticipation of the Knocking*: two large ceramic pots brimming with petunias in the entryway, a row of solar-powered lanterns that lined the walkway to the front door, a thin but gloriously blooming crepe myrtle my parents had probably fought the homeowner's association to plant. I thought about stealing one of the petunias to tuck behind my ear but thought better of it and rang the doorbell instead.

My mother was at the door in a flash, her magenta maxi dress floating around her like the petals of an orchid. She was still strik-

* During the Knocking, a man and his parents come to a woman's parents' home, armed with a bottle of either gin (old school, traditional) or schnapps (the J. H. Henkes' "aromatic" brand, not messy frat-party fare). Afterward, the family asks the woman whether she accepts the proposal. Back in the day, after the Knocking, an envoy was sent out to make sure the suitor was good enough for the lady in question, collecting info such as his family's medical history, whether his uncle was an alcoholic, and if anyone had a predilection for wife-beating. Nowadays, Ghanaian families just stalk their daughter's boyfriends on LinkedIn.

16

ingly beautiful. She hated when I said that
— "Still! Am I abrewa★ already?" — but it
was true. Dealing with my, Tabatha's, and
Daddy's bullshit for a quarter century plus
somehow hadn't put a crack in that silky
smooth skin of hers.

"Where's Frederick?" she asked.

Probably, I thought, *because she's pre-
served in brine.*

"Nice to see you too, Momma, you look
lovely," I said. I stepped around her and
gave Auntie Abena, who had come to Chicago for a short trip that, so far, had lasted
four months, a nod. "Auntie."

"Yes, where is that fine boy you said you
were bringing?" Auntie Abena said.

"He's not coming," I said, toeing off my
shoes by the door. Saying it out loud stung
more than I'd anticipated, and I took a
deep, settling breath to recalibrate. "It
smells amazing in here, Auntie. Did you
make nkatenkwan?"

"How did you know *I* didn't make it?"
Momma said.

I shot my mother a disbelieving look.

★ Old lady. You start out as a "sister," progress to
an "auntie," and in the midnight hours of your
life, become an "abrewa." My grandma, eighty
years young, still declines the title.

17

Despite being the picture of the perfect Ghanaian woman, my mother's skills in the kitchen were notoriously lacking. She could crank out a reasonable kontomire, throw together an ampesi that Grandma wouldn't side-eye, but anything more complex was a wash. If it weren't for our omnipresent crashing aunties, I probably would've grown up on takeout.

"Where's Daddy?" I shouted, walking down the hall to drop off my bag in my room.

"Looking at himself," Momma shouted back. "Tell him he has to hurry up. Christopher and Gregory will be here any minute." When I circled back into the kitchen, she grabbed a hold of my arm, turning me around to face her. "So why isn't Frederick here? It would have been good for him to watch, for when he knocks."

Frederick, knocking, for me? When we first started dating, I'd seen it. Frederick standing at my door, bolstered by the parents I had never met, a bottle of ostentatiously expensive gin tucked under his arm. The image seemed preposterous now. Still, at its resurgence, my body ached with yearning.

"We broke up," I admitted in a small voice.

Momma's eyes widened. Then she released me, smoothing her hands down her dress with a huff.

"Ah, well, lawyers don't make that much money these days anyway." She narrowed her eyes critically at my hair, reaching up to fluff the crop of tight curls. "You know, I don't think this hairstyle is helping you. You know how these men are; they like their women with hair down their backs. Before you leave, you should try on one of my wigs. And we can take you around church; a few nice young men joined the congregation recently, and Sister Lisa has said some of them are looking —"

"I'm going to check on Daddy," I said with finality.

But before I could step toward my parents' bedroom, the doorbell rang.

It was Chris, right on time at ten thirty. Chris was the most punctual Black person I had ever met, a peculiar match for the perpetually late Tabatha. Thankfully, his patience was about as infinite as his love for my sister. At least from the outside, their relationship was by the book. Chris and Tabatha dated for the appropriate amount of time — three years, long enough to prove that Chris was serious, not so long that his intentions could be questioned. He was respectful, tall (which Daddy liked), African American (which Daddy liked a little less), and had recently landed a six-figure job as a mechanical engineer three months after walking the stage at the University of Illinois at Urbana-Champaign. When Tabatha insisted on moving to Evanston to pursue her MBA after graduation, Chris left his beloved college town behind and followed her north, spending hours in our living room chatting with our father and sipping Muscatella. We all knew it was only a matter of time before he knocked, but when?

And then, last week, I got the phone call. Chris cleared his throat and asked me to please find a way to get Tabatha out of the house, and within minutes, the entire Appiah family, both domestic and international, knew that *when* was *today*.

"Hi, Angie," Chris said, his smile a little shaky. He had spritzed on too much cologne, but otherwise looked smart in his blue button-down and dark wash jeans. He clasped a thin box that I knew contained the ceremonial liquor he would use to make his request. Behind him stood a heavyset middle-aged man. Chris's father, Gregory Holmes, I remembered, just before clapping his large hand in mine. Chris had done his research. You can't come alone to ask to marry a Ghanaian girl. My parents would have laughed him all the way back to Urbana.

"It's nice to see you again, Angela," Mr. Holmes said. "How's medical school going?"

"Well," I said, dismissing the many sleepless nights and the tearful breakdowns alone in a corner of the campus library in one woefully inadequate word. "Hard, but I'm enjoying myself."

Mr. Holmes inhaled deeply, as though my admission had shifted something deep and old inside him back into alignment. He was sixty-something years old, of the generation that remembered scorched churches and sundown towns, and every young Black person's success seemed to loosen the scars left by the state-sanctioned violence he had endured in his youth. He placed a heavy hand on my shoulder and squeezed, peering down at me over his bifocals.

"Good," he said. "Good. We're proud of you, you know."

I smiled. Old Black people were always proud of me. It felt undeserved; *my* parents had grown up free.*

"Thanks, Mr. Holmes."

I led them into the living room, where my

* Free to grow up as people, not people *asterisk*.

father now sat, arranging himself like an Ashanti chief on our blood-red couch as if he hadn't been preening in the bathroom seconds before. I'd disliked the decor in my childhood home for some years now, with its garish gold curtains, lavish green throw rugs, and custom coffee table with Gye-Nyame* engraved into the sides. It seemed desperate, a too-transparent proclamation of our family's Ghanaian-ness. It was as if my parents — who'd been born in Ghana, educated in Ghana, then shipped off to England in their twenties for jobs that didn't exist at home — had grown insecure in their heritage. When we first moved to the States, their habits and mannerisms had still been distinctly Other. Growing up, Tabatha and I had taken off our shoes before entering the house, folded our hands behind our backs when scolded, and were careful never to hand things to our elders from our left hands. But those habits were extinguished within a quarter of the time that it took for them to be ingrained in our parents in the first place. Even my parents' accents had become something oddly inimitable, no

* Adrinka symbols represent proverbs. Gye-Nyame, the most ubiquitous of these, symbolizes the supremacy of God.

longer the thundering brogue I used when describing to my friends what a Ghanaian accent sounded like, but something slightly English, slightly American, with a touch of a vague African something mostly audible in the *r*'s and *t*'s. The last time Momma went back to Tema and tried to haggle in Twi in the market, the seller accused her of being a foreigner and tried to charge her double. After that, our house was suddenly shrouded in red, gold, and greens, in adrinka symbols and carved ebony elephants. I was a bit surprised that Daddy hadn't broken out the kente cloth for the occasion.

Daddy didn't stand until Chris and Mr. Holmes stopped in the center of the living room. He regarded them with a cool smugness for a half second before languorously getting to his feet, moving with the syrupy slowness of a man who considered himself a great benefactor.

"Chris, good to see you!" he said, clapping him on the back with one hand. With the other, he reached for Mr. Holmes's hand. "Oh, Greg, Chris was telling me you were coming into town. How was the trip?"

The niceties continued. Daddy asked after Chris's mother, who unfortunately could not make it, and oohed and aahed over

23

pictures of Mr. Holmes's new BMW. When they settled into their chairs, Daddy shot me a look, reminding me to execute my duties as eldest daughter and serve our nice guests. I put on my most serene smile and asked them whether they would like anything to drink (orange juice for Mr. Holmes and water for Daddy and Chris), any biscuits* — *We have some good shortbread, you really have to try some* — and shuffled to the kitchen to help prepare the arrangement. The presentation had to be perfect — biscuits arranged so that not a crumb fell out of place, glasses filled to three quarters height with just two cubes of ice in Daddy's water, napkins folded into neat triangles, all balanced on a large silver serving tray. The first time Chris came over and my father sent me to the kitchen to prepare the tray, he had seemed uncomfortable being served. Now he barely acknowledged me before plucking a biscuit from the plate.

"How's Dorothy doing?" Mr. Holmes asked. I sighed internally; gathering my

---

*Yes, biscuits. The British imparted their particular brand of English on us, and some things stuck. For example, I am still convinced that *football* is the correct way to refer to the sport Americans like to call "soccer."

parents was like herding cats.

"Oh, she's doing well. She'll be out in a minute."

Daddy gave me another look, this one saying, *Go check on your mother,* and I obliged with a nod and slipped out of the living room and into my parents' bedroom.

I found Momma in front of her vanity wearing a gray sheath dress, her magenta maxi dress discarded at her feet. She gave me a chagrined smile, as shy as Dorothy Appiah could look.

"I looked out of place," she explained. "All of you are in muted colors, and I thought we should match, you know, for the pictures . . ."

She was nervous. Of course she was; the Appiahs were among the first crop of Ghanaians to immigrate to Naperville, and Tabatha the first of the children to have a Knocking. All eyes would be on our family, taking notes on how successfully we translated the marriage traditions through a Western lens. Any photographs we took would likely be circulated through WhatsApp groups across the country, and Dorothy Appiah was not about to give any cause for salty aunties to cluck about the mother of the bride trying to "steal the spotlight."

"You looked great before," I said truthfully, "and you look great now." I turned my body toward the door. "Come on, Ma. Hurry out before you miss the whole thing."

Momma didn't miss the whole thing, and neither did Auntie Abena, who snuck her nosy ass into the living room under the guise of sneaking some biscuits and ended up sitting on the couch next to Mr. Holmes, interjecting like Tabs was *her* daughter.

I did, though. Because just when Chris cleared his throat and said, "Actually, I have a reason for coming here today," I got a notification on my phone: an email from SCORES@nbme.org.

Your score report is now available, the subject said, and my heart took off in a gallop. My Step 1 score.* I hadn't been expecting it so soon; my upperclassmen had told me to expect to wait six weeks after the exam, and it had barely been two. And yet here it was. The main determining factor for the trajectory of my medical career, the

---

* Step 1 is the first of three major Step exams required to get an American medical license. The exams are designed to be pass/fail, but as residency programs have gotten more competitive, they have been used to "weed out" applicants. No one cares much about how you do on the other two Step exams, though there's talk about changing that.

test that determined whether I had a hope of matching to the specialty of my choice,[*] sitting in my email behind an unassuming link. I rushed into my bedroom to open it, tapping my foot impatiently as the PDF loaded on my phone —

A 209.[†]

I'd passed, but barely. I stared at the number in numb shock, feeling the tears I had held back all morning prickle the corners of my eyes. I had gotten 240s on all my practice exams. I'd studied for twelve hours a day for a month straight. How could this have happened? How could I have *let this happen? So much,* I thought, *for proving myself as more than the Affirmative Action*

---

[*] After medical school, you apply for residency in your specialty of choice. You then rank all the institutions where you interview, and they rank their applicants. All this info goes into a magical box, and then, in March of your fourth year, you open up an envelope that tells you where you'll be spending the next two to six years of your life in indentured servitude!

[†] An objectively awful grade. The average Step score is in the 230s and climbs every year because no one rises to the occasion more than a medical student who has banked $300K on getting into their chosen specialty.

Candidate.

On the other side of my closed door, my father's unrestrained laughter mingled with Mr. Holmes's, and I felt a smothering sense of loneliness. The father of a man who loved me so much that he wanted to be mine forever would never sit with my family nibbling on Walkers shortbread. After all, the one man I'd convinced to commit had left me out on the literal curb after just half a year. *Dorothy's first daughter is a doctor, but she's still unmarried, can you imagine?* the Appiahs still at home base would say among themselves. Up until today, they could have added, *Oh, but at least she's brilliant,* and for me, that would have been enough.

But now, they couldn't even say that. I was not only alone, but also a failure. *All of that potential, wasted,* they would say instead. *What a shame, what a shame.*

What a shame indeed.

I lay in bed, facedown and unmoving, until the Holmeses took their leave and my bedroom took on an orange hue. Being in my childhood room felt less like an escape and more like being trapped in a curated exhibit on Childhood Overachievement. Plastered on every wall were reminders of what I *should have been* before this Step score. The newspaper clippings announcing my induction into the National Honor Society. Trophies from the National Science Bowl regionals and Destination Imagination, from spelling bees and science fairs through the years. Stacks of Princeton Review books, AP workbooks from every available class, a placard next to my diploma marking me as Parkview High School's class of 2010's salutatorian. Markers of excellence, of a girl who always worked twice as hard,* who was the best of "the best and the brightest," not a girl who barely passed. Tabatha's bedroom was much more typical, covered in *Twilight* posters and clippings from *Seventeen* magazine, but Tabatha had grown up with a chiller, saner version of Momma who had allowed such trivialities. My version of Momma had been convinced that simply looking upon the image of a shirtless man was enough to get me pregnant.

Joke's on her, I thought. *If she'd known back then how disastrously bad I would be at keeping a man, maybe she would have let me spend a little more time ogling Taylor Lautner's abs.*

* As every Black kid has heard, "to get half as far."

29

My door slammed open so hard that it nearly ricocheted off its hinges. I looked up to find my sister glowering over me, her hands on her hips.

"You know your bestie has been blowing me up," Tabatha said. "She's freaking out because you aren't answering her texts."

With a sigh, I pulled my phone out from my pocket. I'd silenced it shortly after receiving my score in an attempt to shield myself from notifications from my class group chat, which would inevitably be full of Step-related humble-bragging. I had ten messages from Nia (all some version of Are you alive?) and thirty more from the "Sanity Circle" group chat brainstorming progressively more grisly ways that I could have been murdered en route to Naperville. I smiled in spite of myself.

Sorry to disappoint, I typed. I am, indeed, still among the living. When I looked up again, Tabatha was peering down at my face.

"You okay, sis?" she asked. "Momma told me about what happened."

My heart rate skyrocketed, and I rolled onto my back, looking up at her in terror.

"How did she find out?" I said, my mind racing. Had I somehow accidentally hit a button and forwarded my Step score to my mother? Had she hacked into my exam registration account and taken a peek for herself?

Tabatha raised an eyebrow.

"Um," she said, "because you told her?" When I looked at her blankly, she added, "About Frederick?"

The relief I felt was washed over almost instantly by despair, and I groaned, wiping my hand down my face.

"There are no secrets in this house, are there?" I said.

"Not a one," Tabatha declared. She closed the door behind her with a click, then dropped unceremoniously onto the bed next to me. She was still dressed in a chic jumpsuit from her outing, completely unaware that her boyfriend had spent the morning requesting her hand in marriage.

"Look at you," she said. "Sulking. Just like old times."

"I'm not sulking," I insisted. "I just have a stomachache."

"Yeah, sure, a stomachache," she said. "How are you so bad at lying? Even to yourself."

"How are you so bad at minding your business?" I snapped.

Undeterred, Tabatha sat up on her elbows and flicked me on the forehead.

"My big sister's emotional well-being is

totally my business," she said. "Anyway, what I came here to say was good riddance. No offense, but your boy Freddy was a jerk."

"No, he wasn't." I sighed. "Frederick was actually a gentleman most of the time. He just . . . wasn't that into me."

Him and everyone else. How many times had I thought I'd made a genuine connection with a member of the shittiest sex, only to be shrugged off like an old coat at the nearest opportunity? So many that I had practically lost count. But Frederick had seemed so different. After all, he'd done something groundbreaking: called me his girlfriend. He had looked at me and seen a future, seen something more than an ethnic, erudite fling to show off to his friends. He had wanted something more than an Ass. No one before him had managed that, no matter how poorly they fit the script for what a *fuckboy* was supposed to be. I'd made it to almost twenty-five before convincing a man to commit to me, and even he hadn't made it a year before saying "never mind."

A tear slid down my cheek, and I swiped it away, annoyed. To her credit, Tabatha didn't say anything for a long time, letting me mire in my misery. Then she sighed.

"Angie," she said. "Be honest with me.

Were you that into *him*?"

I rolled onto my side to give her an incredulous look.

"What do you mean, was I into him?" I said. "I was with him, wasn't I?"

Tabatha rolled her eyes.

"You know what I mean," Tabatha said. "Did you *like* him?" Then she grinned, kicking her voice up to a grating pitch. "Did he make you feel all warm and gooey inside?"

Impossibly, I laughed.

"Never make that voice again," I said, but I knew the answer to her question. It was one I'd turned around in my head over and over again ever since the excitement of being chosen had worn off, even before Frederick became distant. "I guess? Or at least, I *wanted* to like him. I didn't have a reason not to. I just . . ."

"You didn't have a spark," Tabatha finished for me.

I closed my eyes. Yes, that was true. Frederick and I hadn't had even the semblance of a spark. But I'd found our lack of chemistry comforting. With Frederick, there was no haze of hormones to cloud my judgment, no rose-colored lenses for red flags to hide behind. No opportunity to do what I did best, which was to throw myself heedlessly into another person and let them

33

drain me dry. A spark was like a sprig of parsley next to a steak: nice, but not necessary, for love. Not objective. I had looked at Frederick, with his three-piece suits and silver tongue, his law degree and his easy, ready smile, and thought, here is an investment that is low risk, high reward. No need for a will-they-won't-they, no hours spent second-guessing intentions and ruminating over lingering touches. Frederick's romantic interest was explicit from the start; after all, we had picked each other like items off a menu. I would have to learn to love him, and I was more than okay with that. Frederick had felt safe, until he hadn't.

I told Tabatha as much. To her credit, she didn't say anything for a long time. I was thankful for that. Not even a year ago, Tabatha might have responded with a pithy statement about how I needed to work on my self-esteem, and I would have been forced to kick her out. But a year out in the real world had taught her that she didn't know everything, and so when she opened her mouth to speak again, I listened.

"You know what, sis," she said. "I think you're thinking too hard about this. Love isn't a test. There aren't right answers. You can't get into anyone's head and puzzle together whether or not they can love you, or you can love them. You just have to jump in blind and accept the chance that you might get hurt."

Lucky for me, I'm bad at tests too, I thought bitterly.

"Well, some of us have better odds than others," I muttered.

Next to me, I felt Tabatha stiffen, gearing up to protest. I closed my eyes against her defiance. No matter how much Tabs tried to empathize, for her, my romantic troubles just didn't compute. Growing up, she'd been Baby Appiah 2.0, with most of my book smarts but none of my diffidence. When we first moved to America, I buckled under the weight of my otherness. The abrupt transformation from being an individual to just another "African booty scratcher"* shattered my first vestiges of self-esteem, and I spent the next nearly twenty years picking up the pieces.

"You know, you're *always* saying shit like that." I could feel her glaring. "That it's easier for me, or something."

Because it is, I thought. Like it or not, Tabs checked off all the boxes for "universally hot Black girl": light skinned enough

* Okay, but why has every African immigrant in America been called this?

35

to pass the paper bag test, slim-thick, with hair that was always laid and makeup that was always tasteful. When Tabatha wanted someone, she hardly had to ask herself if they wouldn't want her back for something she couldn't control, if she was too chubby or too dark or too loud, because she wasn't any of those things. Maybe Tabs and I were different because of natural temperament, or because she was younger and more effortlessly American. Or maybe she had simply been born with the more acceptable set of characteristics. Most people knew how to love a girl like her. They didn't really know what to do with one like me.

"Fine. Whatever. Let's say that it is," Tabatha said then, breaking our uneasy silence. "But what I'm saying is that you don't make it easier. You're always thinking about how men don't like you because of *x* or *y* or *z*. But the truth is, Angie — you're part of the problem. You only go for the low-hanging fruit, and you act all shocked when half of it is rotten."

Good ol' Tabs. Always delivering her toughest love with a heaping spoonful of disdain. I winced, throwing my arm over my eyes.

"Geez. Down, girl," I said without bite.

Tabatha pursed her lips, swatting my

shoulder.

"Well, I guess I should allow you at least forty-eight hours to wallow in self-pity before ripping you a new one," she said. "But at least come out and eat with us. Auntie made nkatenkwan . . . and if you make me wait any longer for it, I'm gonna steal all of your meat."

"Like hell you will," I said, launching myself out of bed and onto my feet. Quick as a cat, Tabatha sprang for the door, muscling me out of the way, and for a moment, in pursuit of the best cut of goat, I left my grief at the door.

THREE

"Are you sure you can't stay any longer?" my father asked. He leaned against my doorframe with his arms folded, watching me stuff my pajamas into my duffel bag. His expression had all the mournfulness of the family pet watching his favorite visiting college kid pack at the end of a break. I would have felt worse about my quick escape if he hadn't spent all of dinner last night interrogating me about my grades.*

"I have a meeting at one with Dr. Wallace," I reminded him. It wasn't a complete lie; I did have a meeting at 1:00 p.m. with Dr. Wallace — in two weeks. But I also had almost twenty-five years of Immigrant Parent experience, and I knew that the best

---

* "The first two years are pass/fail, Dad," I complained. "Pass/fail? Do they not give you a percentage when they hand you your papers? What does that number say?"

way to avoid a guilt trip when trying to make an early exit was to come up with a school-related excuse.

"Well, next time you should come home earlier," he said petulantly. "You have a car, and you live close. You need to commit more time to family."

Miss you too, Daddy, I thought.

"I'll visit soon," I said, skirting past him. Momma was already at work, a small blessing. "I promise."

"Okay," he said, following me out the front door. He pulled me into a hug that would have been comforting if my skin hadn't been crawling with anxiety. "Drive safe. Tell Nia I said hi."

Last night's nkatenkwan had only temporarily delayed my despondence. After twenty-four hours of high-intensity exposure to practically all the potential triggers for my impending breakdown, I was in need of two things: (1) an exit plan (achieved) and (2) a distraction. I'd texted Nia, but she had planned for my absence by finally scheduling the bread-making class I'd given her for Christmas and wouldn't be home until late. Michelle, who had journeyed with me from our Midwestern college to our Midwestern medical school, was still on her Step study block, and wouldn't be free to hang for another week. A bummer; I couldn't very well go sit in my apartment alone with my thoughts. I would have to entertain myself.

Thankfully, it was summer in Chicago. Every Friday to Sunday, there was bound to be a niche street festival or four to explore, a free concert, a park performance of *King Lear.* I scrolled through the city calendar of events, selected an art fair in Pilsen that was only twenty minutes from my apartment, and went on my merry way.

Evidently, the entire city had the same idea.

"Y'all don't have to go to work?" I muttered, grinding my teeth as I drove farther and farther away from the festival, looking for a free parking spot.* *This is fine,* I reminded myself, tamping down on my frustration before it could bubble over and turn into misery. *You have nothing but time to burn. Besides, it'll be nice to explore the neighborhood.*

Eventually, I found parking about a mile and a half away from the festival entrance. Outside, the bright afternoon sun flared in full force. Somehow, I had forgotten that a

---

* With these loans, ain't nobody got funds for $20 city parking.

world existed outside my sphere, one that consisted of city noise and summer color. I thought back to my last few months, which I'd spent holed up in various libraries studying for Step or hiding away in suburbia at my parents' house and realized that I hadn't been properly out in a long time. My world had narrowed to me, Nia, and the occasional interloper,* and the abrupt expansion to so much more stretched my senses thin. I popped my headphones in and selected an upbeat song, the soundtrack for my reintroduction to my bright new world.

Pilsen had a grungy charm, I decided. I'd wandered its streets before, but almost always at night, almost always after drowning my post-exam sorrows with Michelle at some bar. A shame — a neighborhood like this deserved to be appreciated sober and in the light of day. Practically every building featured a colorful, heavily detailed mural, and the juxtaposition of cultures — Mexican, Chinese, Gentrifying Yuppie — meant that every block hid a pleasant surprise.

About a mile into my walk, a gated clearing came into view, an interruption of brick

* A category that includes my now ex-boyfriend, given that he left me on read for most of the spring.

and awnings with lush green and pink and yellow. It was small, barely half a block wide, but glorious. A flaking hand-painted sign at the entrance designated the area as LYDIA'S FLORAL ARRANGEMENTS URBAN GARDEN, EST. 2013, and another read, PUBLIC ACCESS ENCOURAGED. Despite the inviting message on the sign, Lydia's garden was unoccupied. The gate creaked noisily as I entered.

Inside, the garden was even more breathtaking than I expected. Butterflies fluttered through the air, and squat, fuzzy bumblebees buzzed over the petals of bright orange daylilies. I knelt in front of a rosebush so perfect that my mother might have tried to uproot it. My fingers hovered over the unblemished white blossoms, just barely brushing against the velvet-soft petals.

Frederick used to bring me flowers. On our first date, I told him that I hated them as gifts ("they're so much work to prep, you can't really do anything with them, and they die, like, instantly"), and after that, every time I saw him, he had some for me — a fat blue hydrangea blossom, a bushel of baby's breath, a half dozen red roses. At first, I thought it was our little joke. I would hunt around my apartment for the most ridiculous container for them — empty coffee

42

canisters, Diet Coke bottles, and, once, a whole saucepan — and put them in a place of honor in the living room for him to find. At first, Frederick had played along, egging me on . . . but after a few weeks, the flowers stopped coming. And then one day, when we were out to eat, he'd told me that I was ungrateful. "I bet every woman in this room would love to get flowers from their man," he'd insisted, and I realized that, all along, he hadn't been getting those flowers for me. He'd been getting them for himself: to prove that he was the kind of guy who got girls flowers.

And deep down, I'd known that.

Suddenly, I felt fragile, like a cheap glass teetering at the edge of a counter, only a nudge away from shattering. I knew I was headed into a vicious cycle, and fast: unmitigated sadness I had no right to feel, followed by self-loathing, because of course I still felt it. I sat down on the sun-warmed stone of the garden path, tucking my knees to my chest and watching the dark splotches of my tears splash and spread on my jeans. What was *wrong* with me? It was like Tabs had said. I didn't love Frederick, and he hardly liked me. I was too brash for him, too unpolished. He wanted a poised, political wife, and I had been willing, for a while,

43

to flatten myself to fit that mold. And for what? Eight-year-old Angie had dreamed of white coats, not white weddings, and instead of focusing on studying for the last major hurdle in the way of that dream, I had let myself be distracted, anguishing over how to fix a relationship with a man I didn't even want.

"Excuse me," a voice said.

I yelped in shock, my hands flying instinctively to cover my face. The cords of my earbuds caught on my arms, sending my earbuds flying and cutting my music off halfway through "In Fantasia."

Okay, so the guy kneeling in front of me was cute. Real cute. I hadn't gotten a particularly good look, as I was presently trying my best to disappear, but it had been enough for my body to know that it was attracted to his and that alone made me want to push past him and go flying out the garden gate.

Cute Boy laughed good-naturedly as I swiped at my tears, trying in vain to gather the scattered fragments of my dignity.

"Kishi Bashi?" he said. "You've got good taste."

It took me a moment to realize that he was talking about my music. My volume had been turned all the way up; no wonder

I hadn't heard him approach. I sniffed, accepting my earbuds back as he handed them to me.

"Thanks," I said numbly, finally letting myself look at him. Good god, was he hot. Maybe not to Nia, who would probably say he was too lean, but he was exactly my type — tallish, with thick, black eyebrows and an unabashedly sunny smile. He was some kind of brown, maybe South Asian, probably Latin, and dressed simply in black joggers and a burgundy hoodie that was, embarrassingly, almost the exact same color as my shirt. He had his longish hair pushed back and secured with a thin headband; his inevitable girlfriend was probably desperate to cut it.

"Are you okay?" he asked, and I winced. "I don't mean to bother you, but . . ." His smile became sympathetic. "You looked like you needed bothering."

"I'm fine," I said, stretching to my feet.

Now that the initial shock had worn off, I was wary. That a boy had approached me in the wild was not particularly unusual. I was still my mother's daughter, after all. Men finding excuses to stop me in the street had ceased being a compliment and become more of a nuisance not long after I hit puberty, and I had since perfected the art of wheedling myself out of unwanted conversations. Every now and then, though, I wouldn't *want* to escape. I would find the guy charming, and we would banter and flirt, exchange numbers, and talk for a good length of time before he abruptly ghosted, or worse, I discovered that he wasn't actually on the market.

This was not one of those times. Cute Boy was attractive, but he had atrocious timing.

"It's okay if you aren't fine," he was saying. He stood up too, shoving his hands deep into his pockets. "I won't judge."

I narrowed my eyes.

"So is this what you do?" I asked. "Hide out in the bushes like some kind of troll, and then pop out to offer comfort to all the crying girls who come into this garden?"

He laughed.

"Who's hiding?" he said. He pointed at a bench a few feet away, only somewhat obscured by a row of delphiniums. Blood rushed to my ears; how had I missed him there? "I was just sitting there, minding my business. You're the one who came barging into a public garden to have a cry."

"You've been here this whole time," I said, my stomach sinking.

"Well, yeah," he said. "I was going to leave you alone, but you sounded pretty miserable. Though, I will admit, the whole thing was pretty cinematic, what with this backdrop." Just as I was about to sink into the earth, he added, "Nothing to be ashamed of. I've had a couple good cries here myself."

That gave me pause. Not just because he was making light of my breakdown, but because he'd offered up his own. I couldn't remember the last time a man had told me that he cried without shame.

"You have?" I said.

"Oh yeah," he said. "To answer your question, though, I usually come here to draw." He ducked his head, suddenly shy. "And. Um. Actually, I was hoping to ask you a favor."

Here it goes, I thought. *Let me guess, the favor is going to involve me holding something for you. And surprise! That* something *is your dick —*

"I was wondering if I could draw you."

My heart stammered in my chest. It was a strange request but flattering all the same. And I could tell that he was serious; I could see now that he'd left a small book and a pencil pouch on the bench.

"Oh," I said.

Cute Boy seemed to have used up all his bravado on his initial approach, because

47

now he could barely meet my eyes.

"Sorry," he said, "I know it's kind of a weird thing to ask —"

"No," I said quickly. When his smile faltered, I added, "I mean, no, it's not weird. Okay, who am I kidding, it *is,* but I don't mind. You can draw me."

He smiled so widely you would've thought I'd offered to pay his rent. And he had *dimples. Christ.*

"Oh. Okay! Great!" he said, noticeably more animated. "My name's Ricky, by the way. And you are . . . ?"

"Angela," I said. "Angie."

"It's nice to meet you," he said, then, all business, headed back to the bench.

At Ricky's direction, I sat, cross-legged, in a patch of sunlight on the ground across from him. The foliage around me left dappled shadows across my legs but spared my face. He instructed me to put my hands on my knees, then changed his mind and had me fold them in my lap. When he was satisfied, he pulled his sketchbook onto his lap and began to draw.

The early summer breeze shifted through the trees, still carrying with it the sting of spring chill. Without my music, I could hear the loud stillness of the city, cars zooming down the street only tens of feet away, birds chirping, Ricky's pencils scratching against paper. The places where the sun touched my skin felt warm and light, and I took in a deep, cleansing breath. I felt loose and liquid and languid. It was the most at peace I had felt in months.

"You can move, you know," Ricky said after a while. I opened my eyes to find him looking at me with amusement.

"Doesn't my pose matter?" I asked. He smiled, switching out his graphite pencil for a colored one.

"Not anymore, not really," he said. "I just wanted to get your face right." Then he stuck his tongue out, teasing. "This isn't the Royal Academy; I don't need you to stay put for six hours for your portrait."

"Nice of you to wait" — I checked my phone for the time — "fifteen minutes to tell me that." I bent forward in a stretch, making a show of shaking out my kinks. "Are you almost done?"

"Yup," he said. "Just hang on a second." He pulled a corner of his top lip into his mouth, his eyebrows furrowed with concentration. I watched him as he switched between colored pencils automatically, using only red, yellow, and blue. After a few more minutes, he grinned up at me. "Okay. Here."

I sat next to Ricky on the bench, accepting the sketchbook when he handed it to me. In the millisecond before it could exchange hands, it occurred to me that he could like to draw but be terrible at it and I would have to praise this stranger for highlighting my worst features —

I needn't have worried.

"What the hell, Ricky," I said, dumbstruck. By cross-hatching the primary colors together, Ricky had managed to bring a new, shimmering dimension to the garden, merging and blurring the flowers and leaves into a mere suggestion of themselves. And the image of me — it emanated peace and contentment and none of the turmoil I was feeling in reality. He'd made me so beautiful, and so effortlessly. My throat tightened, and I felt my eyes well with tears again.

"Do you like it?" Ricky asked.

"O-of course. It's stunning," I stammered. The tears I tried to hold back trailed down my face, and I sighed and wiped them away before they could fall onto his small masterpiece. "Oh no," I said, exasperated. "Sorry. I can't seem to stop doing this today."

"Hey, it's okay," Ricky said in a low voice. Then he added, "Do you want to talk about it?"

"No offense, Ricky," I said with a snort.

"But why do you care?"

Ricky's expression didn't change. Instead, there was a flicker of strain behind his eyes, like a light being turned off and then back on again, gone and back so quickly that I might have missed it if I hadn't been specifically searching it out. But then his smile disappeared altogether, and he leaned back on the bench, rubbing his chin thoughtfully.

"I . . . Honestly, I don't know," he said finally. "I just knew that if I didn't talk to you, I'd regret it."

You are not an experience, Rational Angie said, but Hopeless Angie had already taken over. This close, I could see that Ricky's eyes were the color of Coca-Cola, the kind in a glass bottle, clear mahogany in the shifting afternoon light. That he smelled like freshly laundered clothes and spearmint gum. My gaze drifted to his exposed forearms — not muscular, exactly, but masculine, with roping veins and long lines of sinew. I wanted to ask him what about me he thought he would miss. I felt like he would answer truthfully, and that that answer would fill me.

"Fine," I said. "But . . . *law of equivalent*

exchange,★ okay? I need your tales of woe too."

If he was offended by my demand, he didn't show it. Instead, he let out a bark of laughter.

"Oh my god," he said, looking at me with awe. "Is that a *Full-metal Alchemist* reference? Are you a *weeb*?† See? I knew it. I knew you were kin."

His smile was so damn bright that I had to avert my eyes. Thankfully, he was too busy fiddling with the zipper of his hoodie to notice. I thought at first that he was removing it because he was too warm, but instead he pulled the lapels apart to show me the symbol on the shirt he was wearing underneath it.

"An Earthbender,‡ really?" I said, chuckling at his enthusiasm. I would give the man

★ Basically, the law of conservation of mass, but make it anime and add attempts at necromancy.
† Short for *weeaboo,* or someone who is really, really into anime.
‡ In the greatest Western animated series of all time, *Avatar: The Last Airbender,* the world contains benders, or people who can manipulate one of the four elements: earth, water, fire, and air. A better way to sort personalities than Hogwarts houses, in my very humble opinion.

credit where it was due; he was very good at cheering me up. "Would've pegged you for Air, actually."

Ricky looked genuinely affronted.

"An *Air*bender? Me?" He scoffed. "What would give you that idea?"

"Your sunny disposition?" I posited. "Your general spontaneity?"

"Me?" Ricky said. "I'm not spontaneous at all."

I snorted, gesturing in an arc around us.

"Ricky. Hate to break it to you. But, uh . . . why am I here, talking to you right now, if you're not spontaneous?"

"I thought we established that my talking to you is part of a great cosmic plan," Ricky said, smirking. "No, but really, I'm not. I angst over every decision I make. It took me years to build up the courage to just say fuck it and do what I wanted to, you know? I almost ended up going to law school because of that."

"Law?" I swallowed, imagining Ricky, hair slicked back, socializing with Frederick and his seedy lawyer friends in the back of a bar that straddled the line between classy and drug front. "That's . . . huh."

"Yeah, I don't see it either. My grandpa did, though, so I entertained it for a bit," he explained.

"Really?" I asked. Immigrant parents pushed their kids into medicine all the time, but, as Momma had astutely observed, *Lawyers don't make that much money these days.* "Does he work in the field?"

Ricky laughed.

"Nah," he said. "He's a carpenter. Like it or not, I clearly got the art thing from him. He mostly builds custom furniture these days." He pulled out his phone, beaming with pride. "Like . . . check this out."

He skimmed through a series of photos showcasing beautifully sculpted, detailed vanities. One of them even had an interactive mirror, the likes of which I had only seen on the internet. I gaped.

"That's *amazing,*" I said. "He should've just taught you to do this! Why even bother with law?"

Ricky shrugged.

"Pretty sure he just likes the billboards." He smirked. "You know. Gutiérrez and Sons. 'We bring the hammer!' "

"Didn't work on your dad?" I asked.

"My dad," Ricky said without skipping a beat, "is a piece of shit. So . . . no."

He sounded bored as he said it, not impassioned or even angry but weary, the way you'd get over rain that never stopped or a drain that never completely came unclogged.

"That was very un-feminist of you, by the way," he said, chugging along as if he hadn't just dropped the Daddy Issues bomb on me. "Jumped straight to Dad. Why can't Mom be the potential lawyer parent?"

I scrunched my nose.

"How'd you know that that wasn't my next question?"

Ricky squinted one eye at me.

"Because it wasn't."

"You're right. I'm problematic." I watched a striped caterpillar inch its way up one of the bench's legs. "So you decided to be an artist even though your grandpa was pushing for the J.D. because your dad is, what, unworthy?"

"First of all, I'm a graphic designer," he said. "I illustrate on the side. But yeah, pretty much. So, what do you do?"

"Ricky uses evade," I said, smirking. "It's not very effective."

If Ricky was offended by my nosiness, he didn't show it. Instead, he laughed and shook his head in disbelief.

"And now a Pokémon reference." He grabbed my hand, sandwiching it between his. "Jesus. Who are you? I mean, other than perfect."

My heart seized in my chest at his touch.

Oh my god, Angie, you are insane, I thought. Not even one day had passed since I'd been dumped by Frederick, and I was trying to catch feelings for a complete stranger. And an artsy boy, no less: the most likely subtype to ruin my life and destroy my credit.

I slid my hand out from between his and nestled it between my thighs. I watched Ricky's eyes track the movement. Then they ticked back up to mine, his lips curling into a smile.

"Charming me will get you nowhere," I said, even though it was getting him everywhere.

Ricky tapped his foot. I followed his gaze over the garden, out onto the sidewalk at the entrance, where people still passed, walking in their troupes, not sparing the spill of nature in the middle of their city even the slightest glance.

"I'm starting to think you're a bit strange," Ricky said without malice. "I think a normal person would know that they're just supposed to awkwardly pretend I didn't say anything."

"Oh, talk about the pot calling the kettle black," I said, chuckling. "Regardless, you *did* say something, so I'm not going to ignore it. Unless you don't want to talk about it. We can make fun of pedestrians instead." A young man with a most unfortunate hairline walked in front of the gate. "For example, someone who loves homie over there really should tell him to just give up, shave his head, and grow a beard like everyone else —"

Ricky held his hands up. The tension hadn't left his shoulders.

"Okay, okay. Can't let you go off attacking people because of me," he said. "And don't think I'm letting you off the hook. Law of equivalent exchange, right?"

I shrugged, but I was smiling. "Let's see what you've got first."

"My dad isn't really in my life," Ricky said. He scraped the ground with the heel of his shoe. "Grandparents did all the raising. He only used to really show up to ask for money. He was fine when I was younger, I guess, but now . . . Now I'm competition. So he just tries to piss me off."

I whistled. "Ah." Then: "Does it work?"

Ricky and I talked for two hours. I didn't realize how long we'd been sitting there, on a creaky aluminum bench in the middle of a tiny block garden, until our secluded space began to fill with people. Despite the heat, we were pressed together, shoulder to shoulder, fingers touching but not overlapping, breathing in tandem. The conversation had started out about his dad, who I agreed sounded like trouble, then about his grandparents, who, in direct contrast, sounded incredible. I told him about my Step score, about how, after years of watching my hard work translate into success, I suddenly had to contend with failure. (I didn't tell him about Frederick, because, well, he'd already seen me crying. No use making myself look even more pathetic by letting him know that it was over some guy.) We talked about art, with the vague promise of going to the Art Institute together sometime soon, then politics. I talked about how disappointed I had been in my classmates' silence about unarmed Black people being executed by police when they could be so loud about unjust exam questions. He talked about how, over the years, the friends he had grown up with in Logan Square had been pushed out of their homes by rental hikes, only to be replaced by wealthier, whiter families who repainted their brightly colored sidings with palatable, neutral tones. ("My grandparents were lucky. They own their house but . . . the neighborhood doesn't quite feel like home anymore.")

I felt like I knew him, even though I

didn't. I remembered Tabatha's advice, given years ago after a failed situationship. *Don't think too hard about things. Just live in the moment.*

"You have totally derailed my afternoon plans, you know," I said. I stood up and stretched, humming in contentment as my vertebrae clicked one by one.

Ricky chuckled, watching me intently from the bench with an odd expression on his face. The razor-thin intensity of his focus made me suddenly bashful, and I sat down again, weaving my fingers together.

"That wasn't my intention," he said slowly. "What were you planning on doing?"

"Oh, nothing much," I said. "Was just going to check out the art fair, then go home and take a nap." I shrugged. "You?"

Ricky smirked. "Nothing planned," he said. "I worked a couple weekends this month, so I took PTO today as a gift to myself." Then he tilted his head. "The art fair sounds cool. We should go."

I shook my head in disbelief. This boy really had no shame, did he?

"We?" I said. "By god, you are persistent."

"Hey," Ricky said. "It took a ton of guts for me to talk to you. I'm trying to get my money's worth."

I didn't believe him, that it had been hard

59

for him to talk to me. For a guy like Ricky, I suspected that it had been as easy as breathing.*

But it didn't matter. I'd silenced all my internal reservations sometime after he'd put the finishing touches on my drawing, and, despite my protests, I knew damn well that I was going to be spending my next hour gallivanting through a random street festival with a guy I'd met in a garden who was definitely going to disappoint me. I suspected he knew this as well, judging by the crooked smile he gave me as he stuffed his supplies into his backpack.

"Come on," Ricky said, slinging his bag haphazardly over one shoulder. "I want some elephant ears."

And, like a fool, I followed him.

Hanging out with Ricky was . . . *fun.* Despite my protests, he paid my $10 festival entrance fee ("You make negative money right now," he teased), and ran from booth to booth with all the enthusiasm of a toddler let loose on a playground. He stopped at

---

* "The good boys should be a little scared of you," my dad had said once. "If he can make your heart beat with a few words, run away! That one has a lot of practice."

nearly every booth, hitting up the artists to discuss technique, pointing out small quirks in each of their styles. *This one uses gouache,* he would say, or *Whoa, do you see how she's built up the texture here? Genius.* When he spotted a booth featuring anime characters in period clothing, he spent fifteen minutes debating between a poster of Vegeta with a monocle or Sailor Moon in French rococo before eventually purchasing both. Six months with a partner who ducked his head with embarrassment every time I showed more than lukewarm interest in anything "childish" had made me a dull girl indeed, but after only a few hours, I could feel Ricky drawing me out. All I had to do was say that I liked something, and he would be tugging my hand to drag me to investigate or disappearing for several minutes only to return with it in hand. Which was exactly what he had just done, with a plate of funnel cake, retrieved after I offhandedly mentioned that I hadn't had it in years.

"I thought you said you wanted elephant ears," I said, as he handed me a fork.

"So you don't want any?" Ricky teased, drawing the plate away just before I could stab into the powdered fried dough.

"No, I just . . ." I ducked my head. *I just*

*need you to stop being so sweet so I can like
you less, okay?* "Let me get the next thing."

Ricky gave me a curious look, then broke
off a piece of cake and popped it into his
mouth.

"You're not used to people doing things
for you, are you?" he said matter-of-factly.

My mouth dropped open in protest.

"I . . . That's not true," I said.

"Yeah?" he said with a smirk. "Then . . .
you'll take this?"

He reached into the front pocket of his
backpack and pulled out a small folded
paper bag. I watched him beadily as he
reached in and produced . . . a Water Tribe
pendant. It was a solid piece, with the heft
of stainless steel, and a thick chain to support its weight. I didn't know whether to
balk or laugh.

"What if I wasn't a Waterbender?" I said
instead, and Ricky scoffed.

"The whole healer thing? The fact that
you can be *ice cold* when you want to be?"
he said. "All Water Tribe. You could be nothing else."

"Well, then you just made quite the move,
considering we just met," I said, turning the
pendant over in my hands. "Don't you know
what it means to give a nice Water Tribe girl

a necklace?"*

The moment the words escaped my mouth, I wished I could take them back. *Too far,* I thought, watching as Ricky's smile flickered with unease. Our banter may have been easy, but Ricky was still a stranger with whom I was having a momentary adventure. Jokes about our betrothal were probably crossing the line.

"Well," Ricky said, a heartbeat too late to be natural, "are you going to wear it?"

"If I don't, what will you do with it?" I said.

Ricky looked thoughtful for a moment.

"I could return it," he mused, "but the guy who made it is a local artist, and he made a good sale. I can't very well disrespect his craft like that. So . . . I guess it would sit in my dresser until I came across another Waterbender worthy of it." He undid the latch, holding up the necklace in an offer.

I imagined him stepping behind me, his fingers brushing the back of my neck as they fumbled with the latch, his body radiating heat onto mine. My breath catching as his hands splayed over the back of my neck. *Do you like it?*

* Hint: it's a proposal.

63

Just the image was giving me palpitations. No way was I letting it become a reality.

Giving him an apologetic smile, I took the chain from him and quickly fastened the pendant around my neck myself. When I looked up, Ricky was giving me that *look* again, the one he'd given me back at the garden that made me feel like I was under a microscope. Not heavy or sexual, like he was undressing me with his eyes, but somehow more intimate, like he was taking me apart and putting me back together again in his head.

"When did you get this?" I said, breaking the silence.

"When I got our water," Ricky said. He cocked his head, regarding me with a smile. "It looks nice."

Thank goodness for the gift of melanin. If I had Michelle's complexion, I would have been beet red. Just in case my embarrassment was still apparent, I walked purposefully in front of him, heading toward the end of the street, where a large stage was set up. This close, the music, before just a distant thumping, was deafening. A small group of people sat on the curb by the stage, eating their festival food and slurping from pineapples filled with piña coladas, chatting with one another as the DJ tried his best to gain their attention. A troupe of girls danced drunkenly to the music, spinning in lazy, uncoordinated circles. The dance floor would fill up in a couple of hours, when the festivalgoers had a bit more to drink, but for now, it was sparse.

"I think we've seen everything," I said. The Water Tribe pendant, though cool to the touch, felt hot against my clavicle.

"Yeah?" Ricky said. He sounded almost mournful.

I nodded, looking to the stage. To my amazement, the sun was straddling the horizon. Nia had sent me a text an hour and a half ago announcing that she was coming home, and my response (Me too, boo!) had turned out to be a lie.

The song changed to a bluesy cover of "In the Pines" that I recognized from my playlist of TV show soundtracks. I closed my eyes, letting the speakers blast the words into my body. We listened to the first chorus in comfortable silence, swaying and holding on to what we both had to know were our final moments together. Our knuckles bumped against each other, but neither of us shifted to make space, relishing in those small, innocuous touches. I realized, chagrined, that I wanted him to hold my hand.

"My girl, my girl, don't lie to me . . . Tell me

where did you sleep last night," Ricky sang softly next to me. I turned to him, surprised that he knew the song, and he smiled down at me, his dimples popping into view. For a brief moment, I felt like a girl in a movie, like all the previous day's misfortune had occurred just to lead me to this place, to this boy. Maybe it wouldn't be so bad to like Ricky. He liked me, right? That was what all this was about — his drawing, our day at this festival, the gift he had practically slung over my neck. And why wouldn't he? Already, we seemed to slot together like adjacent puzzle pieces, our tastes in music and media, interests, and values aligning almost exactly. It was as though the heavens had seen me crying and dropped the perfect guy to wipe away my tears right at my feet. I didn't believe much in fate, but maybe Ricky hadn't been so far off when he said that our meeting was a part of a *cosmic plan.*

"My girl, my girl, where will you go? I'm going where the cold wind blows," I sang back, just a little louder. Ricky's eyes brightened with delight, so genuine that it made my chest hurt. We sang the last bit together, bellowing at the top of our lungs without a care for pitch or tone or decorum.

"In the pines, in the pines, where the sun never shines, I WOULD SHIVERRRRR . . .

the whole night through!"

When the song ended, we buckled over in unison, erupting into peals of laughter.

"Oh man, you are super talented," I said, "but *so* tone deaf."

Ricky waved me off, still braced on his knees.

"Yeah, well, I wouldn't quit med school for a music career if I were you," he said, wiping away tears. We grinned at each other stupidly for a moment, and then he straightened.

"I guess you have to go," he said.

"Yeah," I said, suddenly subdued. Goodbyes were always strange, but this one felt especially hard. "Well," I added, "you have my number."

I didn't need to look at Ricky to know that he was doing that overly intense staring thing again.

"Yeah," he said. He stepped closer, like some part of him resented the space between us. His gaze dropped rapidly to my mouth and then traveled back up to my eyes, and I tracked it, sucking in my bottom lip instinctively. He was going to kiss me. It would be a perfect kiss to close an almost perfect day, just awkward enough with my hands full of funnel cake that we would probably share a laugh afterward, and I

67

would definitely fall for him then.

I couldn't let that happen. I stepped away abruptly.

"Can I see you again?" Ricky said, undeterred.

I tilted my head, considering.

"Are you asking me out on a date, Ricardo?" I said teasingly, tracing the raised swirls of the Waterbender symbol on my pendant.

Suddenly, the air between us grew cold. I watched Ricky's expression cycle between panic and chagrin before evening out to a smile that didn't quite reach his eyes.

I knew that look. Fucking hell. I thought about what I'd thought of him, when he'd first bent over to ask me if I was okay: *No way is a guy who looks like that gonna be single* —

"Um," he said. "Sorry. No, I didn't mean to give you the wrong idea . . ."

It was always me with the wrong idea. Always me somehow "reading into things" —

"But I'm already seeing someone." He looked away, chewing at his inner cheek. "Sorry."

Even expecting it, I felt like I'd been slapped.

Ricky had the nerve to look put upon, like

I had done him a disservice by daring to define what we had in romantic terms. To think that I'd thought of him as sweet, *child-like,* even, when he was really just another fuckboy wasting my time. Old Angie would have given him what for. *How would your girlfriend feel knowing that you spent all this time and money on some random chick? The fuck is wrong with you?*

But I wasn't Old Angie anymore. Being with Frederick had taught me restraint, and I knew that cussing out the boy who, only seconds ago, I had been prepared to make out with in the middle of an art fair on Halsted probably wouldn't make me feel better. So, instead, I bestowed him with my most dazzling smile.

"On second thought," I said cheerfully, "please *lose* my number." I shoved the rest of the funnel cake into his hands.

"Angie," Ricky started.

Too bad for him. I'd already heard every excuse in the book, and despite his creative talent, I doubted Ricky could come up with an original one. Turning on my heel, I found a space in the throng and practically dove through it, marching my way toward my car. Over the music, I could hear Ricky call after me again. The *audacity.*

Turning on my phone, I scrolled to Nia

Johnson and hit "call."

She picked up after one ring.

"About time, girl," she said. "You coming home?"

"Yeah, I'm on my way," I said, gritting my teeth. "But I have to tell you about my day. Because you will *not* believe this shit."

FOUR

"In conclusion, you are way more reliable than any man will ever be," I said to Nia, stomping up the stairs to our shared apartment. On the other side of the door, I could hear Nia cackle.

"Yeah, well, I could have told you that," she said. "I can hear you, hang up."

I unlocked the door, toeing my shoes off and flinging them in the general direction of our shoe rack. The moment I crossed the threshold, I felt a warmth settle into my bones. Momma hated that I called my apartment in Hyde Park my home. "This house right here is your home," she liked to say, but I hadn't felt like myself in Naperville in a long time. Home was a cheap two-bedroom walk-up that I shared with my best and oldest friend and occasionally a foster kitten I would try to convince said friend to let me keep. Within its walls, I was no one's eldest daughter and no one's older sister

71

and I didn't have to *prepare a tray.* I could just be Angie Appiah, without edits.

"Honey, I'm home!" I shouted, throwing my hands into the air.

"Wifey!" Nia yelled from the kitchen. She hustled to the door to greet me, her T-shirt dusted with flour, and pulled me into her arms. I sank into her softness like a best friend–sized marshmallow.

"You're like a puppy, you know that?" I said. "You always act like you're scared I won't come back."

"I know what your parents are like," Nia said, kissing her teeth. She deepened her voice to a surprisingly accurate imitation of my father's. "Angela! What is this *B+* ? Clearly you are off playing the fool in the city. Come study at home; we definitely won't lock you in your room with your books. Maybe you can even find a nice husband under your pillow."

"Ha," I said humorlessly, remembering the realities of Step again.

Nia pulled back and held me at arm's length, her eyes flitting over my face in concern.

"Oh, honey," she said. "You've been *through it,* haven't you? You okay?"

"I'm fine," I said. I wasn't, not entirely, but the thick cloud of misery I'd waded through yesterday had lifted over the course of the day. It was as though my mind had simply decided that it was tired of being sad. *Or,* I thought, *as if that stupid cheating cute boy hit a hard reset button in your brain.*

"Every day I thank the Lord that he made me a lesbian. Liking straight men is a curse," Nia continued. "I'm sorry about Frederick. And about this new guy, too." She zeroed in on my neck. "Though I've got to admit that Water Tribe necklace is dope."

I'd forgotten I still had it on. Swiveling the chain around my neck, I unhooked the latch and held the necklace out to Nia.

"You want it?" I said. "You can have it."

Nia laughed, wagging her head.

"Nah, girl, keep your trophies," she said.

"Fine," I whined. I wandered into my bedroom and dropped it unceremoniously into my pile of tangled costume jewelry. "At least Frederick's trophies all died. Small mercies, I guess."

"All those fucking flowers," Nia said, rolling her eyes. I snickered as I walked back into the living room; Nia had seen the genius behind my flower pranks, even if Frederick hadn't.

We settled at the dining room table, and I sprawled out across it, inhaling deeply.

73

Against all odds, I felt . . . relieved. Regardless of the disastrous result, Step study block was now officially behind me, leaving me with three precious weeks off with no commitments, no lectures, no exams. It was the most freedom I would see until my fourth year. Whenever I said this out loud, Nia would scoff and inform me that *some people have jobs and haven't had a summer since college.* I would remind her that she had once complained to me that she'd binged all the good shows on Netflix and now had nothing to watch, and that she hardly went a day without reminding me how glad she was that she'd never have to study again. *Oh gross,* she'd say, pointing at my computer screen. *What is that?* Half the time "that" would be a harmless histology slide, which for all intents and purposes consisted of amorphous pink blobs, but she'd insist that the dark purple nuclei triggered her trypophobia and skitter away squealing. Once, for fun, I'd shown her what schistosomiasis of the eye looked like, and she'd nearly reintroduced both of us to her lunch.

But now, instead of trudging to campus for an eight a.m. lecture or to the library for fourteen hours of caffeine-powered studying, I would be doing my best to sleep in until after Nia came back from work. I would take a pole class like I'd secretly always wanted and, afterward, eat back my calories with my fill of Jeni's ice cream. Now that Frederick was finally out of the picture, I could just *do me.* And I was the only one, it seemed, who could do me right.

"You're handling all of this exceptionally well," Nia observed. She hadn't stopped staring at me since I sat down, assessing me for any cracks in my facade.

"I know." I peered up at her through my lashes. "I mean. What else can I do? I've emailed Dr. Wallace to come up with a contingency plan, and I'm going to stay the hell away from men. Everything else is kind of out of my hands." Tom, one of our annoying downstairs neighbors, turned on his music, cranking the volume up so high that I could feel the bass through our floorboards. But I didn't have to wake up early tomorrow, and I was too drained to care. "What I'm saying is . . . I guess I decided there was no point in being miserable anymore."

Nia held my gaze for a long moment. It had been eleven years since she'd slammed her tray down next to mine in our high school cafeteria and declared us "Sisters in

75

Blerdom,"* and I'd yet to meet anyone who understood me more. If I had anything to hide, Nia would see right through me. But, for once, I was laying myself bare.

After a moment, Nia rolled her eyes and sighed dramatically.

"Wow," she said. "You're actually okay. What a disappointment."

I gave her an incredulous look. She ignored me, twirling a coil of her hair around her finger.

"Sanity Circle convened," she said, "and we just knew that you were gonna be crushed. A decision was made" — she reached over and placed a hand over mine — "to give you your birthday present extra early." Then she tilted her head, holding back a smile. "But, seeing as you're fine, I guess we'll just wait until it comes up."

I perked up, both touched and embarrassed that my imminent breakdown had been the topic of a round table discussion.

"My present?" I gave Nia a mournful, wide-eyed look that I knew was more cartoonish than cute and held out my hands. "Please? Pretty please?"

"I don't know," Nia said, even as she stood to retrieve it. "Markus, Michelle, and I

* Blerd = Black nerd.

agreed that this was for a rainy day . . . so you better act like you're *devastated* when we call them."

"I'll put eye drops in," I insisted. "Trust me. I've had a lot of practice crying over the last couple days. I can do it."

Nia's laughter boomed through the apartment as she disappeared into her room. A moment later she returned with a gold envelope. Eyeing her, I peeled it open and found . . . concert tickets. To see *Beyoncé.* I nearly fell out of my chair.

"They're shitty seats, chill," Nia said, practically bent in half with laughter as I gaped down at the precious, pristine slips of paper in my hands. The eve of the Best Day of My Life was marked in black blocky letters: JUNE 5, 7:00 P.M. Two days before the Scariest Day of My Life, when I started on the wards. I'd been so lost in my head about my Step exam and Tabatha and Frederick that I'd forgotten to stalk tickets to the tour.

"Fuck a man," I said, holding the envelope to my chest in shock. "All I need is you."

Nia smirked and patted me on the head.

"About time you figured that out," she said.

Dr. Wallace's office hadn't been renovated since the 1970s. The chestnut wood paneling, once fashionable, had lost its sheen over the years, and no one in maintenance had bothered to reapply its lacquer. Still, it was a spacious office and private to boot, and Dr. Wallace took advantage of that space by filling it with books, boxes of unopened academic journals, and various paraphernalia from conferences past. It was the office of a true academic, meaning that it was only about three years away from being featured on an episode of *Hoarders.*

"Sorry about the mess," Dr. Wallace said, as if the mess were new. She pushed her monitor aside to look directly at me. "So. Step didn't go so well."

I sagged in my seat. When I first started medical school, Dr. Wallace had been a mythical figure. The sole Black woman on the tenure track at our institution, she had a résumé that would have made my parents weep: undergrad at Johns Hopkins, medical school at Yale, residency and fellowship at *the* Brigham.* But her achievements had not stopped with her training: Dr. Wallace had carved herself a niche in gastrointestinal

* And she said it like that too, with her chest, not doing that coy "residency in Boston" thing that so many of the Harvardians like to do.

sarcoidosis,* and her serious, round-faced facade graced half of the hospital billboards down the interstate. I had emailed her to make my introduction a week after matriculating into medical school, and she'd been checking in with me every few months since. Disappointing my parents sucked, but at least it was par for the course; disappointing Dr. Wallace made me feel like a failure.

"It didn't," I said. I sighed. "I know. I've closed a lot of doors for myself."

"Okay," Dr. Wallace said, not entertaining my self-flagellation for even a moment. "First question: What specialties are you interested in?"

I bit my lip. I still didn't really know. It had taken me years just to realize that I even *wanted* to be a doctor outside of my parents' influence. When I was born, my father had raised me into the air and declared, "Our firstborn will be a doctor!" and for most of my life, I'd gone along with my destiny. The determination of my career path seemed a small price to pay for their sacrifices, and a natural one; after all, I was academically "gifted," and medicine was a respectable field.

* Something so subspecialized that I'm honestly not sure what it is either.

But then, one day, something changed. I had been shadowing in the Emergency Department, as was the premed tradition. It was a slow day, and I was bored stiff; most of my shadowing shifts consisted of trailing after whichever resident* had gotten saddled with me and pretending to understand medical lingo. The Emergency Department techs wheeled a patient — a man, early thirties, Black — into one of the many empty rooms. He asked for pain medications, but when pressed for details about where he had pain kept giving us different answers. "My shoulder," he'd said the first time. "My back. My stomach." Every part of his body that we touched evoked a reaction, but further questioning was met with either silence or beratement — "Why are you asking me all these questions when I'm in pain?"

"This is what we call a 'seeker,' " the

* A quick overview of medical hierarchies. A medical school hopeful is a premed. After you get into medical school, you become a medical student. You then select a specialty and become a resident. If you want to pursue further specialized training, you can become a fellow. At the top of the hierarchy is the attending, who practices autonomously.

resident said when we returned to the computer. "Look at his heart rate and blood pressure. Rock solid. He's looking for a fix."

"A seeker?" I asked.

"You know," he clarified, giving me a pitying look. "For IV pain meds. Gets them high."

I wasn't so sure. The man's behavior reminded me of my father's. When he had appendicitis, Daddy had lain around the house, stone-faced aside from the occasional grimace, and vacillated between refusing and demanding our attention until Momma got tired of his mood swings and dragged him to the hospital. Four hours later, he was in the operating room.

There were no other patients for me to see, so I returned to the man's room. Upon my entrance, he scoffed.

"The student," he said. "Y'all really are just playing with me at this point." When I raised my hand, he jerked away and fixed me with a scowl. "Don't you push on me again."

"I won't," I promised. "Look — I want to help. Can you please tell me what happened?"

Thirty minutes later, I got a story. He was a forklift operator in a nearby warehouse, and two days before his arrival in the

Emergency Department, had been rammed in the gut by one of his coworkers. The pain had been terrible, but initially manageable, thanks to a friend's leftover Percocet. When I relayed the history to my resident, his eyes nearly bugged out of his head. One STAT CT scan later and the man had been swarmed by a frantic surgical team and injected with enough IV narcotics to send him to nirvana.

Up until that day, pursuing a career in medicine had seemed like another box on my life's to-do list. But without my interference, that man could have sat in the Emergency Department for hours. Maybe he would have gotten sicker. Maybe he would have died. And for what? Because the team had mistaken his distrust for criminality? Because he was young, Black, and not kissing their asses? I imagined a lifetime of patients like him. I imagined feeling a sense of satisfaction that went beyond grades and trophies and the approval and envy of Naperville's coalition of Ghanaian parents. I felt . . . necessary.

"I know I want to go into a field where I have a long-standing relationship with patients," I answered truthfully. "And that I probably don't want to do surgery. But that's as far as I've gotten."

Dr. Wallace nodded, leaning back in her office chair.

"Okay, so that makes things a little easier," she said. "We would have been in trouble if you wanted to go into a specialty like orthopedics or plastics.* No interest in dermatology, right?" When I shook my head, she turned back to her computer, clicking through her folders. "With that score, a nonsurgical specialty is more realistic. You can still match into internal medicine, pediatrics, psychiatry, et cetera, if you play your cards right. What ended up happening with that project you were doing first year? Did you get an abstract† out of it?"

"Yes," I said. "And a poster presentation."

Dr. Wallace beamed.

"Good." Then she turned her monitor toward me. "Here. This is a list of clinical research projects that are actively seeking help. Go through them and see if anything

* All competitive specialties with high Step 1 score cutoffs — I would basically have no chance with my score.
† A research abstract is a short summary of a research project, and, while getting one published in a scientific journal isn't as prestigious as a full paper, it still looks pretty nice on a med student's CV.

interests you and let me know. I'll introduce you to the PI.* Since your score is lacking, you're going to need to bulk up the scholarly work section of your application."

There was a humming sound; Dr. Wallace had printed the list for me. Ducking underneath her desk, she retrieved a small stack of papers from her printer, then riffled through her drawers. Having found her stapler, she pressed them together and, with a flourish, handed the documents to me.

"Look," she said. "I want to be honest with you. You are a Black woman with a low Step score. They are going to use that to confirm their bias that Black students underperform." When I lowered my head in shame, she rapped her knuckles against her desk to bring me back to attention. "So you need to do two things to prove them wrong: do well during your clerkships† and stack up on publications."

"What about community service?" I asked,

---

* Primary investigator, in this case, the attending running the research project.

† Like an apprenticeship. During your third year of medical school, you get a one-to-three-months-long crash course through every specialty. You're graded on your clinical performance. The standards are legendarily opaque.

hopeful. I'd spent much of my first and second year coordinating free clinics, an experience that had continually reminded me why I was torturing myself into this field.

Dr. Wallace smiled. It was the same smile you gave a child who told you that they wanted to be an astronaut when they grew up.

"You know, your heart is in the right place, Angela," she said. "And you have done a lot of good work already. But think of your service as sprinkles on an ice cream cone. It might help you stand out, but it won't get you through the door." She let her words linger, then tapped the list she'd given me. "Make sure you pick a project you can get done in your third year," she said. "A literature review, or maybe a meta-analysis. Something where the data is sitting in a database, and you just have to comb it out."

"Okay," I said. I scanned the list of projects, making mental markers next to the ones that sounded doable. I tried to ignore the sinking sensation in my gut. The current third-years looked exhausted from rotations alone. How was I supposed to study

for my shelf exams,* look good on my clinical rotations, *and* work on research?

"Chin up, Angie," Dr. Wallace said.
"You're a strong student. You're going to do
great things." She leaned forward and patted my hand comfortingly. "You just have
to jump through a few hoops first."

* Shelf exam — a three-hour specialty-specific
exam taken at the end of every rotation.

FIVE

Dr. Wallace's list sat, unaddressed, in my backpack for a week. This was by design; I had the next year and a half to jump through hoops, but only a few more days to *turn up.* Besides, there was still much to do. I shopped for business casual clothes for my rotations,* submitted my requests for my clerkship sites, and, most importantly, prepared myself for Beyoncé. Nia's gift was twofold — concert tickets *and* a long-awaited reunion of the Sanity Circle. And now that the whole crew was getting together, every single one of us had to be on point. We had a dress code and everything. If I couldn't be smart, goddammit was I going to be cute, and my whole squad too. We had "Partition" on. *We been dranking.*

"Turn around again," I told Michelle, who

* An emotionally scarring experience in itself, thanks to the Ass.

had shown up at our door in leather pants and red pumps that screamed Sandy from *Grease*. "Look at how good your butt looks, girl!"

"Study block booty," Michelle said, wagging her hips. She was already two shots of Patrón in, which, for Michelle, meant that she was a whiff of beer away from plastered. She turned around, grabbed her chest. "Study block titties too. All that stress eating was good for something!"

"Oh, that lil' thang?" Nia said from her doorway. She spun into view, thick brown curls bouncing, grabbed a hold of the doorframe, and dipped backward as the bass dropped low in the song. Then she turned and dropped, jiggling her impressive bum in her black jumpsuit.

"Okay, okay, I lose," Michelle admitted. "Though you'd better be careful. If Markus's girl sees you do anything like that, she's going to turn the car around."

"Diamond gon' have to chill," I said. I reclined on the sofa, satisfied with our work. We looked good. Faces beat for the gods. Hair laid. Bodies right. Diamond was going to be mad regardless.

She was, of course. When we opened the door, Diamond was right behind it, her smile strained as her eyes flickered from girl to girl. I refrained from rolling my eyes and opened my arms for a hug instead.

"Hey, Diamond," I said. "How was the drive?"

"It was good!" she said a little too cheerfully. She looked good too, dressed according to the code in a backless black dress. If she would just look in a mirror and see that she had nothing to worry about, I would like her a lot more. "Markus drove the whole way. He's *so sweet* like that."

My attention shifted to Markus, who was hanging behind his girlfriend and giving us a shy smile. I thought about holding back for Diamond's sake, then changed my mind and threw myself into his arms. His laugh was breathless, but he squeezed just as tightly as I did.

"I am so mad at you," I told him. "The fuck you been? You never call! You never write!"

"But I'm here, aren't I?" he asked. It had been two years since I'd seen him in the flesh, inexcusable since he lived only a two-hour flight away. Our grainy phone cameras hadn't done him justice. I brushed my hand over the back of his head, feeling the transition from coarse curls to stubble and skin.

"Whose idea was this fade? Had to be yours, right?" I asked Diamond, who had accepted a drink from Nia and was, bless her, trying her best not to cause a scene. "We couldn't get this boy to a barber if we put a knife to his throat."

"Hey!" Markus said. He was currently being enveloped by both Michelle and Nia, and the former was drunkenly kissing his neck. Sensing danger, I waltzed over and drew Michelle away to a couch, complimenting Diamond on her hair. On cue, Michelle wrapped her arms around me instead and kissed me, very tenderly, on the cheek.

We sat down, briefly caught up, and called a Lyft. I pretended not to notice Nia stuffing a flask into her cleavage, made sure everyone else had their tickets (I didn't trust Michelle to keep track of hers, so I kept it in my bag), and forced everyone to pose for pictures while the lighting was good. Then we were strutting out the door, looking like the hottest new hip-hop girl group featuring Omarion.

The venue was packed when we arrived, even though we were an hour and a half early. Nia somehow got her flask through the security check, and we joined the other thousands of excited Beyoncé stans in the stadium. As expected, the level of Black Girl Magic was through the roof; everyone was showing up and showing out just in case the Queen decided to bestow them with a glance. We ogled the prices of concessions, then went to scope out our seats. They weren't great, but that was okay; the massive screens currently projecting an ad for a local radio station would give us enough of a view. Nicki Minaj was blasting over the loudspeakers.

"I need to pee," Michelle announced, two minutes into "Super Bass." I turned to Nia, who was busy rapping along with Markus, and offered Michelle my hand. We made our way, wobbling on high heels, down the stairs. A petite girl in a gold sequined dress stepped out in front of us, her steps certain in her spiked stilettos. Her long black hair swished and shone as she walked, and I marveled at just how *pretty* everyone in attendance was. The girl seemed to have the same idea as us; we trailed her through the extra fly crowd until we reached the bathroom. It wasn't too hard to find; about thirty other ladies had had the same idea as us and were lined up outside. Michelle grit her teeth as we sidled up to the back of the line.

"I'm gonna piss myself," she declared. "What if I use the men's? There's like, no guys here anyway, right?"

I looped my arm through Michelle's just in case she decided to turn that idea into action.

"Girl, of course there are guys. *We* brought a guy."

"Where's the support, Angie?" To my horror, she tapped the girl in the sequined dress on the shoulder. "Hey. You. My friend's a wuss. Wanna sneak into the men's with me?"

The girl giggled, a tinny, happy sound. She had large, round eyes, with brows that turned up like a Precious Moments doll.

"I don't know if I can use a urinal," she said hesitantly.

"I'm sure we can figure it out," Michelle said. She widened her stance and dropped into a squat. "Maybe we can back it up over it like this?"

"You realize men's rooms have stalls, right?" I interjected. "Besides, the line's moving. You'll make it."

Michelle did make it. No one pees faster than a bunch of girls terrified that they're going to miss "their song" at a Bey concert. The line at the mirrors was another beast entirely, though; whatever time our fellow concertgoers had saved Valsalva-ing* the pee out of them was immediately squan-

---

* You know when you bear down to take a dump?

dered on making sure that their falsies were hanging on just in case their faces made it on the jumbotron. I squeezed past a row of girls reapplying their lipsticks to get to a sink. The girl from the line squeezed through beside me. She smiled. It was the same smile lone travelers had given me in hostels in Europe, inviting and shy and a little bit brave.

"I like your cat eye," she said. "I can never get mine to look that clean. Plus, it's hard to get eyeliner that's black enough."

"Drugstore, eight bucks," I said, smiling back. Aside from cherry-red lipstick and foundation, she wasn't wearing much in the way of makeup. "I have it with me, if you want me to do yours?"

She smiled brilliantly, revealing the tiniest, most charming gap between her two front teeth.

"Could you?"

We dried our hands. I located Michelle, who had found a sink on the far side, and gestured to her to join us. We made our way to the back wall, and I took the girl's chin in my hand and tilted her head up.

"What's your name?" I asked, uncapping

Congrats, you know how to do the Valsalva maneuver.

my liner.

"Camila," she said. "Yours?"

"Angie," I said, then pointed to Michelle, who had an arm wound tightly around my waist. "The octopus is Michelle."

"Nice to meet you, Camila," Michelle said, squeezing tighter.

"Okay, now stay still. This eyeliner isn't super forgiving, so if I jack your face up I'm making a run for it, okay?"

Camila laughed, then schooled her face into neutrality.

"Okay, okay. I'm trusting you!"

She was right to trust me; I'd been doing the same cat eye on my own face for the last three years. Camila maneuvered her way to the mirror to examine my handiwork, then giggled, pleased.

"Looks like I won't have to beat you up," she said. She looped an arm through the arm that Michelle had not already claimed. I would have found her easy touch presumptuous in any other situation, but Camila was like a puppy in the rain, lost, adorable, and searching for the first person who would offer her shelter. Who was I to turn her away? "I think you guys are sitting close to me. I'm in section 324. Do you think they'll care if we sit together?"

I looked down at her, surprised and a bit

impressed by her gumption. Before I could respond, Camila continued, her tone taking on a pleading edge.

"I'm here with my boyfriend," she explained. "He's not actually a fan, but I kind of made him come. But now it's kind of weird, you know, 'cause it's *Lemonade*? I don't want to be singing 'Sorry' at him by myself?"

"Okay," I said. "You can join us, but just warning you — my friends are a *lot*."

Together, we walked to our section. Camila flashed the stadium worker a dazzling smile as she showed him her ticket, which was for the section to the left of us in the sparsely populated bleachers. He gave her a beleaguered look, just enough to let us know that we were inconveniencing him, and then let us through.

"We made a friend!" Michelle announced to the group, breaking out of my hold to bound toward Nia and company.

"Us too!" Nia said.

I peered around her, to where Diamond and Markus were standing, Diamond with her arm around a new guy who was not Markus, her face alight with the most genuine smile I'd seen on her since we'd met. From this distance, I could tell that the guy she was talking to was cute. My body knew that it was attracted to his before it could register that it had felt this particular attraction before, to his even brown skin and arms that were not thick with muscle but instead threaded with sinew and thick black hair that looked so much better up in a ponytail and would probably look best mostly hacked off —

You have got to be kidding me.

The boy turned around, a ready smile on his face. It was Ricky. Of course it was Ricky. And of course Camila was peeling away from me to lope toward him, because he was her boyfriend, of course he was, and my stomach was sinking deep into the cradle of my hips and the alcohol that I had drunk two hours before burned the back of my throat.

I'm seeing someone, he'd said, and the person he was seeing made *sense* for him. Even with my head swimming, I could appreciate how good Camila looked tucked underneath his arm. When Nia had asked me whether I was okay after the festival, I had said yes, and I had meant it. But now? I felt like I'd been sliced with a hundred papercuts and then dunked into a vat of alcohol.

Our eyes met, and Ricky's expression went blank. I wondered whether mine mirrored his, whether our friends could trace the path of our gazes and catch wind of the tension between us. Michelle was already excitedly introducing herself to Ricky, who had an arm slung over his perfectly sweet, perfectly fun girlfriend, and I wondered if he would recognize her from the stories I'd told him in the garden as my *crazy Korean friend.* Then Diamond was pulling me forward too, and I remembered to reassemble my face into something of a smile, the kind that probably would not reach my eyes, the deadly smile that only Nia would recognize. Except today she didn't, because the Weeknd was playing over the speakers and she was too drunk to notice.

"This is Ricky," Diamond said. "He lived across from me my freshman year! I just saw him sitting over there by himself —" She pointed across the bleachers, where Camila had said she was sitting. "Small world, right?" She looked up at Ricky, too excited to notice that he was doing a piss-poor job of matching her fervor. "Ricky, this is Angie. She's one of Markus's good friends."

Ricky's eyes flitted up and down my body as if he couldn't help it, and I praised whatever Higher Powers There Be for at least ensuring that I looked fine as hell on the day that I ran into him again. He looked nice too. He was dressed smartly in a navy short-sleeved button-down and black jeans. He opened his mouth, closed it, opened it again, clearly at a loss for words.

"Nice to meet you, Ricky," I said, and thrust out my hand. I held his gaze in a dare. After a pause, he recovered and took my hand to shake.

"Nice to meet you too, Angie." He tilted an eyebrow up in a subtle question, and I clenched his hand tighter in a warning.

"Angie did my makeup in the bathroom," Camila announced, beaming.

I gave Camila a thin smile.

"The artist is only as good as her canvas, Camila," I said.

"Pretty sure it's the opposite," Ricky said. Camila swatted his shoulder, but I only stared coldly, taking pleasure in the way his smirk slowly lost its luster. Then, with a nod and a wave, I moved around them to the other side of Nia, as far away from them as possible.

It's him, I wanted to tell Nia. *The boy from the garden. The one who gave me the Water Tribe necklace.* But then the stadium lights were dimming, and the jumbotrons surrounding the stage lit up with an image of Queen Bey's eyes, her lips, her thighs. It was impossible to stay upset then, not with the excitement pulsing through the stadium. I screamed as loud as I could manage, my voice melding with those of the thousands of other stans in attendance.

Once Beyoncé's curvaceous silhouette graced the stage, I was hype. When she opened her mouth to send forth her outrage, I echoed it with all the feeling in my body, eyes clenched tight, joining the chorus of ecstatic-angry fans. Because, really, who the fuck did Ricky think I was? Who the fuck did any of these men who played games with the hearts of women like we weren't real, breathing, feeling people deserving of respect think they were? I wondered if Ricky would recognize himself in the lyrics, and if he would, at the very least, feel bad. Probably not. He'd probably already rewritten history in his head and absolved himself of any questionable behavior by assuring himself that he'd only wanted to be kind to a damsel in distress. I wondered whether he understood that *Lemonade* was about men like him, who could smile in the faces of the ones they loved all the while betraying them.

And then the chorus hit, and I forced myself back into the moment and far away

from this man who, God willing, I would
never have to see again.

SIX

The Sanity Circle started the next morning much like we had ended the night, in a groaning heap across the Appiah-Johnson living room. There had been plans, of course, to split off between the couch and our respective bedrooms, but all of those had gone to shit after we'd decided to sit around rehashing our college glory days after the concert instead of going to bed. We ended up falling asleep where we sat, blankets distributed unevenly among us, leaving us with kinks and aches in places we didn't know we could get kinks and aches.

"That's your foot in my back, Markus," Michelle said. She had an arm over her eyes. I didn't feel too sorry for her. She'd earned that hangover.

"Everyone alive?" Nia asked. We all grumbled in the affirmative and no one moved a muscle until, several minutes later, Markus rolled off the sofa to pee. The next twenty minutes involved stacking bathroom use such that one person was always peeing and another brushing their teeth at a given time, hydrating ourselves via water from the few clean mugs leftover over from the previous night's shenanigans, and discussing which greasy brunch place was least likely to have a wait.

It was not until we got to Yolk that Diamond revealed her treachery.

"How many?" the hostess asked.

"Five —" I started to say, but Diamond cut in.

"Actually, seven please." She gave me an apologetic smile. "Sorry, I invited Ricky and Camila."

I nearly rounded on her, but then remembered that, to Diamond, Ricky and I had only just met yesterday, and that he was the only person who was actually her friend and not just an associate by proxy. I closed my eyes, held back a sigh, then opened them and gave the hostess my most dazzling smile.

"Great," I said. "Seven."

Nia was not drunk this time, which meant that the strain in my voice did not go unnoticed. A moment after we'd found a corner to chat away our ten-minute wait in, she looped an arm over my shoulders, an-

102

nounced that *we* needed to pee, and guided me to the bathroom. Michelle stared after us but said nothing. I winced. I knew I'd have to do damage control for that later.

"Okay, so what was that?" she said the moment the bathroom door had swung shut.

I held up both hands, then dived down to make sure Camila hadn't made it there before us.

"Michelle is going to be mad," I said. "Couldn't we have done this later?"

"Oh please!" Nia said. I realized then that she was actually annoyed, not just hunting for gossip. "You were grumpy all last night. Then just now! Why were you so damn salty? Yeah, maybe Diamond could've told you she was going to invite her friends — who you made absolutely no effort to talk to, by the way — but don't you think you're being a punk about this?"

I flinched, properly admonished. Nia had put in a lot of work organizing everyone just to make me happy, and I'd managed some-how, someway, to not be. *Always over men,* I thought with a pang of guilt.

"I'm sorry," I said. "I had so much fun yesterday, Nia. Honest. I just —" I threw up my hands. "Ricky is Art Fair Guy."

Nia stared at me, hands still on hips, brow

103

still creased, but eyes stuck in a wide stare. She shook herself out of her trance, then said, "Okay, what?"

"That day after Tabatha's Knocking. When I went to the art fair, and I hung out with a random guy I met? That guy was Ricky."

"The one who gave you the betrothal necklace?" Understanding flashed over her face, then delighted horror. "Holy shit!"

I nodded once, then shrugged.

"Yeah. Well."

Nia kissed her teeth, then shook her head in disbelief.

"Men!" Then she whipped back toward me, looking me up and down with concern. "Wait . . . You okay?"

"Oh my god, Nia, it was one day." I ran a hand over the back of my head, into the close-cut crop of dense curls. "Am I really that fragile?"

"Do you really want the answer to that?" Nia said flatly.

"Maybe not," I said.

"Thought so." She peered around me at the stall. " 'Kay, well, that's actually a pretty decent excuse, and I actually need to go. Wait here."

In my mind's eye, I could see Michelle, arms crossed and silent, preparing her tirade — *You and Nia are always leaving me out,*

104

and I get that you go back further than me, but we've all been friends since college and it isn't fair to me — and winced. From her stall, Nia gave a long, satisfied sigh, clearly unconcerned about Michelle's impending ire. Michelle never got after her for excluding her, most likely because Nia did not give a singular fuck. "Get over it, it's not that serious," she had said the one time Michelle had tried to confront her six years ago.

When we returned to the group, they were already piling into our seats. Neither Ricky nor Camila was anywhere in sight. I would have been more relieved if Michelle hadn't been giving off fury in waves.

"You were there a while," she said, flipping through the menu aggressively.

"Yeah, 'cause Angie had to take a dump," Nia said. "Ange. Wanna split a Chunky Monkey with me?"

"I kind of wanted the apple blintzes," I said. "But . . . I also want an omelet . . ."

"I'll get the blintzes, you get the omelet," Michelle said. She said it nonchalantly, but everyone at the table, save Diamond, knew that it was her way of settling a score that did not need settling. I pursed my lips, decided on a Santa Fe omelet, and had just started smiling hopefully at our waiter when I saw Ricky come through the door.

His hair was down today; that was the first thing I noticed. It had a subtle curl to it that hadn't been as apparent the other times I'd seen him, and it fell across his face in a way that was both appealing and really fucking ridiculous, like he was trying to be Mexican Fabio or something. I'd probably been staring at an especially dumb lock for a full five seconds before I realized that he had come alone.

"Hey, guys," he said. "Sorry I'm late." He walked over to the empty chair across from Diamond.

"Where's Camila?" Markus asked. Next to me, Nia snorted. I elbowed her under the table.

"Sleeping in," Ricky said simply. He picked up the menu, flipped it around in his hands. "All the brunch spots in Chicago, and you guys go to Yolk?"

"What do y'all have against Yolk?" Markus said. "It's delicious! The food is bountiful! There are many locations and reasonable wait times!"

"He's mad because Angie said the same thing," Diamond explained in a stage whisper. Ricky's gaze flitted to me, and I looked pointedly at Diamond when I answered.

"I never said it wasn't delicious," I said. "I'm just saying there are a million other non-chain places we could have tried."

"You mean *you* could have tried," Markus accused. "I don't live here! You think I can just roll up anywhere in Nashville and order red velvet French toast?"

"It's Tennessee, Markus," Michelle deadpanned. "They'll probably deep-fry your red velvet if you ask."

"First of all, leave Tennessee alone —" Markus started, just as the waiter sidled up to our table.

We ordered, giving Diamond the last pick so she could have more time to deliberate. Ricky barely glanced at the menu before making his decision, like, despite his protests, a true Yolk regular. Once the orders had been placed, the coffee poured, and the menus cleared, we settled back into casual conversation. I chatted Nia and Michelle up about an article I'd read online, only occasionally tuning in to the conversation happening on the other side of the table. Seeing Ricky here, among my closest friends, felt surreal. I felt like I was reliving our afternoon in the garden, but instead of feeling the heat of the sun on my face I felt the gust of an overzealous AC, and instead of feeling impossibly close to him I felt like there was an uncrossable chasm between us. Even their discussion, which was currently about a prank Diamond and her roommate had played on Ricky and his in college, sounded like it was echoing through a distant valley. Two people, sitting at the same table, with mountains dividing us.

My phone buzzed.

Hey. It was from Ricky.

My eyes flickered over to him. Ricky looked like he had before, listening intently to something Markus was saying. I flipped my phone back over with a thud.

"What's up?" Nia asked, looking from my phone to me in alarm.

"CNN News alert," I said. "Some guy in Florida wrestling a gator."

"Fucking Floridians," Nia said.

Michelle turned on her phone.

"Wait, I didn't get that alert —"

"Sorry, did I say CNN? I meant Vox," I amended. My phone buzzed again. I ignored it.

"Another alert?" Nia asked with a knowing smirk.

I silenced my phone. This time I felt Ricky look at me, and I leered back out of the corner of my eye, channeling as much contempt into the look as I could garner. He turned back to Markus, a hint of discomfort on his face, and offered up a punny joke that they all laughed at.

The food arrived, and we set upon it like rabid wolves. I'd never seen anyone stuff an entire half slice of French toast into their mouth, but Markus somehow managed. Michelle and I divided our dishes in half and doled them out to each other with the automaticity of an old married couple. My phone stayed flipped, facedown and deceptively quiet, on the table. I was glad that at the very least Ricky didn't try to talk to me. There seemed to be an unspoken line between conversations at our table, one that was reinforced by the way Nia had turned her body away from them. That was probably why I missed the fact that the other side was now focused on me.

"Angie. Angie!" Markus said.

My chunk of omelet fell off my fork halfway to my mouth.

"Whoa, sorry, yeah?" I said, ears hot because of course Ricky had seen that bit of inelegance.

"You do your pediatrics rotation at Rogers Children's, right?"

I blinked. I didn't know that Markus knew that Rogers Children's existed.

"Yeah," I said.

"I knew it!" Markus said, puffing out his chest. He jostled Diamond next to him, who rolled her eyes. "See, baby, I do listen!"

109

Then he leaned forward, his whole body alight with the excitement of a child with a dirty secret. "Ricky volunteers at Rogers! He does Child Life stuff there. Small world, right?"

For the first time during this meal, I let myself look at Ricky with more than a passing glance. We met eyes instantly. I knew all about the tragedy of his mother's passing; how had he failed to mention that he volunteered at the children's hospital affiliated with my school?

"Yeah," I said. Neither of us looked away. "Crazy."

If Markus was disappointed that I hadn't been more excited about his discovery, he hid it well, and he didn't try to force interaction between us again. I appreciated that about Markus. He always knew when to drop what needed dropping, and when to pry. And he knew how to lighten a heavy mood with a stupid story — this time about the time he'd caught pneumonia as a kid and Child Life had tried to send him a guy in a Barney suit to cheer him up.

"I was sick as a dog, but I knew a demon when I saw one," he said. "Kicked Barney right in his dino-balls, hard as I could. He went down like a felled tree, just tipped right over. My momma was mortified but she couldn't stop laughing for long enough to help him up. Barney was over there rolling on the floor, in excruciating pain, because I played soccer and I knew how to punt —"

We laughed. At some point, our waiter put down our bill. We ignored it and Nia talked about the time in college Markus had sleepily kicked her in the crotch and we laughed some more until said waiter sidled up to our table ten minutes later to ask if there was *anything else we needed,* and after that we took the hint and left.

"I'm tired," I announced. I wasn't. I yawned anyway to add credence to my claim.

"Me too!" Markus said. "What do you think is wrong with me, doc? WebMD says I got the 'itis."*

"WebMD is a better doctor than me right now," I confessed. "Let's go home, Nia?"

Nia hummed in agreement.

"We're going to walk through Millennium Park before we head out," Diamond said. "So . . . ?"

"Yeah, I guess this is it," Markus said. "Happy early birthday, Angie. Don't hurt

* Or, according to Wikipedia, "postprandial somnolence."

yourself working too hard."

He opened his arms wide for a hug. I gave it to him enthusiastically. We said our good-byes like we said our hellos, except this time Diamond was too busy chatting it up with Ricky to be upset by the number of female parts coming into contact with her man.

Later, after we'd sent Michelle home and Nia and I had settled into our Uber, I finally checked my phone. There were three texts from Markus, all gifs cut from TV shows of people tearfully waving goodbye. One from Dr. Wallace asking if I had selected a project from her list yet. Six from Ricky.

Ricky: Hey.

Ricky: Confession. I did not honor your request to lose your number. Sorry.

Ricky: Actually, scratch that. I'm not sorry. I didn't want to. Because cosmic influence, you know. It would've been bad for my karma to mess with fate

Ricky: For real. Big city, and we all ended up at a Beyonce concert. I don't even like Beyonce! That's got to mean something, right?

Ricky: Markus is gonna choke if he keeps eating like that

Ricky: Angie. I know you're mad. But can we please talk? Just to clear things up?

I stared at the texts for a full minute, my brain short-circuiting because no way was he still trying to endear himself to me, the girl he'd taken for a ride, not even twenty-four hours after I'd caught him out with his girlfriend! Maybe when we were still sitting on a bench in Lydia's garden, doing a deep dive into each other's vulnerabilities, invoking fate had felt appropriate. Now, it seemed like a joke. To think, for a time I'd thought Ricky was *different.* Special. Emotionally intelligent and accessible in a way that was rare and precious in a guy.

But I'd been wrong. He wasn't special at all, just a palette-swap of the "irreverent manchild" model with which I was already intimately familiar. I'd be stupid to miss him. *Dick is abundant and low value,* Tabatha used to say, shortly after discarding a potential suitor. And this particular dick was of the bargain-bin, dollar-store variety.

"You all good?" Nia asked. She had asked me that question countless times over the last few days.

113

"Yeah," I said. This time, though, it felt less like the truth.

114

SEVEN

A week later, the Beyoncé concert, brunching with my best friends in the world and some guy who refused to remain a stranger, my orientation to the pediatrics rotation — all of it would feel like a dream.

"Angela," Momma said. It was 6:15 a.m., far too early for an Appiah Family Confrontation, but my parents had never been particularly considerate of my time. I had woken up to three missed calls from them near midnight, all followed by panicked voicemails — *Angela, call us right now.* I'd listened to them while walking into the hospital and obviously feared for an emergency, only to find that I'd fallen into their trap.

"Your father and I have been looking online.* People have gotten their Step 1 exam scores back. Have you gotten yours?"

* Fuck Student Doctor Network forums for keep-

115

Twenty-four years, eleven months, two weeks and four days old, and my parents were still hovering over me like flies over horseshit. I found an alcove in the hospital hallway, far enough away from the nurse's station that I could have some privacy. There was no use in lying to them; they already knew the truth.

"Yeah, they came out," I said.

My parents said something to each other in Twi, too quickly for me to pick out the words.

"Email us the score report," Daddy demanded. Ever since I'd left his house, he'd gotten into the habit of speaking in a voice an octave deeper than his usual tone in an effort to sound authoritative. Instead, he sounded silly, like a child imitating an adult.

I sputtered, indignant. Tabatha had started her MBA this year, and not once had they demanded to see her grades. This kind of indignity, it seemed, was reserved only for me.

"I," I said firmly, "am pre-rounding on my patients right now. In the hospital."

"It'll take you only a moment to send it," he insisted. "Why won't you just forward it

ing my parents abreast of my medical school goalposts.

116

to us now? Did you fail?"

Unexpectedly, a ball formed in my throat. *You're fixing this, remember,* I told myself. After the Beyoncé concert, I texted Dr. Wallace back about my chosen project. It was a literature review on DVT prophylaxis* — boring, but achievable. Still, it was hard to escape my shame, especially now that I was surrounded by my classmates again. The anticipation of finally being released onto the hospital wards had been sullied more than once by gunners† "accidentally" revealing their high scores. And instead of helping me look forward, my own parents saw fit to berate me.

"No, I didn't fail," I admitted. "I just didn't do well."

There was a hushed gasp from the other end. "Awurade Onyan-kopon," I heard

---

* If you've ever had the misfortune of being admitted to a hospital, you might have gotten shots of blood thinner one to three times a day. This is to prevent you from getting blood clots in your legs during your period of immobility and is called DVT (deep vein thrombosis) prophylaxis.

† Med school's overly ambitious professional test-takers who like to find ways to brag about their academic accomplishments to cover for the fact that, without them, they're sad and boring.

117

Momma mutter. I set my jaw.

"See, this is what I was telling you," Daddy started. "You were spending all that time in the city playing the fool, instead of coming home to study in peace. Playing around with a boy who can't even drive some small distance to come honor your parents —"

Anger spiked through me. Nia, with all her wisdom, had predicted this reaction almost verbatim.

"Momma, Daddy, rounds are coming up, and I have to see my patients," I said. "Can we please do this later?"

"Fine," Momma huffed. "But we will discuss this. Call us when you are done."

"Sure," I said, knowing that I would be doing no such thing. Then I hung up. My heart galloped in my chest and my eyes stung with tears. *You care too much about what Mom and Dad think of you,* Tabatha had said once. *You just have to tune them out.* But Tabatha *could* tune them out. She was their precious, pretty baby girl, deemed too sensitive for the form of "correction" they liked to dole out on me. If she ignored them for a few weeks, they would accept her back with open arms. I, on the other hand, would have to return on my hands and knees.

"Breathe," I muttered to myself. I glanced

down at my patient list. A week into pediatrics, and I'd already crossed it off my list of possible professions. Hospitalized kids were depressing, but they definitely helped put things into perspective; my parents could be insufferable, but some parents were worse than that. Besides, I hadn't been lying when I told my parents that I had to pre-round. The first step to proving myself worthy to future residency program directors was to ace my clerkships, and I was not about to let my parents' pearl-clutching sabotage that.

I stepped out of my alcove, adjusted my stethoscope around my neck, and continued to my next patient.

"Angela," my attending, Dr. Berber, said. "What are the adverse effects of Depakote* in pregnancy?"

An hour after my phone call with my parents, I stood outside my patient's room, clutching a wrinkled wad of paper — my note, written carefully in the wee hours of

---

* The brand name of a medication used to, among other things, prevent seizures. One of the joys of medical education is learning both the generic and brand names of every medication (correct pronunciation and spelling not required).

119

the morning before my prerounds. My patient was a two-year-old who had come in with a febrile seizure. I knew it was a febrile seizure. My resident, who stood, hip cocked, behind me, knew it was a febrile seizure. Even my attending, who had taken a look at the patient's chart and history — thirty-month-old with an uneventful birth history and no known medical problems coming in with two days of upper respiratory symptoms and a fever to 101.4 — had deduced that it was a febrile seizure. The kid was already bouncing around his room comfortably, and his dad, who'd come into the Emergency Department practically foaming at the mouth in distress, had finally been assuaged. Most importantly, my patient was a kid, not a pregnant woman on Depakote.

And yet here I was.

"Umm," I said, my heart jumping in my throat, "what's the generic form of that again?"

My resident gave me an encouraging smile.

"Valproic acid?"

"Oh. Neural tube defects."

"Correct," my attending said. "So. Why aren't we starting Timothy on any anticonvulsants then?"

"Um. Because he had a recent upper respiratory illness, and a high fever. So it's a febrile seizure, and we don't treat that with anti-convulsants." I paused, aware that my answer was insufficient but not sure why. I looked to my resident in panic. She was looking at her iPad and typing away, no longer interested in watching me flounder through this pimp session.* I was on my own.

"Did you ask what the seizure was like?"

"Um. Yeah. His dad said he found him shaking in bed, and then he went limp."

"Okay, but how long was the seizure? Did he have another one after that? Was he confused or listless for some time afterward? Did he wet himself during it?"

Heat rose to my cheeks.

"Um . . . I . . ."

My attending looked over his glasses at me with bleary eyes. I could feel myself being measured and found wanting.

"All right, Angela," he said, in the slow, deliberate tone you'd use on someone who was just learning English, "I have an assign-

* "Pimping" in medical school lingo refers to the act of asking medical students a series of esoteric and unanswerable questions in a public setting in an effort to humiliate them into learning.

121

ment for you. Go read about seizures in pediatric patients and teach us about it tomorrow after rounds."

Behind me, my resident let out a huff of impatience. *It's just the first block,* I tried to remind myself. *I don't have to know everything —*

But, clearly, I should have known that. So much for acing my clerkships. My residency application was going to be a disaster. A face came to my mind, of a fourth-year I didn't know, his voice echoing disdainfully across the empty auditorium: *Maybe the white kids always get AOA* because we work harder.*

For the rest of rounds, I kept my mouth shut. Questions I wanted to ask were scrawled messily in the corners of my notes. They were too stupid. They were things I should've known. If I had known them, I would have done better on Step 1. I would

---

* AOA — Alpha Omega Alpha Honor Medical Society — recognizes the tippy top of your medical school classmates. Almost required to get into the big-bucks specialties like orthopedics and dermatology. The selection process has been decried as racist, because somehow, despite being "objective," most of the inductees end up being white.

122

look them up on UpToDate* later.

A few doors away, I heard the strumming of a guitar, the sharp lilt of childlike laughter, and clapping hands, and my heart rate spiked. Child Life, helping one of the other teams' patients deal with their illness through play. It was an honorable job, done by the kindest, most open specialists and their devoted crew of volunteers, and I avoided them like the plague. Because Child Life could mean Ricky, and I did not need boy-related anxiety on top of my regular school-related anxiety compromising my clerkship performance.

Thankfully, Ricky hadn't tried to reach out since the Sanity Circle brunch. Maybe getting so summarily ignored had given him a hint. Still, every time I walked into a patient room, I peered through the window in the door first, checking to ensure that he wasn't sitting there, speckled with finger paint and smiling hopefully up at me.

"Hey," my resident said, "don't be torn up about Dr. Berber. He asks a lot of those 'guess what I'm thinking' questions."

I looked up at my resident. Her name was Shruti, and even though I'd been scuttling

---

* The reference site your doctor is pulling up when you ask them what your rash is.

around in her shadow for the last week and a half, this was the first time she'd spoken to me like I was a human. I wasn't even sure she knew my name. Still wasn't. Regardless, I appreciated the gesture.

"Thanks," I said.

"Yeah, like, come on. It was a febrile seizure." Her lips quirked like she was going to smile but then decided against it. "Kid's gonna be okay. You've been helpful, so just keep doing what you're doing."

But what am I doing right? I wanted to ask. I spent much of my day mindlessly refreshing labs and stealing snacks from the nutrition rooms. On call days, I sat around in a mixture of anticipation and trepidation of new admissions, using the downtime to read through the dense text of my pediatrics shelf exam review book. I didn't feel helpful. Until this very moment, I'd been positive that the only thing I'd been contributing to on the team was Shruti's insanity.

"Thanks," I said.

The next day on rounds, I was prepared. I showed up bright and early at five thirty in the morning, long before the day intern came in, and found Shruti in the workroom.

"You really shouldn't be here yet," she said, rolling her eyes. She had passed the point during her twenty-eight-hour call where she cared at all about tact or the state of her hair, and barely looked away from her computer screen to address me.

I smiled. I was exhausted — I'd stayed up late studying and woken up early to get to the hospital — but not as exhausted as she was.

"Do you have anyone I should pick up?"

Shruti gave me a grim look and rattled off a one-liner about a child she'd admitted overnight, a twelve-year-old with cerebral palsy coming in after an aspiration event. Then she turned bodily away from me and left me to stalk the chart.

I started off hopeful. I'd come early for this precise reason: to read about my new patient and have enough time to research the management of their medical problems so that when Dr. Berber inevitably pimped me I could sound like I at least kind of knew what I was talking about. But any hopes I had of that were dashed the moment I opened little Miss Marisol's chart. The extra hour I'd budgeted would not be enough to cover even half of the complications she'd had from her cerebral palsy. Twelve years old with a medical history so long and depressing it made my eyes cross. Poor baby.

After thirty minutes, I gave up on chart

stalking and headed to see Miss Marisol herself.

I saw Marisol's mother first. She was wide awake, sitting straight backed in a recliner, woven pink yarn pooled in her lap. Even as she regarded me, her knitting needles moved mechanically in her hands.

"Good morning," she said.

"Hi," I said. "I'm Angie. I'm the medical student on the team."

She gave me a sympathetic smile. She had probably met dozens of medical students over the years and pitied each one.

"It's nice to meet you, Angie," she said. "I'm Marisol's mom. You can call me Mercedes." She tilted her head in the direction of the hospital bed. "Marisol's the hospital's favorite little drama queen. She likes to come in with a bang and settle out right after."

I peered around to the drama queen in question. If I hadn't read her chart, I would never have believed Marisol was twelve. Lying in bed, blanket tucked in under her contracted arms, she reminded me of a fawn. Her eyes stared, listless, into the distance. If it weren't for the lurching of her chest, I would have thought she was dead.

"Hi, Marisol," I said, hesitantly sidling up to her bedside. "My name's Angie. I'll be

126

helping to take care of you."

Marisol didn't track me. This close, I could hear the rattle of her breath. I pulled out my stethoscope.

"Need me to help you lift her up?" Mercedes said. "So you can listen to her lungs."

I nodded, and Mercedes quickly hoisted her child into her arms. Marisol made a keening animal noise in complaint, her first real sign of life. Mercedes's eyes flickered to mine then — kind still, but defiant, the battle-ready look of a mother who has had to prove her daughter's humanity over and over again. I knew then that I'd been caught. I didn't know what to do with Marisol, how to interact with her, and it showed in my awkward, stilted movements, my furtive glances back at Mercedes, my hesitance to touch her.

My next movements were more decisive. I lifted the back of Marisol's shirt in a clean, clinical sweep. Her skin was tawny brown and perfect, marred only by the raised line of the surgical scar down the middle of her back. I placed my stethoscope to her back and listened, trying to isolate the staccato of her upper airway from the sound of air moving through her lungs.

"She does have crackles on the right," I

surmised after a moment of careful listening.

Mercedes looked satisfied.

"Yeah, your resident thought so too."

She placed her daughter back into bed so I could finish the exam, and I checked her gastrostomy tube site, looked at the rest of her skin for cuts or bruises, tried my best to look into her mouth (she didn't like that), and called that a day on my exam.

Marisol had been in a hospital a total of 788 days ("But who's counting?" Mercedes said) since her birth. When she was well, she was a delight. Being mostly nonverbal didn't stop her from attempting to sing along to her favorite song, "Call Me Maybe" by Carly Rae Jepsen, or pulling pranks on her older brother. When she was sick, well. She was like this. She didn't take any food by mouth. Attempts to overcome her oral aversion in her infancy had been thwarted by her Marisol-level stubbornness, and it had taken a year to find a feeding tube formula that she could tolerate. Because of this, she'd never learned how to swallow. Her baby cousins didn't understand that, especially three-year-old Sammy, who had only wanted to share his birthday cake and thought the best way to do it was to slam a chunk of it into Marisol's mouth. The cake had most likely gone down the wrong pipe, considering her tenuous oxygen saturation levels and the presence of crackles in her right lower lung fields. Many efforts were under way to help her cough out the offending particles, including chest physiotherapy and all sorts of nebulizers. She was also on antibiotics.

"Good," Dr. Berber said after I finished my presentation. Then he turned into the room without pimping me at all.

"Wow," I mouthed to the open air, and trudged into the room after him.

EIGHT

Marisol did get better quickly. Aspiration pneumonitis, Shruti called it, and I scrawled that in a corner of my notes because until that moment, I hadn't known pneumonitis was a thing. Dr. Berber switched off service and Dr. Mallort, whose questions I actually understood, came on. I spent the next few days presenting patients, studying for my pediatrics shelf, ignoring my parents' phone calls, and parsing through studies for my literature review. I got a little bit better at being a peds third-year student, a little more helpful, a little less annoying. Shruti called me by my name.

I got comfortable, and I forgot to watch my back.

We could hear Marisol's laughter from outside the door. After four days of treatment, she had perked up considerably, an impressive improvement, considering we'd been throwing around the concept of intubation* when she was first admitted. Marisol laughed at most things, though, and so I didn't think much of it, until my feet crossed the threshold of the room and I heard his voice.

Of course, there Ricky was, sitting in a chair across from Marisol, paintbrush in hand, finishing off what appeared to be a pink butterfly on her cheek. Doing his job. Volunteering for Child Life, like the saint he was pretending to be. Looking, to my chagrin, very good in his paint-splattered white T-shirt and jeans. And Marisol was beaming at him like he was the most interesting, amazing person in the world. My wretched loser heart still skipped a beat.

"Hey, team," Mercedes said, blissfully unaware of my internal conflict. Ricky turned to glance at us, then did a double take. I shrugged his way, keeping my eyes pointedly on Dr. Mallort and Marisol as I presented her case. I could feel Ricky staring, like he always did when we ran into each other. Didn't his grandma teach him better? Still, I talked through all the ways that Marisol had improved since admission, her rock-solid vitals, and ended with "I

* I really didn't want to put this little girl on a ventilator, but it wouldn't be her first time.

131

think she's ready for discharge today," without breaking a sweat.

"I agree with student doctor Appiah's assessment," Dr. Mallort said. "You're looking good, Marisol."

"You mean we can go home?" Mercedes said. "Thank god. She's starting to get antsy."

"You can go home. Just give the team a couple of hours to get everything together," Dr. Mallort said. Marisol laughed, her pink glasses glittering with the movement, and I took that as my cue to leave.

We hadn't gotten far from the room before I heard the patter of footsteps behind me.

"Angie, wait," Ricky said.

I swore under my breath, then swiveled to face him.

"Oh. Hi," I said, plastering on the smile I reserved for annoying parents.

Ricky scooted to a halt in front of me. Behind me, Dr. Mallort and Shruti stopped too, and my ears burned with embarrassment.

"I'll meet you at 4062?" I said to my team, hoping desperately that they would leave and not bear witness to my third and most unfortunate reunion with Ricky.

Dr. Mallort opened her mouth to protest, but Shruti, bless her, spoke first.

"Okay, see you there." She looked pointedly at Ricky, then at me, and smirked before walking away.

Once they were out of earshot, I could drop the nice-girl act.

"What's up?" I said. He still had his paintbrush in his hand, like he hadn't thought to put it down before taking chase.

"I . . . Look, I just wanted to apologize."

I scoffed.

"Apologize for what?"

"Well, for crashing your brunch for one," Ricky said. "I knew when Diamond offered that I was intruding. It was clearly an 'old friends' thing —"

"Apology accepted," I said. "I'll see you around."

"Angie, come on," Ricky said. "Look, I didn't mean to give you the wrong idea before. I just . . . I thought we were getting to be friends. But you've been weird since, and —"

And there it was. *Friends.* My mind shuttled back to that day in the garden, a day that felt like eons ago. To the press of our thighs together, the hungry pressure of his gaze. The bashful smile he'd given me when he confessed that he'd felt compelled to talk to me. I'd made out with guys before and not felt that level of heat. And today, he'd

133

practically taken flight in pursuit of me. He'd even left a child behind to do it! There was no mistaking it; Ricky was on me like a dog on a bone. I wasn't a stranger to friendships with straight men; Markus and I had been tight since freshman year of college and had none of these theatrics. I didn't know what Ricky wanted, but *friendship* wasn't it.

I considered just walking away. I knew I was about to be that girl, the uncool, overly clingy one who has the nerve to expect emotional accountability from people she's only just met. But maybe because I was tired, maybe because I was already getting beaten down by the posturing of my third year, maybe because I was sick of the Fredericks and the Rickys of the world making me question my own otherwise keen EQ, I couldn't take it anymore.

"Stop it," I hissed. "Stop acting like you weren't coming on to me. Like you don't have a girlfriend who'd be pissed if she knew that you kept running me down! We are not going to be friends. We are not going to be anything. Leave me alone!"

It was not my first time erupting on someone, but it was my first time doing it to someone who didn't expect it. Ricky's smile crumpled; his hands dropped to his sides. For a terrifying moment, I thought he was going to cry. But then his face shuttered and became cold. I could never have imagined that he could look like that — like someone who could hate.

"Well damn," he said. "I was just trying to be nice. Not every guy who's nice to you is hitting on you, you know."

I laughed humorlessly.

"Nice? You've got to be joking," I said. "You are *not* nice." Then, before he could say anything else, I spun on my heel and stomped all the way to room 4062.

Nia got home late that night. She had begun taking an improv class at the undergrad campus when I started on the wards, which meant that her Tuesday and Thursday nights, previously all mine, were now shared with ten other comedy hopefuls. I sent her a text (You won't believe who I ran into in the hospital today) that I knew she wouldn't respond to for the next two hours and studied in petulant silence. Nia was the only one of my crew I really trusted with stories like this. Michelle, who drew men to her like flies to honey, couldn't empathize with my romantic woes. Markus always thought I was being overdramatic and needed to "chill." I'd once whined to Tabatha about a short-lived flame, and she asked, perplexed, *Didn't you only go out with him, like, three times?* But Nia understood, because she was just like me — unlucky in love, but somehow always falling into it.

And now here she was, positively twirling through the front door.

"Honey, I'm home!" she sang. I shrugged off my blanket to go greet her and stopped in my tracks at the entryway. Nia looked . . . amazing. Like, "done up" amazing. Her curls glistened with mousse, and her makeup was especially done, complete with contour and red matte lipstick. She was twirling in a green vintage dress that billowed around her, looking for all the world like the poster child for the pretty fat girl performative femininity she was always railing against. It was not an outfit one wore to improv on a Tuesday.

"Okay, so I know you've got something to tell me, but first I have a confession," Nia said.

I crossed my arms and looked her up and down.

"Clearly. Who's the girl?"

At my invitation, Nia launched into a long description of her new sweetheart, a person named Shae, interspersed every few seconds with a declaration of how "cool" they were.

I guided Nia to the couch and grasped her hand as she spoke, my chest seizing intermittently with quiet despair. The last time Nia had been this goo-goo-eyed over someone was with Ulo, and that was two years ago. My best friend had been falling in love and I'd been too deep in my books to notice.

"They're a copywriter, like, full-time for a PR agency. But they also write poetry on the side." Nia leaned forward and added, in a whisper like a secret, "They've let me read their work and oh my god. They're just incredible. The things they can do with words . . . ugh! Girl!" She waggled her eyebrows suggestively. "Makes me wonder what else that mouth do."

"They sound great, Nia," I said. "Where'd you guys meet? In improv?"

Nia bit her lip.

"Well, no. Um. Actually, we're . . . uh . . . taking the class together."

I blinked owlishly at her. Nia tucked her hair back behind an ear, as sheepish as I'd ever seen her.

"You mean the class you've been taking for two weeks?" I swatted her arm. Suddenly the getup made sense. "What. The. Hell?"

"I'm sorry! I'm sorry! I was going to tell you, but you've been busy. And also. I may have broken a cardinal friendship rule. I did it for the pussy, so I know you'll forgive me. So tell me you forgive me first?"

I laughed. Nia took my hands out of my lap and held them, looking up at me with sad puppy eyes until I stopped.

"No way, you crazy girl. What did you do?"

"Well. You know at the Beyoncé concert" — my pulse quickened, somehow already knowing where this was headed — "me and Camila started chatting. And somehow it came up that I liked women, and so Camila, bless her heart, did that thing. You know, the 'I know a lesbian' thing . . . and I tried to brush her off. But then she showed me a picture."

Nia held up her phone. On the screen was a person just as cool as Nia had described. They had a clean undercut, with thick silver-beaded dreads piled into a bun at the top of their head. Their skin was a smooth, even slate, the undertones so cool that they looked more blue-black than brown. They had an angular face, all high cheekbones and sharp eyes; even in the pictures where they were smiling, they looked fierce. I could see why Nia kept calling them cool. They reminded me of a Final Fantasy character.

Behind the phone, Nia was beside herself.

"Look how hot they are!"

"They are hot," I agreed. "So . . . Camila set up a date?"

Nia squeezed my hands in hers.

"Well . . . No. Camila didn't."

Just as I had feared.

"No." I shook my head. "No way. Nuh-uh. No."

"They're really good friends, okay, and Ricky offered to introduce us, and it was just gonna be a one-off —" She paused, noticing how I had not stopped shaking my head. "Okay, Angie, I get that getting Ricky to set me up wasn't cool or whatever, but shouldn't you be happier for me?"

I threw my hands up in resignation.

"I chewed Ricky out today, Nia," I said. "He tried to say hi to me and I tore him up."

Nia dropped her hands into her lap, her expression shifting quickly from annoyance to delight.

"You. Did. Not. Right there in the hospital?" When I nodded, she squealed and kicked her legs. "Angie. Oh my god, Angie, why?"

"I don't know why," I said. All the righteous indignation I'd felt this morning had since dried up, leaving only uncertainty and shame. Why had I yelled at him? Between

Diamond and Shae . . . none of Ricky's close friends seemed to be guys. Maybe Ricky just started all his friendships with dogged pursuit and lingering gazes. Maybe . . . I'd only seen romance and tension because I'd wanted to.

I looked up at Nia, Nia who had been at my side for over a decade now, who was practically glowing with the kind of hopeful giddiness that I hadn't seen in her since Ulo. There was no way I was going to screw this up for her.

"It doesn't matter," I said. "I'm so happy for you, Nia. Tell me if my insulting their friend freaks them out and I'll apologize the next time I see him. Which is bound to happen, given my luck."

Nia bit her lip.

"It won't be luck." She reached into her pocket and produced a flyer. In loud block letters, it announced, SCHOOL'S OUT — CLASH OF THE CLASSES — an improv competition that was this Saturday at 8:00 p.m. and featured performances by crews with names like the Maniacal Magikarp and the Lot Lizards.

"Ha," I barked. And then I logged the event into my calendar.

140

NINE

"Girl, what are you doing in there?" Nia yelled from the living room. She'd settled on the couch twenty minutes ago, already dressed for her show in her loud teal team tee. I, on the other hand, was running late. Some of that was out of my control; weekend rounds* with Dr. Mallort had gone long this morning, and one of my patients had decompensated† in the early afternoon and had to be transferred to the Pediatric Intensive Care Unit. Still, I'd gotten back to the apartment with forty-five minutes to spare . . . and had squandered half of that time looking at myself mournfully in the mirror.

"I'm sorry!" I said. "I just . . . I can't figure out what to wear."

* The best part about medical education is getting only four days off a month.

† Fancy word for getting really sick, really fast.

141

Over the course of my pediatrics rotation, my self-grooming had taken a nosedive — during my first week, I'd worn makeup every day, twisted my hair before bed every three. But those fifteen to twenty extra minutes of sleep I gained back by forgoing those habits had proven invaluable, and the kids didn't especially care what I looked like. My self-neglect was normally totally worth it, except for today. Today, I looked busted, and none of my last-minute primping seemed capable of fixing that.

"I shouldn't have donated all my fun clothes," I complained, flipping through my closet with frustration. Work-appropriate dresses, work-appropriate blouses, work-appropriate blazers — nothing that delivered the message *I'm not trying that hard but I look good anyway.*

Groaning, Nia stomped into my room, gently pushed me out of the way, and yanked a sundress out of my closet.

"This dress is always cute," she said. "Wear it with your brown sandals. And quick. We should be leaving in five minutes." Before she could skulk back into the living room, she whipped around and gave me a smile that was all teeth. "I thought you didn't care what Ricky thought of you?"

I sputtered with indignation.

"Excuse you," I said. "I don't care what he thinks! I care what *I* think! I've spent the last week looking like hot garbage, and I want to feel cute today." I shimmied out of the shorts I'd selected and threw the sundress over my head. "So sue me!"

"I'll do just that if you make me late," Nia said. Her keys jangled: a two-minute warning. "Either way, you ready to face him today after your little stunt this week? Because there's, like, a ninety-nine percent chance he's going to be there tonight."

I scoffed, slapping my legs with lotion.

"It's not like I have to sit with him," I said.

"Of course you don't," Nia said. "You just have to say hi and find a seat somewhere far away. Just don't make it weird."

But of course I ended up sitting next to Ricky. It had been unavoidable, the way everything between us seemed to be, and I'd known that from the moment we walked into the small campus auditorium and found Ricky and Shae coming through the opposite entrance. I clenched my fists as my stomach, already in knots over the concept of running into Ricky again, nearly leapt out of my throat at the reality. But then I looked up at Nia — my best friend in the whole world, my soul sister, and the expression on her face almost turned me into a puddle.

Nia looked . . . happy. Not that Nia didn't always look happy, but these days she seemed to carry a load on her shoulders that I hadn't been able to define (Stress from her job tutoring high school English? Typical millennial angst?) but looking at Shae seemed to lift that burden right off. It was as if she were about to float off into the sky.

No way was I going to screw this up for her.

"Nia!" Shae yelled, waving us over. They were just as striking in person, their features softened by a sunny smile.

Nia's beam brightened, and I almost had to turn away from the blinding intensity of their bliss.

"Hey, baby," Nia said, bending down to give Shae a peck on the lips. I rolled my eyes and looked away as Shae grasped her by the collar and pulled her into a deeper kiss. Over Shae's shoulder, I could see Ricky doing the same, though he was also smiling from ear to ear.

"So," I said when the lovebirds finally came up for air. "You're Shae."

"Yup! And you're Angie. It's nice to finally meet you. Though," Shae added with a wicked grin, "with how much I've *heard*

144

about you, I kind of feel like I already know you." I kept my eyes determinedly off Ricky at that, focusing instead on the hand Shae extended for me to shake.

"You're necking my best friend, we're on hugging terms," I said, bypassing it for a hug instead. "Oh, and, I know this goes without saying, but if you hurt Nia, I *will* come for you."

"Well, duh. That's how it should be. Ricky, why aren't you threatening Nia? Don't you love me?"

Ricky balked, not expecting to be the subject of our collective focus.

"Because I don't believe in fighting losing battles!" he sputtered. "Nia would destroy me!"

Nia gave me a gleeful smirk before letting her face go unreadably blank. I schooled my expression, knowing what was coming next.

"You think I can beat you up because I'm fat?" she asked.

Ricky's bronze skin took on a greenish undertone.

"No, that's not what I —" he started, but it was too late; both Nia and I were buckled over in laughter.

"I'm just playing you," Nia said. "I would *indeed* beat that ass."

"Okay, okay, knock it off," Shae said, patting Nia's back as she wiped away tears. "You're going to give him a heart attack."

"I'll be okay," Ricky said humorlessly. "You're an excellent actress. You'll crush it up there."

"And I'm funny too!" Nia said, beaming. She held her hand out for Shae, who took it. "Speaking of which. We've got to go. Get the show on the road." She turned to me. "If I bomb, boo me. I learn best from negative reinforcement."

"I'm not booing you —" I started, but Nia and Shae were already skipping away toward the stage, kicking up their knees and giggling like children.

Ricky and I watched them go in silence that was oddly comfortable, like anxious parents sending our kids off to school. As the moment stretched thin, I remembered that we were now alone. So much for my grand escape. *This is okay,* I told myself. *Time to put your big-girl pants on.*

"They're going to be okay, I think," I said, breaking our silence.

Ricky turned to look at me, and I pretended not to feel the weight of his gaze. Instead, I focused on Nia's and Shae's figures as they clambered onto the stage. When I turned back to him, he looked up

146

to the ceiling.

"Y-yeah," he said lamely. "I guess we should find seats."

Even as he spoke the words, I could see that he regretted them. Clearly, he had also come to this show with a getaway plan that had been thwarted by the timing of our arrival. I took a deep breath, then shrugged and turned toward the seats. Ricky trailed after me, hands in his pockets, his discomfort evident. The auditorium was thankfully sparse, and so I took my time selecting a spot, pausing at every other row before finally settling on a seat four rows from the front. I stepped in and sat down, saving Ricky the end seat.

"Planning an easy escape?" Ricky asked as he folded into his spot. My face must have fallen, because he added, panicked, "From bad improv, I mean."

Might as well address the elephant in the room. I closed my eyes and steeled myself.

"Listen, Ricky . . ."

Next to me, I felt Ricky stiffen.

"No, wait, Angie, you don't have to —"

I held up a finger. I'd been rehearsing what I would say to Ricky since the second Nia and Shae had locked eyes, and I was *not* going to let him let me chicken out.

"No, I do. Because if I don't, I'm going to

be awkward around you forever. Which I would be okay with if I wasn't secretly wishing for this thing between our friends to work. You and Shae seem close, so I'm guessing we'll be seeing each other around after this. I just want to clear the air." I took a deep breath, then met his eyes in a determined gaze. "I shouldn't have yelled at you that day in the hospital. I was in my feelings, and that wasn't the appropriate way to deal with them. I'm sorry."

This time, Ricky looked like he might actually be sick. I studied his face with the same intensity with which he always seemed to be studying mine, looking from his wide eyes to the nervous bob of his Adam's apple to his reddening ears, nearly concealed by the darkness of the room.

"It's . . . it's really okay," he managed. His gaze dropped to his hands. *Where had all that supernatural confidence gone?* I thought. *Was this the same boy who had chased me down the hospital hallway during rounds?* Suddenly, Ricky seemed small, like a chastised child flinching against the threat of a slap.

"I don't like asking people to move so I can go to the bathroom at shows," I said. Ricky looked up at me, recognizing my peace offering as I presented it. "You know

148

that awkward shuffle you have to do to get past people? I hate that. And I'm . . . not tiny. I know when I've put my entire ass on someone's head and they have to pretend I haven't. Their whole neck stiffens up. Hence," I gestured widely to our seats, "the end of the row."

Ricky's smile emerged slowly across his face, unfurling like a fern in the sun.

"You don't mind inconveniencing me, though?" he said.

I hardly had time to ponder the curious way my heart thudded in my chest before the lights went out and a roving spotlight appeared. An epic theme that the sound team had definitely stolen from a Marvel movie blasted over the speakers.

"Ladies, gentlemen, and ruffians!" an unseen voice said. The spotlight settled at the center of the stage, and the curtains slowly shifted open to reveal a tall, reedy man wearing a blindingly green T-shirt that read LOT LIZARDS. The audience thundered with applause and assorted whoops; the Lot Lizards were evidently quite popular. "Welcome to Clash of the Classes! I'm your host, Ian McLaughlin. And yes, that's my real name. How many of you have been to an improv show before?" The applause was robust. "Any first-timers?"

I joined the smattering of claps, and next to me, Ricky chuckled.

"You might be the only person in our generation who hasn't seen improv," he said, and I made a face at him, glad for his quick thaw.

"Well, about time you got with the program," Ian said from the stage. He flashed a smile that transformed his face from boyish to rakish. "Now, here are the rules —"

The next two hours were a raunchy, raucous affair, full of jokes about genitals and the current political climate. When Nia bounded across the stage, mouth wide in excitement that was simultaneously exaggerated and authentic, I wooed so loudly that Ricky winced. Nia and Shae's team was clearly unseasoned — there were times when a team member lost track of the scenario and the rest of the team had to scramble to save their misstep — but they were far from deserving of any boos. The Lot Lizards and Maniacal Magikarp, the veteran teams, were consistent and lauded for it, and I found myself laughing so hard that I could almost forget how awkward this whole situation was. And that was the thing. It really wasn't that awkward. Ricky was an unselfconscious participant, loudly repeating my suggestions for themes when Ian ignored them, leaning out of his chair with pride when Shae landed a good joke. With Frederick, I'd always had to wonder if my unbridled laughter was too loud, too unladylike, if it was *unbecoming of a future doctor.* But Ricky took my joy and reveled in it, egged it on. He added commentary to the jokes onstage just to watch me break out in tears, beaming with satisfaction every time I doubled over.

If Fate was what kept bringing us together, She and I needed to have some words. It seemed cruel for Her to force this man, who pressed every single one of my buttons and seemed determined to have me in his orbit, into my life. I thought of Camila, of her sweet, gap-toothed smile, and how she had trusted me immediately upon our meeting. How would she feel if she knew of the unholy thoughts I was having about her man?

Later that night, after Nia and I returned to our apartment and said our good nights, I would lie on my back and stare at my ceiling and think that I had been far too forgiving of myself. Because, yeah, sure, Ricky might not be *nice,* but apparently, neither was I.

TEN

The page came late, around 7:00 p.m. Shruti and I were an hour away from sign-out. Neither of us had eaten dinner. Shruti leaned back in her chair and groaned before flicking her pager off its holster and holding it up to her face. Then she jumped to her feet.

"Trauma, ten minutes," she said. She looped her stethoscope over her neck. "Let's go, Angie."

I tamped down my annoyance. At the beginning of the block, I'd been morbidly excited for pediatric traumas. But kids hurt themselves all the time, always doing the dumbest things and always right before Shruti and I could sign out to the night team and go home. Running to traumas usually meant watching orthopedics set some kid's arm after they fell off the monkey bars or jumped off a dresser or failed at parkour. They quickly lost their novelty.

This was neither of these.

The trauma bay was bustling with people by the time we arrived: nurses, my favorite orthopedics resident, an older man I recognized as one of the pediatric Emergency Department attendings. For some reason, the tone seemed somber; all the previous traumas had felt like an interdisciplinary happy hour. In the corner, one of the nurses spoke into a radio and a staticky voice responded. With a world-weary sigh, Shruti turned to me.

"Hey," she said. "So. The patient who's coming in is a fifteen-year-old. Gunshot to the head. It's going to be messy, and there's going to be a lot of bodies in here. Normally, I like for you to be involved, but I think for this one, try to make space."

Gunshot to the head. Fifteen. I had hardly processed her words when the bustle picked up again. The ambulance transporting the patient had arrived. Shruti sprang into action, snatching back boards and then jumping on the computer to put in orders they would need; from far away I could see the words *massive transfusion protocol* and *CT Head* on the screen, and then he was here.

I felt like I was in a fishbowl. The boy on the stretcher looked like one of my younger cousins, except his face . . . his poor face. I couldn't look at him any longer, so I looked at everything else, at the cervical collar placed uselessly around his neck, at the scraps of cut-away clothing that flapped under him. At the rest of his body, splashed with blood, but otherwise pristine and untouched by the violence that had been done to his face; a lithe body, he was only fifteen, he probably played sports, maybe ran track and field for his school —

Someone pulled me bodily out of the trauma bay. A cup of water was shoved into my hands, and a gentle but firm missive to go home whispered in my ear. Instead, I stared blankly through the glass. The boy was obscured from view by the hustling bodies. They had started compressions. Shruti's voice firmly but calmly called out orders from the foot of the bed. A passing nurse muttered that the kid was pretty much already dead, and had anyone called his family? I imagined his mother. She was probably the kind of woman who would call me honey in the grocery store. Did she know what had happened to her son? Or was she sitting at home completely unaware, rewatching her favorite episode of *Scandal* and not thinking to check on her teenager before curfew? Would she pick up the phone when we called, or ignore it to finish the

154

episode? What sound would she make when she heard the news?

I didn't have to wonder long. Behind me, a high, keening scream punctured the air, and when I turned around, I saw her. She was younger than I had pictured, and heavier, but even from this distance I could see the resemblance. The police officers who had escorted the ambulance to the hospital formed a wall with their bodies around her, blocking her from rushing in and interrupting the code, and she shoved against them, her screams devolving into heart-wrenching sobs.

"Do you know what happened, ma'am?" one of them asked her. "Was he involved in anything he shouldn't have been?"

I felt sick. How dare he ask her a question like that while her son clung to life by a thread only a few feet away? Would that question save him? Would it give him back his face? Shaking with fury, I walked back to the workroom and silently gathered my belongings. I remembered the young man from the Emergency Department so many years ago, brushed off as an addict even as his abdomen filled with blood. For both this boy and that man, the message was implicit — whatever suffering they were enduring, they must have deserved it.

The bright colors of the children's hospital took on a dim, sinister edge in the evening light, the chalky round eyes of the children in the third-floor mural becoming dark and bottomless. I sat down on one of the couches in the lobby, leaned my head back against the headrest, and closed my eyes. Home was only a fifteen-minute walk away. I'd been doing that walk for two and a half years, but right now, going into the vast openness of the night felt daunting. I inhaled. Just downstairs, a boy was dying. He had been full of potential, full of a future that had likely now been extinguished. I exhaled.

I wasn't familiar with death. Being an ocean away from most of our relatives meant that the passing of a family member was something Tabatha and I experienced only in abstract. We even looked forward to funerals, excited for the freedom we could enjoy when our parents traveled back to the motherland to pay their respects.* In tenth grade, when my great-aunt Gifty died, I had

* Ghanaian funerals are multiple days long. You have to invite the whole town, and there better be (1) food and (2) party favors, or everyone will talk shit about how you did your family member dirty by being cheap for their going-away party.

nodded passively as my father flipped through photographs of her walking through the market with me wrapped onto her back. It was as if he wanted the images to trigger a memory of her, hoping to inspire in me even a sliver of the loss that he felt. After all, Great-Aunt Gifty had been his second mother. She had helped pay his school fees and housed him in her small London flat when he first moved there for pharmacy school, cooking for him, cleaning up after him, and asking for nothing in return but his gratitude. A true Ashanti woman, she treated my dad like one of her own children.* He flipped through page after page of our old photo albums, trying to imprint her visage into my mind, trying to keep her memory alive within his offspring.

But I'd felt nothing. Instead, when my parents returned from Ghana with funeral favors in tow — fans, mugs, posters, and napkins adorned with Auntie Gifty's stern face — Tabatha and I had laughed at the

* In matrilineal Ghanaian societies, only the children of the women are considered truly part of the family — after all, their parentage is unquestionable. Thus, a man might treat his sister's children (his nieces and nephews) as more of his own than his biological children.

garish designs. Once, Momma caught us snickering over a keychain with her name in bright pink bubble letters and snatched it out of our hands.

"You have been protected," she said, her voice trembling with a deep, soul-dampening disappointment that Tabatha and I would crumple under for weeks. "You don't have to even *look* upon suffering. All you have to do is work hard, and study, and be kind. And *this* is what you choose to do instead."

But I had looked upon suffering now, and my brain could hardly process it. It kept going back to that destroyed face. One eye had been perfectly intact. I mentally filled in the rest — full lips, like his mother's, on a wide mouth. It must have been close range. Was this going to be my life now? Watching person after person die? In just three short years, would I be in Shruti's position, looking down at the body with clinical indifference, shouting out orders with barely any recognition for the horror that was in front of me?

"Oh. Hey, Angie."

Startled out of my thoughts, I looked up — and nearly leapt out of my seat. A smiling, goofy bright blue Barney the Dinosaur knockoff loomed over me. Before I could ask *Why the fuck,* it took off its head, and revealed, of all people, Ricky.

Not that his appearance was that surprising. Ever since our truce at the improv show, Ricky and I had been running into each other quite often. I knew when to expect him these days. He was a regular volunteer, here for three hours on most Tuesday and Saturday afternoons, and I'd interrupted many of his paint sessions to evaluate my patients. Still, I'd yet to see him in costume. The juxtaposition of the ridiculous image before me and the horrific one in my head was too bizarre to reconcile. I burst out laughing, and then . . . just didn't stop. I must have looked hysterical, but it was nice to laugh, even better to realize that I still could.

"All right, har-dee-har," Ricky said. "I'll have you know I'm wearing this for the kids. Regular Dino guy couldn't make it."

"The family jewels still intact?" I asked, harkening back to Markus's story with a less fortunate, similarly dressed Child Life volunteer.

Ricky's eyebrows lifted with recognition. He had his hair up in a ponytail, secured back with a sweatband, and his whole face shone with sweat.

"Yup," he said. "No punters in this group."

"Lucky you," I said. "Why are you still here, anyway? It's seven p.m. On a *Saturday.* I didn't even know we had volunteers this late."

Ricky placed his hands on his hips, a comical picture given that he was still wearing mitts.

"There's a kid on the oncology floor who's stuck here getting induction chemo. His birthday was today, so we decided to throw him a party. He likes dinosaurs. Though, he didn't like how inaccurate Arnie the Ankylosaurus over here is." He tapped his giant dinosaur head affectionately.

"To be fair, he's right. Where are his spikes?"

"He has spikes!" Ricky said. He did a surprisingly graceful twirl to display the back of his costume. As promised, the suit had a few paltry triangles sticking out of the back, and a tail that ended in a spiked ball.

"Apparently, ankylosaurus tails 'don't actually end in maces,' " he continued. "That kid is only seven and is already an insufferable nerd. It's pretty adorable." He spun back around to face me, his expression thoughtful. "It's crazy to see these kids so sick. Like . . . cancer seems too grown up for them, you know? They should be out playing with friends or getting in trouble at

160

school. Not here."

The boy from the trauma bay's face flashed through my head again. My expression must've changed, because when I met Ricky's eyes again, he looked concerned.

"Everything okay?" he asked.

"Yeah, um . . ." I shrugged. "I just saw something really messed up today."

Ricky seemed to get my implication, that describing something as "messed up" in a children's hospital meant that it was *supremely* messed up. He nodded sagely, then dropped onto the couch next to me.

"You want to talk about it?" he asked.

I shook my head. It didn't feel right to talk about it, not when the boy's body was probably still cooling in the trauma bay.

"Let's talk about something else," I said. "Like, what got you into volunteering here?"

Ricky shrugged.

"One of my childhood friends got in trouble when we were in high school, so his mom made him start coming here to teach him a lesson. Of course, I tagged along. But then it turned out volunteering here meant playing Call of Duty with the teenagers who were stuck here forever, so it wasn't actually a punishment. We made a few friends." He paused to wet his lips. I read between the lines. Some of those friends didn't make it.

"And I just never quit. Thankfully, work is pretty accommodating — I just go into the office earlier on the days that I'm here. And since I'm a veteran volunteer, Child Life mostly lets me do what I want."

"Is that why you're the paint guy?" I asked. Other volunteers seemed to be tasked with whatever needed doing: reading with kids, playing games with them, or playing music, but I'd only ever seen Ricky here with a brush in hand. "I only ever see you doing that."

He nodded.

"The 'paint guy.' Sure, I guess," he mused. "I mean, there are real art therapists here too. I mostly help stave off boredom." He rocked back to his feet, Arnie's body sloshing around him. "I need to go change out of this."

"Oh, okay." I tried to keep the disappointment out of my voice. "Nice running into you. Have a good night."

"Wait," Ricky said. "It'll take me like three minutes to change. Are you headed to the parking garage?"

I shook my head.

"No, um, I walk."

Ricky looked aghast.

"But it's late! And dark out!" He looked down at my hand, from where my keys hung. "Oh good, you have pepper spray. There's creeps out there, you know."

"Sounds like something a creep would say," I said, enjoying the way Ricky instantly seemed to clutch his pearls.

"Wow," he said. "I was going to offer you a ride!"

"So," I said, tilting my head. "Are you not going to offer me one anymore?"

Ricky shook his head and started waddling toward the office. Just before he disappeared from view, he pointed back at me.

"Don't go anywhere!" he shouted.

I nodded. Distantly, I could hear the door to Child Life slam shut. The air in the lobby felt still, and suddenly I was alone with my thoughts. Part of me wanted to go back to the trauma bay, to see whether the scene I'd left was still intact. Had they been able to resuscitate the boy? I doubted it — his blood pressure had barely registered on the monitor, and Shruti hadn't looked hopeful. Had they let his mother into the bay?

"You ready?"

I whipped around. Ricky was behind me, dressed in joggers and a thin T-shirt. Out of Arnie the Ankylosaurus, he'd become a boy again. A boy whose every word I stowed away in the back of my mind to revisit when my mind was idle. A boy, I reminded myself,

163

who was very much not available.

I dragged my hands down my face. He'd said it himself: *Not every guy who is nice to you is hitting on you.*

"Yeah," I said, hoisting my bag farther up on my shoulder.

We walked farther into the hospital, toward the bridge to the parking lot. Ricky was talking, relaying the events of the birthday boy's party, but I found myself staring off into hallways as we passed. Maybe Shruti would run into us. Maybe one of the nurses, or worse, another sobbing person who looked eerily like the good side of the boy's face.

The humid air hit us all at once. I realized Ricky had opened the door to the parking lot.

"You are so far away right now," he said. He looked concerned. "You can tell me what's up, you know."

I sighed. There didn't seem to be a point in hiding it anymore.

"I saw a kid who'd been shot in the head today."

Ricky's eyes widened.

"Shit."

"Yeah." I shrugged. "There're no words, right?"

"None at all," he agreed. He swore again.

164

"Are you okay? You can't be, right?"

I thought about it. Was I okay? In general, yes. Less okay than everyone else in the trauma bay, for whom a dead child was par for the course. But not devastated like I ought to be. I would sleep okay tonight. Two years ago, I'd felt the same way cutting into my cadaver for the first time. There had been a voice in the back of my head saying, *You know this is messed up,* but it was all too easy to turn the volume down.

"I guess," I said. "It's not really about me. I'm not the one who's dying. Or who might lose a child." I remembered the mother's sobs, the officers barricading her with their bodies and trying to determine if his death was his own fault. "You know the worst part, though? His mom showed up. And the first thing the cops did was basically ask her if her kid was gangbanging." I bit the inside of my cheek to keep my rage from boiling over. "I mean, Jesus Christ, she just found out that her son was *shot.* Can she get a minute to deal with that?"

Ricky shook his head. Despite having made a children's hospital his home for almost a decade, he looked shaken by my description. *This isn't normal,* I reminded myself. If someone had told me they'd seen what I'd seen a year ago, I would probably

165

be a bit traumatized too.

"That is . . . ," he said. He rubbed his temple. "Angie, I don't know what to say."

What was there to say? Only a miracle could save that boy now.

"I don't expect you to," I said. "It just . . . It made me think. I've been so lucky. No one in my family has any serious health issues, but that doesn't mean anything. Like, them being alive and well isn't a given. I could get a call tomorrow that, I don't know, Tabs was in a car accident. Or my mom had a heart attack." I wagged my head, shaking the images away, along with the accompanying guilt; I hadn't called my parents in a while.

Ricky was quiet for a moment. Our footsteps echoed through the lot. He didn't speak again until we stopped at a car, a white Honda Civic. The most practical of cars, I thought. The doors clicked open.

"I get that. My grandparents are elderly," he said then. His eyes met mine over the top of the car. "I think about them dying all the time."

Oh. I looked down at my hands.

"Of course. That makes sense."

He shrugged, then opened his door.

"Does it? Oh, sorry for the mess. You can throw that in the back."

166

I looked at the "mess" he was referring to — a duffel bag and a half-empty water bottle — and laughed. If this was a mess, he should see the inside of *Nia's* car.

"This is nothing. Thanks for dropping me off." I tossed his bag in the back and piled into his car. A pine tree air freshener hung from the rearview mirror, a new one, by the fresh, nostalgic scent that hit me the moment I shut the door. "How old are your grandparents? Are they pretty healthy?"

"My grandpa is in his early seventies. I have no idea about his health because he won't go to the doctor," he said, starting the engine. "He's lived a 'clean life,' doesn't smoke, barely drinks, and is still pretty spry, so he thinks he doesn't need to. I mean, I think he just doesn't like speaking English at his appointments and is too proud to ask for an interpreter."

All those medical school lectures on health-care disparities, and it hadn't occurred to me that someone I knew would be impacted by a language barrier.

"I didn't know your grandparents didn't speak English," I said.

"They do. Enough," Ricky said. "My grandpa doesn't like to; he'll do it for work but that's pretty much it. Abuela's mostly fluent, though. She learned before they came here. She used to teach classes at the church for kids who'd recently immigrated. So she goes to the doctor all the time. She's been trying to get Abuelo to go forever, but he's stubborn as a mule."

Just like my dad, I thought. Despite his background in clinical pharmacy, my dad preferred to stick his head in the sand about his health. Every year, Momma had to drag him kicking and screaming to the clinic for his annual physical, and we were yet to convince him to get a screening colonoscopy.

"So, you're bilingual?" I said.

Ricky smirked, then said something in Spanish. I didn't catch any of it, but my heart still stuttered in my chest. He could have just told me my breath stank and I still would've thought it was sexy.

"Come on, you might just know the one phrase," I said jokingly. "For real though, that's cool. It's not a given. I can't speak Twi," I admitted. "My parents kind of just forgot to teach me."

Ricky nodded in understanding.

"I'm the do-over," he said. "My dad isn't fluent. They thought he'd pick up English faster if they didn't teach him. Turns out the only thing he picked up was 'asshole.' " His jaw clenched. "He's the real reason

Abuela goes to the doctor, though. He's always in the hospital for dumb shit, and so she's always there too. And one day, she figured that she should get herself checked out. I can thank him for that, I guess."

"You're angry," I observed.

"Yeah, well." Ricky shrugged. "He's a leech. He's been leeching their money, and now he's leeching years off her life. The stress . . . it's not good for her. And for what? It's not like he's going to change anytime soon."

"Ricky," I said, "he's her son. Of course she's going to worry about him."

"Respectfully, Angie," Ricky snapped, "I don't think you can relate."

I clamped my mouth shut. The sudden turn in conversation, and in his mood, gave me pause. Ricky let out an all-suffering sigh, then shifted the gear into reverse.

"Sorry," he said. "Where am I taking you?"

Drop it, Angie, Nia's voice said in my head, but I had never been known to listen.

"You're being unfair," I said. "To me, but especially to your grandma."

Ricky shifted the gear back into park and turned bodily in his seat. "How am I being unfair —"

"It is not your job to decide whether or

169

not your dad is worth saving," I said. "Your job is to support her." I thought about the boy in the trauma bay again, about his wailing mother. About how she probably wished her son could have grown up to be a middle-aged fuck-up instead of dead. "Do you think it helps with her stress to have you mad at her too? You really don't think it's making it worse?"

For several long seconds, I was convinced that Ricky was going to kick me out of his car. I knew I was out of line, but I didn't care. He needed to hear it. What he really needed was a therapist, but I wasn't his girlfriend or his sister or even really his friend, and he would have to have that conversation with someone who fit that description.

But then a smile broke out across his face, so wide and bright that I had to blink away.

"My god," he said. "I have never met anyone like you. How are you like this?"

I squinted at him, suspicious.

"I feel like that isn't a compliment."

He shook his head vigorously.

"No, no, I promise it is," he insisted. "You bust my balls every. Single. Time. I see you. You don't even hesitate. Just bam! Truth."

"That's me, the Truth Fairy," I said drolly. "Your jokes, however, leave much to be desired," he shot back. "Okay, fine. I'll think about what you said. Jesus. But first, let's get you home."

As I spat out my address, it occurred to me that Ricky would now know where I lived. That we couldn't claim to be strangers in that regard. When he settled to a stop in front of my apartment, I became acutely aware of the small space in the car, of the heaviness of potential. Did I hug him? Was it right to do that? If he'd been anyone else, I wouldn't have thought about it. But with Ricky, it felt dangerous.

"Thanks for the ride," I said instead. "The conversation wasn't too bad either."

"Of course," he said. He shifted the gear into park and gave me a tender smile. "Have a good night. I'll see you around, probably? Since we keep running into each other."

"Yeah," I said.

"Or maybe it can be on purpose," he said. "I usually volunteer on Saturdays. We can get lunch?"

I smirked, shaking my head. *A professional trapeze artist, this one.*

"How's Camila?" I said instead, meeting his eyes in a challenge.

Ricky's smile didn't waver, and he didn't look away.

"Don't know," he said in a deceptively

cheerful tone. "She dumped me a couple weeks ago." His voice took on a harder edge. "Why? Can't get lunch with me unless I'm single? You only hang out with Markus when he's got his girl with him?"

I looked down at my feet. Sure, I'd been goading him, but I'd expected him to balk, not announce the end of his relationship.

"Markus and I met in our college anime club," I said. "You and I met because you decided to hit on me in a garden." A car squeezed slowly past us in the narrow city street, and we both watched it pass through squinted eyes. "It's different."

Ricky's hands hadn't dropped from the steering wheel, and now they squeezed, the leather squeaking audibly under his tightening grip.

"I didn't . . ." he said. Then he bit his lip. "Look. I was drawn to you. I don't know why."

"Because you were attracted to me," I supplied. *It wasn't just my imagination. Admit it, Ricardo. Admit why we're here even now.*

"You're a pretty girl," Ricky confessed. Then he turned to face me, his jaw set. "But I didn't mean anything by it, honest. I thought . . . I *think* you're a cool person. I like hanging out with you." He swallowed. "I don't want anything more than that."

172

God, what an emotional roller coaster he'd put me through in the last minute. I wasn't sure whether to feel flattered (*So you do think I'm pretty*) or rejected, and so I settled for the next best thing — relieved. Outside of Sanity Circle, I couldn't recall meeting anyone so willing to show me their hand, let alone throw all their cards on the table. Besides, he'd given me what so many of my paramours of the past had denied me: ground to stand on. I would take it.

Still, there was no way I was giving him a hug now.

"Okay," I said. I reached for the door handle. "Text me next time you're in the hospital. If I can get away, we can get lunch. Cool?"

Ricky nodded. He was looking at me in a curious way, an odd, serene smile on his face. His eyes were bright, illuminated by the streetlights outside.

"Cool," he said. He lingered by the gate until I stepped in and pulled it shut, and then drove off into the night.

ELEVEN

"Oh man, I could *definitely* get used to this," Shae said, patting their stomach and practically purring with contentment. "That was delicious. What is it called, again?"

"Double chocolate fudge surprise,"* Nia said from the kitchen. The recipe was one of her oldest inventions, created when we were in high school, and it was one of my favorites. Normally, the double chocolate fudge surprise came out only for special occasions, and because my birthday had been celebrated with Beyoncé, I'd assumed I wouldn't taste it this year. Lucky for me, Nia considered impressing her new partner to be worthy of whipping out her best work.

"What's the surprise?" Shae asked, opening their eyes to give Nia a suggestive smile.

---

* Or, as I used to call it, DCFS. That is, until my peds rotation familiarized me with the Department of Child and Family Services.

"Is it something nasty?"

"I sure hope not," I interrupted. "Seeing as I've been eating it for years."

I hadn't meant to sound bitter, but apparently I had, because Shae grimaced and Nia let out a long, all-suffering sigh. It was just . . . ever since Shae and Nia had made things official, I'd been seeing a lot less of my best friend. Our previous romantic relationships had taken up space in our lives, but never like this. Nowadays, Nia was notably MIA most of the time, too busy hanging out with her hot, fun S.O. and her new troupe of gay comediennes* to save time for her Day One.

Not that I had a problem with that. Nia was happy, so I was happy. *Extremely* happy, in fact. I was extremely happy for Nia and not at all jealous that she wasn't around as much anymore.

Still, today was a nice change of pace; Nia and Shae had opted to veg out in our apartment instead of Shae's, where I could at least be their third wheel.

"Don't worry, Angie," Shae assured me. "I'm not going to steal her from you." They shared a conspiratorial look with Nia. "Or, you know, we could set up a trade. Your bes-

* Lovingly called her "lesbrigade."

175

tie for mine."

I balked. Ever since Camila and Ricky's breakup, Shae had been very transparent about trying to nudge us together. Whether this was out of guilt for snatching my best friend from me or due to some insider knowledge about Ricky's true intentions was unclear — either way, it was just uncomfortable enough that, most of the time, I ignored them.

Lucky for me, I had a Knight in Shining Armor* in the kitchen.

"Didn't Ricky just get out of a relationship?" Nia said, speaking my thoughts out loud. "I'm not handing over my best friend to be a rebound for yours."

Shae made a noise in protest.

"It won't necessarily be a rebound," they said. "The boy just loves him some love. He's quick to get back on the ol' horse." They gave me a rakish grin that forced me to remember why Nia liked them so much. "Not that you're a horse, Angie. You know what I'm saying. He's a relationship guy. His picker is a bit off, though; Camila was a dream compared to the chick he was with in college. But you seem cool, so —"

"You're not doing the best job of selling

* Or in this case, Knight in Sailor Moon Apron.

him, babe," Nia said plainly.

"Doesn't matter how you sell him," I grumbled, scraping a strip of OPI Never a Dulles Moment from my thumbnail. "Ricky's not interested, and neither am I."

It was true. Since the day in the lobby of the children's hospital, Ricky and I had been . . . friendly. We talked about art and music and complained about our best friends abandoning us for each other. Twice a week, we got lunch in the small café on the first floor, sometimes coffee, if he came in early. We'd even planned a study session this weekend at his favorite coffee shop in Bridgeport. It was easy talking to Ricky now that we'd ripped away the blanket of uncertainty. The electric chemistry I felt the first day we met had quieted into a comfortable compatibility, the way I felt with Markus, or with Nia.

And that was a good thing, I told myself. I wasn't above admitting that I still thought Ricky was a snack. That he smelled nice and looked even better and made me feel like I was two seconds away from belting out Destiny's Child's "Apple Pie à la Mode" every time he smiled at me a certain way. But I also wasn't a damn fool, and I'd gotten the message loud and clear — Ricky wasn't into me like that. Gone were the more untoward comments, and he was always careful these days not to touch me, folding his hands together, leaning away *ever so slightly* from my friendly nudges.

I respected that. That's how it should have been from the beginning. After all, he thought I was a cool person, and I felt the same about him. No reason to complicate things beyond that.

After all, dating Ricky *would* be complicated. I'd tried the "make a relationship work in medical school" thing once already, and it had almost ended with me throwing the last six years of grinding down the drain.* And Frederick had popped into my life at just the right time — about two years before I applied to residency, just enough time for our relationship to stabilize for me to factor his needs into my rank list determinations.† What business did I have pursuing a fledgling attraction to a guy who threw up more flags than a football referee and prob-

* You'd think that one exam that you get to take one time wouldn't have this effect, but alas — students with my Step 1 score have only a 50 percent chance of matching into residency.
† Because there ain't no way that I'm letting a man who isn't my husband or anything close have any say in my future career, and that's that.

ably had more ex-girlfriends than DMX* when I had my hands full trying to become a whole doctor? Besides, Momma would pitch a fit if I tried to bring home a *Mexican artist.*

"Okay," Shae said, disbelieving. "Whatever you say. Your sexual tension just *happens* to be thick enough to cut with a knife, but yeah, neither of you are interested."

"Shae," Nia warned, leaning over the back of the couch to kiss them on the cheek. Then to me, "Please pardon my eager little beaver over here. They were not a huge Camila fan."

"And I was right not to be!" Shae said. "Have you seen what she's been posting these days?" They didn't wait for my answer to pull out their phone and hurriedly pull up Camila's social media page. Indignantly, they held it up to my face for me to see.

Poor Ricky. Camila's most recent photos featured a new addition: a well-dressed white dude with great hair and even better pectorals. She had some plausible deniability for the first few pictures, but as I scrolled up through her feed, the photos got more and more compromising. There was no

* As listed in his hit song "What These Bitches Want."

179

doubt about it; Camila had a new boo, and, judging by the timing of her posts, he'd overlapped with her old one. I cringed at the most recent picture: a photo of Camila in a hot pink bikini, staring up at her "kicked out of the third episode of *The Bachelorette* contestant" boytoy like she was about to rip off his swim trunks. The tag? #Mancrushmonday. *Yikes.*

"This is . . . bad," I admitted. No way that Ricky didn't know about Camila's new Instagram-official boyfriend, and yet, during all our interactions, he seemed fine. We talked about his patients, about what nerdy show we were watching, and never about his ex.

"It's fucking disrespectful, is what it is," Shae fumed. "Can you imagine?"

I couldn't. I had thought that Frederick had done me dirty, but at least he hadn't flagrantly dumped me for another person and then announced his infidelity to the world.

My phone buzzed in my pocket — Tabatha was video calling me. She never video called me out of the blue; Tabs couldn't bear to be seen "looking anyhow" even by her sister, and so our calls were always planned. My heart took off at a gallop. This could mean only one thing.

180

"I think Chris proposed," I said to Nia.

"Oh my god, what?" Nia said, ripping off her apron and running around the couch to stand over my shoulder.

Shae watched us, confused. "Who's Chris?"

I gave Shae an apologetic glance.

"One sec," I said, and answered Tabatha's call.

Sure enough, Tabatha answered the call with her hand to the camera, a glittering hunk of a rock on her ring finger. Before I could stop myself, all three of us were squealing in excitement, all while Shae looked on in bewilderment.

"My sister!" I explained. "She's engaged!"

Even during the Knocking, it hadn't felt completely real. But now that I could see a ring on her finger and her damp, mascara-tracked face, it hit me. My baby sister, the same kid who used to cry when she didn't get a chocolate in the checkout line, the girl I would read bedtime stories to on the nights when both of our parents worked late, was getting married! Before I could stop myself, I was crying too. Nia, a softie at baseline, had already fetched tissues.

"When?" I asked.

"Just now!" Tabatha said. She swung her camera to the side and suddenly Chris was

181

in view, beaming with pride. "It . . . It was perfect."

As she described Chris's proposal, I let myself bask in her happiness. Chris was such a good guy. He'd reached out to me for help with the Knocking, anxious to honor both Tabatha and our family properly. For the proposal itself, the advice he sought was much more vague. I'd told him what she told me — *private, meaningful.* And so he'd taken her on a trip to Michigan and rented a room at the resort they had stayed at during their first trip together. They had spent the last three days lazing by the river, hiking along the trails, and enjoying each other's company. Tabatha had, of course, been suspicious, but when two evenings came and went without Chris popping the question, she had let her guard down . . . only for Chris to drop down on one knee the evening before they were set to return.

Sitting here, surrounded by love so sweet it made my teeth ache, I felt a deep, throbbing longing. "Why do you want to be in a relationship so badly?" Michelle had asked me months ago, when I was still swiping through dating apps in search of *the one.* "You know they can suck, right?"

I don't remember the answer I gave at that time. It had been something flimsy, a dismissive response to what I'd thought was a dismissive question. Who didn't want a relationship? Hadn't we all grown up watching the same romantic comedies, reading the same young adult vampire novels, and dreaming of the day that another person looked us in the eyes and declared themselves ours?

Except, now I knew better. I knew why I was losing Nia. It was because, when Nia looked at Shae, she saw a home. She saw a person who accepted her as she was, with all her bumps and crevices and cracks and beauty and graces. Just like Tabatha accepted Chris and vice versa, and my parents accepted each other. Forever was a long time for a twenty-three-year-old, and yet here was my baby sister, promising it without hesitation.

And none of the stories I read could have ever hoped to capture dedication like that.

I dropped my backpack with a thud on the bench next to me. Ricky's chosen coffee shop, Jackalope, turned out to be only a fifteen-minute drive from my apartment, and without even tasting a drink, I knew I would be back. The colors I'd seen on its website were only more vibrant in real life — the walls were painted bright orange and yellow, teal and highlighter pink. The table we picked was nestled underneath a shoulder mount of a large hare with suspiciously real-looking antlers: the shop's namesake. We had arrived at the shop at the same time, stepping out of our cars simultaneously, and the smile that had graced Ricky's face upon seeing me had almost knocked me out. Like my presence was the biggest box under a Christmas tree and it had his name on it —

Stop it, Angela.

Knowing that Ricky just wanted to be friends should have made things easier for me, and to a degree, it did. My daydreaming took on a much more innocent edge now that I knew it could go nowhere, and his small favors — like getting me a latte, as he did now — didn't send my mind into a flurry. Because I knew they were just that, favors. Ricky liked doing things for people. It made him feel needed. Before the improv show, he had taken Shae out to dinner, and he'd already stopped by my apartment on an evening when I was working late to help Nia change out a flat. From him, a latte wasn't a hint or a romantic gesture. It was just a latte from a guy who wanted to show off his favorite drink.

And a necklace . . . is just a necklace.

Ricky's gaze dropped to my collarbone,

his grin broadening.

"You're wearing it!" he exclaimed.

My hands jumped instinctively to the Water Tribe pendant, and I flushed. I'd been wearing it to the hospital lately; it worked wonders as an ice breaker for my teenage patients.

"Yeah, well," I said. "It's pretty. Thanks."

I focused on unloading my backpack, but I could still feel the triumph coming off him in waves. The table groaned in complaint as I dropped my ob-gyn shelf review book onto it, then my *First Aid** text, and, finally, my laptop.

"Those look heavy," Ricky observed.

"Yeah, 'cause they are." I watched him open up his laptop. "So, what are you working on?"

"I'll show you. But wait a second," Ricky said. He pulled out his phone and opened up a timer application. "When me and Shae were in college, we'd do this thing," he explained, "where when we were working on a project, we'd give ourselves seven minutes to talk, then thirty minutes to work. Rinse and repeat."

"Ah," I said, "so that's what this is about.

* Every medical student has, and intends to someday burn, a copy of this book.

185

Your position for a quirky Black bestie's just opened up, and you're interviewing candidates." I stuck my tongue out at him. "Weird way to grieve, Ricky."

Ricky rolled his eyes and punched the timer on.

"Starting now, I guess."

I snickered. "You realize I was premed once, right? You think I didn't pump out these study exercises like a pro?"

"Yeah?"

"Yeah," I said. "Except it was seven minutes every hour."

"Oh, of course. You even sound like a freaking premed," Ricky said. "We used to look left and right to make sure you guys weren't lurking in the bushes somewhere before complaining about how much work we had to do, because you'd always pop out to talk about how none of it compared to organic chemistry."

I laughed.

"Guilty! But where I went, we didn't bother you art school students as much. You guys lived in a studio."

"Ha, well then I would've definitely been a target," Ricky said. "Majored in poli sci and English."

I did not know that.

"You're self-taught?" The little green

186

monster in my chest I'd last felt the first time I'd seen his work lurched again.

"I took a few classes my senior year once I figured out what I wanted to do," he explained. "But yeah, for the most part."

We talked a bit about school then: the evolution of his career aspirations ("I want to open my own design firm someday"), the study abroad trip to Colombia he'd gone on after his sophomore year, the year-long power struggle with his grandfather when he decided to pursue his passion instead of translate his very law-aligned coursework into a doctorate.

I slapped at his laptop playfully.

"Let me see what you broke your grandpa's heart for, then."

He flipped it around. Unexpectedly, it was a brochure, and a dry one at that. My face must have dropped because Ricky slumped forward onto the table and laughed out loud.

"What do you think graphic designers do, Angie?"

I threw up my hands. "I thought you were drawing!"

Ricky's shoulders still shook with mirth.

"What?"

"You should see yourself," he said. "Pouting like a baby!"

187

I was really pouting now. "Leave me alone. I can't control my face."

"You really can't," Ricky said. "You're like a cartoon character. Everything comes out through the face. The rest through your hands."

I looked down at my hands, and, lo and behold, they were fidgeting with my earbud cords in my lap. I balled them into fists.

"You're observant," I said.

He smiled lazily.

"I like looking at interesting things."

Before I could figure out whether he'd just insulted me or hit on me, the timer went off.

"That's it. Time for you to hit the books."

When Ricky had suggested meeting in the coffee shop to help motivate me to study, he hadn't been playing around. He was a drill sergeant. All my attempts at sneaking in conversations were rebuffed. He barely looked away from his computer screen to direct me back to studying, sometimes by pointing at my books, once by stepping on my toe when he caught me on my phone. Eventually, I gave up on distracting him and actually started doing practice questions. There were a thousand of them in the bank, a number that seemed impossible in the six weeks I had for my ob-gyn rotation. I'd been paralyzed by that number, by the low returns, by the fact that one hour of studying would get me through only twenty. That my one day off a week, the one day I had away from Labor and Delivery and the disapproving attendings and the emotionally friable residents had to be spent grinding. Maybe that's why I'd avoided it, why I'd let myself sit and stew in my bitterness instead of trying to keep myself from failing my next shelf.

The timer went off, and I jumped up in shock. I'd done eighteen questions in half an hour. Not bad. If we kept this up for two more hours, I'd get seventy done, which was way better than zero.

"You must be very smart to have gotten into medical school," Ricky said, "because you totally lack discipline."

"Jerk," I said. "I'll have you know I was very productive, despite you breathing down my neck."

"You really think you'd have gotten anything done without me here?" Ricky said.

"Of course," I said. "How do you think I got this far? Start the timer."

"Yes, ma'am," Ricky said, punching it on. Then, without asking permission, he reached across the table and picked up *First Aid.*

189

"So," he said, opening up the book and flipping idly through the pages. "Shae said your sister got engaged the other day. Didn't that already happen?"

I snorted.

"Marrying a Ghanaian girl is complicated, okay," I said. "The day you and I met was right after the Knocking. It's like . . . the traditional engagement?" I pursed my lips, trying to think of the best way to explain it. "Chris's dad basically came with him to tell us he was planning on proposing."

"So . . . ," Ricky said, "it's the same as asking permission to propose?" He puffed his chest out, dropped his voice an octave. "Like, 'Sir, I would like to ask your daughter to marry me'?"

I wagged my head, laughing.

"No," I insisted. Then I considered it. "Actually, though, maybe? But I don't know, it's *heavier* than that. You have to seal the deal with a drink and everything."

"What kind of drink?" Ricky asked. He seemed genuinely curious, resting his chin in his palm and giving me his rapt attention. Who would have thought we could come so far in a month — from squabbling on the peds floors to sitting in a coffee shop across from each other, discussing Ghanaian engagement traditions? *Maybe he's stor-*

190

ing this away for future reference, Hopeless Angie said in a small voice, and, annoyed, I shoved her back into the hole from which she came.

"Gin," I said, "or schnapps." When Ricky's grin grew devilish, I added hastily, "Not *that* kind of schnapps."

"Yeah?" Ricky said. "You mean I can't go lay claim to a Ghanaian girl without figuring out what schnapps flavor she favors?" He narrowed his eyes, then pointed at me. "You look like a whipped cream kind of gal. Wait, no, peppermint. Definitely into Peppermint Patties."

I crossed my arms, pretending to take umbrage.

"What's that supposed to mean?"

Ricky rubbed his chin thoughtfully.

"Hear me out," he said. "I'm guessing you spent most of college hiding away in a library, yeah? Probably not partying too hard. Definitely not wasting your precious study time getting trashed."

I raised an eyebrow, curious about where he was headed.

"Okay . . . ," I said.

"Except," Ricky continued, "on those nights after your big organic chemistry exams, or whatever big premed test you had to take. Those were nights you truly wanted

191

to forget. But you couldn't stand the taste of liquor, because, unlike your college-aged brethren, you hadn't spent the last several months burning off your taste buds with bottom-shelf vodka. Enter . . . the Peppermint Patty. Highly efficient and tastes like dessert."

I winced at the accuracy, recalling a time that Michelle accidentally squirted a line of chocolate syrup down my chin instead of into my mouth at a spring break house party.

"You sound like you have a lot of experience," I said instead.

"Not really. Just did a lot of people watching back then. Gotta imbibe in moderation, considering I'm genetically predisposed to like it too much," Ricky said. Then he gestured for me to continue. "So. You give the gin, or maybe the schnapps, and that's it?"

"We send the rest of the liquor to the head of the family," I explained. Tabatha's bottle of schnapps had already been shipped to my great-uncle's house in Tema. "And then, most times, the groom gets a list."

"A list?" Ricky asked. Done teasing, he now looked intrigued.

"A bride price," I clarified. "Stuff he has

192

to get. Like cloth, jewelry, sometimes cash
—"

When I glanced back at Ricky's face, his jaw was practically on the floor.

"Hold up. What you're saying," Ricky said, "is that you get *sold*?"

Now my indignation was real. I closed my laptop with a sharp snap, knowing that I was wont to knock it off the table if I gesticulated any harder.

"No!" I said. "Of course not!"

Ricky was not convinced.

"The guy exchanges money and goods for a woman," he said, "and that's not a sale?" He pushed his hair out of his eyes, and I realized that his concern was now genuine. "Angie, I get that it's tradition and every-thing, but —"

"You've got it totally wrong," I asserted. I'd really only come to understand my own culture's engagement practices in the last year, and, though I'd reacted similarly when I first learned about them, I now felt the need to defend them. "It's the exact op-posite. It shows that the woman has *value*. She's precious, and whoever intends to marry her needs to *earn her* first. And it's not like the family blows the bride price! They put it aside for her in case the guy turns out to be a dud and they need to help her escape." I scowled. "It's better than a dowry, where they treat the women like a burden."

"Okay, okay," Ricky said, holding his hands up in surrender. "I didn't mean to imply that your traditions were misogynistic, or something."

I sucked in my bottom lip, dropping my gaze to the timer. *Two minutes left.* Suddenly, I wished that Tabatha's engagement hadn't come up, that Ricky hadn't pressed me for details, that I hadn't provided them. Chris's reaction to the Knocking traditions had been immediate acceptance, and he had merged into our household so seamlessly that Momma had taken to joking that he probably had Ghanaian ancestry. "He looks like a village boy from Obosomase," she teased, watching him pile his plate with waakye at one of the Naperville Ghanaian shindigs. She'd made her preference for the ethnic makeup of her daughters' future husbands explicit long ago, down to a ranking system: first, a Ghanaian boy,* then Nigerian ("the alata fo are like our cousins"), then assorted West African, followed by Black American or the larger African

* And not just any Ghanaian, but a Christian, southern one.

194

diaspora, and finally, reluctantly, an oborɔnyi,* with no consideration for anyone else. Once, during Tabatha's short-lived fling with a sweet, very eligible bachelor named Adesh, Momma had called me up in hysterics. "You have to advise your younger sister against what she is doing with this boy," she had said. "*Sri Lankan?* That is too many traditions!" If Ricky's first thought about the Knocking was that it was misogynistic and antiquated, then he wouldn't stand a chance against Dorothy Appiah's assessments.

I must have been quiet for a long time, because across from me, Ricky sighed. Then, unexpectedly, his hand covered mine. I looked down at it in shock, then back up again, focusing just over his shoulder so I wouldn't meet his eyes. He hadn't touched me on purpose in a long time. The places where our skin met burned like live wire. It took all the discipline Ricky claimed I lacked to not pull away.

"Hey," he said. "I'm sorry. That was rude. You just taught me something really neat

* A white dude, and even then, only if he could handle his *shito* (a spicy paste made from peppers, onions, and dried shrimp that we use as a condiment).

195

about your culture, and I shouldn't have been judgmental about it. Thank you for taking the time to explain."

I slipped my hand out from beneath his under the guise of picking up my ob-gyn review, my heart hammering away in my chest.

"It's fine," I said, wondering if he could see my hands tremble as I turned the pages. Out of the corner of my eye, I could see Ricky smile, slow and syrupy, like he knew exactly what effect his little flirtations were having on me. *The pretty ones,* I thought, *are the worst.*

"What I want to know, though," he mused, "is how much *you're* worth. Four cows? Sixty yards of cloth? Your weight in gold?"

I huffed, even as I willed my pulse to slow.

"Don't worry about it. You couldn't afford me," I said. "How much time is left on that clock?"

TWELVE

It had been two and a half months since my last meeting with Dr. Wallace, a short interim for an audience with someone of her station. But Dr. Wallace had a vested interest in my matching into a residency program. As the face of the Diversity and Inclusion Committee, she had fought tooth and nail for every Black student who had walked through the hallowed halls of our medical school over the last fifteen years, and her ability to continue doing so was at least in part contingent on our success in the Match.* So when she called for a

* Every fourth-year medical student, after deciding on their specialty, applies to a wide slew of programs. They rank said programs. Said programs rank them. And on a fateful day in March at 12:00 p.m. EST, the students open an envelope to find out where we will be completing our two to seven years of indentured servitude.

check-in meeting, I wasn't entirely surprised. Besides, I had something else I wanted to discuss.

"I saw that you honored* peds. Congratulations," she said. "Peppermint?" she offered, waving toward the latest addition to the disaster of her desk: a clear glass jar of mints.

Remembering Ricky's declaration that I was a Peppermint Patty, I shook my head.

"Thank you," I said. Dr. Berber, of all people, had given me a glowing evaluation. *Angela is always upbeat and ready to learn,* it said. *Her fund of knowledge is impressive for a fresh third-year.*

"Ob-gyn might be harder," she said. "But you'll do fine. Keep this up, and I think we'll be in the clear for your residency apps. Now. About your project."

I'd finished the first draft of my DVT prophylaxis literature review weeks ago, and it had been sitting, unaddressed, in my PI's, Dr. Donoghue's, email inbox ever since. I told Dr. Wallace as much, and she scowled, crossing her arms.

* Med school grades are as follows: Pass, High Pass, Honors. As perfectionists, most medical students are devastated to get anything other than an Honors.

"That's not good," she said. "There are some big conference deadlines coming up. Email him again to check in." She tapped her chin. "What about another project? Just in case this one falls through. There were a few others on that list that I thought looked promising."

My hands curled on my knees, and I sat up as straight as possible, meeting Dr. Wallace's eyes directly. That was the best way to get her attention, I'd learned; be commanding, don't slouch, avoid self-deprecation. Come prepared with hard data.

"Actually," I said. "I want to do something else. An . . . original project."

I told her, then, about the boy in the trauma bay. About his mother, and the assumption of his guilt. About the man from years ago in the Emergency Department ("I wrote about him in my personal statement, actually"). And then, about my idea.

"I want to look into specifically Black patient perspectives on physician-patient communication," I said. I pulled out a folder from my backpack, removing printed copies of the relevant studies I had found thus far. "There's a lot of data out there already about how physicians are more likely to undertreat pain in Black patients, and how we're more likely to miss serious diagnoses. There's also a lot of data about what factors contribute to patient satisfaction, and what patients think physicians could do better. Some people have looked into medical mistrust in the context of medicine's role in maintaining racial hierarchies. But . . . there's this intersection that's just . . . missing." I met Dr. Wallace's stony expression with my own. "I want to address that."

Dr. Wallace took my papers from me, riffling through them one by one. Then she lowered them onto the desk in front of her.

"You're very passionate," she said after a long time. "And driven."

"But . . ." I filled in for her, quirking an eyebrow.

"But," she said, "a project like this is risky. For one, you will need IRB* approval, which will slow you down. You might need to find funding for transcription services. You'll have to collect the data yourself, and code it yourself." She rubbed her temples.

* The Institutional Review Board is a committee that reviews research proposals to make sure they're ethical, preventing researchers from going off the rails and, say, letting Black people die from treatable diseases to "observe the natural course of disease" (literally the Tuskegee Syphilis Study).

"This isn't something you can finish in one year, Angela."

"I know," I said. "But I think I can make some serious headway —"

"And," Dr. Wallace added, "it's a 'Black' project."

Oh. I sat back in my chair, trying to process what I'd just heard. Dr. Wallace leaned back with me, folding her hands on her desk.

"What," I said finally, trying to hold back the disgust from my voice, "is that supposed to mean?"

"Why are you in my office, instead of, say, Dr. Bauer's?" Dr. Wallace asked. Her glasses glowed with the reflection from her desktop monitor. "Because we share an experience, right? Because I am able to peek beyond the frosted glass and tell you honestly about the bullshit that is going down on the other side." She picked up my papers again, and with a firm thud, lined up the sheets before stuffing them back into my folder. "And what I'm saying is that, at this stage in your career, you are better off marketing yourself as a clinical researcher than another Black health disparities one."

Before, I had been just one of many *Black kids with a bad Step score,* and now, my attempt at creating original research was just *another Black kid looking at health disparities.* Even though I knew she was just trying to help me, I felt betrayed. Dr. Wallace had always seemed like a source of unending wisdom, but now I felt like we were out of sync. Like she looked at me and saw only a liability. She reminded me of my parents, summarily destroying my enjoyment of anything that wasn't directly aligned with her specific vision of my future in medicine.

"I didn't come to medical school to become a clinical researcher," I said slowly. "I came to be a doctor." I stood up, grabbing my folder from her desk. "I'll email Dr. Donoghue about my DVT prophylaxis review."

Someone else may have asked me to stop, or even apologized. But not Dr. Wallace. It wasn't her style to do or say things she thought she could regret. When I walked out of her office, she told me to have a good day, and asked me to please close the door gently behind me. Whatever. I was tired of being told what I could or couldn't do.

I was Angie fucking Appiah, and no matter what a stupid, outdated test said, I had brains for days. I was going to do whatever I wanted, and I was going to do it well, and when my work was finally done, everyone who tried to hold me back would look upon the spoils of my labor and know that they'd screwed up.

"Yikes," Michelle said after I'd told her about my meeting with Dr. Wallace. Throughout our first and second years, Michelle had been a pivotal part of the Sanity Circle, the only one who fully understood the endurance course that was medicine. I probably wouldn't have survived preclinicals* without her by my side, which meant, of course, that the Powers That Be had snatched her away from me for our third year. The only rotation we shared was ob-gyn, which meant that our conversations had to be brief; the residents in Labor and Delivery were allergic to fun.

"Yeah, yikes is right," I said. Dr. Donoghue, likely at Dr. Wallace's nudging, had responded to me with a revision to our review, and I'd implemented his changes without flourish. It felt cheap, like getting into residency was a game rather than a goal. "It's okay, though. I did some digging, and I found an attending who sounds interested. Danny Reed? He's a hospitalist, so he doesn't normally work with students,

* The first one to two years of medical school, prior to starting clerkships.

203

but he's, get this" — I lifted my hands in scare quotes — "another Black health disparities researcher."

Michelle grimaced.

"Don't piss off Dr. Wallace," she warned. "She's big leagues."

"I won't piss off Dr. Wallace," I said. It was strange; I was upset with my mentor, but I still thought the world of her. "I've still done everything she's asked me to do. And I still appreciate her. It's just that —"

"Umm . . . ," a nasally voice interrupted. "Why are you just sitting there? Don't you see that patient in antepartum?"

I jolted, then turned to look at Gwen, my assigned ob-gyn resident. She'd somehow gone from hunching over her computer and pretending I didn't exist to looming over us and scowling like she'd just caught us eating her lunch.

"I'll go see the patient in a minute," I said slowly.

"I'm sure you will," Gwen said. She made a point of rolling her eyes before pivoting and walking back to her computer. Michelle could probably see the murderous intent behind my glare, because she pinched my arm.

"It's okay," Michelle said. "Go see that patient. We'll talk later."

Grumbling, I walked to room 2, where the patient was boarded. Her eyes snapped to mine the moment I opened the door. She crumpled the bedsheets at her sides in a white-knuckled grip.

"Sorry for the wait, Ms. Herring," I said.

"What wait? I just got here," Ms. Herring said. A mechanical hum droned in the background — her blood pressure cuff going off. She looked nervously at the monitor. "What does it say? Is it high?"

I blinked at her. The cuff hadn't even finished running yet.

"It'll take a minute," I said. *She's terrified.* And no kidding. The sheet outside her room that summarized her reason for her visit had told me that she was twenty-two years old and twenty-six weeks pregnant. Younger than me. I still forgot that I was now firmly within the age of what was considered socially acceptable for motherhood. Yet most days I could barely take care of myself, let alone a tiny, fragile human.

"My cousin's blood pressure was really high during her pregnancy. She had preeclampsia. She's fine now, and the baby too, but . . ." Her eyes glazed over with fear. "I used her cuff at home. The top number was one fifty. That's high, right?"

"It is, but let's see what this one says."

A few seconds later, the monitor produced a number — 145/95. I watched Ms. Herring's heart rate spike before my eyes.

"See," she said, "that's high."

I clicked through her chart. Ironically, she'd only ever come to the doctor for birth control. Her blood pressure at all those visits was always normal.

"You're right, it is a bit high," I said. "But it's okay. You did the right thing. You're here now. Our job is to make sure nothing dangerous is happening."

I examined her, clumsily. Somehow, I felt like she'd transmitted her anxiety to me, turned my usually sure movements jerky. I asked her a slew of questions: Any headaches? Blurry vision? Abdominal pain? Nausea, vomiting, constipation, diarrhea? And she nodded every time and looked more and more frazzled with each passing second. I'd just lifted her sheet to check her legs for swelling when the door to her room slid open.

"Hello, Ms. Herring, I'm Dr. Jansen," Gwen said, an angelic smile on her face. "Thank you for talking to our medical student." She cut her eyes to me. "Well?"

I rattled off Ms. Herring's history and listed all the symptoms she endorsed. I

206

could see Gwen getting bored the longer I spoke.

"Hmm," she said. "Did you do an ultrasound?"

Had my nerves not been already shot to hell, I would have laughed. Do an ultrasound? I could barely tell apart fluid and not-fluid on ultrasounds,* let alone do one. She went to medical school too, she had to know that that wasn't part of the curriculum. But a moment went by and she added, "Well?"

"I'll go get a machine," I said. It took real effort to keep my face neutral. *Just three weeks, Angie. You can do this.*

Of course the ultrasound machine was just around the corner, where Gwen could have easily grabbed it on the way to the room. I allowed myself a second to fume as I unplugged it from the wall and wheeled it to Ms. Herring's room.

Gwen was surprisingly gentle with Ms. Herring. She eased her back on the exam table and made a comment about her Betty

---

* I don't know how many times an eager attending has tried to explain to me the difference between the staticky gray of the liver and the staticky gray of the lung on an ultrasound — it's still all Greek to me.

207

Boop tattoo that made her laugh, and when that laughter turned to tears, she produced a small box of tissues from her scrub pocket and rubbed Ms. Herring's back soothingly. When it was time for the ultrasound, she got the baby the moment her probe hit skin. I'd known after day one of the rotation, when I'd watched a woman fill a bedpan with blood during an incomplete abortion,* that ob-gyn wasn't the specialty for me, but I still felt a twinge of awe when I watched the residents do procedures with skill and ease.

After presenting the patient to our attending, we walked back to the workroom in silence. There were still eight hours left in my shift. I wanted to cry.

"Okay, so you clearly don't want to do ob-gyn," Gwen said out of nowhere. "So what do you want to do?"

My blood pressure spiked so quickly it gave me a headache. *Breathe, girl, breathe.*

"I don't know yet," I said.

"Well, you better figure it out soon," she said. "Because you'll have to at least *try* to impress them there."

* Did you know that if your placenta doesn't completely detach, you just never stop bleeding? Yeah, I didn't. I do now. Heeellllllll no.

208

Gwen held open the door to the workroom for me, as if that small courtesy could make up for her awfulness.

"I hate her," I whispered later to Michelle, after Gwen had left the room. "Oh my god, I hate her so much."

Michelle gave me a sympathetic look. Her resident was equally burned out, but significantly less toxic.

"Well, at least you have tomorrow off," Michelle said. She dropped her head into her hands. "I have a *freaking* Monday. Ugh."

"At least you can get some errands done," I offered. My phone dinged in the front pocket of my scrubs, and I pulled it out.

Ricky: You still in the hospital? Need a re-up? He sent a photo of the self-serve coffee canisters from the downstairs café.

I smiled. Yeah, I responded. And oh my god yes. Please.

Michelle leaned toward me, turning my hand over to reveal my screen.

"Who you texting — ? Ohhhh." She leered at me. "It's *Ricardo.*"

"Michelle, chill, it's not like that."

My phone dinged again. You're in the L&D, right? Third floor?

"Are you sure?" Michelle said. "Because it looks to me like he's about to wander all the way to Labor and Delivery just to *hand*

209

deliver you coffee."

"He's just like that, Michelle," I assured her. How was I supposed to maintain my cool-cucumber status when all my friends gave me the same knowing look when Ricky so much as shot me a glance? "We've been through this already, remember?"

"Aw, come on," Michelle said. "When did you break up with Frederick again? Aren't you missing" — she dropped her pitch, affecting a sultry Southern accent — "a man's warm embrace?"

"Nope," I said, popping my mouth on the *p.* Michelle snickered, patting my arm in sympathy.

"Okay, sweetie," she said. "But just know . . . the relationship types don't stay single for long. Get in there before someone else does."

At the thought of someone else, my stomach dropped. After Camila, I hadn't even considered the possibility of another woman in Ricky's life. Which was ridiculous. He was a good-looking guy, and, despite my initial misgivings, a total sweetheart. There were probably a thousand hot girls in a ten-mile radius waiting to snap him up. And if one did . . . where would that leave me?

"There's nowhere to get," I said, just as Ricky responded: I'm here.

210

Checking to make sure the coast was clear of residents and waiting antepartum patients, I dashed out of the workroom and into the waiting area. To my horror, Michelle followed, giving me a look that said *I ain't missing this shit* when I rolled my eyes at her.

We found Ricky standing in front of the L&D check-in counter, shuffling his feet awkwardly. Gladys, the unit secretary, was clearly dressing him down, looking at him disapprovingly over her red horn-rimmed glasses. He had two cups of coffee in hand, and his brown skin was flushed with mortification.

"No, I need to know who you're here for," Gladys was asking him. "And I don't see an Appiah on our list. Are you sure she's at this hospital?"

"She's not a patient," he tried. "She works here —"

"Hey, Ricky," I said, rescuing him from further questioning. Behind me, Michelle was trying, and failing, to stifle her laughter. I turned to Gladys. "Afternoon, Gladys. Sorry, this one's mine."

Gladys gave me an unamused shrug and turned back to her computer. Finally released from his interrogation, Ricky sagged with relief and handed me my coffee.

"How's the day going?" he asked in hushed tones. Then, looking left and right: "You still working with La Diabla?" he added, invoking Gwen's nickname.

"Yeah, but careful, I think she can hear through walls," I said. I accepted the coffee from him, trying to ignore the brush of our fingers as the cup exchanged hands. Behind me, Michelle cleared her throat.

"Oh hey," Ricky said, startled. "Michelle, right?"

I could tell that he was thinking back to the Beyoncé concert and remembering why he'd been there in the first place.

"Nice to see you again, Ricky!" Michelle said, just a bit too cheerfully. "Don't mind me, just stretching my legs. Sitting in that workroom is for the birds."

Ricky raised a questioning eyebrow at me, and I shook my head, helpless, as Michelle started doing lunges behind me.

"Well, I should let you guys go," he said. Then, without preamble, he reached for me, loosely cupping my elbow. "We're still on for tomorrow, right?"

My eyes darted down to his hand, then back to his eyes. It was an innocent touch, and feather-light, but it felt like he was breaking some unspoken rule. He'd been touching me a lot more lately: brushing his fingers past my back to squeeze behind me, nudging me to get my attention. Nothing I would've noticed coming from anyone else . . . but Ricky *wasn't* anyone else, and so of course I did.

"Yeah," I said. He smiled and, dropping his hand, took a swig of his coffee.

"Cool," he said. "Then, well, I'm heading home. I'll pick you up around two?"

"Sounds good," I said, feeling Michelle's eyes bore into the back of my head. She hardly waited for the doors to the L&D to shut behind me before rounding on me, jabbing me forcefully in the chest.

"What. The. Hell," Michelle said. "I am so freaking appalled." She pulled out her phone, typing a message to the group chat that made my pocket buzz a second later. "What do you mean, 'he's just like that'! With *who*?" Her expression grew grave, and she placed a hand firmly on my shoulder. "Angie, I can't believe that I have to be the one to tell you this . . . but that man wants to screw you into the carpet."

I winced against her crudeness, but Michelle didn't spare me even a half second to recover before barreling over me some more.

"Where are you even going tomorrow?" she asked. "For your little not-date?"

I crossed my arms, preparing myself for

an excessive Michelle response.

"King Spa," I grumbled, as Michelle sputtered in disbelief. "What! I told him I was stressed out, and he thought it would be fun. I know I was supposed to go there with you first, but it's been two and a half years since we moved to Chicago and we still haven't managed, so —"

"Yeah, yeah, whatever, you have betrayed me, okay," Michelle said, waving me off. "I don't care about that. I want to know why you're lying to yourself so thoroughly. Look!" She held up her screen, where I could see that Nia had responded: Yeah, Shae thinks it's only a matter of time. "Even his best friend thinks he's into you! So why don't you?"

"Because!" I said. "I believed him when he said he wasn't interested! And even if he was . . ."

Even if he was . . . I paused, simmering. *It wouldn't last.* It was just as Michelle had said. Guys like Ricky didn't stay single for long, and girls like me . . . Well, we were exciting in theory, interesting as a concept. Bright and shiny when we were new and our outspokenness was "refreshing" and our exoticness* exhilarating. Eventually, when

* A word that should probably apply only to

reality settled in and they realized that, actually, they did want the kind of woman that society told them they should — thinner than me, paler than me, less educated and more in awe of them than I ever could be — they left. Just like Frederick had left and every man I'd dared to let into my heart before him. But those men hadn't really been my friends, and Ricky was, so why change that? Why take something that felt good and right in its current form and try to morph it into something that could hurt?

I told Michelle as much. She listened, the furrow in her brow deepening with every word. Then she scowled.

"Why do you feel this way about yourself?" she snapped. "Like you're not enough, or something?"

"I don't think I'm not enough," I said plainly. "I think I'm too *much*." A door slammed shut in the distance, and I winced, wondering if our absence had been noted. "I . . . Never mind. We should get back to the workroom before Gwen realizes I'm gone."

Michelle looked at me like I'd grown a second head.

---

endangered species but has been frequently used to describe me.

"Um, no we shouldn't, because what the hell, Angie," she said. "You realize he can just like you, right? That it doesn't have to be any more complicated than that?" When I didn't say anything, she crossed her arms. "I wish you'd just told me that you weren't interested in him or something. That would be way less depressing."

Depressing or not, it was true, and I wasn't about to apologize for my reality.

"It's fine," I muttered. Then I looked her in the eye. "*I'm fine*. Ricky and I are friends, and we are just going for a nice day at the spa together. Just like with the girls."

"Fine," Michelle said. "Just . . . if you do like him" — she held up a finger when I opened my mouth to protest — "I said *if* — then can you not do that thing you always do? Where you let yourself live in limbo to stop yourself from getting hurt? It's different if you actually want to be his friend, but if you're mucking around in no-man's-land just because you think that it's safer there, I'm going to be pissed. Because you're too grown for that now, and I'm too busy to help you pick up the pieces when it inevitably doesn't work out."

I recoiled.

"What do you mean, what I always do —"

Before I could demand an explanation,

216

Michelle marched ahead of me and into the workroom. Through the sliver of the open door, I could see Gwen waiting for me, clicking her pen menacingly. I groaned. It was going to be a long shift.

THIRTEEN

Ricky pulled up outside my apartment the next day at two o'clock sharp, his face lighting up in a smile that put his dimples on full display. For the twenty-four hours since Michelle had accosted me in L&D, I'd turned her words over in my head. *Mucking around in no-man's-land?* Michelle and I had known each other for six years (and as many heartbreaks, given my tendency to fall for every man who could keep up a conversation with me) and she had never accused me of contributing to my own misery. And yeah, Michelle had a penchant for the dramatic, but she was also frighteningly astute. I would have asked her for clarification, but Gwen was on me like white on rice, and so I never got the chance.

"Congratulations!" Ricky said when I popped the door of his car open.

"For what?" I asked, clambering inside.

"For making it to the weekend without

murdering La Diabla," Ricky said.

I groaned, throwing my bag into the back. It landed with a thud; Ricky had suggested I bring my books to the spa. *It's a whole day affair,* he stressed. *You might want to get some reading in. Nothing medical though — you're relaxing, remember?*

"Ugh. You're right. I deserve a medal," I said. "You know what she said to me yesterday after you left?" I brought the pitch of my voice up a few octaves and talked through my nose. " 'You med students are always soooo slow. Why haven't you gotten me gauze yet? Come on, chop chop!' "

Ricky took his eyes off the road just long enough to give me an incredulous look.

"And you didn't *chop chop* her upside her head?" he asked, shaking his head in disappointment. "But what of your dignity, Angela?"

I snorted, then dropped my seat back. Ricky never seemed to mind long, tangential stories about my day. If anything, he egged them on, picking up on loose threads from prior conversations and inviting me to expound on them. I never felt like he was humoring me, or simply waiting his turn to talk about himself. But of course, he was like Markus — a girl's guy, a grandma's boy, used to the kind of aimless chatter Frederick had once described as exhausting. And yeah, it was nice, but I couldn't just give him brownie points for, gasp, actually being interested in what I had to say.

"Seriously," Ricky was saying, incensed. "It's nuts that they can just talk to you like that without any consequences. She grades you, right? Have you talked to anyone in your school's administration about her?"

"The administration?" I scoffed. "Ha! No. There's no point. They'll tell me that I should work on accepting feedback."

"Then what are they there for, huh? What do they get paid the big bucks to do if not protect you —"

I smiled lazily, watching him rant about the injustice of my mistreatment with genuine indignation. The sunlight poured through the windshield, setting his golden skin aglow. Poor Camila. She had no idea how good she'd had it. There was no way her new meathead boyfriend was getting this charged up about her work drama. Though to be fair, I thought, Ricky and I were friends. Friends listened to each other. Maybe if we were dating, he would have been different.

And then I stopped that thought in its tracks, because we were not dating, and, contrary to popular Sanity Circle opinion, I didn't want us to be. Or, more correctly, I was content with keeping our relationship as it was. What we had now — singing along to Ricky's "top 40s from the early 2000s" playlist, joking about his problematic clients, enjoying each other's company without any expectations — was more than enough.

Too soon, we were pulling into the surprisingly packed parking lot of King Spa.

"This is it," Ricky announced, shifting into park.

The entrance to King Spa was flanked by two statues of lions, appearing simultaneously grand and gaudy in its surrounding strip mall. Inside, a hypnotic flute melody played over the speakers. Ricky bounced with excitement all the way up to the reception desk.

"Maximum relaxation is ahead of you," he assured me. He gave me an earnest smile. "I promise, this place is the best. It's like a serotonin factory. I come out feeling great every time."

Ricky paid for both of our entrance fees ("You can buy me dinner when we get inside") and showed me how to use the bracelet key to open my locker.

"Have a nice soak. I'll meet you in the sauna area in half an hour?" he said.

Then he left, heading toward the men's

baths. I watched him go, bemused. He was so . . . chipper today. It was cute.

I shuffled into the ladies' bath area and located my locker. Already, I'd caught sight of more flesh than I was used to seeing all at once. The old women were especially flagrant blow-drying their hair in the mirrors with their towels draped uselessly over their shoulders. The younger women seemed almost as unperturbed; there were groups of them huddled together, giggling and gossiping like they were hanging out in a café. It was like any women's locker room except none of us were wearing clothes.

A few years ago, I wouldn't have been caught dead in a bikini, let alone naked with a bunch of strangers. I'd been too self-conscious, hyperaware of the stretch marks on my bum and the stubborn bits of cellulite around my thighs. But even my brief time on ob-gyn had forced me to be gentler to myself. I saw so many bodies all the time, many with features that I hated on myself and found human or even beautiful on others. After I disrobed, grabbed a towel, and showered, it was finally time for a bath. There were multiple baths at different temperatures, and I played like Goldilocks, dipping my toes in each one until I found one to my liking. Gingerly, I sank into the almost painfully hot water and closed my eyes. Around me, the sound of bubbling water mingled with the din of hushed conversation, and I let my mind go blank.

Who knows how many minutes later, I was awakened by a splash on my cheek; a little girl, maybe eight years old, had jumped into the water. Her mother bobbed her head in apology, but I waved her off, searching the walls for a clock. I hadn't expected to fall asleep. Well, I supposed, if Ricky wanted to be in my life, he was going to have to get used to me being late.

Eventually, I made my way out of the baths and into the standard-issue spa uniform. I giggled at myself in the mirror — the pink oversized shirt and baggy shorts made me look like a twelve-year-old — and followed the signs to the saunas.

The sauna area was unexpectedly grand, beautiful in an eclectic way. Dozens of similarly dressed spagoers lounged on the plush couches, played checkers on squat tables, ducked in and out of saunas with elaborate entrances and names like the Ocher Room. I watched people at the far end of the room bring steaming trays of food over to tucked-away dining tables. I scanned the space for Ricky and found him sitting on one of the couches. Our eyes met, and he beamed, jumping to his feet.

"So? How was your first King Spa soak?" he said. He had a towel draped around his shoulders and his hair tied into a wet top-knot.

"A little weird at first, but nice. Sorry I made you wait. I dozed off in the bath," I admitted. "I like your Starbucks bun."

Reflexively, Ricky reached up to the top of his head. "Starbucks bun?"

He looked so genuinely confused that I resisted the urge to reach out and tug his cheek.

"You know, like when girls go to coffee shops with wet hair?" I explained. "And they just kind of" — I made a sweeping motion over the top of my head — "pile their hair up? Like that."

For a moment, Ricky squinted at me, and I panicked, wondering if I'd offended him. But then he shook his head, incredulous.

"You always say exactly what you're thinking, don't you?" he observed. "So. Saunas? Or food?"

The smells coming from the cafeteria were mouthwatering, but I didn't think I could handle a sauna with a full stomach.

"Saunas for sure." I scanned the room, pointing to a gleaming, gold pyramid. "That one?"

"Wimp," Ricky said. "That one's barely hot."

"It looks hot," I countered, heading toward the entrance.

Even though he knew better, Ricky followed me in, laughing when I got inside and realized it was about as balmy as a warm summer day. We lay quietly on the gold floor for a few minutes, then shared a look of understanding and shuffled out the door. I let Ricky pick the next sauna ("this one's for the vets") and ended up in a room with a coal fire and a floor so scorching that I had to cross it on the balls of my feet. We sat cross-legged on mats, next to a group of other guests, gathering in a still, worshipful silence as flumes of herbal steam wafted from a central vat. I watched the beads of sweat form on my arms in real time and drip onto the floor. Next to me, Ricky's eyes were squeezed shut, his hands planted firmly on his knees. *What a strange guy,* I thought, following a particularly tantalizing droplet trail from his temple to the hollow of his neck. *Goes to spas on his off days. Hangs out in gardens to draw. Next, I'm going to find out he plays the mandolin.*

After only a few minutes, my throat was parched and my body drenched. I cursed King Spa for making the ladies' uniforms this shade of pink; my pits and back were now covered in wet, conspicuous splotches. I groaned internally and looked down only to find a large stripe under my chest as well. The dreaded under-boob sweat, the least sexy look after cameltoe. Ricky and I had broken past the "poop jokes" phase a while ago, but this felt like a step too far.

Ricky popped one eye open.

"Ready to go?" he mouthed, and I nodded, clambering to my feet and practically running for the exit. I took a gasp of dry, cool air and nearly cried in relief.

"Pretty sure that room was a form of torture, Ricky," I said. I could still see steam rising off my skin.

Ricky snickered, as if the ability to withstand being cooked alive was something to be proud of.

"I thought you said 'fire couldn't kill a dragon'?" he said, referencing a line from *Game of Thrones* I'd dropped last week after guzzling a near-boiling cup of tea with ease.*

"That wasn't fire," I insisted. "That was a humid hellscape."

Ricky shook his head in disbelief.

* One thing Ghanaians took from our British colonizers was a love for tea.

"Don't you come from a 'tropical stock'?" he said, clucking. Then he smirked, amused by his own wit. "Come on, you haven't even done the best part!"

His hand settled on the middle of my back to guide me to our next stop, and then he recoiled. I burned with embarrassment; of course, I was drenched and so very gross right now, and why had I thought going to a place where I would explicitly get sweaty was a good idea?

"Sorry," I said, holding my arms to my chest. "I'm disgusting right now."

The next thing I knew, he'd grabbed my hand and placed it firmly on his chest. Underneath my palm his body was warm and firm and wet. I could feel the ridge of his nipple along the edge of my middle finger, and the steady pounding of his *apical impulse* under the flat of my palm. When I lifted my eyes to Ricky's, he returned my gaze in a challenge, lips stretched in a feral grin. There was no longer any doubt in my mind: Ricky knew *exactly* what he was doing.

Annoyed, I snatched my hand back. Ricky seemed to think toying with me was A+ comedy, judging by the way his grin widened.

"It's a sauna, Ange, the point is to get

227

sweaty," he said. He pointed ahead of us, to a room shaped like an igloo. "This will dry us off."

If the coal-fire room was unbearably hot, the Ice Room was the exact opposite. The sudden shock of cold knocked the breath out of me, and this time, Ricky didn't let me wimp out. We shivered together, my increasingly more creative expletives only making him laugh harder. Eventually, when my cursing turned into threats against his life, he let up.

"Damn it, Ricky," I said, teeth chattering as we exited the igloo. "I thought this was supposed to be relaxing!"

If I hadn't been spending the last month studying every minute change of Ricky's face for meaning, I might have missed the flicker of worry that came before his sheepish smile.

"Come on," he said. "You don't feel good? Not even a little bit?"

I paused, focusing on the sensations in my body. I did. My skin felt like it was buzzing pleasantly, my body light and loose with endorphins.

"No, I do, I do," I relented. "But hopefully the rest of these are . . . less masochistic?"

"They are, I promise."

And they were. We jumped from room to room like schoolkids let loose in a mall, sometimes lying flat against the hot floors, sometimes sitting up straight, backs pressed against walls lined with amethysts and charcoal and clay. One sauna was filled with tiny wooden blocks, and we buried ourselves within them, waiting until the other guests cleared out before tossing them in handfuls at each other. An old Korean woman caught us jogging to our next sauna and chastised us, and we skittered to an amble and then snickered at being caught. By the time we decided to go to the cafeteria, my cheeks hurt from smiling.

It was dinnertime, so most of the other guests had the same idea as us. The line to order food stretched halfway into the dining area.

"We can wait an hour for it to die down?" Ricky suggested. On cue, his stomach growled loudly.

"I don't think you can wait an hour," I teased. "I'm hungry. Want to find a table, and I'll hold a place in line?"

Ricky surveyed the room. Almost all the tables were occupied, but a few groups were clearly finishing up.

"Cool," he said. "Wait, I'm going to run to the locker room and get my phone first.

Can you get me the japchae if I'm not back yet?"

"Yeah, of course," I said, and then I watched him go.

The line was going to take me some time to get through, so I busied myself peering over the heads of the other customers to try to view the menu. Being friends with Michelle had made me familiar with Korean food, but there were options that I hadn't heard of before. Squinting, I searched the menu for something familiar. Should I get the oxtail soup, or just play it safe and get bibimbap? Maybe the budae jjigae? Would that be too much for one person?

"Definitely get the haejangguk," a deep voice behind me said. I whipped around to see the speaker. A muscular Asian guy with a sleeve tattoo smirked back at me; I realized that I'd been musing out loud.

"Hmm," I said. "I've never had that one before. What is it?"

"Hangover soup," he said. He shoved his hands into the pockets of his shorts and gave me a devilish smile. "You know, the kind of thing you eat after a long night out."

I assessed him as he listed the ingredients. Okay. So he was hot. His broad chest strained the shoulders of a spa uniform that was probably a size too small, and his full,

230

pink lips stood in stark contrast to his pale skin. He looked like a proper K-pop star, if they hit the weights and joined a biker gang. And he clearly knew it, given the transparent way that he was checking me out. Probably one of those Asian dudes who listened exclusively to hip-hop, saw the Ass waggling along from behind, and decided to see what I looked like from the front. Old Angie would've been all about this, even if just for the story. Current Angie's mind was further away, in the men's locker room.

But Current Angie was a fool. Why was I pining after a guy who had explicitly stated his disinterest when there was a perfectly good smoking rack of galbi standing right in front of me?

"So, there's no meat?" I said when he was done.

"Oh, there's plenty of meat," he said, his tone heavy with suggestion.

"Eh, on second thought, maybe I want something vegetarian today," I said, glancing back at the menu and steering the conversation into neutral territory.

"Then the kimchi ramen's good," he suggested. He pushed his damp hair out of his eyes. "This your first time here?"

"Yeah," I said. "I've never been anywhere like it." I looked past the cafeteria into the

231

sauna room, staring at the gleaming peak of the pyramid. "It's been really nice, though. I'll be back."

"Did you get a scrub?" he asked. When I shook my head, he whistled. "You need to go back and get one. They take off, like, a layer of skin, but you end up soft as a baby. See?" He held out his arm in invitation. "Feel."

Well, this seems dangerous, I thought. And not just because this guy fit every archetype of the Bad Boy Who Would Definitely Give Me Herpes. Or because I was an arm girl, and his arms showcased a work of art — his actually tasteful tattoos — on a work of art, his generous biceps. My hand hovered over the milky skin of his inner elbow, one of the few spots unmarred by ink —

A hand pressed against the small of my back.

"Thanks for waiting, Angie," Ricky said, but his eyes weren't on me. Slowly, his hand drifted up my back and his arm draped over my shoulders in a show of ownership so blatant that Hot Tattooed Guy raised his eyebrows. My hand still hovered in the air as Ricky guided us toward the counter, only dropping his hold when we got to the front of the line. Numbly, I ordered the kimchi ramen, trying to process what had just happened. Next to me, Ricky was like a stone wall, expressionless and stubbornly silent.

"I'm supposed to pay for dinner," I tried after we'd ordered.

"No," he said, not looking at me.

"No?" I leaned against the counter, crossing my arms. "What do you mean, no?"

"I mean you're not paying," Ricky said, like that was it.

Okay, so now I was pissed off. Maybe when I was nineteen the jealousy schtick would have been cute, but I was twenty-five now and had enough experience to know that it was everything but. Possessiveness wasn't the same as love. It wasn't the same as commitment. It was easy to want my exclusive attention, harder to give anything worthwhile back. And Ricky wasn't giving me *shit*. He wasn't my boyfriend. We weren't even dating. Just because he didn't want me didn't mean that no one else could shoot their shot. If I wanted to have a quickie with Hot Tattooed Guy in the pyramid sauna, I would be well within my rights to do so. Maybe this was what Michelle had meant by *limbo;* up until today, I had felt like Ricky and I had walked a perfect balance, and now, he was mucking it up.

"Fine," I said finally. "I guess I'll find a table then."

I pivoted away, marching into the dining room. In my peripheral vision, I could tell that Hot Tattooed Guy was following me with his eyes, but I was already over him. I was over men, period. I gathered our utensils and arranged them on a free table, biting furiously at my inner cheek.

A few minutes later, Ricky showed up with a tray. I didn't look up from my nails as he set it down gently and returned to the counter to get the next one. When the table shifted with his weight, I kept my gaze fixed on my food, accepting it with a brief "thanks" before picking up my metal chopsticks. Well, I thought, slurping up my ramen, Hot Tattooed Guy was right; the kimchi ramen was a good choice.

"You're mad," Ricky said finally.

"I'm not," I lied.

"You are." He put his elbows up on the table, glaring off into the distance. "Come on, Angie. That guy was clearly bad news."

My anger flared, red hot and dizzying, and I put down my chopsticks.

"What do you mean, bad news?" I asked.

Ricky sputtered. Across the room, Hot Tattooed Guy had rejoined his crew of jacked Asian boys, and they were laughing boisterously together.

"Don't act naive," Ricky said. "He wants

only one thing from you, and you know that."

I leaned forward on the table, popping a soybean into my mouth.

"Maybe," I said, "I just wanted *one thing* from him too."

The tortured expression on Ricky's face should have been satisfying. Instead, it was gut-wrenching. I hated that I had hurt him, even though I didn't know *why.* How annoying. We ate in frustrated silence, heads bowed. Just minutes ago, we'd been having fun. My brain was already creating outlandish scenarios where Ricky would sweep the plates off the table, grab my hand, and declare his love for me. Not that that would ever happen. He would just play with me like he was doing now and tell me that *he hadn't meant it that way* if I slipped up and tried to assign any amorous intent to his actions.

"Look," Ricky finally said. "I'm sorry."

I glanced up from my bowl. Ricky still couldn't quite meet my eyes, but his jaw was set with conviction.

"I was out of line." He rubbed the back of his neck. "If you want to go hook up with that guy, you should. It's none of my business."

I slurped my broth slowly, watching him

over the lip of my bowl.

"You're right," I said, setting it down. "It was none of your business."

Ricky scowled around a large bite of japchae, glancing back at Hot Tattooed Guy's table.

"I'm just saying," he muttered, like he couldn't help it, "you could do a lot better."

That was it for me. Setting my chopsticks down, I pushed my tray away and stood. Ricky's eyes darted back to me, alarmed.

"You haven't finished your food," he said.

"I'm not hungry anymore," I lied. "And I think I need another dip." *And some space. Away from you.*

It was as if Ricky could hear my inner dialogue; suddenly, he looked down at his plate, twirling a chopstick between his fingers.

"Oh," he said. "Okay."

I nodded stiffly, not sparing him another glance. Then, I made for the locker room, careful not to spoil my dramatic exit by slipping on the wood floors. *So much,* I thought, *for a relaxing day at the spa.*

FOURTEEN

I did not get to take another dip in the baths, because the moment I entered the locker room, I heard the obnoxious blast of my ringtone, the sirens from *Kill Bill,* piercing over the ambient background music.*
Mortified, I jogged to my locker, bowing my head apologetically to the other spagoers. A middle-aged, topless woman glared at me as she toweled off her back.

"That's your phone?" she said, clearly pissed that I had compromised the tranquil spa vibe. "It's been going off for the last ten minutes."

"Sorry," I said, my fingers fumbling with my padlock.

"Next time, silence it before you leave," she said, then throwing on her shirt, she walked out of the locker room with a huff.

* A bamboo flute cover of "My Heart Will Go On."

I finally got my locker open, scrambling through my belongings for my still-blaring phone and feeling my stomach sink. My regular ringtone was a lot less abrasive — the *Kill Bill* sirens were assigned to my parents, at Nia's suggestion. "It's like a boss fight theme," Nia had joked. "This way, you're never caught unaware." She was right, but she hadn't considered the unfortunate side effect — I'd now Pavlov'ed* myself into an immediate panic at the sound. It was worse when my parents called like this, multiple times in a row, taking away any opportunity I might have to claim that I'd simply "missed them." That almost always meant that trouble was afoot.

Just as my phone prepared to ring one more time, I gritted my teeth and picked up.

"Hello," I said, settling back on my haunches.

* In case you don't remember from your high school bio class, Pavlov discovered "classical conditioning" when he realized that he could train dogs to salivate to stimuli they associated with food, such as a ringing bell. In this case, I am the dog, Beatrix Kiddo's murder track is the bell, and blaring parental disappointment is my crappy meal.

"Angela." It was my mother speaking this time, though I suspected that Daddy was hovering somewhere nearby. "How are you? It's been a long time since we spoke."

I just called you last week, I thought, *and you chastised me about my waning reproductive potential and tried to set me up with Auntie Abena's nephew.*★

"I'm fine," I said. "I'm actually out right now —"

"Oh, you can take five minutes," she insisted, as if any conversation with her ever lasted only five minutes.

I busied myself by shuffling through my locker's contents as Momma prattled on about the seamstress she had hired to sew our kaba† for Tabatha's traditional ceremony, and then complained about one of her new hires, a woman named Felicia who had signed on for her caretaker job and immediately quit when she realized that she

★ Just in case you think we're into weird European-royalty kinds of incest, every family friend is called auntie or uncle — fitting, as they are just as in your business as any blood relations.

† Traditional Ghanaian dress for women. Made from kente cloth, it normally consists of a peplum top and a long skirt, though stylish variations exist.

would need to clean up after her clients. I offered my typical assurances, humming when appropriate, asking for clarification, but careful not to offer my real opinions — *The design you're asking for is complicated, that's why it's more expensive. Felicia asked you about managerial positions during the interview, I don't know why you thought she wouldn't be prissy* — and lulled myself into a false sense of security that this conversation would be benign.

"Anyway, how is your research project coming along?" Momma asked. "You've started it, yes?"

"Yeah," I said. I could hear the sirens again, but this time they were in my head. "I finished the literature review, at least. I'm just waiting on Dr. Donoghue's final comments."

"Good, good," she said. "You'll have to work very hard, you know. Not like you did with Step." I flinched. *Here we go.* "I was looking online, and it says that, to be an orthopedic surgeon, you need a very high score. You didn't get that, so you'll have to focus on research. This is a good start."

"I have no interest in being an orthopedic surgeon," I said.

Momma snorted, affronted. I could almost see her face through the line — chin tucked into her neck, mouth downturned in a frown.

"And why not?" she said. "They make the highest salaries. Why would you not want that?" When I didn't respond immediately, she clucked her tongue. "You think when I came to this country I wanted to go around cleaning other people's behinds? No! But we needed the money. All this time you are in medical school, are you going to throw it away to be, what?" She paused, considering. "A *psychiatrist*?"

"Maybe!" I said. A woman drying her hair at the counter met my eyes in the mirror, and I lowered my voice. "I don't know. Can we talk about this later?"

"Fine," Momma agreed. "But I want to make sure you have a plan. You're almost finished with this first paper, then? What are you working on next?"

I hesitated. I could avoid the question, but Momma had her nose on me and would call me out. I could tell her that I hadn't picked my next project, but then she would berate me for being unprepared.

Or you could hang up, Tabatha would say. But if I hung up, I would have to pay for my intransigence in pounds of flesh later. So, instead, I told the truth.

"Actually, I've been working on a research

protocol for a new project."

In spite of myself, I found myself describing the project in detail, going into depth about the interview questions that Dr. Reed and I had drafted, the intense IRB approval process, our proposal for funding that was due in less than a month. To my surprise, Momma didn't interrupt, and as I spoke, I felt something warm and unfamiliar blossom in my chest. I was *excited,* I realized, and about *research.* Research had always been a means to an end, a thing to dip my toe in to get to the next step in my path, an activity done out of begrudging necessity. But here was a project that I had conceived myself, that had arisen out of a need that I had identified —

"Is this one of Dr. Wallace's projects?" Momma said when I was finished.

I bit the inside of my cheek.

"No, but —" I started.

"Because it sounds a little . . ." Momma paused, searching for the word. "Fluffy to me. Why haven't you picked one of the projects on her list? I think that would be better."

Her words slashed through me like a knife across my chest. It was like my own mother had sat back and listened to me speak, licked her fingers, and put my enthusiasm out like a flame. And she had done it so dispassionately, with the same regard that she crossed an item off a grocery list. This wasn't the first time, either. I remembered coming back from school and holding up the poem I had written for our county's literary contest. My high school English teacher had held me back after class. *Angela,* she had said, *I knew that you were a strong writer, but this? This is incredible.* She'd given me a list of local competitions and scholarships for aspiring writers and encouraged me to apply. I had come home beaming with pride, validated for once in a subject in which there was no best answer, just one that felt right.

Momma had taken one look at the list, balled it in her fist, and thrown it in the trash.

"How many SAT practice questions have you done today?" she asked instead, her face smooth with passivity.

It had been a decade since that day. Since then, I had moved out. Gotten my own place. Taken on $258,000 in medical school loans, paid my own bills . . . and yet nothing between us had changed.

"I'm not a person to you," I said softly.

Momma sputtered.

"What are you saying?" she said.

"I said," I started, too far gone to turn back now, "you don't think of me as a person. That's what this is all about."

"Ey. Why are you speaking to me in that tone? I'm trying to advise you, and you are getting emotional?" she accused, her voice dropping in pitch. "Your future is not about emotions, Angela. Sometimes you have to hear things that you don't like. Your father and I are only trying to do what's best for your success —"

"Oh stop it," I snapped. The woman at the counter looked at me again, but this time I didn't care, too overwhelmed with frustration. "My *success*? I'm in medical school; I'm not going to go broke. Stop making this about *me* and *my emotions* and be honest with yourself. I'm not a person to you. I'm just a puppet for you to live your dreams through." I ground my teeth. "That's why you treat me like this, right? Like nothing I think or want matters?"

Momma kissed her teeth, and the sound was like gasoline to my fire.

"American children," she scoffed. "Always finding ways to blame their parents. Since when have I said that what you think doesn't matter, eh? Since when?"

"Since literally right now!" I said. "Every time you talk, it's to tell me about all the

244

ways I'm not enough! I don't work hard enough! I don't dress well enough! Even the things I care about — they're not important enough!"

"I promise you, if you can come up with *one* thought that is worthwhile on your own, I will listen to you! But, look at you, even now, behaving like a child! Like you still haven't figured out how the world works —"

That was it.

"Oh, forget this," I spat, and hung up. My brain felt like it was vibrating inside my skull. Before I could get barraged with a series of outraged calls and voicemails accusing me of *disrespect,* I scrolled to my parents' contact information and hit "block." The twinge of guilt I felt was overshadowed by the heat of my rage.

Twenty-five years old, and I was still living with this shit. I buried my face in my hands, surprised to find that they didn't come away wet. Normally, conflict with my parents inspired tears almost immediately, but what I felt today wasn't my typical shame. It was *righteousness.* After all, I had done nothing out of step. My entire life, I had been obedient. I had joined the clubs they'd told me to join, hung out with the friends they approved of, avoided boys when

245

they said boys were bad, sought them out when they decided they were necessary. I had gotten into one of the Top Colleges and then a Name Brand Medical School, and my parents had accepted the awe and envy of the Naperville Ghanaian community but given none of the credit to me. But of course they didn't. Momma had said it herself — none of what had made me successful had been my idea, because my ideas were *stupid* and *childish.* My malleability hadn't earned me their respect; their expectations had only gotten more granular over the years, more unyielding.

But I had to draw the line sometime. Why it had to be now, in the locker room of King Spa, with a boy wringing his hands waiting for me just outside, I didn't know. It was like third year of medical school had stripped me of my last remaining pretenses. And so, if my parents were going to forget that I was an adult, I would have to remind them what they had to lose.

Ricky was sitting on a couch outside the women's locker room when I finally emerged some twenty minutes later. In the aftermath of my Declaration of Independence, I'd forgotten that I was mad at him, and the expression he gave me as I approached, like a dejected puppy, furthered his case.

"Hey," I said. "Sorry I was gone a while."

Ricky stretched out like a cat.

"It's all right," he said, yawning. Then, noticing my stony expression: "Everything okay?"

I shrugged. I felt drunk, my hold on my body tenuous in the aftermath of my emotional onslaught. I wavered on my feet, then sat down.

"Ha. Not really," I said honestly. I gave him a small smile. "Just had a massive fight with my parents. You know. Same old, same old."

"Again?" Ricky said, shaking his head. When I shrugged, he leaned back on the sofa. "Well. We are conveniently right next to something that could help you cool off —"

His eyes darted to the Ice Room.

"Absolutely not," I said, wagging my finger at him in warning. "You are not taking me back into that torture chamber!"

Ricky laughed.

"No, no," he said, then pointed with his chin to the upper level of the spa. "There's a few meditation rooms up there. Maybe we can sit there. Breathe out all of our negative emotions." The creases around his eyes softened. "We probably need it."

247

The meditation room was composed of several long mats separated by six-inch-tall wooden partitions. Red "ion" lights — purported to have a number of questionable health benefits, including the ability to reduce cholesterol, diminish wrinkles, and cure insomnia — were housed in wooden fixtures over each mat. The space was empty but for an old man snoring in the corner with a towel over his eyes. Upstairs, the din of the spa felt far away, drowned out by a tranquil harp soundtrack. I took a deep breath, filling my lungs with the thick, herbal air. Ricky did the same beside me.

"What is that smell?" I said. It felt heady, like I was steeping in a hot cup of tea.

"Jasmine, I think." He gestured for me to walk ahead of him, watching as I sidled from row to row before deciding on a mat. "Not near the exit this time?" he teased.

"Nah," I said. "No danger of traumatizing the general public in this place."

I dropped down onto the mat and stretched, noting how Ricky averted his eyes as he arranged himself on the mat next to me. Then, I tucked my head under the wooden fixture that housed the ion lights. A second later, Ricky slid his head under to join me. His face landed closer than I expected, just inches away. Drenched in red light, I felt like we were tucked away somewhere alien, drifting together on a distant planet. I laughed; my fingers curled nervously on the mat next to my face.

"This is *so weird,*" I said. I looked up at the light fixture above my head, unimpressed. "Also, I'm pretty sure these are just a bunch of red LEDs."

"I'm pretty sure you're right." The light cast his face in an otherworldly glow, and I knew that this image of him, his features simultaneously flattened and sharpened in red, would be etched in my mind from now on. "Thank you for coming here with me, by the way."

I blinked myself out of my stupor.

"Thank you for bringing me," I said in a small voice. "Sorry that I wasted precious spa time fighting with my parents in the locker room."

Ricky's brow furrowed. I watched, fascinated, as his gaze dropped from mine, his eyelashes casting layers of shadow across his cheeks.

"Why do you still talk to them?" he asked softly. "I mean, every time they call they upset you, right? Why not just . . . stop picking up?"

I watched him, waiting for him to regain his resolve and look me in the eye. I knew that his question was layered; for someone who reportedly despised his father, Ricky seemed almost obsessed with him. With what he was and wasn't doing, where he was, how he'd failed his family. I remembered a story he told me once, of returning home after a Child Life shift in high school to find his biological father seated at the head of the dining table, playing Lotería with his grandparents over a bowl of menudo. The week prior, Gabriel Gutiérrez had called his mother from the county jail after instigating a bar fight to demand that she post his bail. Ricky had begged her to refuse. "He's just going to be back in there next month," he'd said. "It's too much money, Abuelita, please." And yet there Gabriel was, dribbling hominy all over his board and bragging about how much his father was going to owe him as if they hadn't just sunk eight hundred dollars springing him out of the box.

"It's like *Groundhog Day*," Ricky had said. We'd been sprawled across the grass in a park not far from the hospital, Ricky watching dandelion fluff float across the sky, me watching him. After a moment, he reached up and snatched a floating seed from the air, rolling the thin white fibers between his fingers. "We just save his ass every other day and expect him to someday appreciate it. And surprise, he never does. Nothing changes."

How do you love someone who hurts you over and over again? he seemed to be asking me now. And I didn't have an answer for him. I knew how I could love my parents, who had provided for me, sacrificed for me . . . but how could he love a man who had done neither?

"You know," I said, "Tabs asks me the same thing all the time." I smiled; my kid sister always came to my defense. "And to be fair, I *did* block them today." When Ricky didn't laugh, I sighed. "How old were your grandparents when they came to America?"

"Young," Ricky said, looking at me directly now. His eyes were black under the light, huge and reflective. "In their twenties."

"My parents were in their thirties." I rolled onto my back, studying the ring of light above my head. "My mom won the green card lottery, and so they decided to come. Dad was a clinical pharmacist back home, and Momma had just finished nursing school. They were reasonably established, so I don't really understand why we left, to be honest. I think the job market just wasn't great in Ghana, and they were hoping for something new."

251

"And so they leapt at the chance to move to the Land of Opportunity," Ricky said drolly.

I chuckled, closing my eyes.

"Yeah," I said. "Either way, those first several years were . . . tough. Tabs doesn't remember much, but I do." I could picture our first home in the States like I still lived in it, a one-bedroom apartment in Bronzeville, smaller than the space I shared with Nia now. Momma, unable to transfer most of her credits over, had signed with a home health agency and worked as a caretaker for three elderly clients. She left for work before I went to school on most days, and so I quickly learned to care for myself, laying out my school clothes, chasing Tabatha down the halls in the morning to force her to brush her teeth. Dad, on the other hand, had taken a job as a pharmacy technician while waiting for his credentials from the United Kingdom to be approved, working the night shift at a twenty-four-hour Walgreens because the pay was fifteen cents an hour better than working days. Their lives had seemed like a constant grind; I couldn't remember a single moment of indulgence between the two of them.

"They worked nonstop," I continued. "Saved every penny and built a foundation for us out of nothing in a country where they knew and had no one. And the only thing they really ask of me is that I make good on their investment." I sighed. "I know I didn't *ask* for them to shuttle us across the world. But I can't act like I'm here now because of my own efforts. Because I'm not. I owe most of what I am to them. They make me crazy, but . . ." I scratched at the mat, running my nail over the ridges of bamboo. "I have to honor them. And I will. I just" — I turned back to look at Ricky, giving him a shy smile — "need some space from them right now, I think."

Ricky rolled over flat onto his back, closing his eyes. The light cast his face into sharp relief, filling the hollows of his cheeks with shadow. In the silence that followed, I studied his face. His lips were tucked into a line, and every now and again a muscle in his cheek would twitch nervously. Ricky always seemed perpetually cheerful. He moved through life like he was new to the world, finding small moments of beauty and expanding them, relishing them. But even I could tell that some of it was a farce, a mask he put on for the benefit of others. Right now, under the glare of the ion lights, I could see through its cracks.

"You know how I told you that Abuelo

wanted me to be a lawyer because of the signs?" he asked.

"Yeah?" I said.

"I lied."

I laughed.

"I figured," I said. "So why, then?"

Ricky shrugged, smiling to himself.

"When my grandparents first moved to Chicago, before Abuelo set up his furniture business, he used to work construction. Met my tío Matteo there," he said. "They both had sons around the same age, but his son became a hotshot corporate lawyer. Made stupid money. Tío Matteo retired, like, fifteen years early." He peered at me from the corner of his eye. "My dad didn't really try at school, but I was good at it. Abuelo thought it was something within my reach, and so . . . pushed me toward it. He never wanted me to work with my body. *The mind lasts longer,* he liked to say."

"He's not wrong," I said. I remembered the week that my mother had thrown out her back after turning a client the wrong way. The pain had kept her nearly bedbound for three days, but she had been most concerned about lost income. *This is why you have to study hard, Angela,* she had said. *So that you don't have to worry like this.*

"I get what you're saying, about feeling

like you have to honor your parents," Ricky said. "I felt so guilty for so long about not just . . . going along with what he wanted for me, even after I realized I didn't want it for myself. It's not like I didn't work hard. I did well in school. I got every scholarship I could, worked my way through college . . . but I didn't come to a new country with nothing but a hundred dollars and a dream, right?" He smiled, rolled over on his side to face me. "Still, in the end, we know ourselves better than anyone. Even the people who raised us. I was able to use my skills to help Abuelo rebrand his business. He used to take whatever carpentry job he could get, but he was really passionate about designing and building furniture . . . and now that's all he does. He has a handful of rich clients who commission a few pieces from him a year, and he makes a lot more than he used to, doing less. And he's been able to hire a few more guys to help out, so these days he's mostly at the drawing table."

Of course. A well-designed website and logo made the difference between a mom-and-pop carpenter and a *furniture designer*.

"I probably would've made a shit lawyer," Ricky continued. "But I'm good at *this*. Whatever it is you want to do . . . I bet you're good at it too. And you should go for it. Your parents want you to do what's safe because they're scared, but if you can prove to them that your way works too, they'll back off."

I blinked at him, touched.

"That," I said, "was wise as hell, Ricky."

Ricky shrugged.

"Just returning the favor. You're always lecturing me," he said.

I gasped, indignant.

"That's not true!" I started. When he laughed at me, I sucked in my cheeks and glared until he laughed harder. But then his expression softened and turned thoughtful. He looked away from me.

"Do you remember," he said, so softly that I had to strain to hear him over the ambient music, "that first time I drove you home from the hospital?"

I snickered.

"How could I forget, Arnie the Ankylosaurus," I teased.

Ricky chuckled.

"Ha. Right." Then he licked his lips, serious. "No, but I mean what you told me. About Abuela."

"Yeah?" I asked encouragingly.

"Yeah," Ricky continued. "Well, I followed your advice. My dad got admitted again. And I drove Abuela to the hospital. That was it. I didn't even go up to the room with her." He opened his eyes then, and they shone with the reflection of the lights. "She was so *happy*, Angie. Singing, the whole way there. All because I got my ass in the car and drove her to the hospital so that she could sit next to her son's hospital bed. God, I felt like such a piece of shit.

"My family is small. So my grandparents have worked to expand it, you know. Abuela has her church friends and her Sunday school kids. Abuelo's all but adopted some of the guys at his shop. I grew up with some of them, you know. Like this guy Juan . . . he's been there like fifteen years and treats them like his parents. But still. I'm her *blood*." Ricky swallowed. "She used to have to wait for Abuelo to close up shop, you know. Sometimes she'd convince one of the guys to drop her off. As if her perfectly capable grandson wasn't just sitting on his hands a few miles away."

"Ricky," I said. The air was thick with his self-loathing. I felt a sudden, irresponsible urge to pull him close, but the six-inch-tall wooden barriers between our mats prevented that. "It's more complicated than that. You're allowed to have complex feelings about your dad."

"But it isn't about my dad," Ricky interrupted. "It's about Abuela. I never considered that perspective, before you. Which is nuts. It's the only one that makes sense." He turned to look at me then, his face open and unguarded. "That's the thing about you, Angie. You just . . . *get* it. You care about people, even when they're kind of shitty to you, but you aren't a doormat. You don't lose sight of who you are in the process. You make me actually stop and *think* about things, you know?" He looked at me unblinkingly, his expression almost grave. "That . . . I don't think you realize how special that is."

I've never met anyone like you, Ricky had said on the night that we decided to be friends. Frederick had once said something similar, but he hadn't looked at me the way Ricky was looking at me now, with something akin to wonder. Instead, he'd grimaced, embarrassed. *Angie,* he'd said. *Can you please just keep your thoughts to yourself for once?*

"I'm glad I talked to you that day, in the garden. I know you feel some type of way about it, but we would've been strangers still, right? We wouldn't be here right now. And that would've been a tragedy. Because this way . . . I get to know you. And I . . ."

Ricky continued, "I consider that a privilege."

I didn't realize that I'd been holding my breath until I felt my lungs seize in my chest. There were only a few times in my life that I'd been left at a loss for words, and this was one of them. I ducked away from Ricky's probing stare, my pulse pounding audibly in my temples. This wasn't fair. He couldn't just open up to me and say all that and *not* expect me to fall for him. And I could feel myself falling, feel a pressure on my chest that was almost painful. Many men had called me beautiful; no one had yet to reach deeper and tell me what they liked about me beyond that. And here was Ricky, going into detail, identifying what I liked most about myself and telling me he liked it too.

"Thank you for saying that," I managed finally. I reached out as far as I could above the partition, hooking his pinky into mine.

Ricky's smile unfolded across his face slowly, first in the corners of his mouth, the lift of his cheeks, the squint and crease of his eyes. How many times had I looked at that face just to watch it light up like this? So many that it should have been embarrassing. But today, something was different; today, it felt like it was made for me, every

259

part of it a match for mine, from the small Cupid's bow in his top lip to the slightly jagged right canine that showed only when he laughed. I wanted to kiss him. I had never wanted to kiss anyone so badly. It was a physical want, like the feeling I got after one too many rum and Cokes, like the pulling I'd felt in my skin after our stint in the Ice Room. The impulse was so strong that I could think of nothing else, and so before I could convince myself otherwise, I closed the distance between us and pressed my lips against his.

My first thought was that Ricky's lips were softer than I had imagined. Fuller than Frederick's, and smooth, like he used scrub or something —

The second was that they weren't moving.

I pulled back, my heart racing in my throat. Ricky's face was carefully blank, his eyes fluttering open and shut in shock.

Shit shit shit shit shit. What did you just do, Angie? I wanted to disappear, or cry, or both, but I couldn't will my body to move, and so instead I stared back at him, waiting for the judgment that would inevitably come.

"Angie . . . ," Ricky started, his voice softer than a whisper.

"Ah-ah!" an unfamiliar voice shouted.

We jolted apart, both banging our heads on the partitions behind us. Skull smarting, I dragged myself out from under the ion lights to find a short, severe-looking woman glaring down at us. Completely unconcerned about the damage she had just wrought to her customers' heads, she pointed her broomstick at a sign plastered on the wall stating, in rainbow Comic Sans font, CUSTOMERS MUST REMAIN TWO FEET APART AT ALL TIMES!

"Too close!" she accused.

I stared at her in disbelief, feeling rather than seeing Ricky sit up beside me. Deux ex Ajumma* coming in with the save. I watched, mystified, as the woman tossed her head haughtily and swept off to go break apart other young lovebirds. Next to me, Ricky was holding on to his head and cackling, his shoulders shaking with mirth.

"So," he said, wiping tears from his eyes, "you down for the Ice Room now?"

---

* Older Korean woman. Probably has a perm, and is rarely seen outdoors without a visor and a roller backpack.

FIFTEEN

"Nia, I don't know what to do," I groaned. I sat at our dining room table, my face pressed against the cherrywood paneling. "Please, oh wise one. Give me guidance."

Nia looked at me askance, squaring up her papers with a thud. Having completed her lesson plans for her tutees, she was now finishing her grading, and did not seem all that invested in my current romantic debacle.

"Easy," she said. "You talk to him. Like an adult."

I buried myself further in the shadow of my arms, shaking my head furiously. For the last week, I had felt like I was losing my mind, and my usual remedies weren't working.* I had kissed Ricky, and he hadn't

---

* Namely, studying, working on research, and listening to the most grisly, least sexy murder podcasts I could find.

kissed me back. Instead, he'd pretended like nothing had happened — though, to be fair, I hadn't given him much of a choice. The moment our Peeping Ajumma stomped out of the meditation room, I filled every available second with chatter, reading every sign in front of every sauna, giving him an overly detailed description of a C-section I attended the week prior, encouraging him to pick up on the story he'd started on the drive in about his least favorite coworker's inexcusable love for clip art. To my immense relief, Ricky played along, turning up the music on the drive back while I tried not to asphyxiate on my anxiety in his passenger's seat. It wasn't until we pulled up in front of my apartment that he turned to look at me, biting that bottom lip *that I had kissed, oh my god,** as he said, "Listen, Ange—"

"Thanks for the ride!" I said brightly, tossing my backpack over my shoulders and throwing the car door open. "I've got an early morning tomorrow. See you later!"

"Wait —" he said, but instead I slammed the door shut. I didn't want to stick around to hear what he had to say next. *Angie, I'm flattered, but . . .* No. I could still see the

---

* And, oh my god, after eating KIMCHI OF ALL THINGS TOO.

look on his face, saturated with red light, his eyes wide with panic. I didn't need the gentle letdown. The "I just really value our friendship" speech. It was better to forget that anything had happened at all.

". . . I think I'm going to try it," Nia was saying.

I sat up straight, wagging away my thoughts. I hadn't even realized that Nia was still talking. I bit my lip, embarrassed to be caught so obviously in the middle of a daydream.

"Sorry," I said sheepishly. "I missed that."

Nia gave me an exasperated look.

"Unbelievable," she muttered under her breath. Then she fixed me with a stony stare. "Girl, you probably just surprised him," she said. She thumbed through her sheets. "Want me to save us all some grief and tell Shae to ask him?"

"If you ask Shae, they'll know that I wanted you to ask, and then it'll become this big deal," I whined.

"It already sounds like it's a big deal to you," Nia said. Then, unceremoniously, she gathered her papers and stalked silently into her bedroom. I watched her go, flinching against her slammed door. I chewed at my inner cheek. Something was clearly wrong, but I couldn't put my finger on *what*. There certainly wasn't trouble in paradise, judging by the compromising position I'd caught Nia and her boo-thing in yesterday when I returned home after my shift. And I didn't think it had to do with work; this block's group of tutees hadn't tried to bribe Nia into writing their essays for them even once. Maybe it was me? I shook that thought away — I'd hardly been around enough to get under Nia's skin, and besides, if I did, she would tell me.

Right?

"Yo, is Nia mad at me?" I asked Markus over the phone as I power walked through the hospital halls.

"How am I supposed to know?" Markus said. "Hundreds of miles away, remember?"

I groaned; Markus was a darling 99 percent of the time, but the other 1 percent he could be the annoying little brother I never asked for.

"Has she *said* anything," I clarified.

"Bruh, you're the one who lives with her," Markus grumbled. At any other time, I would've felt bad about interrogating him; the Sanity Circle was an uncommonly peaceful bunch, and we were so rarely in conflict with one another that it felt awkward when we were. But we weren't in college anymore, and I didn't have time for sleuthing. Besides, Nia was rarely home nowadays; I didn't want to waste what precious moments we had together in a confrontation.

"Come on, Markus . . . ," I said. I stopped in my tracks at the entrance to the academic hospitalist's office space, scuffing my shoes against the slippery hospital tile.

"Nope," Markus said. "I haven't heard anything, and even if I had, I would stay out of it. Just talk to her, Angie, like you always do." He whistled. "Anyway, you have two minutes until your meeting. I know how you like to be late, but you should probably get to that."

"I'll have you know that I'm standing right outside!" I said, feigning indignance.

"Sure, sure," Markus said, disbelieving. Then, his tone softened. "Just chill, Angie. You two will be okay."

But would we be? As I tugged open the glass doors to the office, I tried to recall the last time that Nia had felt distant and came up empty. Sure, we squabbled every now and then, but our anger had always been like a spark — hot, bright, and gone as quickly as it came. Whatever this was, it was cold and lingering. I hated it.

The academic hospitalist area was significantly less grand than Dr. Wallace's office.

There were a few private offices, labeled with the names of the most senior hospitalists, but most of the space was filled with standard-issue cubicles. A few of the hospitalists had personalized their cubicles with pictures of their children; one had a magnetic dartboard hanging from the back of his swivel office chair. Dr. Reed's cubicle, though, was sparse, its only personal touch a four-by-six black frame of him and his husband.

"Oh, Angie," Dr. Reed said, swinging around to face me. With his heathered gray Patagonia sweater, sea-foam-green scrubs, and youthful face, he looked like he could be one of the residents and was regularly mistaken for one.* "Wait. Let me get you a seat."

He stood abruptly and walked around me to steal a chair from his neighboring cubicle, pushing it behind me until the cushion brushed against the back of my knees. I swung my backpack forward, reaching in to pull out my laptop.

Dr. Reed got right to it.

"I've sent our interview script to one of my mentors," he said. "He thinks it's good,

---

* That is, on the days that he didn't get mistaken for a janitor or food service instead.

but he's wondering if journals will worry that we pulled the questions out of our heads. We may need to start with a focus group."

For any other project, I would have cringed at this news; a focus group meant more time, more resources, and another six months to our journal submission deadline. But in this case, he was right. Our data would be stronger if we could say that even the questions were generated by our target population. "I think a focus group is a good idea, actually," I said. "How do you think we can recruit participants?"

Dr. Reed and I brainstormed for the full hour, adjusting the slides in our skeletal proposal presentation according to changes in our plans. We would have to edit the IRB to include a focus group, and though the prospect itself was cumbersome, I felt like we were conspiring to do something good. And Dr. Reed was unlike any attending I had worked with before: easygoing but driven. When he jokingly chastised me for not updating a figure as promised, I didn't shrink under his admonishments or worry that I'd sabotaged a recommendation letter, but rather added it to my list of to-dos. He followed each of his suggestions with *What do you think?*, as though, despite my status as a lowly medical student, my opinions actually mattered to him.

I returned home an hour later to an empty apartment and kept myself busy studying for my ob-gyn shelf exam, which was, impossibly, next week. The sun made its course across the sky, casting our apartment in a warm orange glow until it disappeared entirely and left me working only by the light of my laptop screen. Immersed in my work like this, I could almost ignore the oppressive silence around me. It was as though there were a Nia-shaped space sitting across from me, one that should have been filled with her giggles or a pithy joke but instead was conspicuously empty. It was eerie. Nia and I had been physically apart, sure, but she'd never felt truly gone. If anything, I thought of her as omnipresent, always a text or a call or a not-safe-for-work meme away. But the text I'd sent her before my meeting (Have fun with your friends today! Where are you guys going, again?) had gone unanswered.

But there was no time to wallow, not when I had three hundred practice questions to get wrong. Eye on the prize, Angie, I reminded myself. There would be time to worry about best friends and boys after this shelf. In the meantime, I had to worry about myself.

About eighty-three questions in, I heard the front door open. My pulse quickened with nerves; Nia was home.

"Hey," I said, watching her tug off her shoes at the door. Nia glanced up at me, giving me a smile that didn't quite reach her eyes. She looked cute in a striped romper that I didn't remember seeing in her closet.

"Hey," she said. I trailed her with my eyes as she hung up her keys and made a beeline for her bedroom. My stomach sank; there was no way she wasn't angry with me. Mentally, I card-flipped again through any possible transgressions: Had I talked about *the kiss* too much? Left the dishes out again? Had she noticed that I'd stolen some of her expensive face wash? Her expression wasn't giving anything away. There was no helping it. I needed to take Markus's advice and "just talk to her."

"Nia, wait," I said, standing up.

To her credit, Nia paused at the threshold of her door. When she looked up at me, it was with a placid expression, almost like she was looking through me.

"What's up?" she asked.

"That's what I'm trying to find out," I

said, walking toward her. She watched me cross the room skeptically, like a cat scoping out an unwelcome guest. "Girl . . . what's wrong?"

Nia's eyebrows twisted.

"Nothing," she lied. "What, do you think something is wrong?"

"Yes, of course," I said, disbelieving. "And I've been trying to think about what it could be, and I keep coming up empty. And . . . I don't know, I figured I should just find out from you." I dropped my gaze to our feet. Nia's socks were cute today, pastel pink and patterned with smiling bananas. "Just . . . Whatever it is I did, I want to make it better. And make sure I don't do it again." I looked back up at her, biting the edge of my tongue. "But you have to tell me what it is first."

For a moment, I thought that Nia would blow me off again. Her gaze was hard. I had seen her direct that look at others, people she didn't care about, those she wanted to give her space, but in the decade since we'd declared ourselves besties, never at me. My throat tightened.

Nia sighed.

"Angie," she said. "It's really . . ." Her lips tightened into a line, and suddenly her mask fell away and she squeezed her eyes

271

shut. I watched the transition happen in shock, feeling my stomach sink into an abyss. "The friends I went out with today. What are their names?"

I recoiled, not expecting the question.

"Your friends? You mean, the Lesbrigade?" I asked, flustered.

"They have names. I've told you what they are a hundred times," Nia insisted. "What are they?"

I stared at Nia blankly, trying to remember the people in her new friend circle. I'd seen them onstage at the improv show, and in the photos Shae shared on social media, and yes, Nia had been bringing them up more often these days, but I couldn't for the life of me remember their names.

"I . . . think the blonde's name is Beth?" I tried.

"Beck," Nia corrected. She crossed her arms in disgust. "That's all you got? Really? Because I know that you're working with a resident named Gwen, that she's originally from the Bay Area, wants to do MFM, and sometimes comes to work smelling like patchouli. What do you know about Beck? Clearly not her name."

Flustered, I threw my hands up.

"Okay. So yes, I'm bad at names, and you want me to know more about your new bosom buddies. I can do that —"

Nia let out a huff of laughter, wagging her head with frustration.

"No," she said. "I want you to actually give a fuck about what's going on in my life."

That left me speechless. I had to pull the reins on my defensiveness, shocked that Nia could make such an accusation. To me? Her best friend? As if I didn't ask her about her day every day? As if she hadn't been responding with a halfhearted "fine" for the last week?

"What do you mean?" I said instead, clenching and unclenching my fists.

Sensing a challenge, Nia tossed her head.

"I mean, do you actually know what's going on with me? Do you care? Because it feels like you don't. I try to talk to you, but it all goes in one ear and out the other." She bit her lip. "It's like, these days, no one's problems are as big as yours. Like what I do isn't important."

"That isn't true," I said beseechingly. I took a deep breath; I would have time to parse through her words for truth later. For now, all I wanted to do was to fix us. "Nia, I'm sorry if I've been up my own ass lately. I didn't mean to make you feel like I didn't care about your life. I do, promise.

"But I'm not going to lie. You haven't been around much. You go off with Shae and Beck and . . . the others, and it's clear that I'm not welcome to come too, even if I could." I shrugged. "I just assumed that you wanted to keep us separate."

And I understood that, I really did. Despite her vibrant demeanor, Nia was an introvert. With me always within spitting distance, she'd never really been motivated to find a group of queer friends, even while she craved a place in her community. And now, thanks to Shae and an improv class, she had a new crew of people who shared her experience. I missed her, but I could never begrudge her that, had actually encouraged it for a while. But I'd always felt confident that I would remain her number one. *Hubris,* I thought mournfully.

"You think I'm not around?" Nia said. "*You're* not around. And I get that, I know that medical school is tough. But when was the last time we had a conversation that wasn't about your school, and your problems? You just tack me on as an afterthought."

"I . . . ," I said. The cup noodles I'd had for dinner threatened to come back up. "I didn't mean —"

I watched Nia's eyes well with tears, and

274

reflexively, mine followed suit. Her fingers twitched on her doorframe. Then she swallowed and steeled herself.

"I'm moving out."

Whatever I had expected to come of this conversation . . . that had not been in it. I felt like someone had dunked my head underwater. I remembered us driving up to Chicago a month before graduating from college, scoping out apartments, tittering with excitement about finally having our own place in the Big City. The drama with our first landlord, who had downplayed the severity of his property's mouse infestation. Breaking our lease right before my physiology exam. Moving out in the dead of the Chicago winter to our new home . . . All of it had just felt like another chapter in Nia and Angela's Big Adventure. We had run through the empty rooms of our new apartment, pointing out where we would put paintings and dressers and TVs, rolling down the warped, sloped hardwood floors in our second-hand office chairs. The giddy excitement of knowing that I would be continuing my journey toward doctordom with my favorite person by my side had saturated that memory.

And now it felt like all that had been a charade.

"Moving . . . out?" I said, not understanding. "Wait. What? Why?"

"I just . . . ," Nia said, her voice cracking. "I feel like this is something I have to do. Don't worry about my rent — I'll keep paying it until I find someone else to take over my lease."

I could barely process the concept. Someone else, a *stranger,* living in Nia's room? Sitting in Nia's spot on the couch? Leaving behind hair in the shower that wasn't coiled and brown?

"Nia," I tried. But it was to no avail. Nia gave me one last mournful look, then stepped into her room and slammed her door shut.

Shutting me out. Leaving me behind. For so long, Nia and I had been a reliable source of love for each other. A fountain of validation. Proof that someone out there thought that we were the best exactly as we were. Others could come and go from our lives, but Nia and I were supposed to be *forever.* I hadn't even thought to imagine a future where we weren't.

And now, as I stood outside her room, trying to figure out how my world had gone to pieces, I realized that I would have to.

SIXTEEN

My exam scores for ob-gyn came back glowing: Honors, 95th percentile, the best I'd done on an exam since starting medical school. I glanced at my score, then clicked out of the screen. Apparently, all I had to do to improve my scores was get my heart smashed to pieces.

The silence in my apartment was deafening now. Every creak or groan of the old building left me frozen in place like a startled animal. Lucky for me, I was in the hospital during the majority of Nia's move. Every time I came back to the apartment, there would be more of her gone: her baking tins, her favorite plush blanket, the extra clothing rack she kept in the living room. I'd go to work dreading the operating room and then return dreading running into her on her way out. She seemed to know this; every time I returned, I could sense that her absence was fresh, still smell the light musk of her perfume lingering in the air.

I tried to understand Nia, but I couldn't. It wasn't as if we'd never fought. Normally, our squabbles were followed by a short stretch of tense silence, but before the day was up, we were sitting on our couch, snickering over tea, and brainstorming ways to make amends. And I was willing to do just that. If Nia wanted me to be more present, I could be more present. I could schedule weekly girls' nights, put my books aside to focus all my attention on her. Yeah, I talked about medical school a lot, but I could stop that too. I could adjust my behavior, if she wanted me to. All she had to do was say the word.

But Nia wasn't saying anything at all. She'd dropped off the face of the earth, ghosting me just like all those boys I'd cried about in the past. But this hurt so much more because I could never have seen it coming.

So I avoided the apartment. On my two days off before my exam, I drove far from home to libraries across town, subsisted on blueberry muffins and overripe bananas from dusty cafés, and came home only to sleep. I burned through question banks, filling my mind to the brim with knowledge to avoid leaving space for anything else and powered through my research proposal at lightning speed. Because if I thought too hard about Nia, I would lose my mind.

"Oh, honey," Michelle said, grasping my hand. We sat in the downstairs café of the adult hospital, Harland General, white coats thrown carelessly over the backs of our chairs. We were both playing hooky, having snuck out of our respective rotation orientation lectures to catch up. At the beginning of third year, we wouldn't have dared to sit out in the open like this, in plain view of any of our passing attendings. Now, Michelle slurped her frappe with unselfconscious gusto.

"This is the worst," I said. "She didn't say anything to you, either?"

Michelle shook her head, her gaze dropping to the table. I could tell that Nia's rift from the group was hurting her too; the Sanity Circle group chat had been conspicuously silent for some time now.

"Maybe," Michelle suggested cautiously, knowing that she was entering dangerous territory, "it was just a function of time. Maybe you were outgrowing each other, and it just took you a while to notice."

I nodded miserably. I had considered that possibility, that the Angie Appiah of today was no longer as compatible with Nia as the one from years past.

"Yeah," I said. "Most people aren't still cool with their high school friends, I guess." I sighed. "Medical school kind of feels like it's taking everything from me at this point." My parents, whom I hadn't spoken to since the fallout in King Spa; my weekends; and now my best friend. What was next, the blood of my firstborn?

"Hey," Michelle said, pouting. "I'm still here, aren't I?"

I laughed, knowing that she was only half-joking.

"Yeah, well, we're enduring this hell together, aren't we?" I sagged in my chair, watching the line for coffee grow as the lunch hour came to a close.

"We sure are," she said. "Can't say the same for most of our class, though. Seriously. How many couples broke up this year? So many, right?"

I thought about it. It was true — a good half of our classmates who had entered medical school with significant others had magically become single before the end of our first rotation. It was as though all the nonmedical partners had been seduced by the concept of a "cute doctor boyfriend,"★

★ The "future doctor" perk seems to work out well

280

only to balk at the reality.

"Oh my god, wait, remember the party at Barron's right before study block?" Michelle said, grinning savagely around her straw.

"With Simon Pritchett?" I asked, primed for a laugh.

And of course, she had been talking about Simon, whose illustrious career as class lothario had recently taken on an exciting turn — apparently, he'd gotten back together with his college ex over spring break! This would have been run-of-the-mill class gossip if not for one small detail — he'd also started dating a first-year, Katie Beckert, who had been too excited about her new six-foot-two, strapping, piano-playing, future-doctor boyfriend to realize that the only thing he could commit to was his workout schedule. She'd found out about Simon's duplicity when the ex-ex sent him a nude while Katie was using his phone to take a picture of our class on the dance floor. The ensuing drama had been delectable. An inconsolable Katie had immediately thrown Simon's phone to the ground; an-

---

only for the guys; before I met Frederick, a guy I went on a first date with asked me how I expected "to be a good girlfriend" if I was always working. Needless to say, we didn't go out again.

nounced in very colorful, very explicit language exactly what she'd seen flash across his screen; then bum-rushed the stunned-into-stillness, picture-ready gathering of medical students to tell Simon about himself right to his face. At some point, she'd tried to slap him, but being too short to reach his face, accidentally hit poor Arnold Patterson instead. The night had ended abruptly after that, with the rest of class dispersing from the scene of the crime faster than it'd taken them to get in formation for the picture in the first place and Simon staying behind to finish off the bar's supply of Jack Daniel's while groaning to a highly amused Michelle and me how *he really wasn't a bad guy* despite his infidelities.

"He bought us so many drinks just so we could hear him out," I said, nearly choking on my coffee. I could still remember him babbling into his glass, alternating between making thinly veiled passes at Michelle and complaining about how we "all had him wrong."

"Since when is therapy free?" Michelle said, wiping away tears of mirth. Then she pointed at me. "But anyway, back to you. Not to get all up in your business, but when are you going to let Ricky up in your business?"

Such a nasty mouth for such a small woman. Michelle's reaction to the news that I had kissed Ricky at King Spa was to punch the air and shout, "That's my girl!" Unlike me, Michelle wasn't the type to sit on her hands and wait for a man to approach her; she liked to do the choosing. In college it was par for the course to lose Michelle at a party because she'd decided to go on the hunt, and only slightly less common to be harangued somewhere on campus by one of her discarded former flames, begging us to pass on a message. At some point, her pile of broken hearts grew so high that Markus started calling her the Praying Mantis.

I whipped behind me, checking to make sure we were out of earshot from anyone we could know.

"Ricky has been great," I said, my ears hot. And he had been, remarkably so. Now that I was in the adult hospital, we couldn't have our regular coffee breaks, and so he'd taken to texting me instead. Nary a day passed without a check-in, sometimes a How's studying going, occasionally an article for us to discuss. I messaged him shortly after Nia's announcement, and forty minutes later got a buzz on my apartment intercom from a delivery driver from Dough 24/7 with three M&M cookies, ordered by him from across town. Shockingly, nothing seemed to have changed between us after King Spa; if anything, Ricky seemed to be even more available than before. When I requested his help with learning more about Shae and Nia's new friend group, he obliged without a second thought, and every now and again I could expect a random photo of a member of the Lesbrigade, followed by a question about their name, profession, and preferred pronouns.* It didn't take me long to learn almost everything it was acceptable to know about Beck, Charlotte, Latrice, and Wenji. And even though the realization that Nia was creating a new set of memories with a gaggle of folks I had never met stung something fierce, he made learning about them almost fun.

Michelle studied my face for a moment. She enjoyed being provocative, especially to people who would see her heart-shaped, pert-mouthed face and assume she was just another docile Asian girl,† but I knew that she was forcing me to think about what

* "Is studying your solution for everything?" he teased.
† A stereotype that has never made sense to me, because I have yet to meet an Asian girl who isn't alarmingly powerful.

284

she'd said to me that day in L&D. And talk about poor timing too. With Nia gone, I had a crushing realization: I wasn't first, second, or third priority in anyone's life. Markus could hardly catch a break for long enough to give me a phone call. Tabatha was too wrapped up in premarital bliss and wedding planning to give me much mind these days. Even Michelle, bless her, could spare me a moment only when it was convenient. At first, this revelation had hurt beyond measure, but after several days of alternating between feeling sorry for myself and studying away the pain, I'd come to terms with it. Because I had Ricky, and with him, I could at least pretend to matter.

I didn't tell Michelle any of that, though. It would only make her pity me more, and I already pitied myself plenty.

"Anyway," I said, desperate to change the subject. "I just got my schedule this morning. You know we get only one day off a week on internal medicine, right?"

Michelle wasn't dumb, so I knew she saw through me. Thankfully, though, she took the bait.

"And we're paying thousands of dollars for the privilege!" she declared. "Why did we choose this life again? Like, why? You know what our attending said when I showed up to orientation this morning?"

I smiled and listened to Michelle go on a rant about her quirky neurology attending. *This is you becoming an adult,* I decided. Letting go. Learning restraint. Learning how to go home to an empty apartment, and to interface with friends like this — in stolen moments at work, or in the line for lunch, not sitting at a creaky old dining room table for hours.

I held on to this mantra like a talisman against my despondence for days, and it worked. Suddenly, witnessing Nia's slow disappearance from my apartment didn't hurt so much, or, at the very least, I could pretend it wasn't happening. When I searched through my kitchen drawer for a missing utensil only to realize that it was Nia's, I could pull out my phone and order one online before the misery could settle in. I bought my own overpriced face wash. I was doing okay.

Until a couple days later, when I walked into my apartment after my last day of orientation and found it occupied.

"Oh," Shae said, lowering a box labeled "bowls" to their feet. "Hey, Angie."

I stood, frozen in place, at the entryway, feeling all the anguish I had been holding back burst forward like a tidal wave against a hastily built dam. Somehow, although I'd assumed Nia was planning to move in with Shae, my heart hadn't accepted it as truth. After all, Nia and Shae had only been dating for about three months, nothing compared to the eleven years I'd spent at Nia's side. Shae seemed to know this too, judging by the way they shuffled their feet awkwardly in front of me, shoving their hands deep into the pockets of their artfully tattered jeans.

I heard some clattering in the kitchen: Nia, probably looking for any last baking supplies to pilfer. I watched as she scuttled into view from behind the kitchen wall. She held my gaze as she placed a box very gingerly on the dining room table, her mouth dropping open as if to speak —

I couldn't take this. Swallowing against the toad in my throat, I kicked my shoes off and marched into my bedroom, closing the door behind me quietly. Throwing my backpack onto the floor by my desk, I let my head fall back against the door and inhaled deeply. I could feel my body fighting to produce tears, but I fought back just as valiantly, willing my heart to slow, wishing away the bitterness.

"This is you becoming an adult," I whispered to myself. Behind my closed eyes, I could see Nia in the kitchen, her hair piled into a bun on top of her head, looking at me like I was a stranger. "Letting go. People grow apart. It happens. You have to let go —"

"Okay . . . So what was that?" Shae snapped, loud enough for me to hear them through the walls.

"Leave it, Shae," Nia said with finality.

That was it. I exhaled in a shuddering breath, then trudged to my bed. My slacks came off first, then my button-down top. I peeled off my socks with my toes, then burrowed myself under my covers and co-cooned myself in my comforter.

"No, babe," Shae said. "I'm not leaving it. Why was that so weird? Thought you said she was happy for us?"

"Drop. It." Nia's voice was cold.

Suddenly, I felt like I was drowning, choking against a pain that I had summarily failed to keep at bay. My chest physically hurt, every beat of my heart distinct and excruciating. I'd been heartbroken before, so many times that I had practically lost count. It had always hurt but . . . not like this. *Never* like this. If I could sink into my bed and feel nothing ever again, I thought, it would be preferable to this.

I lay in miserable silence for what felt like

hours, listening to their muffled voices, Shae's litany of sighs, the creak of feet against our — *my* — ancient floorboards. Outside my door, I could sense the tension in the aggressive way that Shae seemed to be filling boxes, the grating sound of tape being pulled taut and papers rustling becoming my white noise.

Eventually, though, the door to our apartment clicked shut, and I was finally alone.

I rolled out of bed and shrugged on a robe. The living room was in immaculate shape, the air heavy with the smell of lemon-scented cleaner; they had clearly cleaned up before leaving. Which meant that this was it. Nia had moved out. I walked through my new space in mournful silence, taking note of what I had lost. She had left her paintings but taken her throw. Her vase — a real one, not one of the counterfeits I'd used to prank Frederick — sat on the living room table, a single fresh daisy in it. Her row of size 11 shoes was gone, and the rack neatened; even my hastily tossed flats had been put in a place of honor on the top row. She had left behind a single pastel-blue apron — her favorite one, I realized, with a start. I ran my fingers along the strap, and knew, with certainty, that we were over.

Suddenly, I didn't want to be alone, and

certainly not here.

From my bedroom, I heard my phone, abandoned on my nightstand, buzz.

It was Ricky. Everything okay? he said. Shae just texted me that it might not be.

Before I could lose my nerve, I called him. I listened to the line ring once, twice —

"Hey," Ricky's voice sounded husky with disuse. He cleared his throat.

"Hey," I responded. "What are you up to right now?"

"Nothing," Ricky said. "Just watching TV." His tone softened. "Are you okay?"

"I'm great," I said hastily. "Can I join you?"

SEVENTEEN

I pulled up in front of Ricky's apartment at 9:15 p.m., a full forty-five minutes before what Michelle would have deemed "booty-call o'clock." It was dark out, the side street where he lived dimly lit by sodium street-lights. I managed to snag a spot right in front of his apartment, and parallel parked with the smoothness of a true, deep-dish-slinging, "no ketchup on my hot dog"* Chicagoan. And now I sat in my car, still gripping my gear shift, trying to figure out what the hell I had just done.

Thankfully, after I invited myself over to his place, Ricky didn't make things weird. If anything, he'd been *gracious.* He responded with a prompt Sure, texted me his address, and gave me tips about where to find park-

---

* No seriously. You might get decked if you ask for ketchup on your hot dog in the city. They're very particular about it.

ing around his apartment. I threw on the first clean outfit I could find — a plain black tee and a pair of denim shorts — grabbed my keys, logged Ricky's address into Google Maps, and fled my apartment. I moved with a single-mindedness I hadn't experienced in a long time, for once not thinking about what I *should have* been doing, whether that was studying or filling out our IRB application or prepping for the wards. All I had was a destination, and a mission to loosen up the knot in my chest. And with every mile I inched closer to Ricky, I felt like my rudimentary plan was working.

Except I had never been to Ricky's place, and now I was showing up under the cover of night. Over the phone, it was easy to pretend that nothing between us had changed. In person, though, I wasn't so sure. Would meeting in person remind him that, the last time we'd seen each other, I'd kind of sort of violated him and then fled the scene of the crime?* Would he go back to how he'd been early in our friendship, when he avoided touching me at all costs?

Ricky was at his door before I could make

---

* It's not like I asked permission to kiss him, after all. And he *did* tell me that he wasn't into me like that. Ha. I hate myself.

it up the stairs.

"Here," he said, sticking his head out and waving me toward his apartment. I power walked down the long hallway, trying to keep my hormones in check. It had been some time since I'd seen Ricky in the flesh, and there was something about how he looked now, in plaid pajama pants that hung low around his hips and a plain white tee, with his hair wet from a shower, that seemed indecent.

"Thanks for having me over," I said, stepping cautiously inside. Ricky grinned, closing the door behind us with a click.

"Thanks for coming over. You've never actually been, right?" Ricky said. The pads of his fingers brushed against the small of my back as he guided me farther inside. *Okay. So definitely still touching me.* I wasn't sure if that realization soothed my fears or stoked them.

Ricky gave me the grand tour. His entire apartment was open concept — the kitchen, dining room, and living room blending into one open space — and well lit. It was immaculate in a way that felt maintained rather than rushed, but then again, I had suspected he was a bit of a neat freak since the first time I'd hopped into his car. Ricky pointed out the bathroom, then led me from wall to wall to show off his expansive collection of framed prints and posters. I spotted the posters he had purchased from the booth at the art fair, hanging in ornate frames alongside several other goofy period pieces: a painting of a cat with a monocle and top hat, Queen Elizabeth but with the face of a possum.* Then there was his collection of prints by his favorite Chicago muralists, and he walked me through those leisurely, describing the recurring characters in JC Rivera's work, laughing when I excitedly identified Hebru Brantley's FlyBoy as the "Black kid with goggles across from the Trader Joe's."

"What's this one?" I asked, pointing to a painting he'd skipped, propped up on top of his bookshelf. It was a vibrant acrylic piece portraying a dancing couple, almost incongruent with the rest of his decor. The iridescent colors reminded me of the drawing he'd done of me in the garden so many months ago.

"That's one of mine," Ricky said, suddenly shy. "It's, ah, based on a picture of my grandparents, actually."

I stepped closer, peering at the two smil-

* "Ricky," I said. "I'm not going to lie. That is *terrifying.*"

ing figures and marveling at how master-fully he'd re-created such a tender moment. When I turned back to Ricky, he'd pulled out his phone and scrolled to the reference image, a photo of a man in a cowboy hat twirling a petite, laughing woman around a dance floor. Next to me, Ricky radiated pride, the way he did every time he talked about his grandparents.

"It's beautiful," I said after a moment. "Why haven't you given it to them?"

"Because I never got around to finishing it," he said, gesturing to the blurred, abstract edges of the painting that I had assumed were purposeful. "Probably never will, if I'm honest. I tried my hand at painting, but . . . it's just not really my forte."

I tapped my finger against my chin, re-membering how Ricky had identified the artists' techniques at the art fair.

"Well, *I* think you're incredible," I mused. "Maybe you should get back on it."

Ricky waved me off.

"I'm more of a digital guy," he claimed. "Come on, let me show you my toys."

He led me to his workstation, an expansive desk with two large mounted monitors and a smaller screen that he explained was actu-ally a graphic tablet. He showed me these with the giddiness of a child at show-and-tell, describing not just the items but where he found them, when, his decisions to arrange them as he had.

"It's a nice place," I said when he was done. Ricky had done well for himself. "That is," I added with a sneer, "for a starving artist."

"Asshole," he said without bite. He shoved his hands into his pajama pockets. "But thanks. So? Want anything to drink?"

I shook my head and he tsk-ed, bringing me a glass of water anyway before whisking away to what I now knew was his bedroom. I crumpled onto his sofa, taking delicate sips as I listened to his footsteps patter against his wood floors. To my surprise, I found myself next to a mound of blankets, so high they almost peeked over the top of the couch. They looked so incongruous next to his carefully folded dish towels, and there were so *many* of them.

"How many of these do you need, Ricky?" I said, lifting layer after layer of blanket only to reveal more underneath. Some were clearly store bought, but a few were knit, and judging by the color schemes of iconic anime characters,* by hand.

Unceremoniously, Ricky returned from

* Any respectable weeb knows that a combo of

behind me and dumped an armful of sheets onto the couch.

"All of them," he said. "We're building a fort."

In spite of myself, I let out a bark of laughter.

"A blanket fort?" I asked giddily. I couldn't remember the last time I'd made a blanket fort, and when I told Ricky as much, his grin only grew wider.

"Oh, then this is definitely a good idea," he said. "Hold on," he added before disappearing into his bedroom again and re-emerging with a stack of pillows. "I know you're a guest, but I'm putting you to work. Help me move these chairs?"

I followed him to his dining table, noting its unique dimensions and its welded steel base.

"Your grandpa make this?" I asked.

"Yeah," Ricky responded, beaming. "The chairs too. It was my present for getting my own place." He ran his thumb against the table edge. "Completely caught me by surprise, because my grandparents were pissed when I told them I was moving out."

"Why were they upset?" I asked, thinking

---

orange, blue, black, and white is pathognomonic for Son Goku.

of Nia and her box of kitchen utensils, the hollow look she'd given me as she placed it on our dining room table.

"I mean, this place is only a fifteen-minute drive away from them, and it's not that much more convenient for work," he said. "They were hoping I'd stay in their home until I got married."

I hoisted one of the chairs up. Unbidden, the image of Ricky, dressed smartly in a black tux and standing, beaming, at an altar, came to mind, and I shook it off.

"So why didn't you?" I asked. "Stay, I mean. You probably would've saved a ton on rent."

Ricky snorted and followed me into the living area, dropping off his chair before crossing the room for another.

"For one, my dad was always there, and he's annoying as shit," he said. Then he gave me a strange look, sucking in his lower lip. "And then, well, you know. Camila."

My stomach turned. I didn't know much about Camila and Ricky's relationship, just that they'd met in college and, like me, were three years out. Had she lived here, in this apartment? Had he . . . started a home with her? I found my eyes darting around the room, searching for any vestiges of Camila's touch, and finding only Ricky.

"Of course," I said, attempting to sound casual even while my skin crawled. "Your grandma's a virtuous Catholic woman. Couldn't be fornicating openly under her roof, right?"

Ricky let out a bark of laughter. He arranged the chairs into a rectangle, gently guiding me out of his way to make sure that mine were adequately lined up with the couch.

"I think she would've pretended not to know, if it kept me home," he admitted. "Okay, so now we have to make the ground."

With professional precision, Ricky lay down layer after layer of blankets, instructing me to line them up to create an even "floor" for our fort. When that was done, he gathered pillows for seating, running back to his bedroom to collect another when one of his chosen pillows proved too flat for his liking.

"You're clearly an expert at this," I joked, watching him search his bookshelf for books heavy enough to hold up the fort canopy.

"Made a lot of blanket forts in my time," he said. He turned to smile at me. "I was an only child in the smallest Mexican family in Chicago. Needed somewhere to play my Game Boy and feel like I was on an

299

adventure, you know?"

I laughed, imagining the Ricky I'd seen from his middle school photo holed up in an elaborate fort, playing Pokémon and humming along to the gym themes.

"And it was a good place to retreat when I was upset," he added, just a bit more solemnly. He straightened and turned to look at me. "I'm sorry about Nia. I know how important she is to you. If it gives you any solace, even Shae doesn't really get what's going on. I don't think . . ." He sighed, pushing his hair back. "*We* don't think this is just about you. Shae says she'll probably come around."

The knot in the center of my chest, which had loosened over the last several minutes of fort building, tightened again.

"What if she doesn't?" I said quietly. My vision blurred with tears, and I blinked them back. "What if this is it?"

When I looked back up again, Ricky was right in front of me, squinting down at me with dark, bottomless eyes. Suddenly, the room felt small. Gently, he cupped my face in his hand. His thumb stroked, very lightly, over my cheekbone, and I took a sharp intake of breath, feeling a frisson of anxiety shuttle down my body like a lightning bolt. Rooted in place, I looked up at his face in search of an explanation and found nothing but tenderness.

"Then, Angie," Ricky said softly, "you find a way to move on."

Then he swept into the kitchen, asking me whether I wanted any popcorn.

Fuck. I clutched the back of the couch, not entirely convinced that my legs were fit to hold me up. I was so sure that I could do this. So certain that I could be cool, that I would withstand being in his vicinity without feeling like I was on fire. But just then, there'd been something in Ricky's eyes that had set them smoldering, and I felt that heat down in the pit of my belly. It was so different from the blank look he'd given me after I kissed him at King Spa, and it scared me more.

"Do you want kettle corn or butter?" Ricky called from the kitchen, like he hadn't just almost stopped my heart. "I've got both."

"Butter," I said, proud that my voice didn't waver. I sat on our blanket fort floor, leaning against the couch and closing my eyes. I listened to Ricky root around his cupboards, then tear open a package of microwavable popcorn.

"Want to pick something to watch?" Ricky said from the kitchen.

"What were you watching before I decided to impose on you?" I asked.

"You didn't impose," Ricky said, dropping to the floor next to me. He gave me a shy smile. "I'm really glad you're here, actually."

I ignored the buzzing in my ears and accepted the remote when he handed it to me, scrolling to Netflix.

"You heard of *One Punch Man*?" he asked.

I nodded. I'd fallen off the weeaboo train in college, but Ricky had clearly been riding it since *Dragon Ball Z*.* Still, Markus kept me abreast of the shows of the moment.

"Yeah," I said. "It looks very stupid."

"It is," Ricky admitted. "But it's also very funny. I'm down to start from the beginning, if you're interested."

"I'm down," I said. The microwave beeped, and Ricky jumped to his feet to retrieve our popcorn as I searched for the show.

"Can you get the canopy up?" he asked, tearing open the bag.

* Entry-level anime for most millennials. Were you really cool if you didn't crowd around the TV once a week to watch Goku spend another twenty minutes screaming and charging a Spirit Ball? (The answer is yes, you definitely were.)

302

I stood, picking a sheet and throwing it over our arranged chairs, then securing the corners by placing Ricky's selection of books on top of each chair. The blanket fort was complete. I stepped back to admire our handiwork, my heart fluttering in my throat. It was a small space, cozy. As a kid, blanket forts had seemed like such innocent fun. As an adult, though, it felt like I was crawling into a trap.

The room dimmed; Ricky had turned off the kitchen light. Ricky himself emerged a minute later, a bowl of popcorn in one hand and a flickering electric candle in the other. *Mood lighting?* I almost teased, but then bit my tongue — because what would I do if he said yes? Instead, I watched him bend to enter the fort, settling into a pillow seat next to me. He dragged a couple of blankets off the couch and tossed one to me wordlessly, and I nodded in thanks, draping it over my shoulders.

"Want to start?" Ricky asked after a few seconds of silence.

"Yeah," I said, and hit "play."

One Punch Man was absurd but hilarious, the perfect show to dispel my nerves. Within five minutes we'd given up on muffled snickers and had burst into full-on commentary and peals of laughter. I always knew when an especially stupid scene was coming because Ricky would lean back against the sofa and watch for my reaction, and every time, I would prepare a clever barb to make fun of his enthusiasm and promptly forget it because the scene would really be that funny. We watched the first episode, then silently agreed to continue to the next. By the third episode, our bowl of popcorn was empty, and I had graduated from sitting up straight against the couch to lying comfortably on my belly and swinging my legs against it. I looked up at Ricky, his face lit by the TV screen and the flickering of his fake candle, and felt myself flood with warmth. To think that I'd ever thought of him as anything other than kind. He had heard, secondhand, that I needed him, and devised a strategy to cheer me up on the spot. Michelle had been right — third year of medical school tore most people apart, but somehow, it was bringing us together.

Ricky glanced at me from the corner of his eye, and I looked away, embarrassed at being caught staring. A second later, something soft and plush struck me in the back; it took me a split second to realize that he'd just hit me with a *pillow*.

"Wh-what — !" I stammered, baffled. "You did not!"

Ricky raised an eyebrow in a challenge, the culprit pillow held in front of him like a shield. When I sat up and snatched a pillow out from under me, he scooted just out of my reach.

Lucky for me, I *wasn't* an only child, and this was not my first time at the rodeo. I lobbed a pillow at him, let him bat it away, and then grabbed another and smacked him against his side. Keeling over with laughter, Ricky dodged my next toss but caught the one after that on the side of his head. Cackling, I scrambled under the canopy for the throw pillows on top of the couch and, finding one, prepared to launch my next attack —

Ricky was faster. Before I could pelt him with my newfound weapon, he caught me across the stomach with a swing, knocking it out of my hands. I reached for my throw pillow again, and he lunged for me, grasping my wrist and wrestling it back with one hand and tossing the pillow out of my reach with the other.

"No fair!" I said, struggling to get out of his grasp. He laughed thunderously, snatching a full-sized pillow and preparing to hit me with the finishing blow. He raised it high, fixing me with a smile that was all mischief.

"Do you yield?" he asked.

"Never," I spat. Then I kicked his legs out from under him.

Our blanket fort canopy came flopping down onto us. I laughed myself breathless as I tried to push myself out from under the cloth, but found myself impeded by something heavy, firm, and warm —

Oh.

I froze, cataloging all the places that our bodies overlapped. Ricky had fallen onto me at a right angle, his head pressed into my stomach, one arm draped across my legs, the other perilously close to my breast. I could feel him chuckling too, his tone tinged with disbelief, and the sound rumbled through my belly. I fought to hold back a shudder, knowing that, pressed against me like this, he would feel it too. Slowly, he pulled himself up, adjusting himself so that his face hovered over mine. The sheet slipped halfway down his back.

He was close. So close that there seemed to be two Rickys overlapping each other, three beautiful, dark eyes, two sets of soft slightly parted lips. My gaze dropped to the hollow of his neck, and I watched, fascinated, as the shuddering of his pulse jumped and quickened.

"Hey," he said, and I licked my lips,

watching as he homed in on the motion. "I'm going to kiss you now. Is that okay?"

I didn't trust my voice to work, and so I nodded instead. The corner of Ricky's mouth quirked with amusement, and then, between one breath and the next, his lips were on mine.

I'd imagined what kissing Ricky — *actually* kissing him — would be like. I'd imagined it would be electric, that it would feel the way touching him felt but times a thousand. But I hadn't expected it to feel like home. The first touch of our lips together was brief, like an experiment, or a question that we both answered with an emphatic *yes*. Warmth trailed down my body, like I'd taken a long draft of wine, and settled in my fingertips and the parts of my body where we touched. We kissed for a long time, my arms twining around his neck, his hands sliding down my sides to clasp me at the waist.

Eventually, Ricky pulled away. His hands came up to cup my face and he looked down at me reverently, his thumbs rubbing circles on the high points of my cheekbones. I felt like a fizzy drink, my body light and buzzing.

"Hi," he said.

"Hi," I breathed. We laughed. He lowered

himself to kiss me again, lightly this time, then, throwing the sheet off us, flopped onto his back. He threaded his fingers through mine, bringing the back of my hand to his lips.

"You're a hard one to catch, you know that?" Ricky said, chuckling. "Which is funny, considering you kissed *me* first."

Blood rushed to my cheeks, and I lifted my free hand to cover my face.

"Yeah. Ha," I said. "I don't know what I was thinking —"

"I knew what I was thinking," Ricky interrupted. "That if you'd just given me a second, I might've told you that I liked it." He reached over and gently tugged my hand away from my face, his voice taking on a husky tone. "I might have told you a lot of things."

I swallowed, flustered by the sight of his reddened lips.

"Like what?" I said, holding my breath for the answer.

"Like . . ." Ricky rolled to his side, drawing me to him again and kissing me once, twice, a third time, "how long I've wanted to do this." He tugged on my bottom lip gently, and my body, released from its prison of doubt, prickled with want.

"Yeah?" I asked after he pulled away.

"How long is that?"

"Since the improv show." Ricky snickered to himself, then flopped onto his back. "Okay, before that. Probably since the day we met, if I'm honest with myself."

My mind shuttled back to the art fair, to the moment when I'd been so sure he was about to kiss me. So I hadn't misread him after all. I remembered what Michelle had told me, after Ricky had delivered me coffee in L&D — *Maybe he just likes you.* My stomach turned in pleased knots.

"You little punk," I said, nudging his arm. "You told me you weren't interested! Who does that?"

Ricky shrugged. I watched him squeeze his eyes shut, clench his jaw. His hand tightened in mine. The shift in the atmosphere was instant, and I didn't understand why.

"I . . . ," he started. Then he cleared his throat. "You know about Camila, right? About how we broke up?"

Oh. Hearing him utter his ex-girlfriend's name a minute after we'd finished playing tonsil hockey on his floor was kind of a buzz-kill.

"Not all of it," I said. "I know that she's with someone else now."

Ricky nodded. It had been months since

Camila dumped him, and he hadn't brought her up voluntarily once. I had thought it was odd but figured that their three-year relationship had just fizzled out. But now, he looked pained, like the memory of her still lingered and hurt. Not a look I was prepared to contend with.

"When she was breaking up with me," he said, "she told me that I didn't actually love her. That she had always known that something was off about us, but she couldn't put her finger on it until she met someone who did." He covered his eyes with his free arm. "And at first, I was pissed. She'd cheated on me, right? Met some other guy and was carrying on right under my nose . . . but then, I realized that I'd been doing the same thing. With you."

My heart skipped a beat, and I averted my eyes, focusing instead on the flickering of the fake candlelight against the ceiling.

"My dad's had about a hundred girl-friends," Ricky continued. "He'd bring a nice lady around, sit her at Abuela's dinner table, and then bring a different one the next week. My mom was the only one he knocked up, that we know of, at least, and he ditched her the moment he found out." He laughed. "She was really sick, you see, and she knew that she probably wouldn't

310

be around to take care of me. So she found my abuelos, and thank god they fell in love with her, because the rest is history.

"But my abuelos have been together for, what, almost fifty years? They're that old married couple you read about. Still totally obsessed with each other. A while back, after a bad breakup, I asked Abuelo how they'd made it work over all that time. You know what he said?" Ricky turned bodily to face me, propping himself up on one arm. His voice dropped into a thick, drawling Mexican accent. " 'Listen, gordito. The secret to long-lasting love is simple. You wake up. You roll over and look at your wife. And you say to yourself, today, I will choose you. I will love you. And you keep doing that every single day until you die.' " He grinned. "It sounds better in Spanish."

I snickered.

"Your grandpa sounds like a wise man," I said.

"He's brilliant," Ricky agreed. "And it makes sense, right? After that, I figured that loving someone, the proper way, I mean, was about discipline. Being disciplined enough to keep choosing the same person you chose fifty years ago, over and over again, year after year, rain or shine." His voice cracked on the last words, and he

311

cleared his throat. "And I thought I could do that. It seemed straightforward enough. And then one day . . . this crying girl comes stumbling into my favorite garden and all of a sudden it's a wrap."

Ricky reached for me then, brushing his knuckles against my cheek. It was as though once he'd gotten permission to touch me, he couldn't stop, like his affection was bubbling up inside him and needed to be released in small gestures.

"What are you saying?" I asked. "That I'm some sort of temptress?"

Ricky chuckled, shaking his head.

"Your eyes have set man's heart ablaze," he recited quietly. *"And you have had your will of him."** He paused. "James Joyce."

I rolled my eyes and bit back a smile.

"You artsy boys are so disgusting," I said, but I leaned in close to kiss him anyway, marveling at the fact that kissing Ricky was something I could just *do* now.

---

* I looked it up later — a quote from *A Portrait of the Artist as a Young Man,* the "Villanelle of the Temptress." The poem itself isn't actually that romantic — mostly the muses of a horny boy blaming women for existing because they pull him away from his religiosity or something. Which . . . I guess also fits?

"I really like you," Ricky said in response, and I warmed under those words, letting their meaning permeate. Ricky had seen the full, unfiltered range of what I was, and he liked me. Just as I was. Angie Appiah, with no edits.

"I really like you too," I said softly. We giggled together, giddy as teenagers. But unlike my teen years, there was zero chance of my momma busting down the door to interrupt.* Nothing stopping me from letting the mouth that was hovering just above mine trail lower, of slipping my hands beneath his thin white tee to learn what he felt like underneath. No one standing in the way of me pulling Ricky's body back over mine and seeing exactly where the night took us.

But I didn't do any of that. *One year until I apply to residency,* I thought. *One and a half until Match. Until I get sent to train somewhere across the country, and you decide to hop on a different horse.*

"You're thinking so hard right now," Ricky said, squeezing my hand. "Everything okay?"

* Not that I'd gotten within six inches of a real human boy as a teen anyway. Too busy being in them books.

I smiled indulgently at him, watching the candlelight flicker across his face. I felt like we'd slammed down on a timer until heartbreak. And now, I was in too deep to come out unscathed.

"Nothing," I said, rolling closer to him, resting my forehead against his. "Just that I'm . . . relieved. I wasn't sure that you felt the same way."

Ricky hummed in affirmation, and then he kissed me again, so slow and deep that I almost felt at peace. When he pulled away, his eyes were bright.

"Me too."

EIGHTEEN

Tabatha crossed her arms petulantly across her chest. When she was a kid, that same stance had signaled an impending tantrum, each one more explosive than the last. Even Momma used to take cover, until the year Grandma came to live with us and introduced her to corporal punishment.* Still, sixteen years later, I knew that that pose meant trouble.

"Why must you always choose the hardest thing?" Tabatha said.

We sat in a ripped-up booth in Robust Coffee Lounge, Tabatha's favorite Southside coffee shop, sharing a plate of banana French toast between us. I looked up from my mournfully empty coffee mug, my finger tracing the rim in slow, slippery circles. Ta-

* Spare the rod and spoil the child might as well be Grandma's favorite bastardization of a Bible verse (Proverbs 13:24).

batha looked especially gorgeous in an off-the-shoulder floral shirt that showed off the slope of her back, and I'd watched about four guys begin to approach her before jumping back at the sight of the glittering rock on her finger.

"What do you mean?" I said, mirroring her pose. "I'm seeing someone, and he makes me happy. Isn't that what you've been wanting for me this entire time?"

"Of course it is," Tabatha said. "But I also want you to be careful. Like . . . sis. He's not your boyfriend, right? Y'all are just" — she waved her hands dismissively — "going with the flow or something?"

"We haven't talked about it," I said, puffing one cheek out. "Why? Suddenly I can't just enjoy myself?"

"I mean, yeah you could, if you weren't clearly in love with this dude," Tabatha said, scoffing.

I bit the inside of my cheek. *I don't know about* love, I wanted to say, but I couldn't deny that my feelings for Ricky were more intense than anything I'd felt for anyone before him. I hated how reckless he made me, how I couldn't seem to think of us together without letting my mind shuttle heedlessly into the future. And Ricky wasn't helping. In the forty-eight hours or so since we'd stepped boldly out of the friend zone, he'd been doing his best to plant seeds about the possibility of a long-term *us* into my head. He talked about attending music festivals that were a year away, posited taking a trip to Puerto Rico in February to escape the worst of winter. Yesterday, he'd even entertained the possibility of me stopping by for an impromptu dinner with his grandparents, a proposition I dodged by insisting that I would be working late.

"That's a pity," he said wistfully. "Abuela would really like you. She likes her women a little feisty, you know?"

I wasn't so sure. After all, Ricky's grandparents sounded kind of old school. How would they feel about him bringing home a Black girl, and a dark-skinned African one at that? Camila was pale, petite, Spanish-speaking. The great-grandkids she would've given them might have passed for white.*

---

* Every culture has some pejorative for Black people, some concern about mixing with us. I didn't remember much from AP World History, but I do remember the image of *Ham's Redemption,* the painting portraying a Black grandmother celebrating her white grandchild, a depiction of the successful blanqueamiento of her family. My teacher breezed through that section, but I had

317

Once the judgment of the most important people in his life came into play, would Ricky realize that, actually, the whole "being Black by association" thing wasn't up his alley?

But if we kept things chill, reined ourselves in, none of these questions would really matter. I wouldn't have to worry about eventually picking between him and Match. I wouldn't have to think about introducing him to my parents, or wonder if he would ever knock for me. I wouldn't even have to think about us breaking up, because without a clear title, we could just fizzle out and fade away.

I stabbed my fork into a slice of French toast, feeling the pressure of Tabatha's gaze on my forehead.

"Girl, at least figure out if you're exclusive," she said. "I realize you didn't get your dating reps in, so you might just not know, but the rules of millennial courtship basically state that if you don't explicitly agree on that, he's gonna be fucking other people."

stared at it for a long time, grateful that the Latin American culture that we were learning about had at least been explicit in their intent to wash the blackness of people like me out like a blight.

I almost laughed. I was uncertain about a lot of things, but Ricky's commitment to serial monogamy was not one of them.

"Nah," I said, "I don't think that'll be a problem."

"Sure," Tabatha said. "Just don't come crying to me when you get chlamydia."

Okay, now I was annoyed. I placed my fork down on the table and fixed my little sister with a stern look.

"You know, just because you're getting married doesn't make you an expert on my love life, okay?" I said. "Drop it. I'll figure things out with Ricky at my own pace."

Tabatha rolled her eyes dramatically, leaning back in her chair.

"You don't have to get mad. I'm only trying to help. But whatever, big sis, I suppose you have all of this handled," she said, in a way that made it abundantly clear that she thought the opposite. Then she exhaled, flattening her hands on the table. "That reminds me. I owe you formal congratulations. You've got Mom and Dad on lock. Blocking them! Didn't think you had it in you."

I gave Tabatha a thin-lipped smile. When I had first texted Tabatha to beware of an impending parental blowout, she hadn't believed me. But hardly a day had passed before her phone was overloaded with texts and voicemails from our parents, first demanding that Tabatha speak to me about unblocking them, then asking her to check in to make sure I was okay, and, most recently, to ask her to ask me if I would like them to ship me anything from the Ghana shop.

"Yeah, well," I said. "Had to be done." It would be a lie to say that I didn't miss my family, but the peace of knowing I could walk through the hospital halls without hearing a diatribe about my unworthiness was worth it.

"You done good," Tabatha insisted, seeing my crestfallen expression. "You know how it is with Mom and Dad. Sometimes, you just have to" — she made a snipping motion with her fingers — "before they get the picture. When the time is right, you can put it back together again."

"I hope so," I said, thinking of Nia. Despite the outpouring of support from Michelle, Tabatha, and my not-boyfriend, I still carried Nia's loss like a boulder on my back. And with every passing day, I felt more and more sure that she was never coming back.

"Back to loverboy real quick," Tabatha said. She knocked back her coffee, holding up one hand when I began to protest. "Maybe, like, don't sleep with him until you figure out if he's in it for the long haul?"

My jaw dropped.

"Not you, *Tabatha Nhyira Akua Appiah,* telling me not to live *my best ho life* —"

Tabatha tutted me. "Yeah, well, some of us can handle it." She pointed at my chest. "You? No way. Your heart is attached to your vagina."

But not sleeping with Ricky was turning out to be a real *endeavor.*

We sat on the couch in my apartment, Ricky's phone faceup on my coffee table and the timer counting down from seven minutes. I dragged my hands through his hair, scratching his scalp as he unabashedly cupped my ass. His hands trailed down the swell of my thighs to the bend of my knees and yanked me farther up his lap, his kisses rapidly going from gentle to stinging. I rolled my hips into him playfully, smiling against his lips as he let out a low, rumbling groan —

The timer went off.

I hopped off his lap, snickering as Ricky tilted his head back against my sofa in frustration.

"Come *on,* Angie," he said, his voice taking on a husky tone that nearly sent me tumbling right back into his arms. "Fuck the timer."

"Ha," I said, heading back to my dining room table and waking up my laptop. Ricky trailed sluggishly behind me. "No can do. I have less than two weeks to finish up my research proposal presentation, I have to study for my shelf, *and* my attending wants me to present a topic during rounds tomorrow." I smirked, taking pride in the still-dazed expression on his face. "Making out with you isn't going to get me into residency."

"It might get you something else," Ricky said suggestively, then, accepting defeat, gave me a chaste kiss on the cheek.

Dating Ricky hadn't turned out to be all that different from being friends with him, minus the heavy petting. Mostly we hung out and worked together, him helping me with themes for my upcoming presentation, me offering opinions on *color scheme* and *structure* for his projects. Since the day we built our blanket fort, we hadn't gone a day without seeing each other in person. Ricky had moved to occupy the space Nia had left behind, and though he wasn't a perfect fit, the ways in which he was different were . . . exhilarating.

"Oh yeah, Ange," Ricky said, flopping into the chair across from me. "It's Juan's son's fourth birthday next Friday, and Abuela's throwing him a party. You want to come?"

The hairs on the back of my neck stood straight up.

"Next Friday?" I said, perhaps too quickly. "No can do. I'm post-call."★

Disappointment flickered across Ricky's face, but he covered it by bending forward to pull out his laptop.

"Oh, okay," he said. I watched him plug in his graphic tablet, spinning his pen between his fingers. Guilt sat heavy in my stomach.

"Is that okay?" I asked, suddenly nervous. Ricky's gaze flickered up to mine.

"Of course," he said, giving me a warm smile. He reached across the table and squeezed my hand. "I know you're busy. It's all good."

Oh, Ricky. Ever understanding, endlessly considerate. *Next time he asks,* I thought, *I'll*

★ Ah, the "call" cycle. When your medical team is on call, they take new patients from the Emergency Department or other teams. Post-call is the day afterward. They tend to run long. I probably could ask to leave early if I needed to . . . but for now it serves as a decent excuse.

say yes.

"Well," I said, "on the bright side, I stopped by Jewel and picked us some snacks for today. Grabbed a few of your favorites."

Ricky leaned back in his chair.

"Yeah? What'd you get?"

"Goldfish," I said, then added with a smirk, "the Annie's kind. Got some pineapple in the fridge, too."

"Ooh, big spender," Ricky said. "You want to bring those out?"

"I got you," I said. I threw open my cabinets, swearing quietly to myself when I found them bereft of goodies. "Oh shoot. I must have left a bag in the car. Hang on a second; I'll go look."

Ricky waved me along, not looking up from his work. I snatched my keys off the wall and dashed down the stairs, a small part of me hoping in vain that my small offering of goods could make up for my flightiness. Frederick's parents lived just outside of Milwaukee, only a two-hour drive away, and not once during our six-month stint had he proposed we visit them. And yet here was Ricky, ready to merge our lives without even a week's hesitation. But was that out of his regard for me? Or simply out of a habit of making a home with every woman he dated? *He loves love,* Shae had

324

said, and Ricky had demonstrated that over and over again, in his effusive love for his family, in the fact that he'd left his grandparents' home for his ex. I threw open my car door, relieved to find the abandoned bag nestled under my front seat. Tossing it over my shoulder, I journeyed back up my stairs, my pace slowed by the whirl of my thoughts. Maybe I should have said yes to the birthday party. Maybe meeting Ricky's grandparents wasn't as big of a deal as I was making it out to be; maybe, as he'd postulated, his grandmother and I would get on like a house on fire and all my hand-wringing would be for naught.

I sighed, pushing open my front door. Inside, I could hear the muffled sound of Ricky's voice. He was on the phone, no longer sitting at the table but standing by it, looking out the window to our building's courtyard below.

"I know it must feel like shit," he was saying. His voice was gentle, like he was trying to lure in a skittish cat. "Okay, yeah, worse than shit. But you're doing good. Just . . . try to power through."

As I approached, the voice on the other end grew audible. It was a man's voice, trembling with an infectious anxiety. The tension felt familiar, and I pondered why for several seconds until it clicked — it was the same panicked tone I heard from my patients right before they were wheeled into surgery; uncertainty, fear, and anticipation rolled into one. Ricky looked at me askance as I stepped closer, giving me a small, hapless shrug, and suddenly I knew exactly who was on the other end of the line.

"Get through this, and I can go with you to the clinic, yeah?" he said. "You just need to make it to the morning, and we can walk in together."

In that moment, my small offerings felt insufficient. I placed the tote bag of snacks gingerly on the table and walked toward Ricky, watching him gnaw at his thumbnail as he listened to his father's exhausted rambling. The blinds cut harsh shadows across his face, the orange glow of the setting sun turning his eyes almost amber. He spoke to his father tenderly, like one would to a frightened child, listening to him describe his withdrawal symptoms with unending patience, offering words of encouragement, assurances of his support, and . . . God, how could I not love a man who loved like this? With his whole heart, even when choosing love was hard? Even when the only thing he could reliably expect in return was disappointment?

I roped my arms around his waist from behind and rested my head against his back. His voice vibrated into my cheek, and I let myself be lulled by the sensation, by the whooshing of my pulse in my ears and the thrum of his heartbeat against the flat of my palm. He twined his fingers through mine as he talked, running his thumb back and forth across my knuckles, and I hummed, content, as my mind formed the words that I already knew to be true. Because Tabatha was right. This . . . *thing* I felt for Ricky wasn't just infatuation; it was something deeper, more fundamental than that. It was love, or at least something like it, and I was tired of trying to fool myself into thinking it was anything less.

Eventually, Ricky hung up. He turned around in my arms slowly, a chagrined expression on his face, like talking his dad through his withdrawal was a source of embarrassment.

"Sorry about that," Ricky said. Then, with a small smile: "I know it's probably bullshit. But he might actually be trying, so . . ."

In response, I grabbed ahold of Ricky's collar and pulled his face to mine. It was a decisive kiss, a declarative press of my lips against his, and I hoped he knew what was in it — an apology, acceptance, a promise to myself to finally see him as more than a liability. When we broke away, his eyes were full of questions.

Before he could ask a single one, I jumped in with one of my own.

"Tabs and I are meeting up on Sunday to go over my presentation," I asked. "Do you want to come?"

And this is how I found myself sitting at a long table in a private study room at our local library with Ricky and my very unamused younger sister.

Clearly all my newly awakened emotions had muddled my judgment. *Introduce Ricky to your sister, he'll like that,* a voice in my head had said, somehow forgetting that my sister was the kind of Grade-A Mean Girl who had once made her eighth-grade teacher cry in the middle of class. I sent her a warning text in advance — Be nice — but, in her typical, boorish Tabatha way, she'd elected to ignore my request. If looks could kill, Tabatha would have burned Ricky to a crisp on sight.

"Hi," Ricky said when we walked in through the glass door of the study room. "I'm —"

"I know who you are," Tabatha said icily. In my peripheral vision, I could see Ricky flinch. Then she turned to me. "Your presentation?"

I pulled out my laptop and plugged it into the projector. My presentation, jazzed up by my personal graphic designer, flashed onto the screen, and I walked up to it as Tabatha hummed approvingly.

"It looks nice," she said. "Eye-catching, but not overdone, you know."

"Ricky designed the theme," I offered, just to see how she would react.

Tabatha didn't disappoint.

"Though, on second thought, those lines over there are a bit distracting," she said matter-of-factly. "But that's not important right now. We can get you something that looks better later."

Ricky shifted in his seat.

"I think it looks plenty good now," I said, already regretting my decision to put Ricky directly in the line of fire. Though, I reasoned, Tabatha was small fry next to my mother; if Ricky wanted to be involved with me, he might do well to get used to sitting in the Appiah family hot seat.

"You wanted my opinion, didn't you?" Tabs said.

Then she proceeded to give it at every possible opportunity. I stood in front of my presentation, holding back a wince when

Ricky offered a critique of one of my sentences only for Tabatha to outright tell me to pay him no mind, shooting her a warning look when she followed up his praise with criticism. Still, in between her swipes, Tabatha doled out useful advice, and I stopped several times during my practice presentation to jot down notes. After the first run-through, she even allowed Ricky to participate, once going as far as agreeing with him on a point about one of my figures. I was proud of my little sister. No matter how often I poo-pooed her "B-School preschool" degree, I recognized her shrewd judgment and her eye for marketing. With my loans in the way, Tabatha would make buckets more than me and soon.

"Thanks, guys," I said, closing out of the presentation. Dr. Reed would have to approve of the final edits, but I had a feeling he would agree with their input. "This was really useful."

" 'Course," Ricky said. He pulled out his laptop, then reached into his pocket for his phone and set the timer automatically. I smirked; I forced him to study with me so often that it had become routine for him. *I've never been more productive in my life,* he'd joked. At first, I'd felt guilty that so much of his day had to be spent watching me click through question banks, but he waved me away.

"I like your company. I don't really care what we do," he'd said earnestly, successfully reducing me to a puddle.*

"What's that for?" Tabatha asked, cocking her head at the countdown on his screen.

"Timer," Ricky said. He explained our study game, then pointed at me with his pen. "Have to keep that one honest."

Tabatha didn't smile.

"What do you do during the thirty minutes?" she asked. "You're not in school, right? So are you just on the internet? Watching sports or something?"

Bless Ricky and his patience. He gave Tabatha his most indulgent smile.

"No," he said slowly. "I do a good amount of freelance illustration work."

He turned his computer around to show off his current project — the album cover he'd started a few days back. I leaned across the table to take a good look. On his screen was a face, androgynous, composed of

*The truth, though — Ricky's just organized. He likes squeezing productivity out of every minute of the day. I think he's relieved that he can cross out "work" and "quality time with his girl" in one fell swoop. An Earthbender indeed.

triangles of varying sizes with lines of varying thickness. The proportions were intentionally off — the nose too long, mouth too wide, heavy-lidded eyes too close together — and the head was tilted to one side and rested on a pair of folded hands. It was beautifully stylized and quite different from his usual work.

"It's coming along really nicely," I said encouragingly. Next to me, Tabatha sniffed. There was no way she wasn't even a little impressed, but I knew that she'd rather eat her foot than admit it. I watched her beadily as she tossed her hair over one shoulder.

"How much does all of this make you?" she said. "Can't be much."

My jaw dropped with mortification.

"Ricky," I said quickly. "You don't have to answer that —"

Ricky's expression shuttered entirely, his eyelids dropping to half-mast as he met Tabatha's gaze.

"Enough," he said simply. Then he snapped his headphones over his ears.

An hour of tense silence later, Ricky shut his laptop with a thud. I met his eyes from across the table, burning with embarrassment. I'd known Tabatha would likely be rude, but I didn't think she would be "ask Ricky about his income with the undertone that it wasn't sufficient" rude. That move had big Dorothy Appiah energy, and it put me off.

"I'm heading out," he said, piling his things into his bag. He stepped around the table to where I sat and pressed his lips to mine in a lingering kiss that I suspected was partially for Tabatha's benefit. "See you tomorrow?" he asked. I nodded. Then to Tabatha, stiffly, "It was nice to meet you."

Tabatha's grin was incisive.

"Likewise," she said.

I waited for the door to swing shut, then counted for thirty seconds to be sure that Ricky was out of earshot. Then, I swiveled in my chair to face my sister.

"The fuck is wrong with you?"

Tabatha placed a hand over her mouth, feigning innocence.

"What do you mean?" she said in a thin, tinny voice.

I glowered at her, folding my arms across my chest.

"That whole thing about money. You know I don't care about that," I spat. "I think what he does is great, and even if I didn't, I'm going to make enough to support a family by my damn self. That was so incredibly shallow."

"It wasn't shallow," Tabatha insisted. She

placed her elbows on the table and leaned forward onto them. "It was realistic. I'm not worried about whether you'll be taken care of financially, Angie. You're about to be a doctor, I know you'll be fine." She gave me a defiant look. "But men can get funny about making less than their girl. I was just reminding him of your situation."

"I didn't ask you to do that," I said. "So you shouldn't have done it."

"Why?" Tabatha asked. "You said so yourself, Ricky's not your boyfriend. So what if I rough him up a bit?"

"So *what*? I like him," I said, seeing red. I'd seen Ricky shut down only once before, the time that I yelled at him in the halls of Rogers Children's. Ricky had thick skin, a trait I took advantage of often when I was ribbing him, but Tabatha's line of questioning had clearly struck a nerve. "You don't get to insult people I like just because you think you're doing me a favor."

The air thickened with tension. I whipped away from my sister, trying to quell my anger. After all, I knew that it was misdirected; I was most angry at myself. My impulse decision to demonstrate to Ricky that I was serious about him had led to him being hurt, and he'd deserved exactly none of that.

After a moment, Tabatha sighed.

"I get why you like him, you know," she said. "He's smart, and you two have this ridiculous vibe. Whatever spark you didn't have with Frederick — you definitely have it with him." She tapped her fingers rhythmically on the table. "And he clearly likes you. Otherwise, he wouldn't be spending his Sundays in a library listening to you drone on about *social determinants of health.* It's just . . ." Tabatha exhaled, and her expression changed, her insolence giving way to concern. "Angie, it would be different if you told me that he was serious about you. If you were moving toward something, you know? But right now, he's just some guy you're messing around with that you're making me meet for some reason."

"He's not just some guy," I insisted. Then I sighed. "We just haven't gotten around to . . . that conversation yet."*

"Well, you should," Tabatha pressed. "Because we both know Ricky's not an easy sell. This thing with his dad . . . It's a lot."

I bristled, knowing where she was headed.

* You know the one — the "DTR," or Define the Relationship conversation. I have DTR'd successfully exactly one time, with Frederick, and we all know how that panned out.

For the first time during this entire disaster of an afternoon, Tabatha had the decency to look ashamed. I'd known that telling my kid sister about Ricky's parentage would come back to bite me in the ass, but I hadn't anticipated that it would come up now, or like this. I understood then what she'd meant last week, when she accused me of always doing the "hardest thing."

"Ricky isn't his father," I said softly. The opposite, actually, I wanted to add. Loving. Thoughtful. Deliberate.

"I know that," Tabatha said. "But he's his family, and if you're trying to do this right, you can't separate him from his people." She sighed. "You're right. I do sound like Momma."

"You do," I said, but I understood. Mollified, I leaned back in my chair.

"I just want you to be careful," Tabatha repeated. "I don't like seeing my big sis get hurt."

"I won't," I promised, and left it at that.

NINETEEN

I had not been looking forward to internal medicine. With every new rotation came a drastic paradigm shift, a change in culture, presentation style, and unspoken expectations for medical students that we frequently and summarily failed to meet. On pediatrics and ob-gyn, I'd felt a need to kowtow to my residents and attendings in an effort to bump up my clinical grades, and the months of sniveling had left me feeling unappreciated, exhausted, and annoyed all at once. And thus, I approached my internal medicine rotation with half of my usual allotted fucks . . . and it was working *in my favor.*

"Hey, hey, Angie," my senior resident, James, said, as I walked back into the workroom shortly after finishing my pre-rounds. He gave me a fist bump. "How's your lady in 35?"

I smirked. "She's hanging in there. No fever overnight."

"Good for her," James said. "You think she can go home today?"

"Probably. Want to switch her over to oral antibiotics? Her susceptibilities are back, and it's sensitive to Bactrim. Oh, and I asked her if she needs any refills for her meds at home. She said she was good."

"Peeerfect," James said. "I'll pend her discharge orders. You're the best!"

Against all odds, I felt like I was finally getting ahold of this whole third-year gig. The wards were a much friendlier place than the lecture hall for a girl like me, who was more motivated by the personal than the material. Here, no one cared if you got a 95 percent on the second-year Micro exam or what your Step score was. In internal medicine, the bodily fluids were abundant, but so was the conversation. Better than peds, where the former was always true and the latter very dependent on developmental age.

My good work on my clerkships hadn't gone unnoticed. Dr. Wallace sent me an email congratulating me on my ob-gyn grades, and Dr. Reed responded to my edited presentation with genuine excitement. ("This is awesome, Angie," he said. "I'm confident we'll get this funding.") From my very first anatomy lecture, medical school had felt like an uphill climb, but it seemed that I was finally strengthening my core.

I got a reservation. Only available time was 5:30 on Thursday — you think you can make that?

I glanced at my phone, smiling in spite of myself. After our disastrous study date with my sister, I'd expected Ricky to distance himself. Instead, he took the experience in stride, waving off my apologies with a chagrined smile. "She clearly would kill for you," he'd said. "I'd probably be the same, if I had an older sister." Then he'd moved on to excitedly sending me articles about a new Peruvian restaurant opening in Logan Square.

"You realize we haven't gone out on a real date yet," Ricky surmised. "You know, where we get dressed up and spend too much on cocktails."

Frederick and I had only ever done "real" dates. My singular ex-boyfriend had taken pride in taking me to restaurants with *atmosphere,* as he called it, places that felt opulent without all the pomp and circumstance. My wardrobe of evening clothes had expanded during the six short months of our courtship, and then rapidly contracted after our breakup; every dress I'd purchased to look good for Freddy had gone straight into a donation pile.

We're pre-call Thursday, so should be fine, I texted back, then immediately opened a window into an online retailer with a fast shipping time. Just as I was typing *bodycon midi* into the search bar, a text banner dropped from the top of my screen.

It was Nia.

Hey Angie, it said. I was hoping to stop by the apartment tonight. Can we please talk?

I froze in my chair, my grasp on my phone tight. Fifteen days. It had been fifteen days since Nia and I had last spoken, a fact that was confirmed by the time mark of our last exchange before this one. In that time, so much had changed that I almost felt like a different person. My past concerns, which had previously been focused on my rotations, my feelings about Ricky, and the direction of my research project, had since dissolved, but my feelings about her reaction to them had had time to fester. Because the longer I replayed our last conversation in my head, the more convinced I was that Nia hadn't been fair to me. We were supposed to be ride-or-die. Neither hell nor high water should ever have come between us, let alone something as asinine as a misunderstanding. And even though I

340

missed her, even though I still couldn't open the door to her empty room without feeling like I was about to be sick, I felt skittish. After all, even when we clashed, we understood each other. I knew Nia better than I knew myself, and our arguments were short-lived because we could see the other's point of view as clearly as we could our own. But every time I tried to parse what could have compelled Nia to abandon me, I came up empty. It felt as if Nia had taken a decade of trust and cracked it like a kola nut.

Still, I texted her back right away.

Okay, I said. I should be done by 5 today. I'll meet you there.

After ten hours of rounding, calling disgruntled consultants, and chasing after outside hospital records on the Harland wards, I turned onto my street to find Nia's car already parked in front of the apartment. The sight of it made my palms clammy.

"It's Nia," I reminded myself. "Your best friend, who you love, who loves you." I repeated this silently to myself as I trudged up the stairs of my walk-up. The more I said it, the truer it felt, and so I kept going. "Your sister from another mister. The sun of your stars. The moon of your life."

The sweet smell of chocolate hit my

nostrils before I was halfway up the stairs. As I got closer, I could hear Nia's voice, smooth and low, singing along to Lauryn Hill. In my mind's eye I could see her swirling around the kitchen, the apron she had left behind tied around her waist and flecks of batter on her cheek. It was a routine I was used to because I'd seen it once a week for years. It was home.

I closed my eyes, breathed in, and unlocked the door.

"Ange?" Nia cut the music off. She emerged from the kitchen looking exactly as I'd expected her to, with her hair piled into a messy bun on top of her head and her flouncy blue apron secured around her waist.

"Hey," I said cautiously.

Before I could mutter another word, Nia crossed the room and enveloped me in a tight embrace. Surprised, I stiffened, and she squeezed me tighter. On cue, my throat clenched with emotion. I'd imagined multiple iterations of our reunion, and most of them began with Nia and me awkwardly shuffling in front of each other and stumbling over our words like strangers. But here Nia was, holding me as if nothing had happened. As if the fifteen days of our separation had been but one.

After a long, quiet moment, she released me.

"Go sit," she said.

I obeyed, toeing off my shoes before dropping my backpack where I stood. Before my butt could hit the sofa, Nia pushed a mug of tea into my hands. I sniffed it.

"Earl Grey," I said.

"Your favorite," Nia said in a singsongy voice. She lifted her own mug to her lips. I stared at her for a long moment, still shocked to see her here, in the flesh, sitting on the couch we'd bought together. Somehow, I expected her to look different, but she was still the same Nia I had always known, down to the last freckle.

"You're a bit early," she confessed, giving me a shy smile. "I wasn't prepared for that. I can usually count on you to show up thirty minutes after you say you will."

"Yeah," I said lamely. Then: "I memorized all of your friends' names."

The second the words escaped, I wanted to snatch them back. My ears burned with mortification, and I opened my mouth to explain — but Nia had already thrown her head back in laughter.

"Girl, what?" she said when her cackles finally died. "You memorized their names?" Then, she straightened, pointing at me with her mug. "Okay then. Prove it."

I rattled off what I had learned during my study sessions with Ricky, interweaving my responses with my opinions about each member of the Lesbrigade's sense of style, comedic timing as observed during their performances at the improv show, and lastly, a rating of how deserving they were of my best friend's time, on a scale of one to ten. By the end, both Nia and I were doubled over with laughter, holding our mugs in viselike grips to keep from spilling hot tea down our fronts.

"You creep," Nia said when we had finally caught our breath. "Where did you even source all of this info?"

"Excuse me, they all have very stalkable Instagrams," I said. "And, well, Ricky helped."

"Oh yeah, Ricky. I heard about that," Nia said, nudging me with her knee. "I lost twenty bucks on that bet, by the way. I could have sworn you would hold out for at least another week."

In the last few minutes, we'd managed to fall back onto our age-old habits, but the reminder that Nia hadn't been around for the evolution of my relationship hit me like a splash of cold water.

"Yeah well," I said. "I guess we don't know

everything about each other."

Nia made a small, soft sound of complaint. Then she placed her mug on the coffee table and stood.

"Wait here," she said. I nodded, watching errant tea leaves swirl around in my mug as she sprang into the kitchen on light feet. From the other side of the wall, there was a clink of glass, the slam of cabinet doors being shut. When I looked up from my mug, Nia was standing in front of me, holding a white ceramic serving tray. On it were two squares of cake, each one three layers and covered with a shimmering mirror glaze. Atop them was a small spiral of spun sugar.

"Whoa," I said as she lowered the tray onto our coffee table. "Someone's been watching *The Great British Bake Off.*"

Nia laughed.

"You could say that," she said. She nudged a plate toward me. "Try it."

Holding her gaze, I used the teaspoon she provided to scoop a bite into my mouth. My eyes nearly rolled to the back of my head. The cake had all the richness of Nia's double chocolate fudge surprise without the heaviness, and there was a familiar floral taste to it that I couldn't quite put my finger on. It was divine.

"Will you make this every time we fight?"

I teased. I spooned a second bite into my mouth, then chased it with a sip of tea. The moment I did, Nia's alteration became obvious — she'd added *bergamot.* Genius. "Because, Jesus Christ, Nia, this is delicious. I mean, don't get me wrong, the double chocolate fudge surprise is good at baseline, but this is next level."

Nia looked down at her lap, smiling bashfully.

"Better be," she said. "Considering I'm getting professional training now."

I placed my mug down on the coffee table so firmly that I had to check to make sure I hadn't cracked the glass. Nia snorted, chagrined, as I composed myself.

"Professional training?" I sputtered.

"More of an informal apprenticeship," she qualified. Then she launched into a description of her new job, at a bakery called Le Menagerie, a small family-owned patisserie run by the matriarch, a seventy-two-year-old woman named Annette. A month ago, Nia had been scoping out the area around Shae's apartment in search of a place to mark papers when she had come across La Menagerie and struck up a conversation with Annette. They'd spent forty-five minutes discussing Annette's foolproof way of making a pâte à choux, and somehow that

346

conversation had turned into an invitation for Nia to join her in her kitchen.

"Her kids and grandkids don't really want to take over," Nia said, "so none of them have really tried to learn her craft. But Annette! She's a savant. She trained in France like fifty years ago, and so she's all about the details, you know. She makes me better. And she thinks I've got a good foundation." She looked up dreamily. "She asked if I would work for her, and I said yes in a heartbeat. I never thought I could be a pastry chef. I've looked into it before; you need six months of unpaid internships before you're allowed to do *anything*. I feel like I've found a cheat code or something. Even if she doesn't end up keeping me on for the long-term, I could start my own business! It's just . . . It's been a dream, honestly."

I could see it, then. I'd walked into this room with my shoulders tensed with worry, but Nia seemed light as a feather. This was not a Nia mired in regret, this was one who finally felt *free.* It was the same look I'd seen on her face when she watched Shae walk toward her at the improv show, the look that had made me put aside my grievances with Ricky.

"That's incredible, Nia," I said. "I'm really happy for you."

I meant it. I was so happy for her. For so long, Nia had seemed a bit lost. She'd graduated college with dual degrees in communications and education but no real plan. For the first three months after graduation, she contemplated applying to culinary school, but couldn't afford to take on any more student loans. After that, she worked at the front desk at an orthodontist's office, but the pay was abysmal and her boss was a creep, and she came home from work every day a deflated version of herself until I begged her to quit. Then, at a medical school party, one of my classmates mentioned a gig tutoring some rich high school kids in the south suburbs. The pay was twice what she had been getting at the office, the hours significantly better. Nia leapt at the opportunity but swore that it was temporary. *Until I open my catering business,* she would say, or *Until I get a real teaching job.* But *until* never happened, and over time, we simply stopped discussing whether it would.

Nia's smile wavered on her face.

"Angie," she said. "I'm sorry. I said all of that stuff, about you treating me like I didn't matter to you, because . . ." She swallowed, grabbing one of the throw pillows and squeezing it against her chest. "Honestly, the truth was that I was treating *myself* that way."

"No," I said, shaking my head. "You weren't totally off. It's okay. I know I was being self-absorbed —"

"Stop," Nia said, interrupting me. "I'm going first, Ange." When my smile faltered, she reached over and flicked my cheek. "Look, I'm not an idiot. I know that you and Michelle are going through the ringer this year. And it wasn't right of me to make you feel bad about telling me about your experiences. Or to quiz you about people you've never met to prove a point." She squeezed the pillow tight. "I still think about what you told me, about the kid in the trauma bay. And how messed up that was. The fact that you two are able to get up and go back to the hospital after seeing something like that is wild to me. And . . . I think it made me feel like my problems were small in comparison. Like, what does my quarter-life crisis matter when you're out there watching people *die*?"

"It's not the same," I said. "Your problems are *different*, Nia. Not less."

"I know that," Nia said. "And I know that if I'd said something, you would've told me as much." She gave me a small smile. "I think, because you aren't around as much, it was easy to fix a narrative on you. I felt *stuck,* and instead of figuring it out, I painted you in my head as selfish." She shook her head in disbelief. "Which is wild, because you've never been selfish. A bit melodramatic, maybe," she allowed, giggling when I gaped at her in faux outrage, "but not selfish. I created another version of you that sucked, and I got mad at it instead of just getting my shit together."

"But you did get your shit together," I said. "This is how it started, right? You've always loved baking. You've always loved talking to people. And now you'll get to do both! And you're so freaking talented that you practically got scouted for a job." I looked down at my hands; she'd gotten the job *before* our fight. Was the set of papers she'd been grading at our dining table on the day she told me she was moving out her last? How many times had she wanted to tell me about the big moves she was making in her life, only for me to interrupt her to talk about *the wards* or *the boy* instead?

"Is it my turn now?" I asked. When Nia nodded, I pressed on. "I'm sorry too. I completely neglected you. You shouldn't have to ask for me to *see you.* I should have done that on my own." I curled my fingers together. "I'm proud of you. But that's not

350

enough, right? I should have been present for you, and I wasn't. And so I'll try to do that, yeah? Just . . . please don't shut me out again."

The smile that Nia gave me was sheepish; her eyes turned down to her lap, pillow clutched to her stomach like a shield. It was so different from the Nia she usually presented to the world. When I first met Nia, I'd been struck by her confidence. She had found me sitting alone in our middle school cafeteria and slammed her tray next to mine.

"Hey, nerd," she'd said, as though we'd been friends for years. "Nice Inuyasha keychain."

With time, I'd come to recognize her confidence for what it was: a front. But it was a solid one, a brave face she could slip on as easily as a favorite shirt. She wore it most of the time, even for me. I was so used to it that I could easily forget that underneath it, Nia was just as afraid of the world as I was. Maybe that's why we needed each other so desperately.

Right now, Nia had stripped that front away, but I knew it would be back. It always came back. It was my job, as her best friend, to see through it. And, over the last few months, I had failed at that job. I'd known that Nia was struggling to define her direction in life, but I'd sidelined that, reassured by her jokes and easy smiles that she was okay. I would have to do better in the future.

I reached for her hand and squeezed.

"I missed you," I confessed. "Can we never fight again?"

"Only if I never wait to tell you that I'm moving out until I'm practically out the door," Nia offered with a shrug.

I shook my head, chuckling to myself.

"Yeah, well, I was too far up my ass to realize that you even wanted to." I blew over my tea. "So. How's living with Shae? By the way, I'm allowed to make a lesbian U-Haul joke about y'all, right? Because come *on.*"

Nia laughed.

"That part was all business, okay? Shae doesn't charge me rent. Plus, they live right across the street from the bakery, and now that my hours are going to be about as bad as yours, I didn't want to commute."

"Doesn't charge you rent, huh?" I said. That made sense; Nia didn't seem in much of a rush to find a subletter. "What a sweet deal."

"It is," Nia admitted. She smirked to herself. "You know what's funny about all of this?" When I swallowed expectantly, she continued. "I'm here right now because of Shae."

"Because of Shae?" I repeated.

Nia nodded.

"I don't know if Ricky's told you this," Nia said. "But the two of them have been thick as thieves since high school. It's actually nauseating; Shae always be on that phone texting him."

I hadn't noticed, though when I thought about it, Ricky did frequently put down his tablet pen to smirk at his laptop and type. Did that mean that all this time, he'd been cheating at our study game and sneaking in conversations with his bestie? All while tittering at me for being easily distractible? I filed that factoid away for future ribbing and nodded for Nia to keep going.

"But a few years back, when Ricky and She-Who-Must-Not-Be-Named got together, Ricky went ghost on Shae," Nia continued.

"I don't know this story," I said softly. I remembered how I'd felt watching Nia pack up her kitchen utensils, and hearing some of that pain reflected in Shae's voice — *I thought you said she was cool with it* —

"Well, he didn't want to," Nia said. "But you know how the guy is. Most of his friends are women. Camila didn't like that and gave him an ultimatum. Them versus her. Didn't even matter to her that Shae

353

isn't a woman; they got lumped right in." Nia tilted her head to one side, considering. "It sounds fucked that he would even consider it, right?"

"Yeah," I said, my fists curling in my lap. If a man I'd just met suggested I get rid of Markus, I would kick him to the curb so quick he'd get whiplash.

"Thing is, those two get each other. So Shae understands why he went along with it. They even let him drift for a while, but both of them were miserable the whole time. Eventually, though, Shae got fed up. Practically banged down Ricky's door." Nia chuckled, as if the memory were her own. "They talked, Ricky told his girl to back off, and the rest is history."

"That was brave of Shae," I said. Not like me. Paralyzed by a fear of being rejected for good, I hadn't even sent Nia a text, let alone showed up at her new place to demand an audience.

"They're a brave person," Nia said. She let the sentence steep for a long minute, then pushed a stubborn curl out of her eyes. "You know what they told me, after we finished moving me out?"

"What?" I asked.

"That finding someone to love you romantically is actually kind of easy," Nia said.

"There's a whole cocktail of brain chemicals at work telling you to obsess over this other person. Plus a rulebook for relationships we've all been given since infancy. Friendship doesn't have any of that, and so finding a person who will hold you down for no reason is rare. Shae has so many coworkers who have a partner but not a single close friend, and they're all desperately lonely because of it." On the next blink, Nia's eyes grew glassy with tears. "They told me that, if I was planning on ditching you, then I better be prepared to never get you back. And I would have to ask myself if whatever you'd done warranted that. And if it didn't, ask myself why I was willing to potentially torch what we had for no good reason."

If Shae had been here in person, I would have hugged them.

"I knew I liked them," I said.

"Shae is wonderful. They . . . really feel like they could be it for me, you know? They love me, and make me feel beautiful every day, and hold me accountable when I act out of pocket. I love them, and I'm loving living with them." Nia bit her lip. Her smile dimmed, and then fell away altogether. "But . . . I'm scared, too. It's been you and me for, like, ever. I'm not even sure I know who I am without you. And now, here I am, trying to find out, and almost losing you in the process."

I scooted closer to Nia, dropped my head onto her shoulder. For every summer vacation, every adventure, every trip, practically every class we could manage, it had been the Nia and Angie Show. Everyone else was supporting cast. Michelle had understood this early on and resented it. Would I be who I was without Nia? Without her kindness that day in our school cafeteria so many years ago?

"Remember when we used to say we'd get old together?" I said. "Buy a ranch? Rent out the space to some hot ranch hands when we started to crave a little romance?"

"Ah yes, cowgirls," Nia said wistfully.

"Never anything serious, though," I reminded her. "Flings only. All of our real love would be reserved for the dogs and each other."

"The dogs!" Nia laughed. "That's right. Ten dogs, all big, sweet, dumb mutts. All the dogs at the pound that no one wanted."

"We were going to give them big human names." I snorted. "Like Fitzgerald and Beatriz and Napoleon."

"Maybe we can still do that," Nia surmised. "All we have to do is convince Shae and Ricky to come along."

I could picture it in my head. An endless field, fat, grazing cows. Fences that needed mending, a bright red barn that we used for storage and, when the time was right, parties. All four of us sitting on rocking chairs on an expansive veranda, watching the sunset over the horizon.

"That," I said, nestling into the crook of my best friend's neck, "would be the dream."

TWENTY

"I'm not a diabetic," my favorite patient, a lively old woman who insisted on being called Miss Bernice, said to me for the third time today. Never mind the fact that she'd been admitted for a diabetic foot infection and had to have her foot guillotined off four days ago.* Never mind the metric fuck ton of insulin we were pumping into her just to keep her blood from turning into simple syrup. Never mind that she'd been injecting herself with substandard doses of that very same insulin at home for the last fifteen years.

"Okay," I said. "What do you mean by that?"

The first two times she'd made this declaration, I'd tried my best to assure her that she most certainly was a diabetic, only to be

* Go to your doctor and get your hemoglobin A1c checked, folks!

brushed off and told that I didn't "get it." This time, I'd clearly given a more satisfactory answer, because she gave me a toothy smile.

"I mean, I'm not a diabetic!" she repeated. "Diabetic is a mindset. It's a label! And I don't label myself. Labels aren't good for anything. All they do is limit you." She peered at me through narrowed eyes. "You look young. You married?"

I stiffened. She'd changed the subject so suddenly that I got whiplash, though the question wasn't unfamiliar. A number of little old ladies had already tutted over my decision to prioritize my career over a man. If they liked me, they'd offer up their okay-looking grandsons. If they didn't, they made some comment about how my youth would leave me soon, and what would I do without a family?

"Um . . . no?" I said.

To my surprise, Miss Bernice clapped her hands together.

"That's right, baby girl," Miss Bernice said. "You don't need to be nobody's wife! When the boys come around, you take what you want and move on, 'cause that's what they'll do to you!"

My eyes widened with amused shock for a

split second before I regained control of my face.

"Okay, Miss Bernice," I said. "Uhhh . . . Thanks for the advice?"

"Just looking out," Miss Bernice said. She flipped off her sheet, exposing her leg, now sans foot. "You wanted to take a look at this, right? Go ahead, Doc."

I smiled and took a look at Miss Bernice's surgical site. I'd long stopped trying to correct Miss Bernice when she called me Doc. When James and I first met her in the Emergency Department, her eyes had gone wide when he introduced me as a medical student.

"You training to be a nurse?" she'd asked.*

"A doctor," I said automatically, and her smile turned bright.

"A doctor!" she'd said, clapping her hands together. "Oooh, I'm proud of you, baby! You too, sweetie," she said off-handedly to James, who laughed, understanding. "But you! How long have you got left in school?" When I told her ("A year and a half, ma'am,") she scoffed. "That's no time! I'm calling you Doc now!"

* Obligatory "not that being mistaken for a nursing student is inherently bad, but it is gendered, and I am not training to be a nurse."

360

I walked out of Miss Bernice's room with a smile on my face, as I always did, and made for the workroom. I had only an hour and a half left until my dinner date with Ricky. My quick post-op wound check with Miss Bernice had taken ten minutes longer than I had expected, given her line of questioning, but now I had finally finished off my checklist.

To my surprise, when I returned to my apartment, Nia was there, lounging on the sofa. Since our conversation a few days ago, she had been making a concerted effort to be present when and however possible. With her grueling new bakery schedule, I knew that frequent visits weren't sustainable, but I appreciated them regardless. But at least I had her today to witness my transformation.

Ricky was always brazen in his appreciation of me. All I had to do was stand up from my chair and stretch to get an approving *Mm!* from him, or a half-lidded, lascivious stare. I caught him looking even when the Ass was clearly out of view, sneaking glances at me from over his laptop. When I was feeling a little saucy, I added some sashay to my step when I walked past him just to watch him gawk.

And so today, with twenty minutes left on

the clock, I was going to preen and primp like nothing he'd ever seen. The falsies were coming out, the foundation, the uncomfortable but dazzlingly effective push-up bra. I was not, as one might say, *fucking around.* If I did this right, my halfhearted vow of chastity didn't have a chance of making it through the night.

"Damn, girl, you trying to get pregnant?" Nia asked when I stepped out of my bedroom in my new dress.

I spun around to show off all the angles.

"No," I said smugly. "Just reminding Ricky exactly who he's taking out tonight." I paused, patting my stomach affectionately. "At least until we eat. This dress is not going to be very forgiving."

Nia laughed.

"Where'd you get it? It's definitely a freakum* dress, but classy. I need me one of those."

I sent Nia the link to the dress, then solicited her opinion on which of my four

---

* You know the one. The "Lawd Have Mercy" dress. The dress you avoid wearing anywhere you think you'll be eating a meal, because you *are* the meal, and also because you'll need to suck in your tum. The "I'm about to steal your man" dress. To quote Queen Bey, "every woman got one."

pairs of heels I should wear. She showed me a picture of the new pair she'd just purchased (purportedly the "comfiest stilettos in the world") and, when I expressed my skepticism, opened a YouTube video review. We watched it, pausing every few seconds to say, "Oh my god, shoes," then pulled up the classic 2006 "Shoes" video to round it out. It felt like Nia and I had reverted right back to our old patterns, but better now, because her happiness was genuine.

Of course I was late after all that. Five minutes before I was meant to leave, Nia and I were still draped across the couch and laughing, and I hadn't even put on eyeliner.

"Hurry!" Nia shouted after me when I rushed into my room to finish up.

La Ventana was packed when I showed up, eighteen minutes into our reservation. They had definitely gone for an Instagram aesthetic, with clean, white tile walls and woven baskets of ivy hanging from the ceilings. The wall across from the bar was painted with a large relief of Machu Picchu as viewed through an open window.

"What's the reservation under?" The hostess, a pretty, willowy woman wearing dark red lipstick, asked.

"Probably Ricky? Gutiérrez?" I asked, my

eyes darting across the room in search of him. The woman nodded in recognition and made for the bar. I trailed after her, my steps measured in my heels.

"We don't seat until the whole party is here," the hostess explained. "I could've sworn he was right there . . ."

It was no wonder she was having trouble locating my date. The woman leaning over Ricky had big, blond Texas hair, and from behind she obstructed our view of him entirely. Once he came into view, though, I wished I could turn back and run. Even with the Beauty Pageant Washout practically shoving her chest into his face, Ricky looked *comfortable.* He swirled his glass languorously, looking genuinely engrossed in their conversation, nodding along to her boring-ass story about waiting too long in the line for the Willis Tower. Suddenly, the effort I'd put into my little getup felt cheap.

"Mr. Gutiérrez?" our hostess, bless her, said. Ricky glanced up and gave us a sunny smile, his eyes darting to me and reflexively flicking up and down my body.

"Angie," he said, sounding a bit breathless. "Wow, you look . . ."

"Well, I'd best let you go, then," the big-haired woman said, giving me a look that was everything but appreciative. She was older than I had assumed from first glance, but clearly *maintained,* her eyebrows arched in that slightly villainous way that could be achieved only with regular Botox. A recent divorcée, or maybe a bored trophy wife, looking for a hot, ethnic young thang to show around her boudoir?

Pamela Anderson's Uglier Stunt Double turned back to Ricky.

"Thanks for keepin' me company, Ricardo," she said.

"Sure thing, Polly," Ricky said. "Have a good time in Chicago."

Calm down, I thought, trying not to jump away from the hand Ricky placed at the small of my back. *They were just chatting. It's normal to talk to strangers at bars; that is half of why bars exist. And sometimes in those conversations, you even exchange names. Seriously, who brings a child into the world and names them* Polly —

"You ubered here, right?" Ricky said after we had been seated and handed our menus. "Their cocktails are really good. You should have one."

I looked up at Ricky as he flipped through the overpriced drink menu. I wasn't dumb. I knew what Ricky looked like. Most hot-blooded heterosexual women would probably find him very pleasing to look at, and look they did, all the time. I was okay with that; as Ricky was already aware, I got hit on in public too. But if it had been me sitting at the bar, waiting for him to show up, I wouldn't have entertained any company, especially not company that looked like it was five seconds away from launching its tongue down my throat.

But then again, it was like Tabatha had said. Ricky wasn't my boyfriend. Sure, we were enjoying each other's company, but he had no obligation to turn down external interest if and when it came. If Polly from Out of Town decided she wanted to have some of Ricky's Tapatío with her papas, he had no reason to decline.

"Everything okay?" Ricky asked. He placed the menu down firmly on the table. "You're quiet."

I smiled, knowing it wouldn't reach my eyes.

"I'm fine," I lied.

Badly, apparently. Ricky's eyebrows knitted together with concern.

"Bad day at work?" he asked in hushed tones.

I thought of Bernice whipping her sheets off to reveal her stump like a magician unveiling their vanished assistant and smirked to myself.

"No," I said. "It was good, actually." I made a show of going over the drink menu. "I'll just get a red wine."

Ricky looked aghast.

"Babe, come on," he said. "All of these great cocktails, and you go for the wine?"

"I'm not your 'babe,' " I muttered reflexively.

The moment the words were out of my mouth, I wished I could snatch them back. Ricky recoiled, his smile sliding clean off his face. Crap. Was it possible for me to just be cool for *one day* in my life?

"But fine, I can try the Chilcano then," I said hurriedly. Then I took a deep breath, placed my hands on the table. "So . . . how was your day?"

"Great," Ricky said, not taking the bait. He opened his mouth to say something else, then, deciding against it, snapped it shut.

We spent the next few minutes in silence, our heads bowed stubbornly toward our menus. I hated the sudden awkwardness between us. It had never existed before, and now I was sorry I had caused it.

"I think the lomo saltado looks good," I tried.

"Yeah, I was looking at that too," Ricky said wearily. He didn't look up from his menu.

"We should get different things, though, so that we can try each other's dishes," I said. "That's how me and Michelle always do it, anyway —"

"Good thing I'm not Michelle," Ricky interrupted, and I looked up, taken aback by his snippiness. I had seen Ricky hurt, defeated, nervous . . . but never angry. I hardly recognized the emotion on him; it didn't suit him. It turned his normally emotive face placid, ironed the ever-present creases at the corners of his eyes and mouth smooth. I frowned, taking a sip of my water. My ice clinked loudly against the glass as I set it down, desperately loud against the silence.

As if I'd summoned him, a short man dressed in all black swept up to our table. I never thought I could be so happy to see our waiter.

"Will you be having any drinks tonight?" he asked. He went over the day's specials, and I paid rapt attention, asking way too many questions about dishes I knew I had no intention of ordering, all to avoid looking toward the glacial being sitting across from me. When our waiter was done with his spiel, I pretended to consider before putting in the order I'd decided on already.

"Nothing for me," Ricky said.

"Really?" I said. "You were just talking about the pisco sour . . ."

"I'm ready to put in my food order, though." He gestured to me, his face carefully blank. "The lady?"

I understood then what was happening. Ricky was trying to cut our date short. I had made a small, *true* comment, and he was reacting by throwing a silent tantrum.

"I think I need a little extra time," I said, giving the waiter my most saccharine smile.

"Extra time. Seems like you need a lot of that," Ricky said. He took a sip of his water, his lips quirking up into an approximation of a smile as his eyes flickered up to hold mine. "You know. Since you're always late."

Sensing tension and wanting no part of it, our waiter chuckled nervously.

"Okay," he said. "I'll come back in a few minutes."

When he scuttled out of earshot, I folded my arms. Ricky did the same. We glared at each other from across the table for a full minute, listening to the din of clinking glasses and spirited conversation.

"Why are you being a jerk all of a sudden?" I snapped, breaking our silence.

"*I'm* being a jerk?" Ricky said with a scoff. "You show up twenty minutes late to dinner, acting salty from the second you walk in, and then you pick a fight and act like *I'm* the asshole for not letting you get away with it."

Oh, this little . . .

"Letting me get away with *what?*" I spoke through my teeth, trying and nearly failing to keep my voice down. "I'm sorry I was late. But you looked like you got yourself some attention from elsewhere in that time, so, honestly, I don't feel that bad."

Ricky looked flummoxed. I watched as the puzzle pieces connected in his mind, and then he shook his head vigorously.

"Polly?" he said. "You're jealous of Polly?" He let out a huff of incredulous laughter. "She's old enough to be my mother!"

"So? She's still hot," I admitted begrudgingly. *And she still looked at me like I didn't matter.*

Our waiter swept by our table, placing a plate of ceviche at the center.

"Courtesy of Ms. Pollyanne Wagner," he said. I met Ricky's shocked eyes over his arm, my eyebrows raised as if to say *I told you so.* When the waiter swept away, he dropped his head onto his hands in shock. Then his shoulders began to shake.

Whatever ire I'd felt before deflated at the sight of him like this, laughing over a small bowl of seduction ceviche, dabbing at his eyes with the corner of his cloth napkin. There was no way he was this clueless. Ricky had such aggressive hot-guy energy.* His ain't-shitness was staggering. Had he really thought that Polly Pocket hadn't been trying to get into his pants?

"This is hilarious," Ricky said. He pushed the plate toward me. "Here," he said. "You take the first bite."

"Um, what if it's drugged?" I said.

Ricky let out a bark of laughter.

"Are you accusing the kitchen of participating in the drugging of their customers?" Then he leaned forward conspiratorially. "Come on. Polly's probably watching. Let's give her a show."

I raised an eyebrow, scooping a spoonful of ceviche into my mouth. Delicious. I hummed around the spoon, closing my eyes as the fresh ocean flavor hit my palate. Maybe this restaurant was actually worth the hype.

"What kind of show?" I asked coquettishly. I pulled the spoon slowly out of my mouth, lavishing it with a languorous lap of

* You know. The quiet, unselfconscious confidence that comes with knowing that you are pleasant to look at and will be allowed to get away with everything short of murder. BDE-lite.

my tongue as I did. Ricky swallowed, and I grinned, amazed at how quickly we had managed to shift the mood.

"That's . . . pretty good," he said, not lifting his eyes from my mouth. When I reached for more, he grasped my wrist and guided the bite of ceviche to his lips, closing them over the spoon. Suddenly, the room narrowed to just the two of us, to Ricky's hand closed around my wrist, his eyes holding mine in a challenge. His grip was strong, like it had been when he'd wrestled my hand away under the cover of our blanket fort. Unbidden, I imagined that hand elsewhere, clasped *just so* around the base of my neck, not quite squeezing, but firm —

"Your drink, ma'am," our waiter said, placing my cocktail gingerly on the table under my still-outstretched arm. "Are you ready to order?"

I jerked backward, leaving the ceviche spoon hanging in Ricky's mouth. Jesus Christ, I thought. Maybe we should get this meal to go. Still, I put in my order, biting back a triumphant grin when Ricky ordered a different entrée.

Thankfully, the rest of dinner went as prescribed. We swapped bites off each other's plates, and I pouted when I discovered that Ricky had made the better choice.

Our first round of drinks became two, which eventually became two and a half when we decided to split a final cocktail. And as the night progressed, I thought of date nights that stretched far into the future, of Ricky's eyes crinkling with crow's-feet as he smiled, of my wrinkled hands offering him forkfuls from my plate. I imagined growing old and arguing about if we *really needed more tomatoes* in grocery store parking lots, Ricky patting me on the bum as I walked in front of him the way my dad sometimes did to my mom. And as the images flickered through my mind, I felt an awful sinking sensation, as hopeless as a cannonball in an ocean. I'd thought there would be an end to the depth of my feelings for Ricky, but somehow every time I saw him, I fell exponentially harder. Tabatha had been wrong. I didn't need to sleep with Ricky to get too far gone; I was already there.

"We overdid it," I declared as he walked and I hobbled out of La Ventana two hours later. The alcohol settled like a thick blanket over my shoulders but turned somersaults in my stomach, and I felt simultaneously pleasantly buzzed and a touch queasy. Chuckling, Ricky reached for my hand and brought it to his lips.

"I think we did just enough," he said. He

grinned dopily, his right dimple popping into view. I resisted the urge to poke it. "You wear this dress just to torture me?"

I laughed, feeling light as a feather, feeling like I could own the world.

"Perhaps," I said coyly. "Is it working?"

Ricky's grin grew wicked.

"I don't know," he said. "Maybe I can walk behind you and find out."

Giggling, I obliged, twirling my hand out of his and falling into my best strut. I could feel Ricky's eyes course over my figure salaciously, and I pondered how a look like that from any other man in the world would have made me run away. From Ricky, though? He could spend the next hour undressing me with his eyes, and I would relish every second. I looked over my shoulder to watch him watch me, waiting for his eyes to tick up from wherever they were now most occupied to meet mine.

A mischievous look crossed Ricky's face, and then he was stepping around me to cut me off, crowding me backward until my back scratched against brick.

"Okay, yeah," he said, pressing into me until my body was crushed between his and the wall. "I would say it's pretty effective." He chuckled, leaning into me. "God. I don't ever act right with you, do I?"

"Ha," I said, watching our chests heave in unison. Our eyes met in a challenge, and in the next second his mouth was slanted over mine, kissing me with an immediacy that left me sagging against him. All at once, my mind went blank except for a euphoric happiness and a sudden, pressing urge to take him home to *finish this*. God, he was hot. I wanted him to touch me everywhere, wanted the hands that were clutching my hips to delve higher and lower and everywhere in between. And afterward, I wanted to sit at my dining room table with him and eat the pancakes that we'd made together and talk about his most recent annoying client and trade funny patient stories and —

"Ricky," I said breathlessly when he pulled away. "What are we doing? Am I your girlfriend?"

The haze of lust whipped away like a curtain being yanked open. This close, I could see Ricky's eyes flood with panic, his body still blocking the light from the street around me. It was the same look he'd given me on the day we met, except this time he was so much more to me than a quirky, handsome stranger.

"Oh," he said, suddenly at a loss. He rolled his lips into his mouth, and then took a step back.

Shit. This had not been part of the plan. I'd asked mostly as a technicality, as a way to soothe my own insecurities. Ricky was supposed to laugh and say, "Of course, Angie, duh," and tease me for thinking I was anything but. Right now, I was supposed to feel validated, then a little sheepish that I'd sought validation in the first place. We were supposed to wander around the city until it was unreasonably late, maybe stop at a bar just to stretch the night out even longer, and at the end he was supposed to ask if I *wanted to come over.* I was supposed to say yes, but only after some gentle cajoling, and when we got to his place let him get a peek at the matching underwear I'd specifically picked out for tonight —

But clearly, I was an idiot. How much of what we had was in my imagination? Here I was, tossing around the concept of *being in love* with him, and Ricky wasn't even sure if I was deserving of a label that didn't require that.

"Say something," I demanded, feeling like I was about to break.

Ricky ducked his head, and the queasiness I'd felt before became outright nausea.

"I . . . ," he said. "I don't know."

I should have known. How many times did I have to get hurt before I would finally learn? True love, the kind that Ricky's grandparents had for each other, that my dad had for my mom, that Tabatha had for Chris — wasn't in my cards. I was the Angela Appiah Experience, a nice ride, a fun time. The girl who taught you something about yourself, who you looked back on fondly while you cuddled up with the woman you decided to actually love in the end.

I stepped back onto the sidewalk. I couldn't look at Ricky, so I stared past him, watching a group of laughing twenty-somethings exit a restaurant across the street.

"I think I should go," I said. I reached into my purse for my phone.

"Wait," Ricky said, placing a hand on my arm to stop me. "No. Don't run off. Let's talk about this, yeah?"

I shrugged his hand off. The tears I had successfully bit back stung my eyes.

"There's nothing to talk about," I said, punching my address into the rideshare app. "I hear you loud and clear. You're not ready to be my boyfriend, or whatever. Fine. I don't plan on sticking around to change your mind."

Ricky staggered back like he'd been slapped.

"What do you mean, you don't plan on sticking around?" he said. "Are you trying to dump me?"

"How can I dump you if we're not together?" I asked, amazed. "We've been doing this . . . *thing* for months, Ricky. I introduced you to my *sister.*" I closed my eyes. *Be careful,* Tabatha had said. Wise beyond her years, that one. "None of this has been casual for me. And if it is for you, then there's no point keeping up this charade, is there?"

"None of this has been casual for me either, Angie, and you know that," Ricky said seriously. He shoved his hands into his pockets, staring out onto the street. "I really like you. I just . . . I was someone's boyfriend for three years. I don't know if I'm ready to be that again just yet."

The breeze blew by, cooler than I expected, and I shuddered. It was already late September. To think that Ricky had occupied a space in my mind for an entire season.

"You can't do relationship shit with me and then tell me you're not ready for a relationship. If you aren't ready now . . ." I swallowed, thinking about how, for someone else, for *everyone else,* he had been ready. And how for me, this meant he would never be. "I'm sure about you," I choked, surprised by how hard it was to admit that out loud. "It really sucks that you don't feel the same about me."

"That isn't fair, Angie," Ricky said, his voice low. "It's just too early for me to be sure. That doesn't change how I feel about you." He pushed his hand through his hair, looking away from me. "It just means I need a little more time."

Time. I thought about Nia, and how she and Shae had jumped in headfirst within weeks of meeting. Of Michelle, who could get a man to practically pledge fealty to her after a day. And then of Ricky, of how countless hours of laughter and discussion and kisses and what had felt like deep, true regard had still come up short.

"You can't just put me on indefinite layaway, Ricky," I said simply. "I don't have time to give."

Ricky didn't say anything, and so I let myself look at him. It felt like this might be my last chance, and so I tried to catalog the parts of him I would miss the most. His strong jaw, locked tight with tension. His hands, curling and stretching at his sides. His smooth, nearly hairless golden skin.

The Ford Focus I had requested pulled up in front of us. The driver rolled down her window.

"Angela?" she asked.

"Yup," I said, taking a step toward the car. I opened the door, preparing to step in.

Ricky grabbed the handle, stopping me from closing it.

"Wait. *Wait.* We're talking about this," he said definitively. "This isn't over, okay, Angie?"

Talk about what? I thought. His initial reaction had been enough; even if Ricky changed his mind tomorrow and told me that actually, he did want to commit, I wouldn't believe him. *You're just saying this because you don't want to lose me, not because you actually want it,* I would think, and that would make me feel even more pathetic than I already did.

"Promise me, Angie," he said beseechingly. "I'm going to call you tomorrow. Promise me that you'll pick up."

My driver sank deeper into her seat with impatience, and I finally let myself look Ricky in the eye again. I'd never seen him look like this, like he was about to fall apart. Panic stretched his voice thin, and his grip on the car door was tight, pulling his skin taut over his knuckles. Maybe at another time, I would have thought that his reaction meant something. Now . . . I wasn't so sure.

I'd thought I could read him. *Look at how he looks at you,* I had thought, so sure that he was the one instead of one of many.

"Okay," I said, and after that, he let me go.

TWENTY-ONE

But Ricky didn't call the next day, or the day after that, or the one after that.

"You okay, boo?" Nia asked, handing me my third cup of Earl Grey of the night. I accepted it with a bleary smile. Even though I was the one who'd just gotten my heart thrashed, I felt sorry for Nia. After all, she was deeply in love with the best friend of its thrasher, and the conflict of interest was probably maddening.

"I have to be," I said, gesturing toward my laptop screen. Dr. Reed had sent me a last-minute batch of edits for our presentation. My team was on call tomorrow, meaning that I wouldn't have the time to implement his changes and rehearse them then; everything had to be squared away today. "I'm too busy to wallow." I gave Nia a small smile. "Thanks for keeping me company, by the way. You really don't have to. You have an early day tomorrow."

"Don't thank me," Nia said. "I still re-member how you took care of me after Ulo."

I laughed, remembering my many late-night trips to the grocery store to grab extra Oreos to help abate Nia's post-breakup suf-fering.

"I'll be fine," I told her. "Go home."

And I would be fine. For the first time since we'd met, I finally knew where Ricky and I stood. I brought up commitment, and he fled the scene. There was no reason to feel conflicted about us anymore. No need to question his intentions or let myself be reassured by how *good of a guy* he was. Like with my internal medicine practice ques-tions, I had gotten Ricky wrong so many times that the right answer now seemed obvious.

Operation Deep Clean went into effect immediately after forty-eight hours of Ricky-related radio silence. I wasn't going to allow myself to sink into a funk of self-inflicted misery by scrolling through his In-stagram or rereading our texts. No. I was going to be proactive against Future Angie, who would doubtlessly want to do those things. I unfollowed him on social media, deleted his number, and set up a study and social schedule so airtight that there would be minimal room for my mind to wander.

Because I was done. And I didn't plan on turning back.

Still, when the day of my presentation came and I didn't get a text from an unfamiliar number wishing me good luck, I had to swallow my disappointment.

"Nice blazer," Tabatha said, peering at me through her camera. She'd stayed up late the night before to give me some last-minute pointers, which included helping me choose an appropriate presentation outfit. When I selected a flaring midi dress, she kissed her teeth. "You don't have to hide those curves to look professional," she insisted, eventually guiding me to a knee-length pencil skirt and a chunky necklace I'd purchased long ago and never worn.

"Thanks," I said. "For everything." These days, I felt like Tabatha had overtaken me in my sisterly duties. Was she really the same brat who used to cry when I got presents on my birthday because she felt left out?

"It's nothing," she said. "Besides, don't thank me yet. You're going to be returning the favor three times over once I get deep into wedding planning." Then her face became serious. "Also. Momma says good luck. And she wanted me to tell you" — she looked left and right, then leaned into the camera like she was sharing a secret — "that

384

she's proud of you."

"Wow," I said. "Proud of me? No way." Had I humbled the great Dorothy Appiah?

"I *know*!" Tabatha said, rolling her eyes. "I almost asked her if she'd hit her head. Anyway, I just wanted to pass that along. Go out there and crush it!"

I pushed open the heavy wooden doors to the conference room where Dr. Reed and I would be presenting our proposal to members of the Beenhouwer Association, named after a physician who had spearheaded qualitative research in medicine in the seventies. The room was unexpectedly small, outfitted with only ten or so seats, and identical to the conference rooms where my teams usually did table rounds.* The room's sole occupant, a round-faced middle-aged woman with chunky blond highlights, looked up from her stack of papers upon my entry.

"Dr. Harrison, Dr. Petrucci, and Dr. Philips should be here shortly," she informed me. Then she gave me a small smile. "Angela, right?"

I smiled back.

* During table rounds, instead of going door to door and seeing the patients as a team, you go over their cases comfortably seated.

"You must be Cynthia," I said. Cynthia had been fielding my formatting questions for the better part of the month, addressing my anxious requests with unmatched patience. I had sent her about five different versions of my final PowerPoint, the subject line of each email some iteration of Appiah Final Version, Promise. "Thank you so much for putting up with me."

"It's no problem," Cynthia assured me. She directed me to the podium at the front of the room, turning on the projector and showing me how to use the pointer.

Over the next several minutes, my judges filed into the room one by one. They seemed relaxed, their white coats either hanging off their arms or nowhere in sight. I opened my mouth to introduce myself, but then, thinking better of it, tucked my lips shut and checked my phone for the time. Just two minutes until showtime, and Dr. Reed was nowhere to be found. Nervous, I glanced up at the screen, where my title slide was projected. After Tabatha critiqued it in the private study room, Ricky had gone out of his way to edit the theme. He'd emailed the revised version to me in the middle of the day on a Tuesday, and when I taunted him about not working on the projects that actually paid his bills, he'd texted back, earnestly, that he'd deemed this more important. I had some downtime today, he said. I wanted to make sure you got it in time. At the time, his conscientiousness had left me simpering; now, it all seemed like part of a pretense. *You asked him if you could be his girlfriend,* I reminded myself, *and in response, he dropped off the face of the Earth.*

Still, our summer fling had been good for something — my presentation looked slick and professional. Even Tabs admitted that it looked like something a consultant would whip up, not a stodgy medical student like me.

Just as the clock hit eleven, Dr. Reed stumbled into the room . . . accompanied by Dr. Wallace.

I froze in place, watching as my mentor rounded the table and took a seat next to Dr. Reed. She gave me a small smile and bobbed her head in greeting. I hadn't met with her in person since before my internal medicine rotation, and I'd most certainly not kept her abreast of this project. Had Dr. Reed looped her in?

"Afternoon, Trish," one of the judges said to Dr. Wallace. "Long time no see. What brings you to the east wing?"

"My mentee is presenting today," she said, nodding toward me. I fiddled with my remote, flooded with warmth.

"We ready to get started?" Dr. Reed asked the room.

"We were just waiting on you," one of the other doctors said, grinning. He clicked open a pen, then gave me an encouraging smile. "Whenever you're ready, Angela."

I cleared my throat. Three months of clerkships had gotten me accustomed to having the undivided attention of frighteningly intelligent audiences, but this time thousands of dollars were on the line. But my judges were relaxed, and Dr. Reed was throwing me a thumbs-up, so I stood, cleared my throat, and began.

"That Black patients in America are more likely to experience significant delays in care is well established in the current literature —"

"You did great," Dr. Reed said when it was all over.

I nodded, still buzzing with nerves. After I finished my proposal, I'd been drilled with questions about our research design, and though I answered them as best I could, every time one of the Beenhouwer representatives lifted a hand to ask me another, my heart took off at a gallop. Still, I'd made it through with most of my dignity intact.

Dr. Wallace tapped Dr. Reed on the shoulder, and he quickly stepped aside to let her join our conversation.

"That was very well done, Angela," she said. "These guys hardly ever see medical students doing the presentations themselves. If you can show that you can secure internal funding so early in your career, it'll look very attractive on your CV." Then her expression softened. "But never mind about that. Even if you don't get funded, you've done an excellent job, and during a busy year, no less."

"I'm not sure how you're doing it, honestly. This was an ambitious undertaking," Dr. Reed added. Then, to Dr. Wallace: "Angie's very reliable, you know. Keeps me on my toes."

"I'm aware." Then, she squeezed my arm. "I'm heading over to clinic. Email me the final verdict, Angela?"

"Of course," I said, stunned. It still felt strange to see her here in the faraway conference room and not behind her messy antique desk. For a woman of such presence, she was shockingly small, barely five foot two. As I watched her leave the room, I thought about how *lucky* I was. Despite her packed schedule, Dr. Wallace saw me as her protégé. She believed in me. I hadn't been angry with her in some time, but the last vestiges of my bitterness fizzled away once she'd crossed the threshold of the room.

Dr. Reed gave me an encouraging pat on the shoulder.

"We should be hearing back soon," he said, pleased. "Do you have to get back to the wards?"

"Yes," I said. No rest for the wicked, and especially not for third-year medical students.

"Well," Dr. Reed said, "take it easy tonight. Don't study. I know you don't like to take breaks, but you should."

"I'll try," I said, touched.

But the truth was that I couldn't "take it easy." Nia needed to be home with Shae, and Michelle was switching to Neuro ICU in the morning and would have to be up early. I would have to spend the night alone, and now, with one less task on my checklist, I had a lot more vacant brain space for me to fill with nonsense about a boy.

I walked back and found the workroom empty; James and his intern had headed down to the hospital to restock on caffeine. I sat down at my computer, leaning back in my stiff office chair until it creaked in protest. My phone felt heavy in my white coat pocket. My vision of this moment had involved calling Ricky right about now. He would have fretted over whether the theme he'd given me had worked on the outdated hospital computers,* asked how the judges had received my ideas. I could imagine his praise — "I knew you could do it, Angie, you're a badass" — and the beaming pride I'd feel afterward. We'd made loose plans to celebrate, decided on where we would pick up takeout. We were going to watch a terrible movie that we both knew would end up serving as a cover for us to hook up on the couch, and it was going to be a wonderful night.

Or at least it would have been, for a woman he could call his girlfriend. For me, who existed somewhere in between, it would only be another confusing memory to fuel an imminent, calamitous heartbreak.

Not a single text, I reminded myself, then ground my teeth and got to work finishing my notes and updating my sign-outs. *Not a call. Not a messenger pigeon, or a bat signal, or anything showing that he ever actually gave a shit about you.*

I finished off my notes and updated my sign-outs, then sent James a text asking if

* Some of which are still running Windows Vista. As Auntie Abena would say, "dees-gost-ing."

he had any other tasks I had to complete. Then I opened up a browser, googling *Chicago Museum Hours*. There was no reason for me to wallow, not when I still had myself. *This is me becoming an adult,* I thought. *Learning to enjoy my own company. Taking myself out for my own damn dates.*

That was how I ended up at the Art Institute.

In the three years since I'd moved to Chicago, I had made plan after plan to go, only for them to fall through at the last minute. It had never occurred to me before today that I didn't have to wait for anyone to make the trip, because someone had always been there. But today, there was only me. And that was okay, because I was excellent company.

I walked up the stairs to the museum, past the looming, oxidized lion statues, through the throng of ambling, slack-jawed tourists. It was a weekday and just past three in the afternoon, and so the crowds in the downtown streets didn't translate into the museum itself. I flashed my student ID for my discounted entrance fee, then added on an audio tour just for fun. Normally, when I went to museums, I had to move faster than I liked to not bore my companions, but today I took my time, stopping at every piece, reading every caption. A rich, deep voice sounded through my rented headphones, informing me about the artist's life, their influences, the historical context of their work. I stood in awe in front of *A Sunday on La Grande Jatte,* imagining a young Seurat poised in front of the enormous canvas, dipping only the very tip of his brush in his oils. I snickered at the thought of Henri de Toulouse-Lautrec hanging out in brothels for "professional purposes," pausing my tour to look up more about his escapades. I ogled Van Goghs that I had seen only in textbooks and leaned in as close as I was allowed to examine the textures of the brush strokes in Monet's haystacks. I took selfies mimicking the expressions of the subjects in classical paintings and sent them to the Sanity Circle group chat.

When I returned to my apartment, I turned my music up to drown out the silence. The song I chose, for once, wasn't a sappy ballad about heartbreak, but a bouncy afrobeats track that I couldn't help but dance to. I blasted it as I looped one of Nia's aprons over my head, singing along to myself as I prepared dinner just for me. I poured myself a generous glass of a red blend that I sipped with my meal, and another that I toted into the living room for a long night of bingeing *The Great British Bake Off.* I lit a massive vanilla-scented candle, dropped onto my sectional, and let myself sink into the cushions. After a couple of episodes, a fuzzy feeling of contentment washed over me. If I were a cat, I would have been purring.

It was funny, how afraid I'd always been of being alone. I'd clearly been missing out; being alone was *lit.*

Just when I'd started to get comfortable, my front gate intercom buzzed. I jolted, nearly spilling my wine on my rug, and steadied myself. My downstairs neighbor had a bad habit of leaving without his keys and then getting upset when we didn't let him back up immediately. Nia used to curse him out through the intercom before opening the gate for him; I guess that was my job now. I sighed, then hit the speaker button.

"Hello?" I asked. "Tom, you can't keep doing this —"

"Hey." A voice I had not expected echoed through the intercom. My blood ran cold, wrenching me out of my cozy, wine-induced stupor. "Um . . . this isn't Tom."

Of course it wasn't, but I wished, more than anything, that it had been. Tom,

394

bumbling, stoner asshole that he was, I knew how to handle.

Ricky, on the other hand?

"I know this is out of the blue," he said. He paused, sheepish. "But . . . can I come up?"

TWENTY-TWO

When I was twenty-one years old, I fell in love with a boy named Sean.

It was not love at first sight. I did not look across the room and see a body that my body knew it was attracted to before my mind could catch up. Nor did I sense the weight of eyes trailing me across the room, because we were at Frank Guo's semi-annual house party and I was too busy trying to make sure Michelle didn't sneak another cup of Jungle Juice. And sure, Sean was cute, but he was cute in a way that I had taught myself to ignore: tall, athletic, with the square jawline and squinted eyes of a future politician. My gaze glossed over him without pause as I surveyed the party, and weeks later, as I lay on my back in bed tracing the path of fading sunlight on my ceiling and wondering how it was possible to feel like someone had wrenched me in two, I would think, "All of this could have been avoided if he'd just left me alone."

But Sean hadn't left me alone. Halfway through the party, Markus sidled up beside me with a shit-eating grin on his face.

"Guess what just happened?" he said, nudging me in the side like the annoying little brother I'd never wanted.

"What," I said.

"Dude over there just asked me if you and I were dating," he said. His eyes darted in Sean's direction and I followed them across the room until I landed on him, chatting it up with our host over the punch. "I think he's gonna try to shoot his shot."

And shoot his shot he did, quite literally, in a clean swoop into Michelle's Solo cup. An hour after Markus's warning and fifteen minutes into a pathetic game of beer pong (Michelle and Nia versus me and a distracted Markus), Sean walked over to our table and plucked the sticky Ping-Pong ball out of my hands.

"No offense," he said with a crooked smile, "but it was getting painful watching you miss."

"Offense taken," I said, assessing him. By that time, I'd had plenty of experience with boys like Sean. Many a corn-fed, all-American white boy had draped his arm over my shoulders to drunkenly declare that

I was *just so pretty for a Black girl,** chalking up their attraction to me to exceptionalism on my part rather than the fact that hotness doesn't come in hues. Some part of them would be sure that I would be honored by the compliment, even more so by the attention, and be put out that I wasn't all that impressed by their interest.

I wasn't all that impressed by Sean's pong skills either, which were admittedly excellent, but there was something about the clear-eyed intentionality of his pursuit that made my heart stammer. Besides, he was actually cute, not just white-with-a-discernible-jawline cute, so when I managed to get a ball into Michelle and Nia's last cup and he swung me into a celebratory hug, I focused for far too long on how nice it felt to be in his arms.

After that party, I couldn't seem to get rid of Sean. We were both premed, so we studied together, ate dinner together, walked the long way back from the library to the dorms just to enjoy each other's company. We could talk about anything and everything, and so we did, seemingly nonstop —

* Funny how every Black girl I've ever met has heard the same thing. Almost like a lot of us are just pretty.

our insecurities, our interests, his difficulties balancing baseball with organic chemistry, my difficulties balancing organic chemistry with biology, our favorite novels, my brief foray into cosplay, his secret, maudlin poetry. We took short drives out to the city to go to museums, and long drives out to the national parks to go on hikes. It was all very sweet and almost platonic until one evening, after I'd said something particularly ridiculous, Sean let out a bark of laughter and swung around to face me.

"Angie, you're incredible," he'd said, snatching my hand up in his. I remembered the look on his face then, the way the evening sun had set his hazel eyes aflame. No one had ever kissed me before. Sean made sure I got plenty of practice.

It was over for me after that. Every thought I had was about Sean. I recounted our conversations to Michelle and Nia almost verbatim. I burned through my monthly allowance buying clothes that I thought he would like and planned my life around our "dates." I wondered if we could get into medical school in the same city, what my parents would think of him, what his would think of me.

Back then, I hadn't recognized that I was getting ahead of myself. Love had seemed so simple. You met someone, you liked each other, you got together, end of. And so when Sean's previously effusive texts became sparse, I told myself, *We don't have to talk all the time.* When his schedule filled up with baseball practices and group projects that came out of thin air, I let myself be convinced that he was just busy. Any doubts I had about us were abated by the occasional "I miss you" text, or once, a $5 fundraiser carnation delivered to me in his name.

Until even these stopped, and I realized, too late, that I'd been abandoned.

"I know you're probably pissed at me," Ricky said when I didn't respond after a few seconds. "But please. I just want to talk. If I say my piece and you still think I'm full of shit, you can kick me out."

You told me you would call, and then you didn't. "This isn't over," he'd said, his body physically blocking me from closing the door on us. And because I never learned, a small, desperate part of me had believed him.

And that part was gnawing at my chest now, even while the rest of me screamed to leave him out in the night. *If you don't hear him out, you'll wonder what he had to say forever,* it said, *and then you'll never get the closure you need.*

"Okay," I said numbly, and then I pressed the button to let him through the gate.

Outside, I could hear the screech of the wrought-iron gate opening. Suddenly, I became self-conscious. Enjoying my alone time had meant being comfortable, which meant cavorting around my apartment in a shapeless nightie and no underwear. Listening to his footsteps start up the stairs, I flew into my room and put my panties back on, then ran into the bathroom to check my face for any offensive crumbs. A little ashy, maybe — I hadn't been generous with the moisturizer after my shower — and so I made a game-time decision to slather my face with a dab of body butter. By the time his steps stilled outside my door, I was poised and ready.

There was a rustling sound, some frustrated noises, and then a knock. I waited a few seconds, bounced back on my heels, took a deep breath — *here goes nothing* — and opened the door.

Instead of a face, I was greeted by a mass of large green leaves.

I jumped back just as Ricky lowered a very large plant to the floor. I stared at it in disbelief, and its long-stemmed white blossoms bobbed back at me.

"You could have told me you were coming," I said. It had been less than a week since La Ventana, but already Ricky felt unfamiliar, and I wrapped my arms around myself to recenter. I couldn't bring myself to meet his eyes, and so I tried to look elsewhere. My gaze lingered on the shadow of his Adam's apple, then dipped down to the smooth expanse of chest exposed by the gaping of his Henley. My mouth went dry. *Okay, eyes it is.*

"You would have told me not to," Ricky said matter-of-factly. He took off his shoes, then bent over to pick up the plant again. "Where should I put this?"

He looked around my living room and, having apparently answered the question himself, carried the plant past me to a corner by a window.

"So you specifically showed up in person to pressure me into giving you an audience?" I said, incredulous. "You realize that you're admitting to taking that choice away from me, right?"

Ricky straightened, then looked me in the eye.

"Yes," he admitted. "And I can't say I regret it." He stepped toward me, closing the space between us, and I looked stubbornly at the floor until his socked feet came into view.

"I missed you," he said. When I rolled my eyes, he stepped in closer. "No, seriously, Angie. I did."

"Well, that's hardly my fault," I said bitterly. "You said you would call."

I heard rather than saw Ricky shift with discomfort.

"I know," he said. "It's not an excuse, but . . . something came up." His hand came to my chin, tilting my face up to his. "How did your presentation go?"

His touch still had *that* kind of effect on me, it seemed. I allowed myself some grace; it had been only a few days, and my body hadn't yet learned that Ricky was off-limits. I closed my eyes and exhaled slowly through my mouth.

"It was fine," I said. My gaze flickered to the plant in the corner of the room. The pot that housed it was admittedly beautiful, a smooth glazed white ceramic with a stripe of blue at the base that complemented my accent wall. Ricky must have picked it out himself. "So. What have you brought me?"

"A peace lily," Ricky supplied. His hand fell away from my face, and he shoved it in his pocket.

"Flowers," I said, unimpressed.

Ricky shook his head.

403

"These ones don't die easy," he said. "They purify your air. Take low light. Low maintenance, but still give you something to take care of." He cocked his head toward the couch. "Mind if we sit?"

Shrugging, I pushed past Ricky, stumbled to my coffee table, and took a sip of my wine. Then I sat back on the couch, crossing my legs expectantly as I watched him settle onto the seat farthest from me. He looked nice, and I wondered if he had dressed for the occasion, parsed through his closet for the outfit that was most likely to curry my favor. We looked silly sitting together like this, him dressed for a date, me in a knee-length, long-sleeved tee with I WOKE UP LIKE THIS written across the chest in bubble letters. Neither of us said a word for a long time, watching the candlelight flicker.

Ricky looked at me askance, his jaw set, and pushed his hair out of his eyes.

"Camila's pregnant," he said.

I had *not* expected that.

"What?" I said. My mind immediately went haywire doing the math. It had been about two months since Camila and Ricky broke up, too long for her to have only just found out . . . unless, of course, they'd been hooking up for longer than I thought. That was unlikely, though; Camila had put up pics of Kirkland Signature Chris Evans practically hours after dumping Ricky; there was no way he would continue to sleep with her after that —

"The baby's not mine," Ricky supplied, interrupting my train of thought. He bent forward, folding his hands over his knees. "Though, honestly, I wasn't sure at first. I found out she was pregnant an hour or so after you left the restaurant, and she just had the ultrasound to see how far along she was this afternoon." He shrugged. "And now here we are."

What a hot mess, I thought. I sucked in a breath through my teeth, then stood.

"You want a glass?" I asked, heading into the kitchen to fetch him one anyway. "It's not the good stuff, but it goes down easy enough."

"Sure," he said. I turned away from him to fill his glass. His stare fell heavy on my back, and I slowed my pour, trying to process the information that I'd just heard. Camila was pregnant and, judging by the fact that she'd called her ex to inform him, initially uncertain about her baby's parentage. I hadn't stalked her social media in a while; I had no idea if she and her new man were still together. I doubted it. Her new boo hadn't seemed the fatherly type.

"You could have just told me," I said, handing him his drink. He took it, placing it on the coffee table without taking a single sip. "It would've taken you two seconds to send me a text."

Ricky shook his head miserably.

"I wanted to," he said. "I almost did so many times, but . . ." He wiped his face with both hands, letting his words hang in the air.

"But you didn't," I supplied for him. "Instead, you let me sit here like an idiot." I looked down at him critically, unmoved by the guilty expression on his face. The longer I looked at him, the more letting him in through the door felt like a mistake. "And now that you've sorted *your* shit out, you're here."

"I'm sorry. You're right. I should have called you," Ricky said. "But what was I going to say, Angie? 'Hey, I know I told you that we would talk about us, but my ex is pregnant and maybe I'm the baby daddy, so can you hang tight for a bit longer?' "

"Yes," I supplied. "Exactly that."

"I couldn't," he said. "Angie, I . . ." He swallowed. "Camila's planning on moving to Tucson to be close to her parents. If the baby turned out to be mine, I was going to

406

go with her."

It took me a moment to process what he meant, and once I did, I felt like I was going to be sick. I remembered when I'd first seen them together, how I'd thought they'd looked good together. *They would make beautiful kids,* I'd thought. *A boy with her large eyes and his long face. A girl with his thick eyebrows and her sweet smile —*

"So let me get this straight," I said, rubbing my temples. "You didn't call me because you knew that if, today, you found out the kid *was* yours, you would've ditched me and gotten back with your ex? I just would never have heard from you again?"

"No. That's not —"

"Ricky," I said flatly, "you *just* told me that you were getting ready to move across the country for her."

"Not for her!" Ricky said, exasperated. "For our kid." He scooted closer to me, grasping my hand and squeezing it beseechingly. "Angie, there's nothing between me and Camila anymore. I'll be honest. I was expecting to feel *something* when I saw her again. I thought it would at least hurt, given how long we were together. But it didn't. I felt like I was talking to a stranger. Even at the obstetrician's office —"

I snatched my hand back. *At the obstetri-*

407

cian's office?

"You went to her appointment?" I said, alarmed. During my ob-gyn rotation, so many of the women had come to their appointments unaccompanied that when I walked into their exam room to find an extra occupant there, I would be thrown off guard. Now the image of Ricky and Camila together came into sharp focus; Ricky standing next to the sonographer as she passed the ultrasound probe over Camila's exposed belly, declaring that the baby was the size of a *peanut* —

Ricky looked up at me with wide eyes.

"Yeah, I did," he said, just a bit defiantly. "I won't apologize for that. That guy she was with ditched her the moment he found out she was keeping it. She was going to go alone."

Even as my fury mounted, I understood. Of *course* Ricky went to her appointment. That was just who Ricky was. Always trying to do the right thing for everyone, all the time. Camila must have known this. As she lay down on the clinic table, spread-eagled and exposed, she must have prayed for her pregnancy to be older, for the chance that her child was also his. Maybe, had he told me what he was doing instead of letting me rot, he could have garnered my sympathy.

408

But at this moment, all I could think of was how, even after all this time, Camila's feelings still trumped mine.

I stood abruptly and pivoted toward my front door. The audacity of this man, really. The peace I had managed to build around myself had just been knocked down with a battering ram, but I would put it together again. There was always more wine, always more museums, always more *Great British Bake Off.* Just as soon as I got this berserker out of my home —

"Angie," Ricky said, storming after me. "Angie, *please.*"

He grabbed my sleeve, and I swiveled to face him, my anger flaring as he closed the space between us. I'd never thought of him as especially tall, but in that moment, the four inches or so between us felt vast.

"You still care about her," I declared.

"Not in the way you think," he tried.

"Liar," I spat, trying to hold back the tears that pricked the corners of my eyes, because *enough* — I had already cried enough over him. "Can you even hear yourself? You drove across the city to go to her appointment to play house and who knows what else, but you couldn't pick up your phone and call me? Couldn't even spare five minutes? Are you kidding me right now?"

"Angie, I —"

"I can't believe that I thought . . ." My voice trailed off as I filled in the rest. That I thought he was different. That I thought what we had was special. That I'd spent the last month feeling *so sure* that we would work, thinking of him not just as my potential partner, but as my *friend* —

"I'm sorry," he was saying. "I was stupid. I felt stuck. I didn't mean to hurt you. I know that doesn't change the fact that I did, but . . ."

"You realize I don't need you, right?" I interrupted, searching his face. "I'm going to be a doctor, and I'm turning out to be a pretty damn good one. I have the most amazing friends in the world. A nice place. Everything I could possibly need —"

"I know that!" Ricky said in a harsh whisper. "You think I don't? You think I don't think about that all the time?"

"Do you?" I said. "Because it feels like you think I'll always be here. That you can just keep playing games with me, and that I'll sit around, twiddling my thumbs, waiting for you to decide that you're ready to commit —"

"I'm not playing games," Ricky said. "I was *embarrassed,* okay? It's a baby. I wasn't sure if it was *my* baby! Angie, you *know* this

410

about me. I'm not abandoning any child of mine, ever. I'm going to be there for all those moments — their first steps, first words; I'm going to be there changing diapers, taking them to daycare, doing *all of that.* How was I supposed to ask you to be a part of that, huh? How was I supposed to tell you that I wanted to be with you, but, oh, also, can you please include my kid in your plans for the future that you've been working so hard for? How was I supposed to, in good conscience, *ask you to do that for me?*"

I sucked in a sharp breath, my fists unfurling at my sides. In the flurry of my anger, I hadn't fully considered what the consequences of Ricky's being a father would be on our relationship. But spoken out loud like that? I imagined arranging my rank list for Match with programs in Arizona, a state I had never even visited, at the top. A small, strange child screaming down the halls when I was trying to sleep after twenty-eight-hour calls —

Ricky squeezed his eyes shut, smoothing his hands down my arms.

"Look," he said, his voice reed thin, his words flowing fast. "I know last week I hesitated. And I know that you think it's because I'm not . . . invested in you, or

411

something. But that's not it. My last relationship was a mess. And the one before that. And before that. I kept going all in with people who weren't ready to go all in with me. I did some shitty things to people I cared about just to try to salvage relationships that weren't worth salvaging. And I told myself, 'Well, this is just what you do for love.' " He chewed at his inner cheek, and I wondered if he was thinking of Shae. "But it wasn't love, was it? It was just me trying to do what I thought was right. And with you . . . it was like I was falling back into old patterns. Jumping in, when I really needed to be holding back. Except it was worse, because the way I felt . . . The way I *feel* about you is just so much more, you know?"

He sucked in a breath, looked down at the floor. This was Ricky stripped bare, I realized. No excuses, no pretenses, just the beautiful, maddening man I had come to know. When he looked back up at me again, his eyes were hard with determination.

"Listen, Angie," he said firmly, and I jolted, jarred by the shift in his tone. "I want to be with you *all the time.* When you're not with me, I'm thinking of when I can see you next. Every time you say you need something, I want to be the one to do it for you.

412

And I thought, 'Look. Of course you feel this way. This girl is smart, she's funny, she's beautiful, her body is *ridiculous*' " — I snorted and ducked my head as Ricky laughed, guiding my face back to his — " 'but give it some time. This is just the honeymoon phase. Get to actually know her, you know?' But I *have* gotten to know you, and that's only made holding back harder. So when you asked the other night if you were my girlfriend" — I swallowed against the ball in my throat, the sting of his rejection still fresh — "honestly, I wasn't sure if we were on the same page about what that meant for me. It's not just a label for me. I'm looking for someone who can be my *family.* I needed to feel like that was something you even wanted with me. And . . . I wasn't always sure that it was." He paused, searching my face for a reaction. "Is it? I'm not talking about right now, or even tomorrow. Just . . ."

All this time, I'd thought I was getting ahead of myself. Always trying to fit Ricky into my future, getting lost in distant what-ifs, instead of just living in the moment. But apparently, he'd been doing the same.

"Are you asking if I see a future with you?" I asked. He gave me a grim nod, and I exhaled, feeling my heart pound in my

413

ears. "I mean. Y-yeah. I do."

Tension rushed out of him like air out of a balloon. "Good," he said.

" 'Good'?" I repeated, and he laughed, all joy, dropping his forehead to rest against mine.

"Yeah," he said. He cradled my face between his hands, breathing my breath, his body radiating heat into mine. "Then it's set, right? You and me? Official, and very serious about it?"

"Yes?" I said. "I guess so."

The first kiss Ricky lowered to my lips was a firm press, a stamp to seal the deal. The second was breathless, his hands steadying my face against his, his body pressing, firm and unyielding, against my curves. God, I could kiss this man forever, and every time would feel like a thrill.

Eventually, Ricky pulled away. We looked at each other, smiled, kissed again. I twined my arms around his neck; he wrapped his around my waist. We stood like that for a long time, my cheek against his chest, his chin balanced on the top of my head, and I closed my eyes, savoring our closeness. Never mind all the pep talks I'd given myself over the last five days, the assurances that I wouldn't let myself be seduced by sweet words when he inevitably turned up

414

again. I'd failed to account for the details, for the crack in his voice as he confessed the depth of his regard for me, for the heart I could feel galloping in his chest. I'd forgotten that I couldn't resist this man. And now, it seemed, I wouldn't have to.

"I'm in love with you, you know," Ricky said into my hair after some minutes. I looked up at him, shocked into stillness by his declaration, and he gave me a small, strained smile. "I just wanted to put that out there, for the sake of transparency. I know it's a lot, and I don't want you to feel like you have to say it back, but . . ."

I almost laughed. *In love with you.* They were words I'd wanted to hear my entire life but had thought might always elude me. Words that felt so foreign that I'd convinced myself no one could actually open their mouth to say them, words that seemed more suited to romance novels or cheesy movies than real life. But Ricky had spoken them like they were indisputable, like his feelings for me were too big to contain, even as his arms trembled around me. It struck me, then, how scared he must've been of confronting me, knowing that I could turn him away. How brave he was to tell me the truth.

It made me want to be brave too.

"It's okay," I said. This close, I could see

his pupils widen. "I'm in love with you too."

The smile that broke out across Ricky's face was resplendent, like the sun peeking through clouds at the end of a thunderstorm, and, reflexively, I returned it.

"Jesus," he said, making a show of clutching his chest. Our laughter bubbled forth unbidden, filling up the vacuum of emotion created by the abrupt departure of months of anxiety. We laughed so loud and for so long that I was sure Tom thought we were losing it, but I didn't care. Ricky loved me. I loved him. And when we kissed again, it was with lips still stretched into smiles and mouths still open mid-laugh, with nothing but the sheer delight of having each other at last.

TWENTY-THREE

I'd never been the one-night-stand type. In high school and college, I'd been as horny as the next hormone-addled young adult, but rather than put my lustfulness into action, I expelled it outward. I read smutty fanfiction and rewatched racy scenes in my favorite TV shows and scrolled through my curated photo album of famous hotties to imagine as my next boyfriend. Cavorting with real boys was unthinkable; the ones in my circle were awkward and smelly and *mean,* and, on top of all that, had the nerve to *not* look like Morris Chestnut. They made jokes about the saggy tits or fat stomachs or funny-looking nipples that belonged to the girls that let them see them at their most vulnerable and traded their girlfriends' nudes among themselves like baseball cards. They spread rumors about who used "too much teeth" and who needed to "wax their bush," and I sat in the ramparts, observing them, and decided that, unlike those other girls, *I* would be discerning. *Only ever with someone who actually cares about me,* I told myself. And I waited for years to find someone who fit that description . . . only to realize that I'd been arrogant. How were you supposed to know if a man cared about you? He could say he cared all he wanted, could bring you flowers you didn't want, whisper sweet nothings into your ear to break down your resolve, but he could also leave, without an explanation, with nothing but an *Actually, I don't think I'm into you like that,* and where would that leave you then?

The only solution was to take Miss Bernice's advice and "take what you want." And at this particular moment, I only wanted one thing.

"Fuck," Ricky groaned against my mouth. His hands found purchase in the flesh at the backs of my thighs, and he hitched one around his hip, grinding into me in a motion so shockingly delectable that it nearly sent my eyes rolling to the back of my head. I flattened my palms against his back, running my nails lightly down his skin and delighting in the way he shuddered against me.

It had all happened so fast. One moment,

we were professing our undying love for each other, giggling as we kissed away each other's tears, and the next, I was pressed against my front door, my whole world narrowing to Ricky's hands on my skin, the friction of his body against mine. We'd kissed like this before, with toe-curling urgency, but always to a limit, always reining ourselves back in before we could go any further. It was almost an unspoken rule, as if sex were a Pandora's box that neither of us felt ready to open.

But now, we were both scrabbling at its flaps.

I pulled away, dropping my head back against the door and looking down at him through my lashes. We stared at each other for several seconds, catching our breaths as we cataloged the effects we'd had on each other — Ricky's eyelids, heavy with want, his pink, glistening lips, the press of his arousal between my legs. After a moment, he leaned into me again, skimming his nose down my cheek and nestling his head into the crook of my neck. He took a deep, lazy inhale, worrying the skin between his teeth. I sighed, arching reflexively into him, then placed my hands firmly on his shoulders.

"My neighbors," I managed in explanation.

Ricky hummed in understanding, trailing his lips in a line up my neck to the angle of my jaw. Then he stepped back, smiling down at me tenderly. *He loves me,* I reminded myself, letting myself flood with warmth again. I took his hand, smiling back. *Look at how he's looking at me. He loves me so much.*

My bedroom was not prepped for a visitor, the sheets askew, yesterday's clothes thrown haphazardly across my desk chair. But Ricky's eyes didn't stray from mine, not until I reached for the hem of my nightgown and pulled it over my head. Only then did his gaze drift down, taking his time to survey my body like it was something to behold. He let out a slow, shuddering breath, ghosting his fingers up my sides.

"Goddamn, Angie," he said, leaning forward to press a gentle kiss against my lips, even as his grip on my waist tightened. Then: "You sure?"

I've never been more sure of anything in my life, I thought, reaching for the hem of his shirt. We snickered quietly as his head got caught in the hole, then, together, tossed it disdainfully across the room.

"Why? Worried you won't be able to handle me?" I teased against his mouth. I felt his laughter rumble into my chest, letting him coax me backward onto my bed.

"I think I'll manage," he said, and, with one last devastating, smirk, slid down between my legs.

Every romance novel I'd ever read described sex as transcendent. Transformative. At the end of a riveting romp with her billionaire/baron/rogue lover, the heroine was supposed to tilt her head back in rapture and experience *la petite mort,* that special moment at the height of pleasure when her consciousness leaves her body, and she ascends into a plane of pure ecstasy.

That moment had always eluded me. After my first time, I'd felt cheated. After all, I'd expected a metamorphosis, a transition into womanhood hailed with trumpets and golden confetti. But instead, there was only pressure, and a paltry amount of pleasure, and when it was all over, I was still the same Angela Appiah, just a little sorer between the legs. And after some time . . . Well, I'd assumed that it was just more storybook lore. That sex was pleasant at best, traumatic at worst, and nothing to write home about most of the time.*

* And for the most efficient results, performed alone, at home, with the help of a Hitachi Magic Wand.

But maybe what I had been missing all along was love. Maybe it was because I loved Ricky that every brush of his fingers made me bite back his name. Maybe because my body had been anticipating his from the moment he kissed me under the cover of our blanket fort that the press of him inside me made me feel whole. Or maybe it was because he was an artist, committing me to memory with the same obsessive focus that he gave to his work, that calling what we were doing "sex" felt inadequate. Because it was too different, too much *more,* than anything I'd done before. Gone were the days of assumptions between us; we learned each other voraciously, eliciting feedback in the form of sighs and gasps, through a whispered *Here?* and a breathless *Yes,* an uttered *Like that.* Practice making perfect. I felt like we were trapped in a void of sensation, my pleasure building his and vice versa, every roll of his hips into mine and lap of my tongue against his skin pushing us rapidly to a foregone conclusion.

"Don't stop," I whispered when we were close.

Ricky smiled down at me, dragged his thumb along my bottom lip. *He loves me.*

"Never," he said. The most heavenly lie.

His skin was smooth, supple, slick with sweat, and when I dug my nails into his sides, his gasp was enough to push me over the edge. But in the precious seconds before my mind went blissfully blank, a single thought filtered through: *This is what it's supposed to feel like.*

After it was over, we lay in bed, staring at the ceiling, catching our breath.

"Not going to lie," Ricky said, "I'm kind of mad that we held out for so long."

I laughed, walking my fingers up the center of his chest.

"We can make up for lost time," I said coquettishly. Ricky gave me a rakish grin, then rolled us over so that he was spooned against my back.

"Can do," he said, pressing a kiss to my bare shoulder. "You're going to have to give me a few more minutes, though. Got to rally the troops again."

I snickered, threading our fingers together across my chest. My whole body felt like it was buzzing, like another version of myself was hovering just millimeters above the first. I felt content. *He loves me,* I reminded myself, as he dragged me closer into his embrace.

A sound like an air horn broke through

our comfortable silence, and behind me, I felt Ricky stiffen.

"Hold on a sec," he said, sliding out from under the covers. I watched him as he swung his legs over the edge of the bed, stepping back into his boxers before circling the bed to retrieve his discarded jeans. He pulled out his phone, his expression turning blank as he looked over the caller ID flashing on his screen.

"Hey," he said. A voice responded on the other end — a woman's voice. Ricky's eyes flickered to mine, and then he stepped through my bedroom door, closing it with a decisive *thunk.*

A chill settled into my bones. I stared at the closed door for a long time, straining my ears to try to hear the conversation on the other side. Ricky was speaking in rapid Spanish, something he did in front of me only rarely, usually during conversations with his grandfather. But those calls were always short, almost transactional, and he'd always felt comfortable having them in my vicinity. For this one, he'd practically leapt out of bed before he could even see who had called.

Why the secrecy? It wasn't like I could understand much of what he was saying anyway. He could have very well carried on

424

his conversation while under the warmth of our covers. Or better yet, waited until after our post-coitus cuddle to call them back.

Then an idea struck, and my stomach sunk.

Was it Camila? Had Ricky fled because he'd known that I'd be able to make out her high, silvery voice over the phone? Maybe the situation with her wasn't as settled as he'd made it seem. After all, it was mighty convenient that after five days of providing a shoulder to cry on and co-ordinating schedules around her obstetrics appointment, Ricky had walked away completely emotionally unattached to his long-term ex. What if Camila found out that, actually, the baby was just small for gesta-tional age,* and now he needed a paternity test? What if his declaration that there was *nothing* between them was a bit of an exag-geration, and Camila was now calling on the other end, begging for Ricky to take her back? Or worse, what if it was someone dif-ferent, someone new? What if Tabatha had been right about the "millennial dating rules," and Ricky's reticence toward com-mitment had been because he'd been decid-

---

* Meaning, the traditional method of dating a fetus by its size wouldn't apply.

ing between me and a handful of other eligible bachelorettes? What if he was talking to one of them now, telling her he was off the market, or worse . . . pretending that he was still on it?

Suddenly, I felt a tidal wave of shame loom over my head. What the hell was I *doing*? So Ricky said he loved me. So *what*? Anyone could say those words if they wanted something badly enough. And it wasn't like Ricky had a great track record when it came to honestly expressing his feelings; he'd sounded just as confident when he'd told me he wasn't interested in me the night that I ran into him at Rogers. Why was I placing any credence in his words, when there were actions right there that showed me the opposite? Who leaves the Girl They Love in limbo, knowing that they might lose her? Who goes off with their cheating ex-girlfriend to do Lord knows what for Lord knows how long, knowing that the Girl They Love is waiting by the phone for them to call? Not even an hour ago, his reasoning — that he'd been unsure about where I stood, that actually, he was worried that he liked me a bit *too* much — had been exactly what I wanted to hear. But now, post-nut clarity was settling in, and with it the rising suspicion that I'd been had. *Really,* I thought, listening to Ricky's conversation drag on, hearing his voice climb with irritation, *you couldn't have told me all of this at the restaurant? You really had to make me wait?* I remembered the expression that had flashed across his face at La Ventana, the same face he'd made after I'd asked him out at the art fair. It hadn't been an expression full of yearning. It had been full of *guilt.*

Good god, what was I doing? I knew better than this. Love wasn't supposed to feel like this.

It was supposed to feel safe. It was supposed to feel like *home.* So why was I accepting something that was so clearly less than that?

From my vantage point on the bed, I scanned the room for our clothes, finding my nightdress pooled on the floor below me. I sat up, pulling it back over my head. When my bedroom door finally opened and Ricky stepped back inside, it was to my tear-stained face.

"Whoa," he said, taken aback by my expression. "Angie, are you *crying?*"

"Who was that?" I asked, swiping at my face with the heels of my hands.

Ricky raised his eyebrow.

"One of my aunties,"* he said slowly, taking a cautious step toward me.

"You have an aunt?" I asked. "Isn't your dad an only child?"

Ricky folded his arms across his chest, suddenly defensive. Gingerly, he placed his phone facedown on my nightstand.

"I call my family friends my aunts and uncles, same as you," he said. He furrowed his brow, delving his hand into his hair. "Okay, Angie, where is this coming from?"

"Where is it coming from?" I asked, aghast. "Ricky. You just told me that your ex is pregnant, and that you just spent the last week 'helping her out.' And now, you're leaving me in bed so you can take a super sketchy phone call. Am I not allowed to feel some kind of way about that?"

"No, you're not. Because you should know me better than to think that me just getting on the phone is 'sketchy,'" he said, his voice saturated with frustration. "Come on, Angie. Don't you trust me?"

Did I trust him? I thought about that question, watching his expression slacken with every second of my silence. If he'd

* One thing common among most non-WASPy cultures is a tendency to refer to every family friend above a certain age as auntie or uncle.

asked me this same question a week ago, when we were still passing our days cracking jokes at my dining table, I would have answered with an emphatic *Yes, of course.* But too much had happened since then. We had regressed.

"I don't know," I said. I brought my knees to my chest, looking down at the crumpled sheets where he'd lain only a few minutes before. "I want to. But I don't think I do."

Ricky didn't say anything for a long time. I could feel the frustration waft off him in waves, hear the crack of his knuckles as he stretched and flexed his fingers. When he finally did speak, it was in a hushed, strained tone.

"I don't know what you want me to do about that," he said. "Because the way I see it, I haven't given you any reason to feel that way."

I sputtered, taken aback.

"No reason? Not one? Really?" I said. "I never know what you're feeling, Ricky. The last time I decided to trust you, you *disappeared.* And now, you can't even stay in my bed for ten minutes after we've *fucked* in it before you're running out of it."

"Look, I'm sorry," he said, in a way that suggested that *sorry* was a generous term. "Next time I talk to my family, I'll make sure I'm still naked in bed with you."

Maybe if he'd been truly apologetic, I could have been assuaged. If he loved me, if there was nothing to hide, why the defensiveness? Why not just laugh, why not just hold me, why not say something like, "Why you bugging, girl?" and tell me stories about this "Auntie" of his? I wished Tabatha could stop being right all the time. She'd called it herself — if I had no doubts about Ricky, if he had no doubts about me, if we could come to my family as a clear, united, star-crossed front, then it would be worth it. If Ricky were stalwart, I could be sure that choosing him over a top residency program wouldn't end in tragedy. If his affection was consistent, if it was predictable, I could give him the deed to my heart.

As it was . . . Ricky was too much of a risk.

I must've muttered the last part out loud, because Ricky wound back like he'd been stung.

"A risk?" he said. His eyes widened, and he laughed darkly, shaking his head. "Yo, what the fuck? Is that what you think, that *I'm too much of a risk*?"

I grit my teeth, not answering, knowing that would be all the answer he would need.

"Ah," Ricky said. "No. Don't bother. I get

430

it." His smile was acerbic. "I know your sister doesn't think I'm good enough for you, right? And you don't think I'm good enough either."

I recoiled. "That's not true —"

"Yes it is, Angie," Ricky said. "That's why you're doing this, right? That's why you're making this hard for no reason. Because you've decided that I'm not, what, rich enough or something? Like you're slumming it with me."

"No! No. That's not it at all!" I said, knowing that it wasn't entirely the truth, knowing exactly what face my mother would pull if I told her about him — *What does he do? Oh. What about his parents? Ay.*
"I just . . ."

I took in a deep breath. How did I tell Ricky the real truth: that my moments alone had been revelational? That they had forced me to recall the three and a half years between Sean and Frederick, and realize that they had been *joyful*? That I could count the number of times that I had cried in that time on one hand? I had felt like I needed romantic love to feel whole, but the truth was that every man I let into my heart took a chunk of it with him, made me feel less when I should have felt *more*. And Ricky had been the worst of them. The

431

uncertainty, the anxiety, he inspired in me? I'd created a version of him in my head, then broken my own heart when he didn't fit neatly into its mold. The Ricky who'd told me he loved me hardly an hour ago felt so different from the one standing in front of me now, teeming with fury because I'd dared ask him for reassurance.

"You realize I'm moving in a year and a half, right?" I said instead. "And I won't be able to tell you where? I'm going to open an envelope and find out. Are you planning on coming with me?"

Ricky blinked back at me in shock, and I held back a snort. *It's not like this is the first time I'm bringing this up. Did you not think Match was relevant to you, Mr. Family Man?*

"I don't know," Ricky said after a heart-beat. "Figured we would cross that bridge if we got there."

If, not when. Ricky had never spoken about us in uncertainties, not since blanket fort. It had always been *when* you meet Abuela. *When* we take that pottery class. *When* we go to New Orleans. For someone who had just claimed to want to be *sure* about his next relationship, Ricky didn't sound so sure about me. All at the first sign of conflict. The corners of my mouth wobbled, and I fought hard against the sob that

432

wanted to break through and won.

"I get how Camila must've felt, you know," I managed. "About not believing that you ever actually loved her. I think you want to love me. But I don't think you know how."

The last vestiges of Ricky's control snapped. I could see the transition happen in his eyes, like an elastic band pulled too tight, or a fuse running out.

"Are you throwing that in my face right now, Angie? Really?" he said. "I thought you were better than that."

I winced, huddling myself closer.

"I guess we don't really know each other as well as we thought," I said, feeling the maw in my chest burst open as I said the words. Then I sighed. "This clearly isn't going to work."

"Wow," Ricky said. Before this, I had thought of his anger as cold, but this time it raged red hot, flaring like a match over kerosene. I looked down at my lap, watching my tears fall in angry splotches. Then he crossed the room, snatching his jeans from the other side of my bed and tugging them over his hips. I kept my gaze determinedly forward as he dressed, focusing on my breathing as he reached past me to retrieve his phone and stuff it into his pocket. He pulled his shirt over his head

433

and when he was done, he settled in front of me, staring determinedly at the space between us.

"Well, this didn't last very long," he said bitterly. "I guess I'll see myself out."

I heard the warning in his tone. *This is your last chance,* he was saying. *Take it or leave it.* And I wanted to take it, more than anything. I knew that I could still do the easier thing and pick him. And then what? Spend the next year and some change living in fear, waiting for the other shoe to drop? Having any of my concerns met with annoyance instead of understanding? No. Enough. Ricky had made his choice the moment he'd decided to leave me high and dry to sit at Camila's side, and now I was making mine.

"Okay," I said. "I'll lock the door behind you."

I don't know how long Ricky stood there, waiting for me to speak. As the time passed, I felt the bluster of his anger fade, watched his shoulders begin to droop. By the end, he looked like a shell of himself, haunted and lost. Then he swallowed, and his expression hardened.

"Fine," he said. "Okay. Fine."

Then he stepped out of my bedroom, and then out through my front door. I expected it to slam, but instead it clicked shut. It seemed like an inglorious way for our saga to end, with a sigh instead of a bang.

TWENTY-FOUR

"Trust who? The doctors?" Mr. Jenkins, my newest patient, said. He let out a booming laugh that seemed to shake the entire room. "Why on Earth would I do that?"

I smiled, scooting myself closer to the edge of the folding chair I had propped up next to his hospital bed. My cell phone was balanced precariously on the end of my clipboard, recording. When I'd first approached Mr. Jenkins with a request to interview him for my project, he'd looked skeptical. "You folks never stop asking questions, do you?" he'd said wearily. But when I broached the topic of the interview, he had taken pause, then waved me over and signed a form consenting to be enrolled and recorded with a flourish. And like with most of the patients I had interviewed thus far, Mr. Jenkins seemed to burst forward with thoughts. After all, no one had thought to ask him his opinions about doctors' communication practices, especially not in regard to whether they were *discriminatory.*

"You're here, in the hospital," I said conversationally. "You're accepting care from the physicians. But you don't trust them?"

"I don't have a choice," Mr. Jenkins said. He leaned back in his hospital bed, tilting his head up toward the monitor. "I can't fix me, can I? Now, don't get me wrong. Everybody here has been real nice. Veronica," he said, referring to his nurse, "has been really attentive. But I don't trust anybody in this place but God." He gave me a critical stare. "You're from the motherland, aren't you?"

I nodded, and, satisfied with his assessment, Mr. Jenkins smiled to himself.

"It's the skin," he declared. "You've got that smooth, dark, African skin. Beautiful, if you don't mind me saying."

"I don't mind," I said. "Thank you."

"What I mean is that I'm sure you and your family are new to this country. You might not know all about what they did to us here." He adjusted his glasses on his nose. "My mother died in the basement of this hospital, back in sixty-three. She came here for help, and they threw her into the back somewhere and forgot about her. Her bowels ruptured. She was thirty-two." He held my gaze for a long moment, his old pain renewed. Then he closed his eyes and leaned back on his bed. "So no, to answer your question. I don't trust the doctors. I just lay here and pray that the good Lord will guide them to treat me right."

I walked out of Mr. Jenkins's room half an hour later, our conversation saved and uploaded to the cloud. It was late, almost eight o'clock at night, and as I trudged back to the workroom I went through my mental checklist. I needed to stop by Dr. Reed's office to put Mr. Jenkins's paper consent form in our folder. I had to forward his recorded interview to the transcription company and check my email to see whether they had sent me any completed transcripts of my prior interviews.

The email from the Beenhouwer Association announcing that we had been rewarded three thousand in internal funding had come two weeks ago. Dr. Reed called me immediately upon its receipt to rejoice, but all I felt upon reading it was the sensation that I had successfully climbed up one rung higher on an infinite ladder. We read over the potential edits to our proposal, which included that we discard the focus group idea and opt for a more open interview style, allowing our participants to drive the conversation themselves. I accepted the critiques, then immediately got to work. In a short time, I had already single-handedly recruited and interviewed fourteen patients, a number that Dr. Reed found incomprehensible.

"When do you have time to do all this, Angie?" he said, exasperated.

"I make time," I said.

And make time I did. On most days, I left the hospital after sunset, sticking around after I'd signed out my own patients to hunt through the wards for more to recruit. I conducted my interviews, walked home, did practice questions over a late dinner, completed a twenty-minute aerobics workout in front of my TV, showered, and went to sleep. Rinse and repeat, day after day.

"That is no way to live," Michelle had said, disgusted, on the rare day that I allowed for an interruption in my routine for a dinner out.

I shrugged. I liked my new, structured schedule, actually. It kept me occupied and made me feel useful.

The workroom was empty when I entered; the night team had probably already left to admit patients. I grabbed my backpack and tore off my short white coat, slinging it over my elbow, then stalked over to the elevators. My heels clacked loudly against the hospital tile, echoing through the empty halls. I pulled out my phone, scrolling to the group chat. Markus had sent a series of increasingly more filthy memes over the course of the day, and I snorted with amusement as I read them, pressing the elevator button for down.

"Excuse me," a voice behind me said.

I jumped, startled. A short older woman stood behind me. Her face was striking — eyes stuck in a perpetual squint and a jaw that was impressively angular under weathered brown skin. Despite her severe features, she gave off an aura of gentleness. She gave me a sheepish smile.

"I think I am a bit lost," she said. She had an accent. "I'm looking for room 5078?"

Something about her felt familiar. Maybe it was the way she shifted her weight from one leg to the other, or the strong bridge of her nose. A part of me was sure I'd met her before.

The moment it clicked, I was flooded with panic. My heart took off like a racecar down a track, pounding so feverishly that I could feel it whooshing in my ears.

Relax, Angie. Not every old Mexican lady is going to be Ricky's abuela.

"Oh," I said, my voice a little shaky.

"You're on the right floor. Just keep headed straight, beyond these elevators, and take a right through the first set of double doors. That should get you close."

She smiled again, touching my arm in gratitude. "Oh, thank you."

I watched her walk down the hall, clutching my phone tightly. My stomach felt like it was lodged in my throat. What was wrong with me, that everything I encountered seemed to remind me of him? When would this end? I had been getting better. Even without my friends physically present to distract me, I'd managed to fill my mind with things* that weren't him. It had felt like recovery.

The woman took a left turn instead of a right. No wonder she'd gotten lost; her sense of direction was worse than mine. I considered leaving her be — it was late, after all, and I had exactly two hours before I ought to be in bed — and then imagined her wandering around the hospital aimlessly and sighed.

* To be specific, an absurd amount of internal medicine knowledge, the lyrics to every song on the iconic 2003 album *The Diary of Alicia Keys,* and a nearly alarming amount of *RuPaul's Drag Race* trivia.

"Ma'am?" I called out, jogging toward her. She jolted, then raised her eyebrows as I approached. "Ma'am, no, that's the wrong way."

"Oh, oh no," she said, chuckling to herself. "I'm very bad at this. Hospitals . . . they're very confusing."

Recalling how expertly I'd gotten myself lost during orientation, I laughed.

"You're not wrong. Here, let me help you." I walked ahead of her back into the common hallway, pressing a silver button to open the double doors I'd meant for her to take. "Go through here." I walked through the doors and to the end of the hall, then pointed to the right. "The numbers get bigger from here. We're at 5072 right now, and so 5078 is just a little bit farther."

The woman clapped her hands together, pleased, then gave me a smile like I'd just told her she'd won the lottery.

"Thank you so much. I can find it from here, I think." She reached over and patted my arm again. "You seem like a nice doctor. Please stay that way."

This was probably the first time I'd been mistaken for a doctor, rather than a nurse or a cleaning lady.

"I'm still a student," I clarified. "But I'll remember that!"

That seemed to satisfy her. With a firm nod, she began a purposeful walk toward the room. I watched her go, suddenly exhausted.

It had been almost a month since I'd ended things with Ricky, and not a day had passed that I hadn't thought of him. Sometimes, the thoughts were innocuous — I considered checking his Instagram to see if he'd posted any new art, or reflexively pulled out my phone to text him about a situation I knew he would find funny before remembering that that was something I could no longer do, or spotted his gifted peace lily out of the corner of my eye.* But other times, my mind went down dangerous rabbit holes (Was he seeing someone new? Or, worse, had he gotten back with Camila?) and I would have to claw myself away from the brink of a nervous breakdown.

"You have to be nicer to yourself," Tabatha said when I called her one day in hysterics, frustrated by my lack of progress. "You know, they say it takes about twice the length of a relationship to get over someone."

* Too heavy to move, and too stubborn (despite my blatant neglect) to die.

443

Which meant that I had ten months* left of this suffering. It felt like a prison sentence, and I marked each day that I managed to roll out of bed and get my shit done as a victory.

My phone dinged.

Don't forget to send me your measurements, Momma said.

I walked out of the hospital into the cool, fall evening, scrolling through my phone for the photo I'd taken of the measurements sheet she'd sent me earlier that week. I'd unblocked my parents shortly after receiving my research funding, and though I didn't feel quite ready to pick up their calls, we had been texting back and forth. Only ever pleasantries, of course — in the evenings, I sent them a good night text, and in the mornings, Momma sent me a floral picture containing a Bible verse. We were so careful not to discuss the cause of our rift, and I didn't want to rock the boat, grateful for our clumsy balancing acts.†

A thumping bassline echoed through the

---

* Because even though our actual relationship lasted all of an hour, I was no longer embarrassed to admit that I'd been sprung on sight.

† Daddy didn't send anything at all, which wasn't unexpected; I figured he would be sore for a while.

stairwell of my walk-up. I'd felt it from the moment I opened the gate to our complex but had assumed that Tom had decided to throw yet another unsanctioned rager and paid it no mind. But when I reached the second landing, Tom's place was conspicuously quiet. I continued up the stairs, confirming what I had already figured to be true — the music was coming from *my apartment.*

Chill, I told myself as I dug through my pockets for my keys. *Nia probably decided to come by and forgot to tell you. You locked the door when you left. There's definitely not a serial killer crouched behind your couch right now, and he's definitely not using the music to cover up your screams —*

My door swung open, revealing, to my astonishment, Michelle.

"She's here!" she shouted, dragging me by my arm into my own home.

I stared at the state of my living room in shock. My coffee table was crowded with booze and bags of chips; the TV was on and blasting Fifth Harmony's "Work from Home" at top volume. And even more shocking — my sister was sitting on the arm of my couch, dressed to kill in a shimmering mini dress and slurping a drink through a straw. Just as I was getting my bearings,

Nia popped out of the kitchen and shoved a cup into my hands.

"What is going on?" I sputtered. I noticed then that Michelle was dolled up as well, her eyes smoky with eyeshadow and hair curled into waves. Nia too, in a mustard yellow bodycon that looked suspiciously like my freakum dress in a different color.

"It's a Friday, and you have tomorrow off," Nia declared. She and Michelle shared conspiratorial grins. "We know because Michelle checked your schedule."

"All work and no play makes Jack a dull boy," Michelle piped in. "And lately, Angie? You've been *boring as fuck.*"

I dropped my backpack at my feet, shaking my head in disbelief. An irrational part of me felt irritated — *But I have to get through thirty questions today to get to a thousand questions by the end of the week!* — but I shoved that feeling down deep and decided to be grateful instead.

"So I'm being ambushed," I said. I took a hesitant sip of my drink and immediately made a face. "Jesus, Nia, what is this, gasoline?"

"Never mind that," Nia said. She raised her glass high. "Bottoms up!"

I forced myself to chug my drink at the same time as Nia did, wiping my mouth with the back of my hand in disgust.

"Tabs," I said, directing my attention to my sister, who was swinging her legs idly and looking up at me with cartoonishly innocent eyes. "I thought you were the responsible one now! You were in on this?"

Tabatha shrugged, twirling her straw around in her Solo cup.

"It's not a big deal." She took a sip. "We're just going out."

I laughed helplessly, offering no resistance as Nia and Michelle pushed me into my room, threw my second-sexiest dress onto my bed, and stood watch by the door as I changed into it and applied my makeup. They snapped their fingers to hurry me along, singing off-key to Lady Gaga and dancing furiously all the while. Before I could finish getting ready, they had already called a rideshare, barely waiting for me to swipe my gloss over my lips to loop their arms through my elbows and yank me down the stairs.

The line into Untitled, my kidnappers' chosen dance bar, was halfway down the block by the time we arrived, but the bouncer took one look at Tabatha and waved us inside. After weeks of solitude, the body-shaking noise, flaring strobe lights, and stale, hazy gusts of artificial fog were overwhelming, like all my senses were being bum-rushed. On either side of me, Michelle and Nia were hype, bouncing up on their heels as Desiigner's "Panda" blasted through the speakers. We beelined for the sparse dance floor, trying not to trip in our heels, giggling at no one in particular.

When was the last time I'd gone out with the girls like this, not as part of a medical school mixer, or after a medical school exam, or following a medical school formal, but just for the fun of it? Years, I realized. I felt like a newborn fawn, my dancing knock-kneed and clumsy, as I tried to will my body back into its old motions. The strobe lights flashed across our faces, catching them in brightly colored snapshots. At some point, Michelle ran to the bar and came back with four shot glasses tucked between her fingers, and we drank and were merry.

An hour or so into our revelry, the first few notes of Juvenile's "Back Dat Ass Up" blasted through the speakers. Nia and I whipped toward each other in recognition.

"Remember freshman homecoming?" Nia said, shimmying with excitement. "Remember how we tore up that dance floor to this?"

I laughed, reliving the afternoons we'd spent practicing in the mirror before the dance, trying to make our asses clap. We'd been wildly unsuccessful but decided to debut our routine on the homecoming dance floor anyway. The assistant principal tried to kick us out for "inappropriate gyrations." Tabatha had been so embarrassed. She probably knew what was coming, judging by how she'd dropped her face into her hands.

"You think we still got it?" I shouted. Nia gave me an incredulous look and then slid right into our dance.

There were parts I'd forgotten. Cues I had to take from Nia, some she had to take from me. But we remembered all the dips, all the body rolls, and this time around we actually knew how to twerk. It was amazing what the body could recall that the mind had lost.

And mine was remembering that I was deeply, desperately loved by many. I hardly had to cry out for my girls to come running to my aid, ready to lift me up when I was down. This was what love was supposed to feel like: uplifting, encouraging, *renewing*. If I had to let go of a love that was not quite that, that was okay. Because I loved myself, and these women had taught me how.

Eventually the song ended and the DJ, grateful for the small crowd we had drawn to the dance floor, announced, "Thank you to these ladies for showing us how it's done!" Nia and I looked at each other and burst into peals of laughter, clutching at each other to stay on our feet. Seconds later, the next song came on, and we kept dancing on the now-occupied floor to a song that matched our heightened energy.

Suddenly, a hand pressed against my back. I jumped away, armed with a ready barb for whichever asshole decided to touch me without permission, and turned.

The man opening his mouth to talk to me didn't look a thing like Ricky. They were both brown-skinned and dark-haired, but that was where the similarities ended. Where Ricky was lean, this guy was burly, his hair swooped back in a standard Finance bro cut that Ricky's tresses put to shame. Still, at this stranger's unwelcome touch, my mind shuttled backward to another dance floor, this one created in the light of day. A steel betrothal pendant hanging heavy against my chest, my fingers still just a bit tacky with powdered sugar. A haunting rendition of "In the Pines" blasting on outdoor speakers, deep, brown eyes squinting down at me, assessing, trying to piece me together —

"Excuse me," I choked, shoving past the man and marching for the exit. I pushed through the crowd of people, tensing against their inadvertent touches. When I finally reached a break in the throng, my march became a jog, and I hastened out of the dance bar, gulping down the fresh night air.

Ten months. Ricky had handed me his heart and I had squeezed it until it burst, and now I was suffering for it. It had been my choice to end us; so why did it hurt so badly?

I sat on the curb outside for five minutes, tucking my knees to my chest, listening to the cars whiz past. A few concerned pass-ersby stalled by me, but, deciding that I was probably another wasted girl having a breakdown on the sidewalk in the middle of River North, kept walking. Ricky would've stopped for me. He was conscientious like that, the kind of guy to double back after grocery shopping to help an old lady load her car. The kind of guy to approach a cry-ing stranger in the middle of a park and ask her if she was okay, then spend the next several hours trying to make her smile —

I felt, not for the first time, doubt. Never mind being a strong independent woman who didn't need no man; what if *I needed Ricky?* What if my attempts at self-determination had actually been self-sabotage?

"Angie! There you are!"

My girls had found me. I looked up at their beautiful, concerned faces from my spot on the sidewalk, cast into darkness by their shadows. My stomach curled with guilt; I'd run off without telling them.

"Sorry," I said. I curled my arms around myself, shivering under the crisp October breeze. "I needed some air."

Michelle, Tabatha, and Nia all exchanged a meaningful look. They seemed to decide something all at once, and I frowned, a bit put out that I had become an agenda for their silent council meeting. Then Nia helped haul me to my feet.

"All right," she said. "So maybe that was a bit too much." She gave me an apologetic smile. "Do you want to go home?"

I wagged my head, sorry that I had cut my friends' fun short.

"No, no," I said. "Just give me a minute, we can go back in —"

Tabatha cut me off.

"No," she said, raising a finger to me in warning. I could sense her admonishment in her glare — *You're doing it again, compromising instead of demanding what you want* — and I sagged. "We're not doing that."

"Okay, fine," I said, properly chastised. Then I straightened, scanning the streets for something else. My eyes landed on a

452

sign in the distance for a diner, announcing a deal: MIDNIGHT MILKSHAKES — $2.99 EACH.

"Let's go there," I said, pointing to the sign. It was at least four blocks away, but a straight shot down the street. "Will everyone's feet be okay?" I asked.

For a crew of practical girls, all of us had chosen very impractical shoes.

"What's a little pain to a warrior?" Michelle said, stomping her stiletto heel mightily on the concrete sidewalk to prove her point. "We can make it down a couple blocks. Come on."

Without further ado, she looped her arm through mine, I looped mine through Nia's, and Nia looped hers through Tabatha's. We took up the whole breadth of the sidewalk, but I couldn't find it in myself to care. Everyone else could make way. Because we were on a mission for milkshakes that mended broken hearts, and together like this, we were unstoppable.

TWENTY-FIVE

This is a good idea, I typed, traipsing down the general medicine floors. I need a change.

My hair, on most days, was a headache. Before third year hit, my barber and I had a tight, unbreakable bond. Once a month, I slid him thirty bucks to cut my hair into its more manageable tapered cut, then spent hours after the appointment in front of my pathology review videos, working the coif on the top of my head into two-strand twists. Depending on how feverishly I prayed to the hair gods, sometimes they held their form the next day in a twist-out.*

I kept my routine going for most of medical school. But I'd been slacking for the last

---

* My 4C hair likes to scrunch down and hide its length, but by plaiting it into twists and giving it a night's rest, it's possible to loosen it up some. But it's also risky. Sometimes I wake up looking like the Bride of Frankenstein.

few weeks, and it was certainly starting to show. Maybe the white people at work hadn't noticed the difference, but the Black people sure did, judging by the cutting way that Miss Bernice asked me when I was *gonna fix my hair* during pre-rounds.

This would look cute, Michelle said, sending me back photos of packs of plastic-packaged weave. Her grandparents owned a beauty supply in Jersey, and she'd grown up learning the difference between Remy and Kanekalon. In college, I'd dragged her into beauty supply stores with me to act as a human shield* but also a brand expert — she could tell me what extensions would turn into a tangled mess on my head, and which synthetic fibers could withstand heat styling the best. After my big chop† in junior year, though, I no longer had use for her expertise. So when, over our hard-earned milkshakes, I asked if she minded doing me a

* The Korean shopkeeper behind the counter let me be when they saw a girl who could be their daughter trailing behind me. I was born after the L.A. riots, but I still remember Latasha Harlins, murdered for lifting an orange juice.
† The term for the moment when Black girls cut off their relaxed ends and embrace their kinky, coily tresses as they are.

455

favor and grabbing a few bundles from the beauty supply by her apartment so that I could get braids, she'd almost been excited at the prospect.

"I always freak the owners out when I buy for you," she'd said, snickering. "They're like . . . 'No, my daughter, this won't work for you . . .' "

You should do a little color this time, Michelle insisted. I feel like the pastel colors could look really cute on you. She sent me a photo of a lavender-colored weave, and I winced.

No way, I said. Not trying to get in trouble for not looking "professional" enough.

Okay, fine, Michelle said. The next photo she sent was of extensions with a black to gray ombre. I stared at it for a long time, intrigued. It would definitely be a different look for me: a little alternative, but neutral enough that it was unlikely to offend even a particularly stodgy attending.

That's good, actually, I said.

Most girls chopped off their hair after a disastrous breakup. Something about drastically changing their appearance gave them power. The woman they looked at in the mirror afterward would no longer quite resemble the one who'd spent the last week crying their eyes out over their shitty ex, and thus, the two women, one pre and the other post a strong pair of shears, could feel distinct.

Lucky for me, my hair was already short, so I would do that trope one better and go in the opposite direction. Besides, I was excited for the chance to be able to *whip my hair* again.

You're the best, I typed. Where should I grab it from you?

Michelle described exactly how to get to the neurology clinic she would be shadowing in the afternoon, and I thanked her, opening up a browser so that I could look up Senegalese twists. I walked toward the elevator with my head bowed toward my phone, then pressed the button to take me up to my last patient's floor.

Behind me, I heard a prolonged sniffle. I paused, then turned to find the same woman I'd encountered at the elevators last Friday. When I caught her eyes, she dabbed them hurriedly with her handkerchief and gave me a brave smile.

"Oh hello," she said. "How are you today?"

Her smile trembled at the corners. I felt a surge of sympathy for her. Just like me, she seemed to live in the hospital; I'd passed by her sitting in the waiting room of her floor, sometimes accompanied by a gaggle of older women, but usually alone. She was almost always hard at work crocheting something, and sometimes, when I had a few extra minutes, I would watch her from across the room, wondering what masterpiece she was creating and for whom. I examined her features in secret, her stout frame, her straight, thin lips, and now it seemed almost funny that I had automatically linked her to Ricky. They really looked nothing alike.

"I'm okay," I said cautiously. "Are you?"

She nodded unconvincingly, then took in a halting, shuddering breath. I stood woodenly for a moment, staring at the elevator numbers flashing above our heads while trying to decide what to do. Console her? Hug her? Would she be okay with a complete stranger's touch? When her sniffles turned to sobs, I settled for a tentative hand on her shoulder. When she seemed to lean into it, I opened my arms wide for an embrace.

Apparently, that was all the invitation she needed, because she dove into them without preamble. I rubbed circles into her back as my elevator came and went, my mouth set in a line. I remembered the boy in the trauma bay, and the way his mother had trembled with anguish even as she pushed against the officers to get to her son. This woman's grief felt similar.

After one long minute, the woman pulled away, her expression sheepish behind her damp face.

"Sorry, sorry," she said, adjusting her sweater. She cleared her throat, dabbing her eyes. "Thank you."

"You don't have to apologize," I said. I wanted to ask why she was crying, who those tears were for. But then I remembered that we were in a hospital, surrounded by tragedy, and decided against it. Maybe she would tell me herself, the next time we ran into each other. I pressed the elevator button again, just as the woman made a small peep of surprise.

"Oh! Look what I've done!" she said, gesturing to my shoulder. I looked down at my scrub shirt to find a few wet splotches, and I laughed.

"Oh, no problem, I've cried on this shirt plenty myself," I said. The elevator door popped open. "I hope you . . . and whoever you love, get through this."

As the door closed, the woman gave me a nod.

"Me too," she said.

I should have suspected that treachery was

afoot the moment I turned onto my street and found a car that looked suspiciously like my family's 2009 Honda Pilot parked a block away from my apartment. All of the clues were there — the clumsy, suburbanite parallel-parking job, the dent along the bumper where Tabatha had reversed into a mailbox in her senior year of high school — but I'd ignored them out of willful ignorance. After all, my parents didn't have keys to my apartment, and though I would not have put it past them to attempt to ambush me at home, they would need a co-conspirator to actually get inside. Specifically, they needed someone with keys. And there was only one other person who fit that description.

Traitor, I texted her when I reached my apartment and smelled the distinct scent of brown stew wafting through the air.

I'm not sorry, Nia texted back instantly. But also, yell at your sis. She's the mastermind. I just dropped off the loot.

Sighing, I opened the door to my apartment. I should have been angrier with Tabatha for forcing this reunion . . . but I wasn't. Distance had never been my style with my family. Even though the senior Appiahs exhausted me, I missed having them in my life.

"Angela?" my mother's voice called from the bathroom. "Is that you?"

"Yes, Momma," I said. My coffee table had a different kind of spread across it this time: duckbilled clips, combs, a spray bottle, leave-in conditioner, gels, braid sheen spray. Hanging up my keys, I approached it slowly, trying to put together just how many of my friends Tabatha had roped into her plot.

Dorothy Appiah emerged from the bathroom behind me, drying her hands off on her leggings. The last time I'd seen her, she'd been fully decked out for Tabatha's Knocking: wig in place, makeup done, dress pressed. The woman standing before me now, dressed in a loose T-shirt with her hair braided straight back in cornrows, was much more familiar.

"It was nice seeing Nia," she said in lieu of a greeting. She made a show of looking around the apartment.* "You've kept this place neat."

I held back a smirk.

"Neat is a stretch." I sagged my backpack off, then shrugged toward the coffee table. "What's all this?"

"Tabatha said you'd decided to braid your

* As if she hadn't already searched every nook and cranny of the place.

461

hair again," Momma said. "You should be saving your money, instead of throwing $250 away at the salon. I told her I could do it." She dove under the coffee table, producing a plastic bag with a row of THANK YOUS running down the front. "I have some hair here; you can find something you like —"

"No need," I said. I bent to open my backpack, producing four bundles of my gray ombre extensions. I watched her eyes widen as she took in the color; Dorothy Appiah was the one person in the world who was actually *stodgier* than my stodgiest attending.

"Don't you think 1B† would be better?" she started, and I cut her off.

"Momma, why are you here?" I said. She flinched, but I pressed on. "We haven't talked in two months, and that was for a reason. It's really nice that you've decided to come by and cook for me and do my hair, but it doesn't change anything about how we got here in the first place."

The Angela Appiah of yesteryear would have said nothing. She would have accepted her mother's showering of love unquestioningly, happy for a return to normalcy. I

† One shade browner than black.

wondered whether Momma had expected to meet that Angela, and if she could accept this new one.

Momma sighed, dropping onto the couch. She looked at me for a long moment, the corners of her mouth downturned.

"I didn't cook the brown stew," she admitted. "Auntie Abena made it. I'm just heating it up."

"I knew that," I said with a smile. I wandered into the kitchen, finding rice warming in my rice cooker and enough brown stew for two simmering on the stove. I grabbed plates from my cabinets and began doling out servings automatically, setting the table for us like the good eldest daughter I was.

"You shouldn't have blocked us," Momma said, following me as I filled our glasses with cold water from my Brita pitcher. "We're your family. That was incredibly disrespectful of you. Your father is still upset about it, and honestly, I don't blame him. It may take some time for him to come around."

I didn't respond for a moment, busying myself by gathering our utensils.

"I would do it again," I said, setting our glasses down hard on the table. "*You* were disrespectful to *me*. I won't tolerate that. Being family doesn't get you a free pass to talk to me however you'd like." I tore off a paper towel for both of us, then sat. "Let's eat."

We ate in tense silence, our forks clinking against our plates. Auntie Abena's brown stew was banging, as usual, and I scarfed it down at resident-level speed.* Afterward, I waited for Momma to finish, then took her plate and mine to the sink.

"You've grown up," she said. I turned to her as I loaded the dishwasher with our dishes. "You have your own place. Pay your bills." She leaned back in the dining room chair. "You're an adult, I suppose."

I rinsed my glass, watching the bubbles gradually loosen.

"Yes," I said, maintaining eye contact. "I am."

"Your dad and I," Momma said. "We don't mean to be cruel." I leaned against the kitchen counter, listening. "You were very studious, and you've always responded to motivation, and we just want to push you to be successful."

* One side effect of not having a scheduled lunch break is gaining the ability to eat wherever, whenever, and however you can. I once saw Shruti consume a Subway sandwich in the time it took her to get down a flight of stairs.

464

"Push me," I repeated with a scoff. "That's one way to put it."

"You've done well, haven't you?" she said.

"I would've done well regardless," I insisted.

"You don't know that."

"Neither" — I wiped my hands roughly with my dish towel — "do you."

We were silent again, and I let us sit in it. Like it or not, I was her blood. Dorothy Appiah was legendary for her stubbornness, but I could hold my own in a battle of wills. After a minute, she seemed to recognize that. She closed her eyes, then smiled to herself.

"Did you wash your hair?" she said.

"Yesterday," I said.

"Come, then."

I sat between my mother's legs on my living room floor, stiffening my neck as she tugged a wide-toothed comb through my dense curls. *This one has hair like banku,* she had said when I was a child. It had been years since she had braided my hair. She had braided for money back then, bringing her customers into the living room of our small Bronzeville apartment and turning the TV to HGTV. She would comment on the houses' French windows and granite countertops with the assurance of someone who would someday have those things, as if our linoleum tiling and MDF cabinets were a temporary embarrassment. I still remembered what she smelled like then, like Pine-Sol and baby powder, like the dusty homes she frequented to take care of her clientele.

Nowadays, Momma smelled like Yves Saint Laurent Black Opium, and her kitchen counters were Caledonia gray granite. But her hands were still quick and precise. I showed her a picture of the jumbo twists I wanted, and she hummed, using the sharp end of the rat-tailed comb to part my hair into squares. The steady pattern of tugs against my scalp, the clack of clips and combs, and the lightly floral smell of conditioner lulled me into a quiet stupor.

"So," Momma said, as she began to twist. "Tabatha says that you're suffering from a heartbreak."

I startled awake. *Fucking hell, Tabs. Tell them all my business, why don't you?* This close, Momma could feel me stiffen, and she chuckled.

"Your sister loves you," she said, as if she'd heard my internal dialogue. "The way she harassed me! 'Your daughter is having a hard time, and she can't even rely on her own mother to help her!' Ay! Awurade. This is why you don't have girls." She handed

466

me the rest of my twist to finish. "You're both so much like me. Your poor father."

My budding fury at Tabatha quelled. She had done good work by trying to assemble my forces. She'd always been our parents' darling, even during her tantrums, and as children she had used that knowledge to her advantage and my occasional detriment. But now? I could imagine her on the phone with Momma, cutting her down through gritted teeth: *What kind of mother are you, huh?*

"Yeah." I shrugged.

"Tell me about this boy."

And so, I told my mother about Ricky. I walked her through our first meeting, our accidental run-ins in the hospital that quickly became purposeful. I told her about Shae, and the Korean spa, and how he'd offered a shoulder for me to cry on when Nia moved out. I told her about Camila, and his initial resistance to claiming me as his. I told her how he told me that he loved me, and how I loved him so much that I could hardly get through a meal without thinking about the ones we had eaten together. I told her about how, after all that, I still let him go.

By the end, my face was wet with tears. I didn't expect Momma to say much. Ricky was, after all, far from her ideal choice for a partner for me — not Ghanaian, not wealthy, not raised in a traditional family structure. At best, she would say *good riddance,* and offer me half-baked condolences, accompanied by the declaration that at least now I could focus on my studies —

"Why did you stop talking to him?" Momma asked instead, matter-of-factly.

I strained to meet her eye, only to be limited by the tug on my half-done braid.

"I told you," I said, gritting my teeth against the pain. "He was wishy-washy. I couldn't tell what he wanted —"

"Sounds to me like you could." She handed me another twist, then rubbed a dollop of leave-in conditioner between her palms. "Nana Adjoa,★ I think you've made a mistake."

I gaped, my fingers almost losing purchase on my twist.

"How," I asked, amazed, "am I making a mistake?"

Tutting, Momma wrapped an extension around the base of my scalp.

"All these friends you have spoiled you.

★ My day name. There's a different one for each day of the week — Adjoas are girls born on Mondays.

You expect people to know exactly how to love you on the spot," she declared. "The man was there for you when you needed him, was he not? Just take your time and see where things go."

Off the top of my head, I could think of about five different women for whom waiting around had ended in heartbreak. Myself included. I said as much.

"Frederick?" Momma scoffed. "That boy couldn't even manage to pay the twenty dollars for gas to come greet your family. This new one — he's sitting in libraries with your sister to help you with something that will further your career, for no benefit to himself. Look at the *behavior,* not the words, Angela."

"Momma," I said, panicked. "But what about you? Daddy was sure about you. You got married, like, six months after meeting each other. You *knew.*"

Momma paused, smoothing her hand down my finished plait.

"We didn't," she said.

It took all my self-control not to whip around and disrupt her work.

"What?" I said, gripping my knees. My mind was racing, the doubt that I had felt since breaking up with Ricky over a month ago ominous and looming now. "But. You met in church in London, right? And then six months after meeting you were married. Why would you — ?"

"Ah," Momma said. "There's been a misunderstanding. Your father and I met *again* in London. We'd known each other for ten years before that."

My jaw dropped. Misunderstanding, my ass! How many times had Momma lectured Tabatha and me about going to church, adding on that we might happen upon a nice, *virtuous* man there, just as she had?

"You're joking," I said.

"I'm not," she said, and regaled me with the true story of how she and my father had met — in their secondary school statistics class. Their story played out like a rom-com: my mother, the stern, sharp village girl, and my father, the jokester from a family of scholars. They had fallen in love over their books, but Daddy's mother, who had her sights set on him marrying the daughter of a close family friend, had discouraged the relationship. Upsettingly, Daddy had bent to his mother's wishes and dumped my mom. Still, they had kept in touch over the years, sending a letter here or there, scheduling slots at the telecoms office so that they could speak over the phone. When Daddy announced that he planned to move to

470

London to pursue his clinical pharmacy degree, Momma had suggested he meet her at her downtown church.

And the rest was history.

"Can you imagine if I'd decided that I would never speak to him again after he told me he was going to take Agatha out instead of me?" Momma said, chuckling. "You wouldn't exist. Your father was my friend. After he left, I didn't put my life on hold for him, or sit around worrying myself about what he was doing. I just kept on living, and eventually he found his way back to me."

I sat in stunned silence, digesting my mother's words as she diligently worked on my head. Her voice was gentle now, soothing, the way you would talk to a baby you were rocking to sleep.

"From everything you and your sister have told me about this Ricky, he sounds like a good man," she said. "But I don't know him from Adam, and you do. Maybe I'm wrong." She hunched down, crossing her arms over my chest and pulling me backward into an embrace. "But, ɔdɔ,* what if I'm right?"

I thought about that question long after we changed the topic, after we turned on

* My love.

the TV to burn through four episodes of *House Hunters* and Momma dipped my finished twists in hot water. Long after I wrapped my hair under my scarf, popped a Tylenol, and painstakingly lowered my tender head onto my pillow. It was impossible to sleep after that. Every time I managed to doze off, another image of Ricky appeared under the curtain of my closed eyelids — Ricky, face blanched in red light, telling me it was an honor to know me. Ricky, then just another Cute Boy, directing me to sit in a patch of sunlight. Ricky, pressing me into a brick wall, his body solid against mine.

"I don't act right with you," he'd said, and when I awoke it was with a gasp, my lips tingling with the memory of his affection.

I sat up in bed, dropping my head into my hands. Dumping Ricky had felt like the right thing to do. *He'd* given up on me. He'd disappeared, and when he came back, he couldn't contend with the pain that he'd caused. That was enough, right? Love was supposed to be simple. You loved someone, they loved you, you got together, end of. All other encumbrances were manufactured, symptoms of larger problems.

Ricky's fingers, tracing the planes of my face with the focus of a man possessed —

I'm in love with you . . .

"Oh my god," I whispered. I grabbed my pillow and screamed into it as loud as I could. Oh my god, I had made a mistake. Ricky knew me. He knew that I was judgmental and opinionated, and that I had no filter. He didn't roll his eyes at my lack of restraint or hide from the important people in my life, like Frederick. He knew who I was, and he liked me for all my faults, and instead of giving us a chance to grow into more, *I had thrown him away* — and for *what*? Hadn't the ferocity of the way Ricky loved been why I'd fallen for him in the first place? A man who loved his grandparents so completely, his father so unquestioningly, would surely love his unborn child. And when that love had to be measured against his feelings for me . . . of course Ricky had felt stuck. Maybe he'd felt stuck the way Nia felt stuck, trapped between deciding on choosing himself and fickle, silly, cowardly, selfish me. Angela Appiah, so petrified of being hurt, so terrified of being loved, that I preferred to hurt myself first.

I scrambled in the dark for my phone, wincing against the blue-toned light. It was just after midnight. My face felt hot as I scrolled through my "recently called" list, my finger hovering over a contact. Sucking

473

in a breath, I called Nia.

She picked up right away. I could hear ambient voices in the background, followed by an abrupt silence; I must have interrupted a movie.

"Hey, girl," she said. "Everything okay?"

"Can I talk to Shae?" I said hurriedly, wringing my sheets at my sides. It was a big ask — after dumping their best friend, I'd become Public Enemy #1 in Shae's eyes. Thankfully, Nia didn't ask questions. A moment later, I heard Shae's voice.

"What do you want?" they asked brusquely.

"Hi. Sorry. I know it's late," I said. "I wanted to ask you something. You don't have to answer." I sucked in a quick breath. "If . . . I wanted to call Ricky, would he want that too?"

Shae didn't say anything for a moment. When they did, their voice was uncommonly gentle.

"Yeah," they said. "I think he would."

My heart fluttered, overcome with relief. *So I've still got a chance.*

"Okay," I said. "Can you text me his number? I, um, deleted it."

"Of course." Shae paused. I could almost hear the gears in their brain grinding. "Angie, wait. If you're going to call him, I should tell you. He's been going to Harland. He's been there pretty much every day this week." They sighed. "He'll probably be there tomorrow, honestly. His dad's in intensive care. Maybe . . . you could try to catch him there?"

"Oh." My stomach dropped, and I had to fight against a surge of nausea. All this time, Ricky had been a stone's throw away. We might have even passed each other in the halls. And worse, his dad was in intensive care, a part of the hospital so chillingly inhospitable that I avoided walking through it.

"Thanks, Shae. I appreciate it," I said. "Have a good night."

Shae snorted good-naturedly.

"Good luck."

I stared down at my blank phone screen for a long time after Shae hung up, my mind whirling. Ricky needed me. He needed me, and instead of being there for him I had spent my time holed up in my apartment, drowning myself in work, trying to forget that he existed. For all his complicated feelings about his father, I was sure that Ricky didn't want him to *die*. He must be suffering, I thought. Whenever I was suffering, Ricky had made sure to be by my side. And now that it was his turn — I was nowhere

475

to be found.

I made up my mind that minute. I had to make this right. *I was going to make this right.*

TWENTY-SIX

I walked into the hospital the next morning with a plan. It was simple — get through rounds, tie up my patients as efficiently as possible, go to the ICU, make myself useful. I rushed through my pre-rounds, keeping my chitchat with Miss Bernice to a minimum.* During rounds, I kept my presentations succinct and didn't engage when my attending tried to waver off topic. There was a possibility that he would interpret my unwillingness to follow him down intellectual rabbit holes as disinterest, but I didn't care. Besides, given the way he'd pointedly avoided calling me by name this morning, I was pretty sure he didn't recognize me with my new 'do. In a few weeks, poor Brianna might be getting herself

* "Why you running out of here, Dr. Appiah?" she said, suspicious. "You chasing after a man? After all I taught you?"

477

a passive-aggressive evaluation from an attending who she'd never met.* I would have to warn her.

Mercifully, James wasn't in a chatty mood either. We worked next to each other in robotic silence, speaking only to run the list† or call our consults. Despite getting a grand total of two hours of restless sleep the night before, I brimmed with nervous energy. It turned out righteous conviction was an even better motivator for me than heartbreak, because I finished my notes in record time.

"Is there anything else you'd like me to help with?" I asked James, dropping the universal line of medical students asking permission to peace out.

James smirked in recognition but didn't let me off the hook.

"You talked to Rheumatology, put in the discharge instructions for Mr. Johnson, and finished your notes?"

I nodded, trying and failing to keep my leg from jostling impatiently under the table. "Sure did. You were on the call with me, remember?"

* Note: Brianna (other Black girl) and I look nothing alike.

† Medical lingo for going over the checklist of tasks for the day.

"Huh. Yeah, you're right," James said. "Well, good. Thanks for all of your hard work today. See you tomorrow!"

"Thanks, James," I said. Hoisting my backpack over my shoulders, I took one step away from my chair, then another, and then bolted out of the workroom before James could change his mind.

My legs took me down the now-familiar path to the ICU, where I'd helped James escort many a crashing patient. When I first came to Harland, every hallway had looked like the next, and every step had felt uncertain. Now I could move on autopilot and trust that I would get to the right place. I could take a back seat in my mind and let myself focus on my objectives. First and foremost — I would have no expectations. There was no guarantee that after everything I'd put him through, Ricky would want to be with me. And, even though the thought of him turning me away made me feel sick to my stomach, I would bear it, because I wasn't helping him to win his favor. I was helping him because I could, and because it was the right thing to do. Second, I needed to join ICU afternoon rounds so I could better understand the plan for Ricky's dad. Afternoon rounds started in fifteen minutes, and so before then, I would need to introduce myself to the attending, whose name was either Dr. Miller or Milner; I looked it up last night but should've written it down, *damn it* —

It wasn't until I tagged open the double doors into the ICU that I realized that I had left out one crucial step. Somehow, in my order of operations, I'd forgotten to call Ricky.

The apprehension that I'd managed to stem came flooding back like a tidal wave. What the hell was I doing? When Shae said that Ricky would want to talk to me, they didn't necessarily mean about one of the most private, stressful aspects of his life. He probably didn't know that I knew that his dad was in the ICU. How would he react when he realized that the girl who'd dumped him after he'd confessed his love had shown up uninvited to stick her nose in his family's business? Would I get in trouble with the attending for wandering into ICU territory? Was it technically breaking HIPAA* if I'd seen Gabriel Gutiérrez's room number listed on a staffing board and not in his chart?

* HIPAA, or the Health Insurance Portability and Accountability Act, protects patients from snooping healthcare workers, among other things.

Numbly, I walked through the ICU entrance, trying to figure out how to fix my mess. Straight ahead, I could see the medical team gathering near the nursing station, COWs* in tow. They would be rounding soon. If I wanted to listen in, I would have to get his grandmother's permission before they started —

Fuck it. I pulled out my phone, scrolled to Ricky's recently reinstated number, and hit "call." It rang once, and I swallowed against the cannonball in my throat —

"Angie?"

It took me a second to realize that I'd heard his voice in real life and not through my phone. In the weeks since I'd last seen Ricky, my mind had convinced itself that I'd dreamed him up. Seeing him in the flesh felt like an impossibility, like I was staring down a specter made solid. And now he was walking toward me, his jaw set in a way it never was in any of my renditions of this moment, his steps stilted. He was lowering his phone from his ear, and I found myself rooted to the spot, cataloging all the ways

* Literally just stands for Computers On Wheels. Sometimes called Jetsons, because every now and then a patient hears us talk about COWs and assumes we're talking about them.

481

he had changed from the Ricky I had last known. His hair looked longer than I remembered it. His shoulders a bit broader, somehow —

"What are you doing here?" Ricky said. His expression was indecipherable, and I felt my heart sink. *What did you expect, Angie, for him to swoop you up* Notebook *style in the middle of the ICU?*

"Shae told me about your dad." I interlaced my fingers, all the bravado rushing out of me at once. I steeled myself. "I want to help."

I could sense Ricky's resistance before he could voice it. He'd stopped a good six feet in front of me, just close enough for us to communicate without shouting, but far enough for me to know that the distance was intentional. Of course it was. I would be foolish to think that I was welcome.

"If you don't want me to be here," I added hurriedly, "I'll leave. I understand if you never want to see me again. I promise I'm not coming here with any expectations. I just . . . want to help. I can ask questions, I can try to explain concepts that you and your grandma might not understand, I can swipe into all the nutrition rooms and sneak you snacks —"

Ricky stared at me incredulously for a

second, and then let out a huff of laughter.

"Jesus Christ, Shae," he said under his breath. He laughed again, and I realized that his eyes were misty. He wiped them quickly with the back of his free hand, and I followed the motion, stunned. Then, to my relief, he gave me a sheepish smile.

"I like your hair," he said.

"Thanks," I said. "I like yours, too."

"You're into the three-days-unwashed look?" Ricky said automatically. "I'll keep that in mind." Then his smile faltered. "Not that we . . . I mean . . ." He sighed, then pushed his hair out of his face. "Angie, you can appreciate that you being here is really fucking confusing for me, right?"

Ricky must have been exhausted, to let his guard down so freely like that. Something like hope twinged in my chest.

"Let me help," I said, closing the space he'd left between us. "Then, after, we can talk?" I reached for his free hand, hanging limply at his side. "Please?"

He didn't look at me, but his fingers twitched in mine. I smiled to myself.

"Okay," he said, and then he turned, heading toward his father's room. I followed, watching his back as he walked, entranced by the way his shirt shifted with the subtle movements of his shoulder blades. I had a sudden, irresponsible urge to rest my head between them.

No expectations, Angie, I reminded myself. An impossible task.

Over the next ten minutes, Ricky did his best to update me on his father's condition. I listened in silence, knowing that none of it was good. Ricky seemed to know this too, judging by the way his jaw clenched and unclenched in between sentences.

After a brief stint of sobriety, Gabriel Gutiérrez had gone on a bender, mixed his downers with more downers and ended up passing out. Who knows when or where that had happened; whoever had dropped him off at the Emergency Department hadn't bothered to stick around to give a story. Ricky understood why his father had stopped breathing — heroin tended to do that — but he seemed perplexed by how that had led to his kidneys not working, or his lungs getting so trashed that they couldn't wean him off the ventilator.

I had my suspicions. My mind whirled with a differential as he spoke, trying to piece him together medically. *Middle-aged man, past medical history only significant for prediabetes outside of polysubstance abuse, found down,* I thought. *The kidneys are prob-*

ably from rhabdo. The lungs . . . aspiration.
Everything else —

We reached the hospital room, and Ricky's hand hovered over the handle. Then he winced, remembering something.

"It's a party in there," he said, suddenly shy. "There're a lot of people."

I *had* noticed a particularly large group of Latinos in the family meeting room earlier today. I smirked.

"So much for the 'smallest Mexican family in Chicago,' " I said, trying not to read too far into the small smile he gave me. Then, before he could stall any longer, I reached around him and slid the door open.

Gabriel Gutiérrez's hospital room was as lively as a hospital room could get. Ricky's family had clearly maxed out the limit of visitors allowed in the room at once; aside from the patient, there were four other occupants. A middle-aged man clapped Ricky on the shoulder as we entered. Reggaeton played over the hospital TV on low volume, and the windowsill was crowded with disposable foil pans and unlit veladoras.

A woman sat on the sofa near the foot of the hospital bed. A bundle of bright, multicolored yarn was gathered in her lap, and a metallic blue crochet needle flashed between her nimble fingers even as she held court

485

for her visitors. At our entrance, she hefted her project off her lap and onto the seat next to her, making to stand. Then she looked up, and we both froze.

"Abuela," Ricky started, walking ahead of me. "This is Angie —"

"Um," I said. "We've met." I gave the Woman from the Elevator a shy smile and held out my hand. "Nice to officially meet you, Mrs. Gutiérrez."

Ricky's abuela scoffed at my hand and tugged me down into a hug, pulling me so close that I could feel her heart beating alongside mine. I swallowed against a lump in my throat, overcome with an emotion I couldn't name.

"My friend," Mrs. Gutiérrez said. She pulled back, only to clasp my face between her two hands. "Ricardo, this is the girl I told you about. *Mi angelita.*" Her eyes flitted from my face to her grandson's, her brows knitting with confusion. "How do you know each other?"

"We're friends," I said hastily, glancing back at Ricky in panic. "I heard about what happened, and I'm here to help."

Mrs. Gutiérrez's eyes welled with tears, and she pulled me back into her embrace again. Then she took me around the room, introducing me to the other visitors. The short elderly couple were the Barreras, Gabriel's godparents. The reedy forty-something-year-old man was Juan, Mr. Gutiérrez's successor for his eventual retirement and Ricky's de facto big brother. Mr. Gutiérrez would be stopping by after work, Ricky's grandmother informed me. I would have to meet him too.

I smiled and nodded and shook everyone's hand, overwhelmed by Mrs. Gutiérrez's instant, complete acceptance. When I was done making the rounds, I stepped over to the patient. Ricky's dad. He was flipped onto his stomach, his face pressed into a beige, plastic pillow at the end of the bed. His back lifted subtly with every mechanical, ventilator-driven breath. Even swollen and distorted like this, I could see the striking resemblance between this man and his son. I shuddered.

"They're going to round again soon, Abuela," Ricky said, leaning against the counter. "Do you mind if Angie listens in?"

"Please," Mrs. Gutiérrez said. She reached down, clasped my hands, and I saw her grandson in her face again. It was the eyes, I realized, not the shape or the size or even the color, but the way they creased beseechingly, the way I could take one look at them and know that they were kind.

"Of course," I said. And so I did.

Over the next three days, I developed a brand-new routine. I put recruiting participants for my study on temporary hold* and made myself the unofficial liaison for the Gutiérrez family. I came into the hospital two hours early to catch morning ICU rounds before absconding to the floors to pre-round on my own patients, then returned to Gabriel's room at the end of the day to check in. Dr. Milner, amused by the feisty little medical student who drilled his team every morning during rounds, took a liking to me, and occasionally whisked me around the ICU to teach me about ventilator settings and Acute Respiratory Distress Syndrome, the lung condition Gabriel had acquired. Afterward, I regurgitated what I learned to Abuela (which Mrs. Gutiérrez insisted I call her, much to my chagrin) in as digestible terms as possible. I called interpreters for major updates and showed Ricky and Juan how to dial for one themselves when Abuela had impromptu questions. True to my word, I snuck them juice

* Much to Dr. Reed's relief. "I was just waiting for you to run out of steam," he admitted.

488

and soda from the nutrition rooms.

When I wasn't with the ICU team, I sat with Abuela. Ricky's looks were all his grandfather, a taciturn, compact man who spoke to me exclusively through his wife, but his personality was all her. She was gracious and excitable and shockingly funny, capable of finding a sliver of happiness even with her only son dying feet away from her. I could see why Ricky loved her so much.

"When I sit for a long time and it hurts, is this also rhabdomyolysis?"* Abuela said, slapping her bum to demonstrate just as Ricky pushed the door open with our Starbucks in hand.

"I don't know," I said, crumpling into giggles. "I'll have to ask Dr. Milner." Then I turned to look up at Ricky, wiping at my eyes.

"Grande iced mocha," he said, handing Abuela her drink. Then, for me: "Tall vanilla latte."

Our fingers brushed as the drink exchanged hands.

"Thanks," I said.

Ricky gave me a long, blank look. Then he

---

* A dangerous syndrome caused by the breakdown of muscle. It is usually seen in people who've been stuck in the same position for a long time.

nodded and pivoted away.

"I'm going to get some work done down in the café," he said. "I'll be back in an hour."

"Okay, mijo," Abuela said placidly.

I watched him leave, racked by guilt. As much as I loved spending time with Abuela, she was Ricky's grandmother, not mine. I knew I was intruding. Even though Ricky accepted my presence, he seemed uncomfortable with it, leaving the room any time we might be left alone together, keeping our conversations strictly clinical, careful to always place an Abuela-sized buffer between us. And that was fine. I was the one who had walked away from us, and now that I had unceremoniously turned back up again, it was Ricky's choice if and when he wanted to accept me back into his fold. *No expectations,* I reminded myself.

I stood.

"I should go too," I said.

Abuela gave me a small, secret smile.

"You love my grandson, don't you?" she said coyly.

Okay, hadn't seen *that* coming. I knew I'd probably been staring after Ricky longingly, maybe letting out some long, lovelorn sighs, but had I really been that obvious?

"U-um," I stammered, unsure of how to

respond, and she cackled, pleased with her-self.

"It's okay, it's okay!" she said. "You don't have to be shy." She patted my arm and gave me a conspiratorial wink. "He's a kind boy. This is hard for him." She looked toward her son, now flipped onto his back. "My son," she swallowed, an ancient, hardened sorrow peeking through, "was never a father to him. He made choices that he shouldn't have, and no matter how hard I have tried, how many times I cried, I couldn't stop him. I have to admit, I gave up long ago on him changing. I have known that I would outlive my son since he was young."

Slowly, I sat back down, not looking away. Abuela's jaw was set, and she looked upon her son's heaving body without flinching. I imagined Abuela twenty years younger, her back a bit straighter, her face less lined, screaming at a man who looked like the one on the vent, who looked like the one I loved.

"Ricky believed, though." She wrung her hands together. "He always thought that his father was capable of changing his own destiny but was just refusing to do so. It's frustrated him his whole life. He could get so angry with me! Every time I give his father money, he would say, *Abuelita, you are enabling him. He's just going to spend it*

491

on more drugs. As if I didn't know." She shook her head, smiled. "I think he was still hoping something would change. But now . . . here we are."

I swallowed against the lump in my throat, for the first time feeling Abuela's resignation. During rounds, when the team talked about Gabriel's case, I could read between the lines. They hadn't said it outright yet, still waiting on a miracle, but we all knew the truth — Gabriel was in a bad way. His chances of making it through this were next to none. He would most likely die here, and . . . Abuela knew this. I suspected she'd known from the beginning, and the sobs that had racked her body when I met her at the elevators the second time had been from grief. She had simply been keeping vigil ever since.

"I used to have regrets," Abuela said. "Maybe if we had sent him to the expensive Catholic school. Maybe if we had not pushed him so hard. Not anymore. My son has brought me many tears, but so much joy as well. And he gave me a grandson who has the most *beautiful* soul." She turned to me then, reached for the hand in my lap. "You too, Angela. You have a beautiful soul too."

I looked down at Abuela, feeling my vision blur with emotion. I opened my mouth to speak but found myself too choked to find the words.

Abuela squeezed my hand, finding them for me.

"Give him some time. He'll come around," she said, giving me a wink. Then she patted my hand. "Go home and sleep, Doctor."

I swallowed, regaining my voice.

"I'll be back tomorrow," I said.

"I know," Abuela said, and then she closed her eyes.

TWENTY-SEVEN

On the fourth day, everything went to shit.

I arrived in the ICU to find Bethany, Gabriel's resident, typing in orders bedside. There was a new machine present, this one unfamiliar, with several huge bags filled with clear fluid. I followed the blood-filled line from the machine into a large catheter in his neck — *Dialysis, then.* I stared at the new setup for a long time, then made eye contact with Abuela over Gabriel's hospital bed. Her eyes were shining, but her lips were thin with resolve. Next to her, Mr. Gutiérrez snored, clearly wiped from an active night.

"Angie! Good morning," Bethany said. She glanced at Abuela, then toward the door. Understanding, I gave Abuela a solemn nod and followed Bethany out. She slid the door shut, then rounded on me.

"It's been a rough night," she admitted.

"Sure looks like it," I said, my stomach

sinking. I wasn't overly familiar with critical care, but during our last lesson, Dr. Milner had explained to me what *pressors** were. I knew enough to know that one was okay, two bad news, three almost always fatal. Gabriel was on *six*. The max, I remembered, feeling sick.

"He went into cardiogenic shock overnight," Bethany said. She had her red hair tied up in a knot on the top of her head, and some errant strands had escaped and hung into her tired eyes. She held out her phone, scrolling to a video of the cardiac ultrasound that she'd taken earlier in the night.

"What chamber is this?" she asked, apparently not too tired to pimp me.

"The right ventricle," I said. "But . . . it looks weird. Is it just the angle, or . . . ?"

Bethany nodded.

"You're right. It's not supposed to look like that," she said. "It's huge. His lungs are toast, and they've done a number on his heart. His kidneys haven't shown any sign of recovery. That's three major organs down, not even counting the pressor requirement." She tucked her lips into her mouth. "You're close to the family, right?"

* Medications used to increase blood pressure.

495

I understood what she was saying, but her unspoken request still sent me into a panic.

"Yes," I said in a small voice.

"I sent an email to your attending this morning," Bethany said, suddenly gentle. "I cc'd Dr. Milner. We asked if he didn't mind you missing rounds upstairs today. Figured all of this could still count as part of your education." She gave me a sympathetic look. "I'm sorry. Are you familiar with goals of care discussions?"

I nodded, my mind racing as I tried to put together my plan of action. Abuela already understood that her son was dying, but did she understand that the next step — the manner in which he died — was up to her? That she could accept him as gone and allow the team to switch their focus to alleviating his suffering . . . or hang on till the last possible second, pummeling him with drugs to raise his blood pressure, dialysis to drag out his fluids, compressions to bring back his heart when it inevitably stopped? Suddenly, I felt like an imposter, a wee medical student playing doctor. None of my shelf exam practice questions could have hoped to prepare me for this.

"Can we get an interpreter?" I asked.

Bethany shook her head.

"Not an in-person one. They don't work

weekends."* When I groaned, she added, "You can still use the phone one?"

I could have laughed. The grainy telephone line? To deliver news like this?

I texted Ricky. The old thread had long been deleted, and our new one was formal and impersonal (Are you here? Yes. What do you want from the cafeteria? A grilled chicken sandwich, please. Thanks.) and my new addition was no different.

Where are you? I typed.

I found Ricky sitting alone in the family room, his laptop balanced on his crossed legs. When I opened the door, he looked up, greeting me with a grim nod.

"What's up?" he said, lowering his headphones from his ears. He had bags under his eyes; I doubted he'd slept much all night. I sat down on the couch diagonally from him, trying to formulate the words. How did you tell the man you loved that his father, estranged or not, was dying? Where was the guidebook for that? Thankfully, Ricky seemed to understand why I was there, because he snapped his laptop shut and put it on the cushion next to him.

* Despite the fact that most people don't tend to wait until Monday to die, the hospital is oddly bereft of services over the weekend.

"There's nothing left for them to do," I said, getting straight to the point.

Ricky wiped down his face with both hands. His left leg bounced, and I listened to the sound of his jeans jostling for a long minute.

Then: "So this it, then?" he said. "He's dying." When I nodded, he let out a shuddering breath. "Shit."

"I know," I said.

"There's *nothing* else they can do," Ricky said, his tone taking on a frantic edge. His hands delved into his hair and gripped, and I watched him, helpless. "They can't just . . . suck whatever is in his lungs out?"

I bit my lip, shaking my head. *It's the inflammation,* I thought. *His lungs attacking themselves. They're supposed to expand, like little balloons. Right now, they're like pumice. You can't suck that out. There's no reversing it.*

"It doesn't work like that," I said lamely instead, but Ricky didn't seem to hear me, still lost in his anguish. Eventually, he braced his elbows on his knees, folding his hands together in front of him.

"Okay," he said. "So now what?"

After a deep, weary sigh, I told him what was left to be done. The longer I spoke, the queasier Ricky looked, his body tight and still with tension. When I was finished, he crumpled forward, dropping his face into his hands.

"You think we should tell them," he said.

"I can say it in English," I said. "You can translate. We can have the interpreter on the line to help out if you get stuck." I looked at my feet, doubt burning the back of my throat. "Unless, you think we should get the team to do it first —"

"No," Ricky said quickly. "They can come after. They should hear it from us first." Then he added, quietly, "They trust you. It'll be better this way."

I looked up at him, watching his knee begin to bounce again. I remembered a story he'd told me, not long ago, after we'd finished the first season of *One Punch Man*. I'd been sitting on my couch, he on the floor next to me. The story featured an eight-year-old Ricky, chubby, naive, and, like many little boys, completely obsessed with his father. Back then, Gabriel had seemed like the coolest person on the planet: suave, stylish, capable of giving Abuela what-for when she was being unfair. Gabriel had picked Ricky up and taken him on a rare trip to Chuck E. Cheese, setting him loose on the arcade with an unlimited pass. Ricky had set his sights on a scooter high up on the shelf of prizes, worth more tickets than he could have dreamed of earning, but somehow at the end of the day, Gabriel had procured it.

"He made me think he was a whiz at arcade games," Ricky had mused. "But turns out he just slipped the kid working the counter forty bucks to hand it over." He'd laughed humorlessly, lifting his arm to cover his eyes. "And of course, it was Abuelo's money, so, technically, not even a gift from him."

Still, Ricky had ridden that scooter until it fell apart.

I wondered whether Ricky was remembering that day in Chuck E. Cheese now, thinking of the last time Gabriel had felt like his father.

"Okay," I said. My hands itched to reach for him, and so I clenched them at my sides, gritting my teeth, and stood, moving to give him space. "I'll give you a few minutes, then. I'll be back —"

Ricky's arms snaked around my waist.

I stared down at the crown of his head in shock, my shins knocking against the base of the couch as he tugged me closer in between his legs. From this vantage point, I could see that his shoulders were trembling. He pressed his face into my stomach, leaving it warm and *wet*. It took me a moment to realize that he was crying.

Fuck. The tears that I'd been holding back for days rolled down my cheeks, and I wrapped my arms around his neck, pulling him close as his tears turned into body-racking sobs. *I'm sorry,* I wanted to say. *I'm sorry this is happening to you. I'm sorry your dad is dying. I'm sorry that I wasn't here to help from the start.*

But sorry wasn't enough, so I didn't say anything at all, just balanced precariously on the balls of my feet and rubbed circles into his back as he broke into pieces in my arms.

Eventually, his breathing evened, and his hold on me loosened. I stroked his hair idly, knowing that he would be shy.

"Are you ready?" I asked softly. I knew it was premature, but I'd seen Gabriel's blood pressures. There was really no more time to waste.

Ricky cleared his throat, avoiding my gaze. His eyes were still glazed with tears, and I wanted nothing more than to kiss them away. But instead, I settled for giving him a comforting smile and a small pack of hospital-issue tissues. He accepted them silently, wiping off his face.

"Yeah," he said, his voice still hoarse. He coughed, then tried again. "Let's go."

As planned, we went into the room before the ICU team. We called the interpreter first, informing him of our plan. Wordlessly, Ricky grasped my hand as we walked toward his father's hospital room, giving Bethany and Dr. Milner a nod as we passed. *Together,* Ricky seemed to be saying. *We're doing this together.*

Abuela was waiting for us when we arrived. Her rosary, normally tucked in a pouch in her pocket, was wrapped around her wrist. She jostled her husband awake, then scooted to the edge of the couch. Her gaze flickered to our conjoined hands, then back to our haunted faces.

"You have something to tell us," she said, giving us a nod. "And we are ready to hear it."

Ricky and I exchanged a glance, and I took a deep breath.

"All right," I said.

And then we began.

I slid the door to Gabriel's room shut, waiting to hear the soft *thump* of the air pressure shifting before dropping my head backward against the glass. Under my closed eyelids, I could still see Abuela and Mr. Gutiérrez's gray, resolute faces, still picture the pale-knuckled grip Abuela had on her husband's shirt.

"How long do we have?" she'd asked, her voice firm even through her tears. *Minutes? Hours? Days?*

Months ago, when I'd watched Shruti lead the resuscitation effort for the young gunshot victim, I'd marveled at her objectiveness in the face of tragedy. But I hadn't seen what happened next. I'd missed Shruti sitting the boy's mother down after the code was inevitably called, holding her shattering body in her arms as she told her that *it was over.* All this time, I'd assumed that being a doctor meant performing miracles. Fixing bodies. Saving lives. I had hardly considered the flip side of that coin: that it also meant looking a patient's family in the eye and telling them to say their last goodbyes. That it meant staring down the permanence of death over and over again, until it stopped feeling like something to be prevented at all costs and instead became something to be occasionally embraced.

I wandered back to the family meeting room. Part of me was tempted to glance at the monitor in the nursing station that displayed Gabriel's vital signs remotely, but it seemed improper to count down a man's death, and so I dropped my head against the back of the couch and tried to understand why I felt like I was losing someone too. A more innocent, naive version of myself, maybe? The one that hadn't been forced to tell the man she loved and the woman she had come to admire that their father and son was circling the drain?

Several minutes later, the door to the family room creaked open. I jumped to my feet, ready to vacate in case Dr. Milner needed the room for a different family, but it was Ricky, one hand in his pocket, the other holding the door open for his grandparents. I gave him a questioning look, and, understanding, he answered with a grim nod. So it was over, then. What had I told Abuela, when she asked how much more time she had with her son? *I don't know, but I don't think he'll last the day.* He had hardly lasted the hour.

Mr. Gutiérrez glanced at me, then back at his grandson, saying something quietly in Spanish.

"He's saying, 'Thank you for everything you've done for our family,'" Ricky translated. His eyes were no longer bloodshot, but I could see the exhaustion in the droop of his shoulders. "And, um, that if you would like, you should come to the funeral."

I gave Mr. Gutiérrez a shy smile, touched.

"Of course," I said.

We stood, looking at the tile, for a long, still moment. There was nothing left for me to say. I'd done what I'd sought to do, and now it was time for me to go home, accept that this was the end of the road, and try to move on with my life. It had been only a few days, but I would miss Abuela. And Ricky . . .

Well, I had almost gotten over him once, right?

Suddenly, Abuela kissed her teeth.

I turned to her, flummoxed by her annoyance, but she had eyes only for her grandson. Ricky staggered backward, wide-eyed and slack-jawed, as she lifted a finger to his face.

"You are still among the living, are you not?" she asked him. "Sé fuerte. Go. Show her."

"Wait," Ricky said, alarmed. "Right now, Abuela? Shouldn't I be going home with you? I can help with making arrangements —"

"You think that we need you for that, little boy?" Abuela said, and suddenly I saw her for the broom-swinging, slipper-slinging

505

matriarch that she was. "Él que no arriesga, no gana. Now *go.*"

Twenty-Eight

"Show me what?" I asked for the third time since we'd left Gabriel's room. For the third time, Ricky ignored me.

"Do you have all of your stuff?" he asked, his voice ragged.

I pulled my backpack higher up onto my back.

"Yes, but —"

"Okay," he said. He looked at me askance, his expression still curiously blank. If it weren't for the grip he had on my hand, I would have thought that he still hated me. I hadn't gotten used to this boy, who was always smiling, looking so grave. But then again, his grandmother had forcibly sent him on this quest with me, not even a full hour after he helped deliver the worst news of her life. "We're going for a drive."

I started, giving him an incredulous look.

"Where?" I asked, trying to keep pace with his long strides.

507

His lips quirked just a little, and I warmed, gratified to finally see a peek of his playfulness. "It's a surprise, okay? Just . . . go along with it for once," he said.

I followed him up one flight of stairs to his car, piling into the passenger seat as he unlocked it. We threw our bags into the back seat in unison.

We drove out onto the highway mostly in silence, but it was a different silence than the one we'd endured over the last several days. Ricky kept his eyes on the road and one hand on the wheel, but the other reached for me, smoothing along my thigh, draped behind my headrest, gripping my hand when we stopped at red lights. An hour and a half ago, we had stood before his grandparents to tell them that his father was dying. The excitement I felt bubbling in my stomach felt reprehensible in light of that. And yet, I still felt it. What did that say about me, that the predominant feeling I had in this moment was *relief*?

"Is it too much to ask you to close your eyes?" Ricky said after he took an exit. I recognized it as the one to his apartment. Was he taking me home? Was *he* the surprise? I laughed the thought away — Abuela had some spice to her, but not "send your grandson away to dick down some girl" spice.

I glanced at him. He looked nervous all of a sudden, chewing at his inner cheek as he scanned the road in front of him. It was a better look than the anguish he'd worn before, but just as curious.

"Okay," I said, closing my eyes. "You'll tell me when to open them?"

Ricky made a noise in the affirmative. With my eyes closed, I could focus on the rest of my senses; the smell of Ricky's car, lemon, judging by the small tree I'd noted hanging from his mirror, the rushing sound of traffic, the squeeze of his fingers in mine. The radio was playing "Untitled" by D'Angelo, and so I hummed along, remembering how I'd flitted around my room in elementary school, belting this song at top volume and pretending to be in love.*

"Almost there," he declared after a moment, as the car stalled to a stop. I moved to open my car door, and he sighed, exasperated. "Stop! You'll run into traffic. Come on. I'll help you."

If Ricky hadn't just lost his father, I might have cheated a little bit. As it was, I decided

---

*With absolutely no recognition of the song's, uh, seductive undertones.

509

to go along with it, letting him guide me blindly down a sidewalk with my arm hooked through his. After only a few meters, we stopped. I heard the creak of a gate opening, and the smooth sidewalk suddenly became mulchy and soft. Even in the crisp fall, the scent of nature was unmistakable.

Suddenly, I knew exactly where we were.

"Okay," Ricky said, letting go of my arm. "You can open them now."

I opened my eyes and looked up.

The woman in the mural was looking down, as though gazing at the garden below her. The corners of her ample lips were turned up in a subtle smile, her head resting on one shoulder and giving a decadent view of her swanlike neck. She was surrounded by clusters of peace lilies, every one of them turned to face her in reverence. Her cropped curls were artfully rendered, and her dark brown skin was even and bright. She was beautiful.

She was . . . me?

Stunned, I stumbled closer to the wall with my head tilted toward the sky. The sounds of our surroundings were lost to me; all I could hear was the pounding of my heart, beating away like a bass drum. No way. It was impossible. When had he —

"Do you like it?" Ricky said quietly from

behind me.

"Like it?" I croaked. "Ricky . . ." *You painted my face on a wall.*

I finally tore my gaze away from the mural to look at Ricky. My trembling hands came up to my mouth, trying to hold back words that were stuck in my throat anyway. Through watery eyes, I took him in. His proud but shy smile. His bright eyes, reflective in the morning sun. The bob of his Adam's apple as he swallowed nervously, his long, dark hair that, honestly, had grown on me —

I loved him. Oh my god. It hurt how much I loved him. I wanted to see that face every day, wanted to roll over in bed in the mornings and watch him wake up. I wanted to hold him close and kiss him breathless and drag him cavewoman-style into my bedroom and do things to him that would make Tabatha blush. I'd been coming to the ICU for less than a week; this mural had surely taken longer than that. And all this, after I had *hurt* him. After I had taken his love and deemed it false. While I was holing myself up in my apartment, determinedly pushing him out of my heart, had he been up on a ladder, painstakingly re-creating my likeness?

"Angie," he said, alarmed.

511

"Oh no," I said. The tears had already started dripping down my face before I could even register that they were there. "Ugh, can I go one day without crying over you?"

"You've been crying over me?" Ricky said sardonically. I scoffed, swiping my face with the heels of my hands.

"Of course," I said. The rush of ecstasy, so soon after despair, made my legs buckle, and I struggled to stay on my feet. "Of course I've been crying over you. I was *so stupid,* Ricky, and I'm sorry, but this is . . . this . . ." I took a shuddering breath. "You made me so beautiful. I still can't . . ."

Ricky closed the distance between us, wrapping his arms around me from behind. I melted into his embrace, and we looked up at his work together. He tucked his head into the crook of my neck and inhaled.

"You know you destroyed me, right?" he said. "I . . . didn't even know I could feel like that. I didn't want to die, exactly . . . but I wasn't too excited about waking up every day either."

I closed my eyes, remembering the hollow look he'd given me a month ago, and nodded, ashamed.

"I'm sorry —" I started, but he pressed a kiss to my neck, silencing me. Then, with one hand on my elbow, he guided me to sit next to him on the bench. I followed him numbly, staggering as I turned back to stare at the mural, still in a state of shock.

"I was so angry, at first," he said, "but even with that, I still wanted to see you. Kept waiting for Fate to kick in again, the way it did in the beginning, you know, when we used to just run into each other. But of course, no dice." He smiled to himself, reaching up to brush away my tears with a drag of his thumb. "I was flipping through my sketchbook one day. And I came across that picture I drew of you, the day that we met. And I don't know. Next thing I knew, I was walking to Lydia's, and asking her if I could have use of her wall.

"I told myself all sorts of things. That you were toxic, and this was for the best.* That painting you would help me get closure," he continued. "You know, *art therapy,* and all that. But really, I think part of me was hoping that you'd walk by and see it. And then, maybe you'd realize that you were wrong about me. And that maybe after that . . . you would come back."

There was only one tree in the garden, and its leaves had begun to yellow and fall.

* I laughed. "Fair," I said.

I nudged one with the toe of my shoe. Even if he had forgiven me, I could still hear the pain in his voice. I tried to imagine if our situations had been reversed, if I would ever be able to look at him again.

"I should have trusted you," I said in a small voice. "I just . . . I was scared." I looked up at him then, my vision blurring. "Ricky, I've . . . I've never felt the way I do about you about *anyone.* You have no idea how much power you have over me. It's too much. It's like I can't be a reasonable human being about you." I bit my lip. "All you have to do is change your mind about how you feel, and I won't be able to function."

"I won't change my mind," Ricky said, shaking his head. He reached for one of my hands, brought it to his lips. "You frustrate me. *So much.* But you also make me better. I *like* who I become when I'm with you." He cocked his head toward my mural, and I followed his gaze toward it, feeling tears prick my eyes again. "I've always wanted to try something like this, but it always seemed like something out of my reach. But I watched you work your ass off every day, throw yourself out of your comfort zone, make yourself learn new things. Always for things you thought were *right,* even when people told you you shouldn't. So screw not

514

being good at painting. I gave it a shot, and I did pretty good, didn't I?" He squeezed my hand. "You know, I posted this mural on my website, and one of the reps from Rogers reached out to me. Wants to commission me to paint over that creepy mural on the third floor." I snickered, remembering walking through the hall in the early morning and feeling the mural's round, chalky eyes trailing after me. "They're offering a *lot* of money for it. Like, maybe 'pay off the rest of my student loans' money."

"That's amazing, Ricky," I said, swelling with pride.

"It's crazy, is what it is," he said. He interlaced our fingers together. "You make me crazy."

I looked up at him. All the lightness from before, his shy smile. It was gone. Now he was looking at me intensely, like he was taking me apart piece by piece and reassembling me in his mind. I remembered, in the beginning, how I used to hide from that stare. Now, I stared back.

"I still can't believe you came back," he said. "I can't believe we're here right now. I can't believe that an hour ago . . ." He let out a huff of incredulous laughter, and I watched his face solemnly. "My dad just died, and I'm sitting here, with you."

515

I ducked my head, suddenly guilty. *Show her,* Abuela had said, throwing her grandson out of the room. Instead of getting the chance to say a final goodbye, he was here, with me.

"And despite that, I'm . . . *happy,*" Ricky finished "Isn't that wild?"

I looked up at Ricky in astonishment, watching as his face broke out into a smile, a real one, the kind that crinkled his eyes and brought out his dimples. I didn't know I could feel happiness like this. So bright, so intense, that I thought it would rend me in two. I closed my eyes, focusing on this moment. His hand in mine, the tendons flexing as he gathered me closer. The tittering of birds hiding in the still-green bushes. The strange medley of smells, of chlorophyll and milled dirt, corn tortillas from the taqueria next door, waffle cones from the ice cream parlor across the street, the light musky scent of his cologne. I knew I was trembling, and that he could feel it.

"I'm happy too," I said after a moment. Then, because he'd said it first the last time, I added, "Nothing's changed for me, you know. I still love you."

And it was easier to say this time because there was no longer any reason to hold back.

"I know," Ricky said.

I nudged him in the side, pouting.

"Okay, Han Solo."

A steady hand on my chin guided my face back to his.

"What, was my grand romantic gesture not enough?" he said. "I know. You came and found me, right? Even though you knew you might not be welcome?" He grabbed my other hand, sandwiched it between his. "I'm never going to forget that, Angie. I'm going to wake up every day for the rest of my life and look at your face and remember that, when I needed you most, you were there for me. For my family."

Every day, I choose, his grandfather had said. My heart picked up speed, and I searched his face for any sign that he was joking. I couldn't find it. Ricky was all firmly set jaw and earnest eyes and when he brought our folded hands to his chest, I could feel that his heart was racing too.

"You know Abuela is already calling you her granddaughter?" Ricky continued.

Oh, Abuela. Not that I was surprised. Ricky had clearly inherited his ain't-shitness from somewhere.

"She is?" I said, snickering.

Ricky nodded, his smile turning impish.

"Oh yeah. She gives me the look every time too. Like, *Get on with it, mijo,*" he said.

He winked. "I told her that I was working on it."

I gaped at him even as he grinned back, clearly proud of himself.

"You're *working* on it," I repeated, my gaze flicking from his smiling eyes to the bit of lip that he'd just wet with his tongue.

"Of course," he said, dropping my hands to scoot closer to me on the bench. "We have to get through a few steps, though, first. Just to make it proper."

"Uh-huh," I said, snaking my arms around his neck.

"For starters" — his nose skimmed over mine, his breath wafting warm over my lips — "we should probably try out the whole 'being my girlfriend' thing again."

"Interesting proposition," I said. "I accept."

Ricky's laugh was more of a rumble, reverberating deep in his chest and into mine. And then he was kissing me, so sweetly it made my heart ache, and I was kissing him back. Dizzy with elation, I pressed myself into his chest and squeaked as he hoisted me up and onto his lap. I splayed my fingers over his shoulders, buried them in his hair. He was real, and all mine, and maybe everything that had transpired had just brought us to this place. I imagined drinking him up like this every day, and for once I didn't feel guilty letting that image blossom into something more in my head. Because I knew he was even crazier than me. Thinking about *the rest of his life,* and whatnot. Definitely planning our wedding in his head. We finally broke away, my braids shrouding us in a quiet, private place.

"Sounds like a deal," Ricky said finally. And then we laughed, kissed again, and laughed some more.

EPILOGUE

I fidgeted in front of the mirror, pulling on the hem of my blue sheath dress. Match Day, the day I had been both dreading and anticipating from the second I submitted my rank list in February, started in one hour. The day when I would learn where I'd be spending the next three years of my life. Poor Ricky'd had to deal with me fretting around the apartment for weeks leading up to this day, including a particularly memorable dinner during which I'd nearly had a panic attack about whether I should have swapped the fifth and sixth institutions on my list.

In contrast, Ricky seemed all too calm about Match. My two favorite programs were outside of Chicago and when I considered moving them further down the list to prioritize local programs, he insisted that I move them back. I tried to explain the ramifications of the Match to him — "You might have to move away from your grandparents, and what if I end up in the middle of nowhere?" — but he insisted that we would "work it out." I'd seen serious relationships break up two months into residency, even less when they were long distance. The nonmedical partners seemed to take residency the hardest, but no matter how often I reminded Ricky that I would soon be working sixty to eighty hours a week, he brushed me off.

Even now, watching me in the mirror from against the doorframe, he looked inordinately unbothered.

"Is this dress too short?" I asked. "I thought it looked good before, but it keeps riding up."

Ricky smirked, scanning the length of my body with shameless admiration.

"I think you look great," he said lasciviously.

I rolled my eyes at him but smiled all the same.

"You're just saying that because it's tight," I said.

Ricky sidled up behind me, pressing a chaste kiss on my cheek while running his hands down the curve of my waist in a manner that was . . . much less so.

"My point still stands," he said, pulling

my ear gently between his teeth. I melted into him, letting him lather my neck with blistering-hot, feather-light kisses, and then, before he could break down my resolve, pushed him away.

"No," I said sternly, pointing at him. "On task."

He chuckled, pressing one last kiss onto my cheek, and then spun me to face him.

"We have an hour," he said, drawing me slowly into him again. "I can be . . . efficient."

Lord, could he be. I considered it. I always found Ricky delectable, but today in particular, dressed in his smart button-down, navy blazer, and a pair of chinos that held his ass up like two loving hands, he looked particularly irresistible. Even Momma, who was still a bit disappointed that neither of her daughters had shacked up with a Ghanaian, cooed, "Ooh, he is handsome," when she first met him.

"It'll take twenty minutes to walk there," I reasoned. "We have to get there ten minutes before, or we won't get good seats. So no."

"Angela Appiah, worrying about being late!" he teased. He lunged for the nearby window, making a show of searching the skies for something. "Are pigs flying?"

I stuck my tongue out at him, and then

stepped into the bathroom to do my makeup.

My entire life, I had been careful. I knew myself, knew that I would give all of myself away for nothing if I didn't hold myself on a leash, and so I made sure I always followed some general rules. No sex before commitment. Always pay for my own first date. Don't say *I love you* until the other person says it first.

But with Ricky, I could be reckless. There didn't seem to be a need to be cautious, not with the man who painted my face into murals and squeezed my hand at his father's funeral. When Ricky's lease ran out, instead of renewing it, he suggested he take Nia's old room, and I agreed without thinking. And when Momma called to ask whether I'd be sending in Ricky's measurements, I did so without question. I spent my newly earned fourth-year free time* taking Spanish lessons and having stilted conversations with Abuela over cups of homemade horchata. I finally convinced Abuelo to go to

* Fourth year of medical school is like the most expensive vacation I'll ever take — sixty thousand dollars for classes no one attends and flights and accommodations for interviews for places where I might not match.

the doctor's, calling into his appointments after he was diagnosed with high blood pressure.

A part of me kept waiting for Ricky to prove that I was making a mistake. That our honeymoon period would pass, and we would go from being lovers to bitter roommates. But he didn't. At Tabatha's traditional, he had looked dapper in his custom-embroidered attire, and somehow won over my aunties so thoroughly that they made a competition out of asking him to dance. He'd eaten fufu properly, with his hands, and helped Momma and me with the cleanup afterward. "I'm a grandma's boy," he claimed when Momma tried to shoo him out of the kitchen. If the mural hadn't won her over, that certainly did the trick.

A year and a half ago, when we stood in Lydia's garden for the second time, I swore that I could never love a man as much as I did Ricky. And here I was, loving the same man, but somehow even more than before.

"You ready?" he asked when we had forty minutes left. Miraculously, I was, and we made the walk to campus.

When we reached the auditorium, the usher, a third-year medical student, directed me down one path, and Ricky into the friends and family seating.

"It's gonna be okay, babe," Ricky said, right before we split up. "Breathe. It'll be over in an hour." He waved to Nia, who had arrived early and saved him a seat, then gave me a brief kiss. "I love you."

"Love you too," I said. I took a shuddering breath and walked down the decorated aisle to sit next to Michelle. She gave me a shaky smile.

"You look bomb," she said. "I told you the blue was a good choice."

"Thanks, boo. So do you." Much to Markus's chagrin, much of the Sanity Circle group chat discussion for the last week had revolved around coordinating our outfits for the post-Match photos. Michelle looked incredible in a red dress that complemented her lipstick.

"Terrified?" Michelle asked. She'd only applied to psychiatry programs on the East Coast, and her rank list had been about ten institutions shorter than mine. She'd been radiating anxiety since the residency application submission deadline.

"Of course," I said. She squeezed my hand.

"We'll be okay," she insisted.

Match Day, like every medical school ceremony, started with a whole lot of pomp and circumstance. Our dean introduced an esteemed physician-scientist as our speaker, who gave a speech about his illustrious career and how we too could be like him if only we were as naturally brilliant and charismatic. We watched a video, stitched together by our alumni, wishing us good luck in residency. Then, one by one, we were called to the front of the room to retrieve our envelopes.

When they called out my name — pronounced *Ap-pie-ah* instead of *Ap-pee-ah* even though I'd given them a pronunciation guide — I walked up to the stage. My professor gave me a reassuring smile as she handed me the envelope. No piece of paper had ever felt so volatile. We were instructed not to open our envelopes until all had been handed out, and I searched the crowd for Ricky and Nia, knowing that the moment the clock hit eleven they would be allowed into our section to celebrate. I caught Ricky's eyes in the crowd. He held up his phone, recording the moment ("I've got to make sure I catch the moment you open it, or I'll have two sets of parents on my ass," he said). He threw me a thumbs-up; I returned a thin smile. I was envious of him, of his assurance that no matter what happened, we would be okay.

"You may now open your envelopes."

With shaking hands, I ripped my envelope open. Heart pounding away in my throat, I scanned the piece of paper until my eyes settled on a line —

I'd matched at my second choice.

My first reaction was elation. I had thought this program was a *reach*! I had gotten along well with the program director during the interview, and we had talked extensively about my project, Physician Communication Practices with Black Inpatient Populations, and my recent oral presentation at the Society of General Internal Medicine on the subject. They'd seemed genuinely appreciative of my passion for disparities over traditional clinical research. But then I remembered that this program was in Seattle, and my heart sank. Chicago had always been home for Ricky. He had a new job that he genuinely enjoyed. Great friends. Family. A budding reputation as a muralist that had taken off after he'd finished the project at Rogers Children's Hospital. Seattle was practically another country for him. Why had I let him convince me to rank it so highly?

Next to me, Michelle was draped across the back of her chair in relief; she'd matched at her number one. We hugged, both exhausted, just as our visitors swarmed in. I laughed as a throng of excited Korean women surrounded Michelle, all clamoring to be the first to see her sheet.

"CONGRATULATIONS, LADIES!"

A set of warm arms wrapped around me and lifted me off my feet. I squeaked in surprise, but laughed as Nia placed me down gently. She smelled like caramel, as she always did these days.

"Thanks!" I said, dampened. With Michelle going to New York, me going to Seattle, and Nia staying behind in Chicago, our Sanity Circle would officially be fragmented. Nia and I had only recently gotten used to living in different apartments, let alone time zones.

An arm slid around my waist, and Ricky laid a kiss on my forehead.

"So?" he asked. "What's the verdict, babe?"

I handed him the paper. He scanned the page closely . . . then let out a whoop of celebration.

"This was your number two, wasn't it?" he said, his excitement palpable and so painfully genuine. "See, I told you it wasn't a reach. You just have to believe in yourself!" Then his face fell. "Wait. Why aren't you more excited? I know you liked your number one a lot too, but I thought these two were pretty much neck and neck?"

I looked up at Nia, who gave me a knowing look. The bestie always understood.

"No, no they were, and I am. I promise!" I said. "But Seattle is so far."

Ricky and Nia exchanged a glance that I found . . . interesting. Before I could ask questions, Nia shoved a frilly pink bag into my hands.

"Treats, courtesy of Madame Annette herself," she said. "You look awesome, and I'm so happy for you. I've got to drive back to work, or my boss is going to kick my ass."

"Oh?" I said, aghast. "You can't stick around for a bit?"

"Nope," Nia said, her lips popping on the *p.* "Don't look too sad, we're celebrating tomorrow, right?"

"Yes, but —"

"Girl, you got a man! Hang out with him!" With a dramatic whip of her head, Nia marched toward the exit. I watched her go with wide eyes, my goody bag still clutched in my hands. Next to me, Ricky looked amused.

"You're so funny," he said. "Come on. Let's head outside."

In the courtyard, clusters of families and friends gathered, taking pictures, exchanging news about their respective matches. I spotted a few of my classmates sitting on stairwells, sobbing into their laps; Match Day was not a happy day for everyone. We walked across the lawn, occasionally being intercepted by my med school friends asking to exchange Match results or take pictures. Ricky played dutiful boyfriend, snapping pictures on their phones, and then requesting every one of them to take a picture of us too. By the time we finally reached the sidewalk, we had far too many different renditions of the same photos of us, courtesy of seven different photographers.

"Where are we going, anyway?" I asked.

"Away from all that," Ricky provided.

"Ugh, you know me too well," I said. Just being out of earshot of the Match Day shenanigans was helping calm my nerves.

We took the scenic route home, winding through a nearby park until we found a bench. I opened Nia's box of treats to find chocolate eclairs — my favorite after Nia's Bergamot Chocolate Sunset, the thrice remixed version of her classic double chocolate fudge surprise. I took a bite, then fed Ricky the next.

"You're worried about me," Ricky finally said. "I told you not to be." He pulled my legs across his lap.

"I can't help it!" I said. "I know you said it was fine, but of course I'm going to feel guilty. I could've ranked a Chicago program higher. I would still have gotten good training at the end of the day." I paused, letting my excitement at matching in one of my dream programs seep in. "I'm happy that you're so okay with it but . . . we can't pretend this won't be harder."

Ricky gave me an unreadable look, and then reached into his jacket pocket. My heart jumped to my throat — *No way** — but then, instead of a box, he pulled out an envelope of his own.

"Open it," he demanded, then busied himself massaging my calves in his lap.

I took it, tearing it open far more carefully than I had my Match letter. I narrowed my eyes, perplexed. At first sight, the paper looked almost identical to my Match letter, down to the formatting and the NRMP logo in the top right corner. But the name listed wasn't mine; it was Ricky's. And the institution wasn't a hospital; it was a company's name and address. A company in Seattle.

* This is out of both pleased shock and panic. If Ricky tried to put a ring on it before Knocking, Momma would confiscate it and pitch it into Lake Michigan.

531

I looked up at him in shock.

"How did you know?" I asked.

"I didn't," he said, laughing. "I just applied to a bunch of design agencies in every city on your rank list. Got a few offers, but I only 'shopped ones for your top five, because I just knew my girl wouldn't drop below those." He dropped my legs to throw his arm around my shoulders. "So . . . I guess we're moving to Seattle."

This man. He painted murals of my face on walls and charmed my most stubborn relatives, and now he was leaving everything he had ever known behind to move halfway across the country for me. And while I was busy doubting the mechanics of it all, he was busy making it happen.

"Thank you. I love you," I said. I wound my arms around his neck. "But also, I really can't stand you. Every city on my rank list? You *crazy boy.*"

He chuckled.

"Well, speaking of crazy," he said. His smile turned coy. "I . . . may have also made a little trip to the 'burbs with the abuelos while you were away for interviews."

I pulled back, not entirely understanding.

"There was a long debate about whether we should go with gin or schnapps," Ricky continued. "I tried to tell them that you were a Peppermint Patty girl, but Abuelo talked me out of it."

He gave me an earnest look, and the pieces clicked together. The man I loved, sitting across from my father in my family's home, sipping Muscatella. Asking permission to be mine forever.

I lifted trembling hands to my mouth. Slowly, Ricky pulled them away, holding my wrists in suspension as he leaned in to kiss me. I let my toes curl from the sensation and wondered if kissing him would always feel like this, like the heat of the sun on the first day of summer or a sip of hot chocolate on a frigid winter day. Like letting myself freefall in love, and for once not searching for where I might land.

"All that's left," Ricky said, breaking away, "is for you to call your parents and let them know if you accept." He kissed the inside of my wrist, holding my gaze. "Though, a warning. I'll be a lot harder to get rid of if you do. So, what do you say?"

I laughed, and for once, when I gave my answer, I didn't have to think about it.

ACKNOWLEDGMENTS

Mom and Dad: I'm sure having a child like me was overwhelming. I never stopped moving, never stopped talking, filled our "Ghana must go" bags with drawings, rambled nonstop about stories I'd made up in my head. But you supported me and my interests from the beginning. You bound my books at Kinko's and taught me that my words had power. You battled my imposter syndrome and reinforced that I have a "big brain" and could, in fact, do it all. I'm so happy to be yours.

Humphrey and Sam: Navigating the world with you is always a delight. You understand how my brain works because yours work the same way. Thank you for being equally dramatic, for being equally loving, for all our dumb inside jokes. Proud to be your big sis.

Justin: Love of my life. You don't even read rom-coms, but you let me read every chap-

535

ter of *OR* out loud to you and offered suggestions that I often summarily rejected, thus sparing the readers your truly awful puns. When I was shaking with anxiety about the process, you were steadfast, like a rock. When I sold, you acted like it wasn't even a big deal, like *Of course you would sell,* because you really do think I can do anything. What an honor to love and be loved by you.

Chris: Holy cow did I luck out with my mother-in-law. Thank you for reading the entire book, for your enthusiastic support during the submission process, for our relaxing girl dates, and for raising a wonderful son.

Linda and Nefti: My IRL Sanity Circle. My sisters. My RIDE-OR-DIES! I joke that I have three brains because you are two of them. Thank you for all the time spent brainstorming plot points, for reading basically every draft of *OR* I have ever written, for baecations and laughter and loving me so hard that I learned to truly love myself. It feels insufficient to call you my best friends. *OR* wouldn't exist without you.

Riss: My writing big sister. You held my hand from across the country, gave me guidance and laughter and genuine, heartfelt care. I could not dream of a better person to be debuting with. Your writing makes me want to weep; it's still shocking to me that you also like mine. (Everyone, go buy *Deep in Providence* by Riss Neilson so that we can fangirl together.)

Shruti: Thank you for kicking my writing into overdrive, reading my revision as I wrote it in real time, for loving Ricky and Angie so much that it made me believe others would too. You're a rockstar, and I love you.

Eunhye, Deje, Mandy, Allison: Thank you for reading that first draft through and giving me feedback that helped guide me, for your enduring support even when you were enduring your own BS. Y'all are the best!

Dr. Vela: Thank you for being my IRL Dr. Wallace. You saw me when I was a wee premed who wrote stories and drew comics instead of churning out abstracts, and you said, "Yes, this one will add something to the field." I love you, and I am always inspired by your willingness to always do what's right. Proud to be a part of #HouseofVela.

Ross, Satish, and Edna — my residency family. We've been through so much: nursing strikes, a pandemic, MICU calls with untenable censuses . . . you name it. Thank you for creating a safe space for me to be myself during residency, for the debriefs after difficult stretches on service, for letting me cry and vent and feel things, for overall having my back.

CJ: Thank you for deciding for the both of us that we were going to be the best of friends, for letting me bounce my whackiest book ideas off you, and for offering even whackier ones in return. You're the best older little brother a girl could ask for.

To Jess, my agent: Thank you for believing in *On Rotation* and in me as a writer, for letting me know it was okay to dream big, for advocating for me in the alien world of publishing, and for working tirelessly to get *On Rotation* sold.

To Lucia, Asanté, and my team at Avon/ William Morrow: You've made my wildest dreams come true! Thank you for shaping this novel into its current (vastly improved) form, for answering my deluge of questions with grace, and for giving *On Rotation* a chance to shine.

Héctor, Tzintzuni, and Rebecca: Thank you for letting me mine you for those identifiable details about your Mexican-American upbringing so that Ricky could feel a bit more real. Hector, thank you for scouring this book line by line to make sure that both Ricky and Shae's portrayals could be respectful and genuine.

Katy: Every Black girl needs a Black girl therapist. Thank you for teaching me the power of no and how to continue to choose myself. I appreciate you so much.

ShirlyGang: My little online homies. I started ShirlyWhirl when I thought no one would be interested in my creations, and you responded with such loving enthusiasm. I learn something from all of you every day.

Kojo and YBLERD: Whodathunk there would be 200+ Black Weebs Who Are Also Doctors out there! My goodness. I really thought that 712 was the only world out there, but there y'all were, being hilarious, being ridiculous, being professionals who also cosplay. You are also all very hot.

And finally, to Mrs. Donna Lehman: When I was the scared, bullied, gap-toothed African child in your class, you saw promise. You went out of your way to pull me out of a bad situation, put me in front of opportunities, and gave me the chance to shine. I genuinely don't know if I would be where I am today without your good-hearted interference. I look at that letter you wrote me when I was a wee third grader, the one where you told me that one day I would be a famous author. Well, I don't know about the famous part, but . . . here we are.

ABOUT THE AUTHOR

Shirlene Obuobi is a Ghanaian-American physician, cartoonist, and author who grew up in Chicago, Illinois; Hot Springs, Arkansas; and the Woodlands, Texas. When she's not in the hospital (and let's be honest, even when she is), she can be found drawing comics, writing on her phone, and obsessing over her three cats. She currently lives in Chicago, where she is completing her cardiology fellowship.

The employees of Thorndike Press hope you have enjoyed this Large Print book. All our Thorndike, Wheeler, and Kennebec Large Print titles are designed for easy reading, and all our books are made to last. Other Thorndike Press Large Print books are available at your library, through selected bookstores, or directly from us.

For information about titles, please call:
  (800) 223-1244

or visit our website at:
  gale.com/thorndike

To share your comments, please write:
  Publisher
  Thorndike Press
  10 Water St., Suite 310
  Waterville, ME 04901